Praise for Cleo Coyle's Coffeehouse Mysteries

ESPRESSO SHOT

"Coyle's Coffeehouse books are superb examples of the cozy genre because of their intelligent cast of characters, their subtle wit, and their knowledge of the coffee industry used to add depth and flavor to the stories. Highly recommended for all mystery collections." —*Library Journal* (starred review)

"Clare visits underground restaurants, temples to high fashion, and the hotel room of a seductive Italian sculptor in her attempts to keep the bride alive . . . A realistic depiction of New York City high and low life. The smattering of recipes, romance, and caffeine-fueled detection add up to a lively tale." —*Kirkus Reviews*

"Enjoyable . . . This mellow-paced cozy includes some surprises . . . Recipes and coffee tips are a bonus."
—*Publishers Weekly*

"Cleo Coyle's Coffeehouse Mysteries, which are among my favorites, can be counted on for great characters, smooth plotting and pacing that keeps readers engaged . . . *Espresso Shot* is seventh in the series and, in my opinion, it's the best one yet."
—*Mystery News*

"Oh, *Espresso Shot* is a fun read! I kept turning the pages long after I should have turned off the light." —*Armchair Interviews*

P9-BYX-382

continued . . .

FRENCH PRESSED

"Engaging . . . Keeps the reader in suspense to the very end, *French Pressed* is well worth reading." —*New Mystery Reader*

"Once again, Cleo Coyle has written an enjoyable, fast-paced mystery that features a perky heroine who has gone from single mother to savvy business owner . . . Readers may be stumped until the very end." —*The Mystery Reader*

"I love Cleo Coyle's Coffeehouse Mysteries and *French Pressed* is the best yet." —*Cozy Library*

"I have read all the Coffeehouse Mysteries and enjoyed them thoroughly. Cleo Coyle has written a wonderful series." —*I Love A Mystery*

"Coyle again entertains, informs, and challenges the reader . . . The clues are there in the open, but we must put them together." —*Gumshoe Review*

DECAFFEINATED CORPSE

"Great characters, smooth plotting, and top-notch writing, it's no wonder these books are bestsellers." —*Cozy Library*

"Author Coyle displays a deep understanding, not only of coffee . . . but also of coffee shop culture. She treats espresso shop work as an honorable profession . . . Coyle knows her coffee so well that even I have learned new coffee bits by reading her books. If you have not yet discovered the Coffeehouse Mystery series by Cleo Coyle, you should . . . I heartily recommend them." —Eric S. Chen, *BARISTO.net*

MURDER MOST FROTHY

"The latest Coffeehouse Mystery is a terrific amateur sleuth tale that showcases the heroine at her best."
—*Midwest Book Review*

"*Murder Most Frothy*, like its title, is a light and lively blend."
—*BookLoons*

"Exciting, delicious fun, with coffee trivia, recipes, a vicarious adventure for those of us at home reading of things we'd rather not face ourselves but understanding Clare Cosi's motives and morals."
—*Gumshoe Review*

LATTE TROUBLE

"Anyone who loves coffee and a good mystery will love this story. Rating: Outstanding."
`—*Mysterious Corner*

"Another delightfully percolating and exciting mystery. The strength of this series lies in the characters who are drawn true to life."
—*I Love A Mystery*

"A delightful series! Clare is a captivating narrator . . . The action is fast-paced and there is a big twist at the end that you won't see coming!"
—*Romantic Times*

THROUGH THE GRINDER

"Coffee lovers & mystery buffs will savor the latest addition to this mystery series . . . Fast-paced action, coffee lore, and incredible culinary recipes . . . All hail the goddess Caffina!"
—*The Best Reviews*

"Full of action and murder with a little romance thrown in on the side. The ending is exceptional and completely unexpected."
—*The Romance Readers Connection*

"There were ample red herrings in *Through the Grinder* to lead the reader astray . . . This is a great mystery in the Coffee-house Mystery series."   —*Roundtable Reviews*

ON WHAT GROUNDS

"A great beginning to a new series . . . *On What Grounds* will convert even the most fervent tea drinker into a coffee lover in the time it takes to draw an espresso."   —*The Mystery Reader*

"A hilarious blend of amateur detecting with some romance thrown in the mix . . . I personally adored this book, and can't wait to read the rest of the series!"   —*Cozy Library*

"A fun, light mystery. Recommended."   —*KLIATT*

"The first book in Coyle's new series is a definite winner! The mystery is first rate, and the characters leap from the page and are compelling, vivid, and endearing. The aroma of this story made this noncoffee drinker want to visit the nearest coffee bar."   —*Romantic Times*

"[A] clever, witty, and light-hearted cozy. Cleo Coyle is a bright new light in the mystery horizon."   —*The Best Reviews*

Visit Cleo Coyle's virtual Village Blend at
www.CoffeehouseMystery.com,
where coffee and crime are always brewing.

ESPRESSO SHOT

CLEO COYLE

BERKLEY PRIME CRIME, NEW YORK

THE BERKLEY PUBLISHING GROUP
Published by the Penguin Group
Penguin Group (USA) Inc.
375 Hudson Street, New York, New York 10014, USA
Penguin Group (Canada), 90 Eglinton Avenue East, Suite 700, Toronto, Ontario M4P 2Y3, Canada
(a division of Pearson Penguin Canada Inc.)
Penguin Books Ltd., 80 Strand, London WC2R 0RL, England
Penguin Group Ireland, 25 St. Stephen's Green, Dublin 2, Ireland (a division of Penguin Books Ltd.)
Penguin Group (Australia), 250 Camberwell Road, Camberwell, Victoria 3124, Australia
(a division of Pearson Australia Group Pty. Ltd.)
Penguin Books India Pvt. Ltd., 11 Community Centre, Panchsheel Park, New Delhi—110 017, India
Penguin Group (NZ), 67 Apollo Drive, Rosedale, North Shore 0632, New Zealand
(a division of Pearson New Zealand Ltd.)
Penguin Books (South Africa) (Pty.) Ltd., 24 Sturdee Avenue, Rosebank, Johannesburg 2196,
South Africa

Penguin Books Ltd., Registered Offices: 80 Strand, London WC2R 0RL, England

This is a work of fiction. Names, characters, places, and incidents either are the product of the author's imagination or are used fictitiously, and any resemblance to actual persons, living or dead, business establishments, events, or locales is entirely coincidental. The publisher does not have any control over and does not assume any responsibility for author or third-party websites or their content.

PUBLISHER'S NOTE: The recipes contained in this book are to be followed exactly as written. The publisher is not responsible for your specific health or allergy needs that may require medical supervision. The publisher is not responsible for any adverse reactions to the recipes contained in this book

ESPRESSO SHOT

A Berkley Prime Crime Book / published by arrangement with the author

PRINTING HISTORY
Berkley Prime Crime hardcover edition / October 2008
Berkley Prime Crime mass-market edition / October 2009

Copyright © 2008 by Penguin Group (USA) Inc.
Excerpt from *Holiday Grind* by Cleo Coyle copyright © 2009 by Penguin Group (USA) Inc.
Cover illustration by Cathy Gendron.
Cover design and log by Rita Frangie.
Interior text design by Kristin del Rosario.

ISBN: 978-0-425-23076-3

BERKLEY® PRIME CRIME
Berkley Prime Crime Books are published by The Berkley Publishing Group,
a division of Penguin Group (USA) Inc.,
375 Hudson Street, New York, New York 10014.
BERKLEY® PRIME CRIME and the PRIME CRIME logo are trademarks of Penguin Group (USA) Inc.

PRINTED IN THE UNITED STATES OF AMERICA

10 9 8 7 6 5 4 3 2 1

*Cheers to John Talbot,
a premium agent and a darn good Joe.*

ACKNOWLEDGMENTS

To begin with, an old joke . . .

"Excuse me, sir?" the tourist asked. "How do I get to Carnegie Hall?"
The cabbie shrugged. "Practice."

Since 2003, the Coffeehouse Mysteries have been published in a quiet fashion, building buzz via independent mystery bookstores, online reviewers, chain store staff recommendations, and even the barista community. While I can't see Carnegie Hall in my future, I offer my sincerest thanks to those of you who have given me the opportunity to practice. Your support of my series has kept it going and kept me going. No kidding, from the bottom of my heart, I thank you for reading.

My second shout-out goes to my publisher, Berkley Prime Crime. In particular, I'd like to salute executive editor Wendy McCurdy for her steadfast professionalism. Wendy's calming character is nothing short of saintly in a profession that comes with ungodly pressures. Major props also go to Allison Brandau, for all of her hard work, as well as former Berkley editors Katie Day and Martha Bushko for their crucial support along the way.

If you've read even one previous Coffeehouse Mystery, then you know how important coffee is to Clare Cosi. Regarding the java she serves up in this volume, I'd like to thank New York City's excellent Café Grumpy, not only for introducing me to the "champagne" of the coffee world, Esmeralda Especial, but for hosting the tasting event at which I had the thrill of shaking the hand of Daniel Peterson, the man who rediscovered the heirloom geisha tree that grows it.

I'd also like to thank Joe the Art of Coffee in Greenwich Village, New York, for their expert advice and outstanding espressos, and Counter Culture Coffee of Durham, North Carolina, for their superior beans. If a superb cuppa joe is what you're after, these fine folks are among the best in the business.

With the greatest respect, I tip my hat to the men and women of the Sixth Precinct, especially its former deputy inspector, who—until her recent promotion—also happened to be the only female precinct commanding officer in a city that employs well over thirty thousand cops. As to the p's and q's of by-the-book police procedure, this is a light work of amateur-sleuth fiction. In the Coffeehouse Mysteries, the rules occasionally get bent.

An additional shout-out goes to Dr. Grace Alfonsi. Not just because she's an amazing physician and hardworking mom, but because she's always helpful to me with thought and advice in matters medical. When literary license is taken in presenting elements in this area, I alone am culpable.

I thank the White Horse Tavern in Greenwich Village for their draft beer, out-of-this-world onion rings, and most of all for still being around after more than one hundred years. The incomparable Metropolitan Museum of Art must also be thanked, frankly, for simply *existing*. My sincerest thanks especially go to their kind employees who answered my questions and the security guards for not arresting my big, dangerous-looking husband when they noticed him taking photos of the employee entrance in his black leather jacket. (Note to aspiring writers: if you ever decide to take reference photos at the Met's Eighty-fourth Street entrance, make sure you bring ID.)

And speaking of Marc . . .

As most of my readers are aware, I write this series, as well as my Alice Kimberly Haunted Bookshop Mystery series, in collaboration with my very talented spouse. Both of us owe a debt of gratitude to our friends and families for their support. We'd also like to thank our literary agent, John Talbot to whom this book is dedicated. John's sincere encouragement and steadfast professionalism over the years have meant the world to us—two writers who intend never to stop practicing.

Yours sincerely,
Cleo Coyle

Coffee should be black as hell, strong as death, sweet as love.

—Turkish proverb

Marriage is a mistake every man should make.

—George Jessel

PROLOGUE

SHE left her building at six for the health club up the street. She'd done this every morning for the last four days, only today something was different. A white sanitation truck had thundered up the block. Now it sat in the middle of the road like an enormous beached whale.

There was no room to maneuver now. No way to get clear, get away. From behind the wheel of the parked SUV, the stalker took a breath, remained steady, stayed calm. With the wedding next week, Breanne's schedule was becoming unpredictable. Waiting any longer would pose problems.

It must be done today. This morning.

After her workout, Breanne returned to her apartment. She showered, dressed, and left for the office at seven fifteen. As her leggy strides ate up the sidewalk, the stalker's gloved hands gripped the SUV's wheel and twisted the key.

The glossy black rental looked like thousands of others on the city streets, but the stalker had taken no chances. The white New York plates had been splattered with mud. A fedora had been purchased, sunglasses worn, a collar turned up.

The location was perfect: Sutton Place, a picturesque nook of the Upper East Side. The area was quiet and exclusive. Best of all, it skirted the Queensboro Bridge, allowing swift and easy egress from a Manhattan crime scene.

At this hour, traffic was still light. The sanitation truck was *long gone. Only two cars moved down the one-way street. The SUV rolled slowly, just behind the target. Breanne nattered as she moved, cell phone plastered to her fair head, unaware of the dark monster pacing her. She looked like a seagull, white and graceful, gliding with ease through the concrete canyons, wings spread, beak high . . .*

The stalker's eye twitched.

She was attractive. So? Even beautiful birds were made to die unfair deaths. This was something the stalker knew firsthand. Breanne's fate was a necessary reckoning: A treasure had been taken. Now a price would be paid.

The stalker's grip tightened on the steering wheel. Several times, this course had been run. An ideal stretch was coming up, where signs warned of active driveways. No cars were parked there. No curbs were blocked—nothing to come between the bride-to-be and certain death.

Everything was perfect. Now it was going to happen. NOW!

The stalker cut the wheel. Tires bounced over the concrete curb. The engine roared, and the vehicle shot forward. Breanne half turned, blond hair flying, finally aware of the threat. But it was too late. In another second, Beauty would be broken beyond repair—

DIE! DIE!

But she didn't.

Before three tons of metal could smash her slender form, Breanne's body was struck by another; a lunging, muscular man slammed her off the sidewalk and into a recessed doorway.

The SUV hurtled past the pair, crushing the woman's dropped cell phone, mangling her designer handbag. The stalker cut the wheel again, banged off the curb, clipped a parked car.

There was screaming, shouting, commotion. The stalker checked the rearview. A man in workout sweats helped Breanne to her feet; a flash of profile told the stalker who he was.

With a raging string of curses, the stalker continued driving the route that had been planned. Breanne and her muscular savior would call 911, report the incident. In ten minutes, maybe less, the police would start looking. By then the vehicle would be off Manhattan's streets.

The SUV made the corner on First Avenue; turned again to the side street that led to the bridge ramp, headed for the Queens side of the East River. There was a place near the warehouses, deserted and dingy. The stalker would ditch the vehicle there. Then a short hike to the subway and back to Manhattan.

It would take a few days to create a new plan, but one would be made, and then it would be done. When the handsome groom saw his bride at the altar, her white gown would be replaced with a burial shroud. Yes, one way or another, Breanne Summour was going to die before her wedding day.

One

~~~~~~

THE way I see it, a wedding is a new beginning, full of hope and possibility. Death is an ending—black, dark, final. Flowers are involved with both, and tasteful music selections, but for the most part, brides and corpses have nothing in common, unless you're talking about the bride of Frankenstein, in which case the bride *is* a corpse.

This particular wedding story involved a bride and several corpses. I was not one of the corpses. I wasn't the bride, either. The one and only time I'd been a bride took place at Manhattan's City Hall, where I waited with my groom in a long line of couples to obtain the proper paperwork, after which my future husband and I were ushered into a room with all the charm of a DMV office. A fleshy-faced justice of the peace in a snug-fitting suit then auto-stamped our marriage license in the midst of declaring us wed, which sounded something like—

"I now pronounce you" . . . *ker-chunk* . . . "man and wife."

I was nineteen at the time.

In calendar years, my bridegroom was barely three years older than I. Sexually speaking, however, Matteo Allegro had traveled light-years beyond. Case in point: our first date.

The life-altering event began with my giving him a chaste tour of the Vatican Museums. It ended in a Roman *pensione* with me giggling naked and blindfolded on a narrow bed, my future husband hand-feeding me bites of gorgonzola-stuffed figs. Eve had the apple. For me it was a Mediterranean fruit drenched in honey and balsamic vinegar.

Dozens more times, I'd succumbed to Matt's perilous charms (not to mention those figs), and by summer's end my fate was sealed. I'd gone to Italy a virgin art student, determined to expose myself to Renaissance genius. I'd returned pregnant with a daughter named Joy.

Matt had been the one to name our daughter, a child he loved dearly (too often from afar), but ultimately Joy's name had not been a good predictor of the years ahead, and after ten difficult laps with my groom around the sun, I forced myself to admit that the magnetic young man to whom I'd passionately pledged my undying fidelity viewed our vows not as a sacred covenant but as a loose collection of suggested guidelines. (His addiction to cocaine hadn't helped, either.)

After our divorce, I'd made a new life for myself and our daughter. We moved to a suburb in New Jersey, where I put together an odd collection of part-time jobs: assisting a busy caterer, writing freelance for coffee industry trades, and baking snacks for a nearby day care center (caffeine free, I assure you).

Unfortunately, my new address across the Hudson and a ream of fully signed legal papers did little to stop my infrequent reunions with my ex-husband. Given his perpetual itches and my own pathetic weakness, the man's magic hands, hard body, and low intentions occasionally found their way back into my lonely, single-mom bed.

Now, with our daughter grown and working abroad, I was back to living and working in Greenwich Village. My marital partnership with Matt remained dissolved, yet our alliance continued in other ways: like the parenting of Joy, for one (the fact that she'd reached legal adulthood was beside the point), and the running of the Village Blend coffee business, for another.

According to Matt's elderly mother, who was bequeathing the Blend's future to both of us, I was the best manager she'd ever employed and the best barista she'd ever met. For his part, Matt was more than simply the owner's offspring; he was an extremely savvy coffee buyer and broker without whom the legendary Blend would be just another java joint.

On good days, my ex and I actually acknowledged what we meant to each other. Even on bad ones, we managed to remain begrudging friends. So, when he asked me, I agreed to help out with aspects of his second wedding, a union with the annoyingly swanlike Breanne Summour, disdainer-in-chief of *Trend* magazine.

For months now, Breanne had been planning the nuptials and reception. Photographers were hired (still and video), flower and cake designs selected (elaborate and expensive), dress fitted (a House of Fen original), and venue reserved (New York's Metropolitan Museum of Art). In sum, the event was shaping up to be a tad more lavish than the unceremonious City Hall *ker-chunking* of the man's first marriage to me.

This was the week that brought us down to the wire. Breanne was moving into panic mode, and her groom-to-be had just moved back into the apartment above our coffeehouse.

"So you're all settled in upstairs?" I asked Matt as he took a load off at my espresso bar.

"Yeah." He nodded. "In my old guest room."

"I can't believe Breanne is happy with your moving back into the duplex. I mean, she does know I still live here, right?"

"It's not for long. Just five days. Frankly, she's happy I'm out of her hair."

I studied my ex-husband's wide, unblinking brown eyes. "She doesn't know you're staying with me, does she?"

"No."

Matt, Matt, Matt . . . "You can stay with your mother, you know. She'd be thrilled to have you."

He glanced away. "I told you already. Joy's coming in this week. I haven't seen her in months, and I'd really like to stay under the same roof as my daughter."

"One last week of us as a big, happy family, right?"

"Right."

"And what Breanne doesn't know won't hurt her?"

Matt shrugged.

I went back to finishing a double-tall mochaccino order: two steaming shots of espresso stirred into a base of my homemade chocolate syrup, a pour of steamed milk, plenty of frothy foam, and a whipped cream cloud as high as Denali. I dusted the ski slope with bittersweet shavings, set the drink on the counter, smiled at the young woman waiting, and turned back to my ex.

"You wouldn't be avoiding your mother because she's been chewing your ear off to cancel the wedding, would you?"

Matt massaged his eyes. "Let's not go there."

"Well, I wouldn't blame you. She's been chewing my ear off about it, too. For months."

"Sorry."

"It's okay . . ."

I moved back to the espresso machine, unlocked the portafilter handle, dumped the packed cake of grounds into the under-counter garbage, then moved to rinse the filter in the small sink. The mochaccino order appeared to be my last of the evening. Gardner Evans was due to relieve me any minute, and most of the twenty marble-topped café tables were empty, which was typical for a Monday evening in April. The tourists wouldn't start flowing back into the historic district for at least another month.

"Anyway," I told Matt, "all of us have enough to do this week to keep us out of trouble. You've got your pals flying here from every country of the coffee belt, don't you?"

"Practically. They'll be arriving all week, but I'll see most of them as a group on Thursday."

"At your mother's luncheon?"

"Yeah."

"And you're going to have a bachelor party with them, oo, right?"

"A bachelor party?" Matt snorted. "She would murder me f I had a bachelor party! Didn't I mention that?"

"*She* who? Your mother?"

"My bride-to-be."

"Breanne would *murder* you? Just for having a bachelor party?"

Matt slipped off his exquisite Armani blazer and laid it arefully on the high bar chair next to him. As he rolled up is sleeves, my gaze drifted up his tanned, sculpted forearms o the open neck of his fashionably tie-free dress shirt.

For as long as I'd known him, Matteo Allegro had been is own man, a hiking-booted, extreme sports–loving ex-plorer. Ever since his involvement with Breanne, however, I wear my ex had been fitted with an invisible collar and leash compliments of some name designer, of course).

"You want a double, right?" I said, moving back to the spresso machine.

"Single."

"But you usually have a *doppio* espresso at this hour."

"Single. That's what I want."

"O-kay," I said.

I ran the burr grinder, which I'd set up earlier with some very special beans, and wondered if a drink order could be Freudian. "Set me straight here. If 'what Breanne doesn't know won't hurt her' when it comes to your bedding down upstairs, then why don't you feel the same way about a bach-lor party with your buddies?"

"Because what Breanne doesn't know will *become* known if paparazzi take embarrassing photos of the thing and post hem on the Net. Or worse, sell them to 'Gotham Gossip.'"

"Oh, I see. So it's more like what Randall Knox doesn't know won't hurt her?"

"Right again."

Knox was the *New York Journal*'s new "Gotham Gossip"

column editor. I'd never met the man, but Tucker Burton,
my actor/playwright assistant manager with an unhealthy
appetite for celebrity prattle, had warned me already about
the guy's rep:

*"Knox is wired into this town, Clare. They say he has tentacles
running around every New York inside track. And when those slith-
ery limbs retract, look out!"*

"Look out?" I said. *"For what?"*

"Bombshells, sweetie. Usually scandalous, always readable!"

"Damn the man," Matt muttered. "Did you know Breanne has some sort of history with him?"

"History?" I said. "What do you mean, history? Were
they lovers?"

"No. Bree says their relationship was professional. That's
all I know. That's all she'll *tell* me. Either way, the prick's
only too happy to publish dirt on her—"

"Or you," I noted.

Matt shook his head. "You don't know the half of it . . ."

"What do you mean? Are you talking about that snarky
item Knox published on Joy?"

Our daughter had been arrested for a terrible crime a few
months back. When the news broke, there was enough dirt
to fill ten pages, let alone a single gossip feature. Strangely,
however, Randall Knox spent some of those precious column inches pretzeling his report so he could embarrass
Breanne, and even Matt, whom he described not as an international coffee broker but as "Breanne Summour's flavor of
the month."

"It has nothing to do with that item on Joy," Matt assured
me. Then he sighed and ran a hand through his short, dark
Caesar. "I don't want to alarm you or anything—"

Few things alarmed me more than my ex saying, "I don't
want to alarm you."

"—but Knox has got some photographer trailing me
around the city, waiting for me to do something embarrassing. Breanne saw the man stalking me one night. She knows
he works for Knox."

"*What?!*"

Matt lowered his voice. "It's one of the reasons I'm bunking with you, if you want to know the truth. This is my place of business, so my being here is nothing unusual. All I have to do at the end of the night is take the back stairs up to the apartment, and I'll have my privacy."

"And I thought you were ducking a fat hotel bill."

"Well, that, too, honestly."

"So what does this photographer of Knox's think he's going to get by following you around?"

Matt sighed. "He snapped me just the other day, picking up a magazine from a newsstand."

"So?"

"So, it was *Maxim*."

I rolled my eyes. "Big deal."

"I know. It's ridiculous, right?"

"Your picking up a lads' magazine is not scandalous behavior. Thousands of men do the same thing every day!"

"I know, but you see my problem, don't you? I could stay in a hotel, but then some pretty young thing might ask me for directions or the time of day near my room door or the elevators that go up to my room, and *bam*, a photo's snapped, a suggestive caption's written, and my wedding's off."

I frowned. "Matt, if you're really on solid ground with Breanne, one stupid photo in a tabloid shouldn't change it."

"Forget it, Clare. You just don't understand."

"Apparently not."

I turned my attention back to pulling Matt's shot—something I *did* understand, thank you very much. After dosing and tamping the fragrant black sand into the portafilter, I locked the handle, pressed the Go button, and began to monitor the extraction process. As high-pressure steam released oils from the finely ground beans, I began to feel better. The aromatics were soothing. They were also very different from the caramelized earthiness of our regular house roast. Sweet and light, these very special beans flaunted naked floral notes, and (to my olfactory nerves anyway) traces of jasmine, honey, and bergamot.

Within twenty-five seconds, the potable perfume wa nearly finished oozing out of the machine's spout, a fine looking *crema* topping it off like a perfectly pulled dark beer I stopped the pull, placed the Village Blend demitasse on it matching saucer, and slid the single shot across the blueberry marble counter.

Matt regarded his shot. "Where's my lemon twist?"

I smiled. "You won't need it."

The espresso method actually wasn't the best way to serve these particular beans. A French pressed or brewed method would have been better at bringing out the amazing flavo characteristics in the single-origin cherries. (And since we'd finally invested in two $11,000 Clover machines for the shop, I could have perfectly brewed Matt a single cup.) But couldn't resist the surprise factor.

Matt gave me a skeptical look until he sniffed his drink Then one dark eyebrow rose. "This isn't our house espresso roast."

"No."

He sipped once, and his eyes smiled. "You gave me th Esmeralda?"

"Yep." For the past week, I'd been in the Blend's base ment, test-roasting the green beans that we'd acquired fo Saturday's wedding. Tonight's test was the champagne of the coffee world, aka Esmeralda Especial.

I was stunned when Matt was able to secure the auction lot Esmeralda beans. Although the Peterson family was stil selling the most recent crop from their world-famous heir loom geisha trees, the celebrated first-place Panamanian Cup of Excellence microlot was as scarce as a sack of Hope dia monds.

Matt and I had explained this to Breanne, and we planne on purchasing other Esmeralda beans; the ones still avail able on the market. But the woman pitched a fit, absolutely insisting that we secure the famous, first-prize, $130-a-pound auction-lot beans for her high-profile wedding guests.

"They've read about the auction lot beans; they've seen the cable stories about it; and that's what I want my guests drinking. The world-record auction lot. Not sloppy seconds!"

Sloppy seconds? I'd wanted to strangle her. The Esmeralda beans still available were among the highest quality on the planet. They were from the same damn geisha trees as the world-record auction lot, for goodness' sake; grown on the same damn farm! But Breanne refused to "settle."

Lucky for us all, Matt had some friends who owed him favors. He made a few calls, and voilá! Two ten-pound bags of the scarce green beans appeared at my doorstep. (And since one pound of coffee yielded approximately forty cups, we now had enough for Breanne's 350 VIP guests to sample.) Along with the Waipuna farm's 100 percent Kona Peaberry, the small lot of Kopi Luwak, and our signature espresso drinks, the Village Blend was bound to make an impression, too.

"Nice job on the roast," Matt said between long, contemplative sips.

"Thanks. I kept it light to preserve the nuances—a nobrainer on the Esmeralda."

"Aren't you having any?"

"I cupped it earlier with Dante—" I tipped my head toward my newest barista, a tattooed, shaved-headed, fine arts painter with a penchant for space and ambient music. (He had some of it playing now: a hypnotic, rhythmic electronic pulsing that would have sent me to dreamland if it weren't for the double espresso I'd consumed before Matt sat down.)

Hearing his name, Dante Silva glanced up from his conversation with the pretty young mochaccino orderer.

"Need anything, boss?" he called.

"No, it's okay."

I wasn't thrilled with Dante calling me "boss," but it was better than "Ms. Cosi," which is how he'd repeatedly addressed me when I'd first hired him. Sure, I'd asked him to call me Clare, but despite Dante's outlaw appearance, the guy had scrupulous manners—no doubt from the same sort of traditional Italian upbringing I'd gotten from my own grandmother. Luckily, our resident slam poetess, Esther Best, held virtually *no* respect for authority, and her routine, semisarcastic address of me as "boss" had finally loosened up Dante enough to break him of his "Ms. Cosi" habit.

Matt knocked the counter with his knuckles. I glanced back to him.

"You off soon?" he asked.

"Why?"

"I thought you'd like to come with me to the White Horse. Koa Waipuna just got into town, and I'm meeting him for a drink."

"Sure. I'm sorry I missed him the last time he was here. We can go as soon as Gardner gets here to relieve me."

Five minutes later, the front door bell jingled, and a long-limbed African American jazz musician with a freshly trimmed goatee strode purposefully across the wood-plank floor.

"Okay, Dante," called Gardner, waving a hand-labeled CD case. "Enough with your Sominex playlist! I just cut a new fusion mix with my group. Let's wake things up in here!"

TWO

∾∾∾∾∾∾∾∾∾∾∾∾∾∾∾∾∾∾∾∾∾∾∾

Walk down almost any of my neighborhood's narrow, tree-lined streets, and you'll see three centuries of architectural history, from Federal, Greek Revival, and Italianate town houses to early twentieth-century apartment buildings. Almost everyone I know has applauded the saving of these landmarks and cried over the treasures that were lost before the historic district was sanctioned. But no one cried hard enough, it seemed to me, over losing the guts of these places.

While the buildings around the Village Blend were now preserved by law, the businesses inside them weren't, and every year that ticked by, more of my neighborhood's legendary establishments folded, their storefronts replaced with the sort of trade you'd find in upscale suburban malls. What made Greenwich Village *Greenwich Village* was drifting away faster than Al Gore's ice caps.

That's the main reason I valued the White Horse. Like my Village Blend, the landmark tavern stubbornly refused to let go of its moorings. Since Welsh poet Dylan Thomas tossed back eighteen fatal shots in its paneled back room fifty years ago, the White Horse has been hyped as the watering hole of literary legends.

True, Norman Mailer used the joint as a second living room, mainly because, as he so graciously put it, "If you invited people to your house, it was not that easy to get rid of them . . ." But I'd also been impressed with the building itself, which was one of the few wood-frame construction remaining in Manhattan. The ground-level storefront originally housed a bookshop. Then the James Dean Oyster Bar took over the space, and in 1880, the White Horse opened its doors.

For the next five decades or so, the tavern poured whiskey for longshoremen working the nearby West Side docks. Then the Village became a magnet for struggling writers and artists and bohemians began to gather there. Today's clientele lived a lot farther up the socioeconomic ladder.

With NYU now owning half the real estate in my picturesque Village, the college crowd was constantly ringing the bar's register. Pub-crawling tourists frequented the place too, along with well-paid or well-subsidized neighborhood regulars who craved good burgers, great onion rings, and ice cold beers. (Local real estate being what it was, authentically bohemian writers had long ago retrenched in other neighborhoods, but sometimes even they returned to the tavern drawn by the legends as much as the tourists.)

This evening, the century-old tavern looked as casually inviting as ever with its upper stories painted summer-sky blue and its stately white horse chess-piece emblems stenciled above the tall front windows.

The manager had gamely put out the café umbrellas, but April was still early in the season for sidewalk seating, and only one of the wooden picnic tables was occupied, despite the mild spring weather.

After an easy stroll under Hudson's glowing street lamps, Matt and I entered the softly lit front room to find Koa Waipuna sitting at the magnificent mirror-backed mahogany bar (the original one, circa the nineteenth century). I hadn't seen Koa in years, but there was no way to miss the man. He was big. And exotic didn't begin to describe him.

Along with his name, Koa had inherited his deep olive complexion and black, expressive eyes from his native Hawaiian father. His frame was heavily muscled, yet he had the delicate facial structure of his Japanese mother. Fluent in Japanese as well as his native Hawaiian, he still wore his long black hair in a samurai-style topknot, an offbeat crowning to preppie khakis, an aquamarine Izod, and polished loafers.

Koa spotted Matt first and grinned. Then he shifted his gaze to me.

"Clare!" He stood and wrapped his beefy arms around me in an enthusiastic hug only slightly less forceful than a boa constrictor's. "I wasn't expecting to see you tonight!"

I'd visited the Waipunas' farm only once in my life, years earlier, when Matteo converted a Kona buying trip into our hastily planned but spectacularly romantic Hawaiian honeymoon. Back then, Koa had been a wild young teenager who refused to wear a shirt, bristled at farm work, and was constantly surrounded by his five giggling sisters. Today he was in his thirties, married with children, and responsible for the coffee farm's day-to-day operations. He was serious as a heart attack, according to Matt, until he set foot off the estate. Then his wild streak returned with a vengeance.

"Come with me," Koa said. Grinning wide, he led us toward the bar's back room. "The gang's all here."

Matt shot Koa a confused look. "The gang? What gang?"

"Oh, uh . . . I just meant that I brought Mr. Koto and Mr. Takahashi along. I hope you don't mind."

"Of course not," Matt said. "I haven't seen Junro since my trip to Malaysia last year."

Matt had mentioned that Koa was working on a business deal with a Japanese company—a plan to host special tours of his estate since Kona-drinking had become pretty popular in Japan.

I was about to ask Koa about it, but I never got the chance. He opened a thin wooden door, and a dozen male voices shouted Matt's name. That's when I saw the hanging banner:

BON VOYAGE
BACHELORHOOD!

Clipped to the banner was the poster of a blown-up photo, obviously doctored. Matt was on all fours with a ball and chain on his foot and a rope around his neck; his beautiful bride-to-be was dressed to the nines in a floor-length burgundy gown, dripping in diamonds, holding one end of Matt's rope like a pet leash.

"Surprised?" Koa yelled over the din.

"Am I ever," Matt replied.

Oh, God. I could see the muscles in Matt's face had frozen. He'd gone slightly pale, and sweat was starting to bead his upper lip. He glanced at me and then behind him, clearly in a panic about Randall Knox's stalking gossip column photographer.

I looked behind us, but there were no paparazzi in sight. Then I glanced around the crowded party room. Apart from the embarrassing poster of Matt and Breanne, there was nothing here to warrant tabloid scandal. Sure, Matt's friends had gotten a good head start on the consumption of alcohol. But it was a *tavern*, after all.

Two of Matt's buddies thrust a mug of beer into his hand, pounded his back, and led him farther into the back room—the same one where Dylan Thomas purportedly drank himself to death (not a good omen).

"I should go," I told Koa, turning to do just that.

"No, Clare, stay!" Koa pulled me back. "Have a drink at least, and say hello to the guys. You know a lot of them—look!"

I did, actually. Some of them were now smiling at me, waving me over.

"This part of the party's going to be tame, anyway," Koa confided.

"*This part* of the party?" I frowned. "Sorry, I need a little more."

Koa pointed toward Matt, now chugging his mug of beer in front of the room's giant portrait of Dylan Thomas. (Actually, the entire room was a makeshift shrine to the dead

Welsh poet, with pictures of his home, framed newspaper
clippings, and a special plaque.)

"Once Matt gets drunk enough"—Koa paused to give me
meaningful wink—"we're taking him to Scores."

"The yuppie strip joint?"

"Gentlemen's club."

Okay, I thought instantly, *I'm definitely staying.*

What Matt did with women—fully clothed or otherwise—
was no longer my business. What he did with his credit
cards, however, was another matter. And I'd never forget
the front-page story of the idiot corporate executive who'd
gotten so drunk with his clients at one of those "gentlemen's" clubs that he couldn't recall racking up seventy
thousand dollars' worth of champagne and lap dancing
charges.

"Matt! Matt! Matt!"

The guys had started chanting for my ex to chug a second
beer.

Good Lord, I thought. *If Matt goes to Scores hammered, we
may lose the Blend.*

"Listen," I told Koa, "Joy's not making much money as
Paris line cook, and she's depending on us. I don't want
Matt 'treating' his friends to the tune of personal bankruptcy.
Got it?"

Koa laughed. "Tell you what. Stick around until we're
ready to take him uptown. I'll get his wallet from him and
hand it to you to hold. How's that?"

"Fine, get me his wallet. Then you have my blessing to
drag him off—as long as you *make sure* not to let *anyone* take
any embarrassing photos of Matt. Breanne would kill him."

Koa laughed again. "You worry too much!"

"You have no idea."

He laughed once more and patted my back. I knew he
meant it to be a light tap, but the force nearly sent me off my
low-heeled boots.

"Trust me, Clare. We'll be discreet."

A strip club. Heavy drinking. And discretion? One of thes
things was not like the others. But then what choice did
have? In the end, Koa was probably right, I decided, an
there was no need to worry.

Obviously, Randall Knox's photographer had taken th
night off, and Matt's surprise bachelor party appeared totall
harmless, anyway: a lot of men, some enthusiastic beer drink
ing, but that was all, really. In fact, I thought, as I calme
down to take a longer look at all the faces in the room, th
gathering was kind of touching.

The men around me had flown here from Brazil, Colom
bia, Costa Rica, Kenya, Ethiopia, the Arabian Peninsula, In
donesia, and the Caribbean, virtually every coffee-producin
region of the world. Some represented small, family coffe
farms. Others owned large estates, exported for cooperatives
or worked in Europe or New York as importers for roasters.

Koa handed me a mug of beer, and I watched as Matt'
friends, one after another, stood up and toasted him, some
times in broken English, often with tears in their eyes.

It was then that I realized what was happening here, an
it was more than just a bachelor party, because these guy
weren't simply my ex-husband's buddies. They represente
the thousand quests my business partner had made to kee
alive a coffee trade his great-grandfather had started, a busi
ness that was still standing, like this tavern, despite th
here-and-gone swells and eddies of the past hundred years.

I smiled, thinking, *Madame should be here to see this . . .*

It was Matt's mother, after all, who'd provided the mone
for the smaller farm owners to even come to Saturday's wed
ding, which would have proved far too costly for most o
them to afford.

With an inspired spirit, I strolled through the crowde
room, saying hello to the guys, many of whom I'd met i
passing over the years. Suddenly, we were interrupted b
some loud demands that the best man now propose a toast.

Matt's closest friend since his youth was Ric Gostwick

Ric would have been Matt's best man, but he was currently serving time in a penitentiary (which was an entirely different story), so Matt asked Roger Mbele to do the honors.

A prominent member of the Nairobi Coffee Exchange, Roger had been like a father to Matt for years. He was also a very old friend of Matt's mother. Eminently dignified, the Kenyan was tall and lean, with craggy features, hair the color of snow, and skin the hue of an earthy French roast. Moving to the center of the room, Roger lifted his half-empty mug and began an eloquent tribute. That's when I noticed the door to the back room opening.

I watched to see who was coming in so late to the party, but no one stepped across the threshold. Whoever had cracked the door appeared to be waiting just outside the room.

My nerves bristled, and I slipped quickly through the crowd of men, toward the door. When I got close enough, I finally glimpsed who was standing there, spying on the festivities. But it wasn't what I feared—some photographer with a zoom lens.

It was worse.

A leggy blond in a business suit stood peering into the room. She wore wraparound, rose-tinted sunglasses that shielded much of her face, but I would have recognized her anywhere. She appeared to be surveying the gathering, and she didn't look happy. No surprise, given her focus on the hanging banner, the one with the unflattering poster of herself holding Matt's leash.

Matt hadn't yet seen her. He'd been distracted by Roger's toast, so I waited for the best man to finish and the gang to raise their glasses. Then I maneuvered through the guys to the center of the room and tapped my half-drunk ex-husband on the arm.

"She's here, Matt."

"Who's here?" He looked down at me, his eyes slightly glazed.

"The woman who threatened you with *homicide* if you had a bachelor party." I pointed to the half-open door.

Matt paled, his mug of beer freezing halfway to his lips.

"I'm a dead man."

THREE

THE door swung fully open, banging like a gunshot against the back wall (and barely missing the framed photos of Dylan Thomas's gravesite and writing shed). The sudden noise quieted the men, and they turned their heads to find Breanne Summour fuming in the doorway.

Regally blond, the statuesque beauty was clad in a form-fitting business suit of pearl gray pinstripes. Her honey-colored hair was coiled in a tight bun, and even though the tavern's lighting was dim and her eyes and much of her face were hidden behind the large rose-tinted sunglasses, there was no mistaking the sharp chin and pouting lips, glossed with her favorite Beaujolais Red lipstick. Sheer black stockings, four-inch pointy-toed heels, and a matching leather attaché completed the sleek trademark look.

Matt winced. "Oh, jeez . . ."

For a moment, nothing happened. Then, in a silent wave, the men parted, allowing Breanne to cut a swath through the room. The ominous bonging of the wall's pendulum clock and the tap-tap-tapping of Fifth Avenue heels across worn hardwood planks were the only sounds in the dead quiet.

Breanne slammed her attaché onto a stout table and popped the leather lid. A moment later, music flowed out of the case, a rhythmic throbbing. As a throaty saxophone began its song, Breanne stepped close to Matt.

Without a word spoken, his broad shoulders sagged, as in relief. And his tense expression—no doubt braced for a tongue-lashing—now visibly relaxed.

It took me another moment to realize what was really happening. Breanne ripped away her tinted lenses, and I finally saw that this was *not* Matt's bride, just a dead ringer for her—or, rather, a dead ringer for a much younger Breanne. Sans rose-colored glasses, the young woman was obviously half Breanne's age. Unfortunately, she was also the bachelor party's featured entertainer, so I could guess what was coming next.

Using a chair for a step, the woman climbed onto a table, where she *definitely* had everyone's attention. With her lips pursed in a seductive pout, she swayed her hips to the prima music and began to unbutton her fitted pinstriped jacket. She released her coiled hair next, letting it fall like a honey-colored curtain; then the dancer slid her hands down her thighs and lifted the hem of the skirt to reveal stocking tops and lacy black garters.

Embarrassed, I looked away, searching the crowd for Koa. He shot me a knowingly amused thumbs-up, and I knew he was the one to arrange this frat-boy prank.

So much for discretion.

The younger guys were going crazy now—buck wild, actually. And I started going crazy, too, frantically pushing my way through the howling, testosterone-fueled mob to the room's windows. I maneuvered the high blinds down to a closed position just in case Knox's "Gotham Gossip" photographer was lurking out there in the night.

Whistles and catcalls erupted around me, and I turned to find Koa at my side, grinning like a Pacific shark. "We really had Matt going there, didn't we?! I thought he was going to drop a rock!"

"Ha-ha, yes, very funny," I said, and was about to add more, but Koa's attention had already shifted back to the dancer, which didn't surprise me. (Men typically preferred staring at a woman rather than actually listening to one.)

Above my head, cloth fluttered down like autumn leaves

The audience hooted, whistled, and howled. I spied Roger Mbele shaking his head, a bemused expression on his face, and that's when I realized the door to the bar's public front room was still wide open.

I moved to shut it and found half a dozen male customers from the bar standing there gawking, eager to get an eyeful of the stripper. When one of the college kids whipped out a cell phone and held it up—presumably to start snapping pictures for the Internet, I shoved the group back.

"Sorry, private party!" I told them and began to close the door in their faces.

But I couldn't shut it all the way. I looked down to find a heavy black boot blocking my efforts. The boot was scuffed and dirty, attached to a guy in his late twenties: too old to be an undergrad, I thought, too skeevy to be a grad student (probably). He was close to six feet and wiry, with a studded leather motorcycle jacket and a black shirt decorated with creepy Day of the Dead skeletons. His skin was pale but flushed, as if he'd been drinking (big surprise). He had a few days' scruff on his jaw, his stringy brown hair was disheveled, and a stud earring of a white skull was snickering at me from one earlobe.

"Who do you have to *know* to get invited to this party?" the guy said, his breath violating my nose with a reeking mix of bad dental hygiene and a great deal of tequila. "Who's the guest of honor?"

"Nobody special," I assured him. "It's just a party. Now, *please* let me close the door."

The man's unblinking stare remained fixed. "Lemme in, lady. I won't drink your booze." He pointed to the Breanne look-alike. "It's the ho I wanna meet."

"Forget it." I pushed harder on the door. His heavy boot remained planted.

"And what if I don't, *bitch*?"

My eyes narrowed. Like most suburban girls, I'd grown up with the usual "be nice" lessons. Good manners were a sign of good character; and the last thing a modest girl would ever want to do was be the cause of an awkward scene. After years working a service counter in this town, however, I'd learned other lessons. To guys like this, for instance, courtesy was a rope to strangle women with.

"Stop giving me trouble, scumbag!" I shouted at the top of my lungs. "Or I'll call our bouncer!"

People in the bar's front room frowned in my direction, but Koa heard my yell (a miracle over the raucous noise) and immediately moved behind me.

"Trouble, Clare?" the big Hawaiian asked, crossing his massive arms.

"Not if this guy steps *away* from the door!" I yelled, this time with close to three hundred pounds of heavily muscled backing.

Eyes shifting to Koa's ham-sized biceps, the jerk's scowl deepened. Finally, he turned around. Heavy boots clomping, he walked back to the front room's mahogany bar. The bartender approached the man as he plopped down and poured him another shot.

I shut the back room door and sagged against it. As the Breanne look-alike finished her act, I studied the vintage tin ceiling. Then I heard a burst of exuberant applause, and a moment later, the statuesque young dancer slipped away. Clothes bundled under her arm, pumps and attaché case in hand, she ducked through the room's back archway, bolting by the tavern's kitchen and disappearing into an alcove that led to the ladies' room.

Roger Mbele walked by me a moment later, his jacket draped over his arm.

"You're not going to the gentlemen's club?" I asked, not entirely surprised.

Roger smiled. "In Kenya, I go to bed when the sun sets, and get up before it rises. I'm too old for late nights." Then he laughed. "Or maybe it's simply a case of jet lag."

He gave me a hug, pecked me on the cheek. "I'll see you at the luncheon, Clare. And Madame, as well."

Roger's departure was followed by some of the other older

partygoers, who also bade me good night. There were empty beer pitchers and glasses everywhere. The party banner had fluttered to the floor, and I found Matt speaking with Dexter Beatty, a Jamaican who sold Caribbean coffees out of three Brooklyn locations. Forty-something, tall, and scarecrow-thin, Dexter almost always displayed a wide grin under his wild Rasta dreadlocks.

"If your new wife can dance like that sweet thing, you are the luckiest dude alive!" Dexter said, knocking Matt's fist. "See you at Thursday's luncheon, mon. And congratulations!"

Matt turned to face me, opened his mouth to speak. Then Koa draped a big arm around his neck, and said, "Okay, bro, now that we got you all hot and bothered, it's time for the main event. We're taking you to Scores!"

The remaining men around us hooted.

"The night is on me," Koa vowed. "So hand your wallet over to Clare. I won't take *no* for an answer"—he winked in my direction—"and neither will she."

I stepped forward, palm up, hand extended.

"Koa, my brother, you're the best," Matt said, rubbing his bleary eyes. "But I'm not going to Scores with you."

Koa looked stricken. "Dude! You can't be serious."

Matt shrugged apologetically. "With the wedding and my daughter coming in, I've got too much to do. I've been going since sunup. It's time for me to call it a night."

"No Scores?" Men groaned in disappointment.

"Just for me, guys," Matt insisted. He smiled at Koa. "You all go. Have a blast."

Koa considered Matt and nodded. "Okay, bro. It's your party . . . but *we're* gonna keep it going!" Grinning, he turned to face the others. "Dudes, it's on! The girls are waiting!"

With more good-byes and congratulations, the men filed out. After everyone was gone, I sidled up to Matt.

"That's a shocker."

"What?"

"*You*—not going to a gentlemen's club with your hammered brethren."

Matt folded his arms. "You've got something to say about it?"

"I don't believe it, that's all." I shook my head. "The eternal boy is *all growed up*."

Matt rolled his eyes. "Again with the 'eternal boy.'"

"Would you rather I use the Latin?" I couldn't help needling him—just a little. *"Puer aeternus?* A man stuck in the adolescent phase of his life."

"I'd rather you get off my back. Believe me, on any other night, I would have gladly gone out with Koa and the guys, but . . ." He sighed, rubbed the back of his neck.

"But?"

"But the sight of that fake Breanne put the fear of bridezilla into me, okay?" He shook his head. "It simply occurred to me that one wild night isn't worth the hell storm that could come down on my head. I'm looking forward to my wedding on Saturday, the Barcelona honeymoon. Why do I need trouble this week?"

"Sounds like a reasoned, mature decision." I smiled then lightly elbowed his six-pack. "Not bad for a man who's chugged as many beers as you have."

Matt finally laughed. Then the pendulum clock on the wall began to bong the hour. "It's eleven already. Let's get out of here."

The front barroom was much busier now and much louder. Tables and chairs were occupied by a mixed group of college kids and older drinkers. As we moved through, I tapped Matt's shoulder.

"Give me a second, okay? I want to use the restroom."

"Yeah, me, too. Chugging beer has its consequences. Meet you at the front door."

I walked past the Dylan Thomas shrine again and into a small, adjoining back area that held an alcove to the ladies' room. That's where I spotted the attractive young dancer again. I froze when I realized *what* she'd attracted.

The obnoxious jerk in the black motorcycle jacket had left the crowded bar and slipped back here, trapping the dancer in an isolated corner. The girl was giving the punk a tense smile, shaking her head prettily, gesturing to her cell phone. He snatched it away from her. She reached for it, but he held it higher, stepped closer.

I hurried back to the bar, waited the few seconds for Matt to return. "I need your help."

"What's the matter?"

"A drunk gave me trouble earlier. He's cornered the Breanne dancer by the ladies' room. We should do something to—"

Matt was already moving. I followed in his muscular wake. The dancer was still standing there and still attempting to be polite to the harassing drunk.

"No. Thank you, kindly, mister. But I don't want no drink . . ."

The girl's backwoods twang was at odds with her hyperpolished Breanne facade. And her little voice was as slight as her figure: down off the stout table, her performance bravado gone, she projected all the sturdiness of a porcelain ballerina.

"Aw, come on," the guy replied with an oily smile. "You musss be thirsssy after all that sexy dancin' . . ."

"I told you, no thanks. Now, can I *please* have my phone back?"

"Not till you give me that private dance I asssked you for. Jusss turn around now, an' you won't get hurt. We'll use the john—"

The scumbag reached out a grease-stained hand for a clumsy grope, but he never got it. Matt grabbed the guy's arm, tightening his fingers around the man's wrist.

"What the hell!"

"Didn't you hear the lady?" Matt said, twisting the guy's arm just enough to make his point. "She doesn't want to drink with you, and she didn't come here to dance for you."

Without shifting his gaze from the jerk's face, Matt pulled the phone out of his grip and handed it back to the dancer. The man stared blankly at Matt. I held my breath as the two remained locked together. When Matt finally released his grip, the other man stumbled back.

"Screw you," he muttered, rubbing the arm Matt had twisted.

Like all bullies, this guy was obviously brilliant at pushing around a weaker opponent. A head-to-head challenge was another matter.

"The lady's with us, okay?" Matt said. "And we're leaving."

"Lady?" The punk snorted. "She's a ho, asshole!"

Matt stepped uncomfortably close again. "Unless you want to experience a *world* of hurt, I suggest you stay here, have another drink, and stay the hell *away* from this *lady*."

Matt took the dancer's arm, then mine, and guided us quickly through the exit. We didn't slow down until we reached the next street corner.

"Lordy," the dancer said, staring up at Matt with wide blue eyes. "Thanks for your help. I thought I could charm my way around that horndog, but he was a real A-hole, wasn't he?"

"Don't you have a driver?" Matt asked. "A guy to watch your back?"

She vigorously nodded. "Normally, I do. But he's down with the flu."

Hearing more of her accent, I placed it as possibly West Virginian—a twang I'd heard when I was raising Joy in New Jersey. A big, friendly family had moved onto our street from a small town outside of Wheeling.

"What about transportation?" I asked.

"The agency's car service is supposed to send a limo over." She held up her cell phone. "All I have to do is call for it. But I kept gettin' their dang voice mail!" She sighed theatrically. "That happens sometimes. I guess there just aren't enough cars in this big ol' city. Anyway, I don't have much cash on me. Not enough for a cab to Brooklyn. I guess I should just take the subway."

"Are you kidding?" I said. "At this hour? With those

expensive clothes and high heels? You may as well shout, 'Mug me.' "

The girl scratched her head. "Think so?"

I exchanged glances with Matt. "Why don't you walk with us," I told her. "We're headed back to our coffeehouse just down the street. You can straighten out your car service problems from there. At least you'll be safe from half-drunk rapists."

"That's a fine idea," she said. "And it'll be my pleasure, too, with this hunky hero here watchin' out for me!"

I rolled my eyes. Matt grunted. Then the girl wrapped her arm around my ex's biceps and we were off.

The weather had turned colder by now, and Hudson Street was practically deserted. We strolled through the shadows on the empty sidewalk, past closed storefronts, parked cars, chained-up bicycles, and the redbrick fronts of restored Federal-style town houses.

The girl continued to coo what a gentleman Matt was. He didn't say much, but I could see he was soaking it up. Her flirting was cute and innocent, nothing like the sophisticated temptress persona she'd projected while performing back at the White Horse. She seemed naive, too, but also funny and open, and (unlike the woman she'd been paid to impersonate) easy for me to like.

She told us she'd been living in New York for only about six months, something I could believe, given her bubbly optimism. The city usually beat it out of girls like her in a year or two.

"I came here to become a Broadway star," she said, "but the only steady work I could get was dancing at a club uptown. These side jobs with an agency pay a lot more, though."

"Agency?" I asked.

"It specializes in look-alike strippers. Funny, huh? They've got guys doin' it, too. There's a Matt Damon and a Brad Pitt. They even got a Mel Gibson, but he's so *old*, I can't imagine anyone wanting Mel to strip for 'em, can you?"

Matt shot me an exasperated look. I bit my lip to keep from laughing.

Curious, I couldn't help asking, "Have you ever done the Breanne act before?"

"Only once, for some guy's birthday party at the *New York Journal*."

Hearing that, Matt grunted and gave me the I-told-you-so look.

"I'm usually tapped to do Uma," the girl said.

"Uma Thurman?" I asked. "The actress?"

The dancer rolled her eyes. "Who else? How many girls named *Uma* do *you* know?"

"Well, I—"

"For Uma, I keep my hair blond like tonight for Breanne Summour, but instead of the suit and briefcase I wear this sweet li'l yellow jumpsuit and carry a samurai sword—"

"Excuse me?" I broke in again. "Did you say a samurai sword?"

"From *Kill Bill*. You know, the movie? Uma played a kick-ass assassin!"

"Wild guess," I said. "When you're dressed as Uma, you don't have any problem with mashers."

"You're right about that one, honey!" The girl snorted. "I just point the tip of my li'l ol' Japanese blade to a certain part of the horndog's anatomy, and he's hightailin' it right down the road!"

We both laughed so hard that Matt had to stop us from stepping into oncoming traffic. We waited for the few cars to pass. Then I looked up and noticed we were almost home. I could see the golden light spilling from the Blend's tall windows just a block away.

"I haven't given up, though," the girl chattered on. "I'm just starting out. I'm going to make my *mark* on this town!" she declared to the century-old buildings.

That's when I heard the pop, like a car backfiring, only not as loud. The sound merged with a hollow thump that seemed much closer. I turned to see the dancer's face had lanched whiter than milk froth. She staggered forward. Her mouth opened to speak, but no words came out. Then she fell to the pavement.

"My God!" Matt lunged to catch the girl, but her body dropped too fast.

Eyes wide and staring, bone china arms spread like a discarded doll, Breanne's look-alike was dead an instant later, her seeping blood on the hard sidewalk the last mark on New York she'd ever make.

Four

⠼⠼⠼⠼⠼⠼⠼⠼⠼⠼⠼⠼⠼⠼⠼⠼⠼⠼⠼

Wiᴛʜɪɴ seconds of the girl's collapse, Matt and I had called 911. Now we stood staring as two FDNY paramedics attempted to breathe life back into a motionless mannequin.

From the grim expressions on their faces, I knew every last vital sign pointed to one conclusion. Resigned to the inevitable, the men snapped off their latex gloves and withdrew.

I stepped back into a nearby doorway and sank like a defeated boxer onto the chilly concrete stoop. Matt followed but he didn't collapse beside me. Instead, he fisted his hands and paced back and forth in a tight pattern, the sizable silhouette of his muscular shoulders continually eclipsing the bloodred flashes of the police emergency lights.

I swiped my wet eyes and returned my gaze to the girl's corpse, pale as moonlight against the dark sidewalk. For a bizarre moment, her pretty form and ruined skull reminded me of Joy's old Malibu Barbie.

Back when I'd been raising my daughter alone in New Jersey, a slobbering pit bull had slipped into our yard and chewed up the doll's pretty blond head. While Joy was still at school, I'd raced to the mall to replace the mangled plaything, determined as any mother to hold off my child's inevitable encounters with the world's brutalities. But there was no running to a store to replace this lost life, no do-over, no turning

ck the clock. The young woman had taken a shot to the
ain, and she hadn't survived. It sounded simple enough to
derstand, but so what? When death was involved, under-
anding and acceptance were two very different things.

I closed my eyes, said a quiet prayer, and realized how
rcefully my ex-husband's lungs were now exhaling breaths.
was horrified by the girl's death, shocked and saddened, but
att seemed to be struggling with a mounting rage. With
where to vent, he threw up his arms at the growing crowd.

"Where did all these people come from?!"

I opened my eyes, surveyed the two Sixth Precinct sector
rs, their radios squawking; the boxy FDNY ambulance
ith its doors thrown wide; and the rubbernecking drivers
w backing up traffic. Four uniformed officers were hover-
g around the scene. One of them asked onlookers to stand
ack, another made a large perimeter with yellow crime-
ene tape.

"They're gawking like it's a sideshow."

"Well, you know what they say." I shrugged numbly.
Dead bodies attract everything, not just flies."

"*They* say?" Matt grunted, folded his arms. "And who the
ll is *they*? Wait, don't tell me. That's one of your *boyfriend's*
tle quips, isn't it?"

Matt was right. Mike Quinn had been the one to convey
at pithy piece of postmortem philosophy. The way Matt
at out the word *boyfriend*, however, reminded me that he
ill hadn't forgiven the detective for arresting him last fall.

I could see Matt didn't appreciate Quinn's use of humor, ei-
er. But his quips weren't meant to be disrespectful, just a
ay to help lighten the relentlessly weighty work of evaluat-
g crime scenes. I was about to make that point when I heard
e fast click of heels on concrete. Two pairs of women's boots
proached us and stopped abruptly in front of Matt.

"Excuse me, sir. You gave a statement to Officer Spinelli?
e said you were a witness to the shooting?"

I looked up. A familiar pair of detectives was standing on
e sidewalk, staring nearly eye to eye with my six foot ex.

Like Mike Quinn, Lori Soles and Sue Ellen Bass worked ou
of the Sixth Precinct on West Tenth.

"We were with the girl," Matt told the women, "but v
didn't see much."

Lori Soles finally noticed me far below her and smiled
recognition. "Clare Cosi? Is that you?"

I nodded and rose off the low stoop—all five foot two
me. (I may as well have stayed sitting.)

Detective Soles gazed down at me, her short, tight cur
making her look like a giant cherub. "I guess I shouldn't b
surprised to find you here. Isn't you coffeehouse just a bloc
away?" She held a small notebook in one hand, gestured
the Village Blend with the other.

I nodded.

Next to Detective Soles, Detective Sue Ellen Bass steppe
closer to my ex. I put both women in their thirties, althoug
Sue Ellen appeared older than Lori by at least five years. An
where Lori had the long, friendly face of a horsey-set blon
Sue Ellen had a lean, triangular look. It suited her personalit
as did her jet-black hair, much longer than Lori's short, blor
curls, though it was hard to tell, since Sue Ellen wore her ha
in a slicked-back ponytail. Both women sported nylon jacke
over blue turtlenecks and dark slacks, gold detective shiel
dangling on long cords around their necks.

I'd first met the pair when they were working undercov
on a special task force headed by Mike Quinn. At that tim
they were trying to bring down a ring of nightclub pred
tors. Glammed to the max, the pair had repeatedly bait
likely suspects at several area nightspots. From what I remen
bered, Detective Soles was happily married. For her, it ha
been just another assignment. But I got the distinct impre
sion from some private banter between the two women tha
Sue Ellen hadn't ruled out meeting future romantic hooku
while on her eight-hour tour of club duty.

"So, Cosi, who's *this* tall drink of water?" Sue Ellen aske
me, jerking her thumb at my ex-husband.

I scratched my head, disconcerted for a moment by h

hoice of words. "Uh, this is Matteo Allegro. He's my . . .
usiness partner." I could have said more, but what was the
point?

She gave Matt's strong form a quick, open appraisal. "Single?"

"Engaged," I said.

"Is that so?" Sue Ellen replied, still looking him over.
Then he's *technically* still available?"

Matt exhaled with what sounded like extreme irritation.
I'm standing right here, ladies, *and* I'm quite capable of an-
wering my own questions."

"He does look capable, doesn't he?" Sue Ellen remarked to
ne with an arched eyebrow. Then she turned to Matt. "In
ases like this, sir, it's best if we direct *initial* queries to the
rofessional on the scene. And since we have one here—"

"Professional?" Matt interrupted.

Ignoring Matt, Lori Soles now addressed me, her pen
poised over her open notebook. "Tell us, Clare, did you hear
he gunshot from inside the Blend?"

"No. We weren't in the Blend. We were headed there, all
hree of us. Matt and I were walking with the victim. We'd
ust left Matt's bachelor party at the White Horse on Eleventh.
We reached this corner, and we were waiting for the traffic
ight to change. I heard a pop, and the woman fell—"

"One pop?" Sue Ellen Bass asked. "Only one? You're
ure?"

"Yes, I'm sure."

Several halogen lamps were turned on just then, and I
ifted my arm to shield my eyes from the glare of tiny suns.
More officers had arrived on the scene, some in uniform,
others in plain clothes, and they appeared to be using the
ight to scour the dark ground—for forensic evidence, I as-
umed.

I also noticed a middle-aged Asian man and a young
white woman in dark-blue nylon jackets. Together they
crouched next to the dead girl and began to examine her
body and head.

"Then what happened, Clare?" Detective Soles prompted.

"It took a few seconds for Matt and me to realize what had happened. Then Matt called 911, and I looked around for any sign of the shooter."

"And?" she asked almost hopefully. But I had to disappoint her.

"The street was empty, the sidewalks, too. Whoever shot her had already ducked for cover."

Sue Ellen glanced at the girl's body for a moment, then back to me. "Did you know this woman, Cosi? Was she a client of yours?"

"Client?" Matt sputtered. "What do you mean, *client*?"

I elbowed Matt. He grunted, and I shot him a look that said, *I'll explain later.*

Sue Ellen stepped closer to Matt, lowered her voice. "Sorry, honey-lumps, I know you can't wait to give me your statement." She winked. "But don't worry. I'll make sure to take it *personally* in a minute."

Matt groaned.

"Go ahead, Cosi." Sue Ellen nodded. "You were saying?"

"The victim wasn't my client," I clarified. "We don't even know her name. We met her tonight for the first time in our lives. She was at Matt's party at the tavern. Actually, she was the entertainer at the party . . ."

I proceeded to give the detectives a rundown of the events leading up to the shooting, making sure they got a detailed description of the drunken scumbag who'd nearly assaulted the girl at the bar.

Scribbling furiously, Lori took everything down.

When I was done, Sue Ellen shook her head. "An exotic dancer, huh? It's no surprise she came to a bad end."

Lori Soles waved over a pair of uniformed officers. She gave them my description of the jerk at the bar and sent them to the White Horse to find the guy, if they could, and report back. Then she got on her radio and had the police dispatcher issue a BOLO, otherwise known as a be on the okout for—an acronym I'd learned a short time ago when a rooklyn cop (unfortunately) had issued one on me.

"So do you think he's the one who did this?" I asked, gesuring to the girl's cooling corpse.

Lori exchanged a glance with her partner. "Both of us arted out in vice, Clare. We've seen this kind of thing firstand."

"What kind of thing exactly?"

"These women play a dangerous game," Sue Ellen said, lding her arms. "They spend hours a day titillating men; it's surprise a percentage of these guys turn out to be pervs and pists. The shooter *could* have been this guy at the bar—"

"That's right, it could," Lori jumped in. "You witnessed im harass the victim, and that's good. We can make a case gainst this guy if we find the weapon on him or even power burns, but . . ." Again, she exchanged a glance with her artner. "It could very well be some other guy."

Sue Ellen nodded. "The girl may have had a boyfriend she lted or lied to about what she did for a living. Or she could ave a whole other stalker scenario going on."

"You mean someone who saw her dance and became sexuly obsessed with her?" I assumed. "Something like that?"

"Exactly." Lori's gaze speared me. "Did the girl mention nyone like that? An old boyfriend? A guy who might have een harassing her?"

I shook my head. "Sorry. She didn't mention anyone like at. Just that the agency hired her to do the job tonight."

"Did she tell you the agency's name?"

"No, but she mentioned it specialized in look-alike stripers. She said they have male performers, too . . ." I told em everything the girl had said. "I'm sure our friend Koa Vaipuna can give you the name and contact number for the gency. The agency was supposed to send a man to look after er—"

"That's right. That's how it's usually done," Lori said. What happened to hers?"

I glanced at Matt. "She said he was sick with the flu, but I suppose it could also be a lead . . ."

"Good." Lori continued to scribble notes.

Sue Ellen frowned at her partner's furious writing. "I still like the scumbag from the White Horse for this," she said quietly.

"So do I," Lori said, "but you know what Lieutenant Quinn always says . . ."

Sue Ellen rolled her eyes. "Yeah, yeah . . ."

Curious, I asked: "What does Mike say?"

Lori shrugged. "Until the case is closed, any lead's a good lead."

"Oh, right. I've heard him say that."

Sue Ellen eyeballed me. "You two still together?"

I folded my arms, not entirely comfortable with the predatory gleam in the woman's gaze. "Yes," I assured her, "Mike and I are seeing each other. *A lot* of each other."

Sue Ellen nodded, getting the message, but I swear she muttered, "Too bad."

"Excuse me?" I said.

The detective didn't repeat her words. "Don't worry, Cosi," she said instead, punctuating her point with a teeth-rattling slap to my back. "We'll nail this shooter, just like you helped us nail that predatory perp at Club Flux last fall."

"She did *what*?!" Matt blurted as I regained my balance.

Nobody answered him, me included, apart from shushing him again.

"Excuse me, Detective . . ." One of the uniformed cops walked up to Lori, handed her a red leather wallet. "Here you go."

"Thanks, Spinelli." She opened the wallet, thumbed through the contents.

"What have you got there?" I asked. "Is the girl's name inside?"

Lori nodded. "Hazel Boggs. Age twenty-two. She may have lived in Brooklyn, but she came here from out of state."

"She'd told us she'd only been here a few months," I said.

"Her occupation aside, she talked more like an innocent than a hardened New Yorker. And her accent had a pronounced twang. It sounded West Virginian to me."

Lori flattened the wallet out, showed me the driver's license photo. "You're good, Clare. The license is from the state of West Virginia."

In the glare of the emergency services halogen lamps, I studied the photo on the girl's license. Her normal look was as different from the super-sleek Breanne act as a new moon from the sun. The girl's regular hair was a kinky dark brown (she'd obviously colored and straightened it). Her pretty, wide eyes appeared to be as blue as Breanne's, but they needed eyeglasses to see, which explained why she'd been squinting when I first saw her. It also explained her bold temptress persona while performing.

To Hazel's nearsighted vision, the faces of the leering men probably blurred together into a single impressionistic landscape. It would have been a good trick to help her performance. All she had to do was dance to the music, and the drooling men in her audience would appear no more menacing than Monet's water lilies.

Still, even with her body swimming in an oversized flannel shirt, her ears holding up clunky, unfashionable glasses, Hazel Boggs's resemblance to Breanne Summour was striking. She had the same facial shape, long patrician nose, model-high cheekbones, pointed chin, and perfectly shaped bee-stung lips.

As I studied the photograph, one of the older plainclothes officers in a suit and tie walked up to us. "A word," said the African American man, staring directly at Lori and Sue Ellen.

The women nodded and stepped away. The older officer gestured to the other personnel around us. He pointed to the ground around the body, and the area farther out—a nearby mailbox and lamppost, some parked cars. Then he spoke some more, slightly shaking his head, which I assumed meant, *No stray bullets on the ground or lodged in nearby objects.*

Finally, all three stepped up to two officials who'd been examining the body: the middle-aged Asian man and the white woman in the dark nylon jackets. The group spoke for a few minutes.

Matt lightly bumped my arm. "Are you going to explain all this to me?"

"All what?"

Matt exhaled. "All this crap about directing initial queries to the *professional* on the scene. The last time I checked, Clare, the Specialty Coffee Association of America wasn't on the NYPD payroll for third-party consulting."

"Dial it down," I whispered. "I helped the detectives with a case a few months ago, and the way the chips fell, they ended up assuming I was a professional private investigator. It's no big deal. Now please be quiet. I'm trying to hear what they're talking about."

It was difficult to pick up the lowered voices, so I moved away from Matt and stepped closer to the powwow around Hazel Boggs's corpse.

". . . a single gunshot wound to the back of the head," the Asian man in the nylon jacket was saying. "Entry wound is evident but no exit wound."

"The witness assures us that she only heard one shot fired," Lori Soles told the group.

"Then your only bullet is lodged right here," the Asian man replied, "inside the victim's skull."

"Let's hope it didn't get pancaked against a bone," Sue Ellen said.

"If there's no exit wound—" Lori glanced down the block, "then the bullet lost velocity."

"That's correct." The Asian man nodded. "The weapon couldn't have been fired from a very close range."

Sue Ellen pointed to the upper floors of buildings in the vicinity. "Could the gun have been fired from a window or balcony?"

"Not possible." The man shook his head. "Look at the angle of entry on the wound. The victim was shot at street level from somewhere directly behind. We'll know more after we get inside the skull."

"Thank you, Doctor." Lori Soles turned to the older plain-clothes officer. "I guess the guys can stop looking for bullets. There was only one, and it's in there." She pointed to the dead girl's cranium.

"We're canvassing the neighborhood now. The shooter may have dropped something . . ."

Just then I noticed a white panel van with a satellite antenna double-parking across the street. Emblazoned on the van's side were three words that sent a chill though my blood: New York 1.

"Oh, God . . ." I muttered. Hazel Boggs's murder was about to make the local news. As a technician jumped out and began unpacking camera equipment, I hurried back to Matt. He looked positively stricken.

"Clare," he whispered, "I have to get out of here."

"Wait!" I grabbed his arm before he could bolt. "These cops will detain you if you try to run. It could get loud. You'll just end up calling attention to yourself."

"But if Breanne sees me on the news—"

"Just give me a second."

I rushed up to Lori Soles, who'd always been the softer touch. "Detective Soles, I'm happy to stick around, but my business partner really needs to get back to our shop. Can you talk to him another time?"

Lori frowned. "*Now* would be better—"

"Oh, let the guy go," Sue Ellen broke in, surprising the heck out of me with an accommodating hand wave. "Spinelli got a statement from him already. And we can track Mr. Tight End down tomorrow. On one condition . . ." She shot Matt an openly flirtatious smile. "He has to give me his digits."

With New York 1's cable news camera approaching, Matt wasn't about to argue. He quickly reached into his back pocket, pulled out his wallet, extracted a business card, and slapped it into Sue Ellen's outstretched hand.

"My cell number's on there," he said before taking off. "Catch you later."

The detective smiled as she pocketed my ex's card. "Not if I catch you first . . ." she promised, her eyes following Matt's posterior all the way back to our coffeehouse.

Five

Fifteen minutes later, I was back inside the Blend.

"Where's Matt?" I asked, approaching the espresso bar.

Gardner Evans glanced up, jerked his thumb toward the ceiling, and went back to crowning a hazelnut-toffee latte with spoonfuls of frothy foam.

I looked around the Blend's first floor and realized I was witnessing an unheard-of customer pattern for a Monday at midnight. The place was packed, and I didn't need a beverage-service management spreadsheet to analyze why.

Sitting around our marble-topped café tables was a base of neighborhood regulars, a handful of NYU undergrads, and a sprinkling of FDNY and police personnel. All of them had come here as a result of the bad business a block away. Murder and coffee, it appeared, were a profitable mix.

"You okay here?" I asked Gardner, scanning the work area. I was unhappy to see him alone. "Where's Dante?"

"Downstairs, getting stuff from the big fridge." Gardner drizzled the finished latte with toffee syrup, dusted it with a fine hazelnut powder, and placed the tall glass mug on the counter for the waiting customer. Three more were still in line.

"Things were dead in here an hour ago," he told me, "and we were going to start restocking and cleaning when we got this rush—"

"Hey, boss!" Dante walked out from the back, each tattooed arm lugging a gallon of milk product. He stashed the jugs in our espresso bar fridge and moved up to the counter. "What the heck's going on outside?"

"Yeah, we heard the sirens," Gardner said. "A couple of customers said someone got whacked?"

"A young woman." I rubbed my eyes. On a good day, they were emerald green, but between the beers and the tears, I figured they were massively shot with red. "Listen, I have to go upstairs and talk to Matt right now, but I'll be back down shortly to help."

"Do you want to open the second floor for this mob?" Gardner asked.

The Blend's upstairs lounge often caught the spillover on busy weekends. But my guys were already into overtime. "Morning comes too soon around here," I told Gardner. "Let's keep the customers on the first floor. No more dining room service, either. Give everything wings—and you can start with two *doppio macchiatos* for Matt and me."

"No problem, Clare . . ."

Gardner pulled a pair of double espressos into paper cups then spotted each of the dark pools with a dollop of foamed milk. (That's the basic translation of *macchiato*: to mark with a spot or stain. Some coffeehouses reverse this recipe, marking a cup of steamed or foamed milk with a bit of espresso instead. At the Blend, however, tradition still ruled.)

I picked up my two steaming paper cups, snapped on flat lids, and pointed to the door. "Anyone who comes in here from the police or fire departments gets free drinks tonight. And start brewing up a thermal urn of the Breakfast Blend. When I come down, I'll bring the coffee out to them."

"Okay, Clare."

"Sure, boss."

"Thanks, guys." I left the espresso bar and began to cut a serpentine path through the crowded café tables. I'd been in a pretty big hurry to get to Matt—until I realized the conversations taking place around me were about tonight's shooting. My pace instantly slowed.

At a table to my right, a group of NYU guys in ripped jeans, T-shirts, and day-old chin scruff were all agreeing that they hadn't seen or heard a thing and they didn't know the woman.

Right. I moved on.

At the next table, a twenty-something girl in vintage seventies fringe leather was speaking excitedly about seeing the New York 1 news van. Her redheaded girlfriend in a neon pink cashmere sweater confessed to a crush on Pat Kiernan, the station's morning anchor.

O-kay. I kept walking.

Three more tables turned out to be a bust: conversations about rent hikes, a lousy love life, and an HBO miniseries. But at the very next table, a couple of guys were talking about the shooting. It sounded to me like they were comparing notes on their separate questioning by canvassing cops.

I slowed to a complete stop.

"Did you hear anything? 'Cause I sure didn't," the first man said. He appeared to be in his early thirties, had a fresh-faced, midwestern look about him with thick blond hair and a J. Crew outfit of pressed khakis, a pale-yellow button-down, and a matching sweater draped over his shoulders.

"You didn't hear anything because your apartment window doesn't face Hudson," the second man replied. "Mine does."

I recognized the second man as a regular Blend customer named Barry. He was a very nice, soft-spoken but brilliant Web designer in his early forties. His brown hair was thinning, and his once-trim figure was spreading a bit, but he had a warm, genuine smile and always took the trouble to compliment our coffee. Like many of my regular Village customers, Barry also happened to be gay, and the man he was sitting with looked about ten years younger and a whole lot cuter than Barry's current boyfriend.

"I actually *heard* the shot," Barry announced.

"Really?" the other man replied. "You heard it? What about Martin?"

Barry frowned and shook his head. "Martin left."

"Oh, *really?*"

The cute guy leaned forward slightly. I smiled, seeing the obvious. Barry, however, remained glum.

"He packed up three days ago," Barry said with a sigh. "So I was alone tonight. This is actually the first time I've come out since he dumped me. Anyway, I didn't know what I heard was a gunshot. Not at the time. I thought it was something harmless, you know? Then I hear sirens and forty minutes later, the cops are pounding on my door—"

"Excuse me," I said.

Both men looked up. Barry smiled. "Oh, hi, Clare. What do you need?"

"Did you just say that you heard the gunshot in the street?"

Barry nodded. "Sure did. It was right under my window, too."

"And where do you live exactly?"

"Two and a half blocks away, on the same side of the street as the Blend." Barry gestured in that direction. "I'm in a second-floor apartment."

"You heard the shot right below you?"

"I'm sure of it."

"And what did you see?"

"Not a thing. That's what I told the police. I went to my window and looked down—I thought it might have been a kid with fireworks or a car tire popping, something like that—but there was nothing. Not a soul."

Barry's story fit with what I'd experienced, too. By the time I'd turned around to look for the shooter, the person was out of view.

"Did you tell the police anything else?" I asked.

"What do you mean?"

"I don't know, I mean . . . You didn't see anything, but did you hear anything after the shot? Say, like, footsteps running, something like that?"

"Well, actually, now that you mention it . . ." Barry scratched his chin. "I did hear some footsteps really close, but they weren't running. They were walking."

"What?" I'm pretty sure my bloodshot eyes bugged at that.

"I heard some footsteps, like you said. But I didn't *see* anyone there, so I didn't mention it to the cops, you know? I mean, why would that matter?"

"Well, if you heard footsteps walking, yet you couldn't see who was walking, don't you think this person could have been the shooter, maybe moving out of sight, say around the side of your building?"

Barry stared at me for a few dumbfounded seconds. "Oh my God, Clare. I didn't think of that. The footsteps *must* have been the shooter ducking into my alley. Oh my God, I should have told the police—"

"It's okay. Listen . . . Why don't you write down this number?" I put down my cups and reached for Lori Soles's business card in the back pocket of my jeans. "This is one of the detectives investigating the shooting. Just call her cell and tell her what you just told me. All right?"

"Okay, Clare. Oh my God . . ." He wrote the number on his Village Blend napkin.

"Don't worry, Barry. You didn't do anything wrong. Enjoy your coffee."

Juggling the two lidded paper cups, I moved to the base of the spiral stairs in the center of the dining room, unhooked the thin velvet rope with the dangling Second Floor Closed sign, and rehooked it behind me. As I clanged up the wrought iron steps, the crowd's raucous chattering slowly dissipated, and my mind started working.

Something isn't adding up . . .

By the time I reached the quiet of the upstairs lounge, I was fairly certain of one thing where the shooter was concerned. I looked around for Matt to see what he thought, but it wasn't easy to locate the man. Most of the room was shrouded in darkness.

SIX

~~~~~~

THE second floor's sofas looked like hulking silhouettes, the colorful throw rugs like gray storm puddles. There were eight antique floor lamps in this large space, an eclectic collection scattered about to give the feeling of a funky, comfortable bohemian apartment, but there was nothing cozy about the room tonight. None of the lamps were turned on. The strongest light came from the hearth at the far end of the room.

Tucked into the exposed brick wall, the split logs were crackling, their high flames flashing like tangerine lightning in the antique coffeepots above the mantel. Fog-gray shadows moved across the old tin signs on the exposed brick walls. The effect was creepy, as if the ghosts of dead customers had come back for some kind of grim midnight party.

Since Matt had taken the trouble to set the fire, I expected to see him in front of it, his muscled frame sunk into an overstuffed couch, his shoes off, his feet up. Instead, I found him standing next to the tall front windows, his body angled tensely for a better view of the activity around the emergency vehicles a block away.

Enough light spilled in from the streetlamps for me to make out a closed laptop computer on the table closest to him, along with a cluster of small porcelain espresso cups, all of which were empty.

"How many have you had?" I asked, walking up to him.

"Four."

"Then you aren't going to want this double *macchiato*, right?"

Matt grabbed the paper cup out of my hand, flipped off the lid, and bolted it.

I blinked. "Guess I was wrong."

"I'm trying to sober up. Not that tonight's events weren't sobering enough already." He crushed the cup in his hand and tossed it onto the table.

I nodded, closed my eyes, and sipped my own *macchiato*, pulling the richly caramelized coffee through the little island of frothed milk. It was profound, in a way, how the tiniest kiss of something sweet and white could transform the heavy impact of something so much darker. The drink's caffeine was energizing, too, and my weary body wanted the stimulation as badly as Matt had wanted his—only not as fast, which, when you got right down to it, pretty much defined our differences.

"Listen," I said, after opening my eyes, "I'm not scheduled for any more hours today, but Dante and Gardner have been dealing with the mob down there alone, so I told them I'd come back on. Do you think you could pitch in, too?"

Matt nodded. "I'll help."

Two simple words, an oasis in the desert. "Great."

The father of my child stared at me for a long moment after that, his jaw working silently; then he peered out the window again. Obviously, the man was agitated. But I got the distinct impression it had nothing to do with the amount of caffeine he'd just consumed.

"Is something wrong? I mean other than the obvious—" I gestured in the general direction of the crime scene, where emergency lights were still flashing red against the century-old town houses.

"Yes, Clare. I think something's *very* wrong, but I don't know how to go about . . ." As Matt's voice trailed off, he shook his head. "Can I talk to you?"

"Of course."

He walked back to the table, but he didn't sit down. Instead, he began to pace to the window and back again. "I've been thinking about it, and I've got some ideas about tonight's murder."

"What do you mean *ideas*?"

"I mean . . ." Matt stopped pacing and faced me, his chiseled features half in shadow. "I'm not so sure the killer was that motorcycle-jacketed asshole back at the White Horse Tavern."

"I agree with you."

"You do?"

I told Matt what I'd just learned from Barry downstairs.

"The man's apartment faces Hudson," I said, "and he swears he heard the shot from right below his window, which means the weapon was fired a block and a half away from the victim."

"Yes, but . . ." Matt scratched his head. "I'm sorry, *why* is that important?"

"It's important because the jerk you threatened at the tavern was *drunk*. The man was slurring his words and unsteady on his feet. How the heck could a guy like that bull's-eye the target of a woman's head from that far away? And in one shot?"

Matt stared at me for a good ten seconds. The half of his face I could see had gone completely pale.

"Matt? Are you okay? Maybe you better sit down . . ."

My ex-husband nodded and took a seat at the table. "You're right, Clare . . . You're absolutely right. And it backs up my own ideas."

"*What* ideas? I still don't know what you're talking about."

"I don't think that bullet was meant for the stripper. I think that bullet was meant for Breanne."

"Breanne?" Now I needed to sit down. "You want to explain your theory?"

As I sank, he rose and went right back to pacing.

"Think about it, Clare. My engagement to Breanne is public knowledge. She's picked me up here in the evenings countless times. I started my evening here earlier, and when we came back from the White Horse, Breanne's look-alike was on my arm. If someone had been waiting in the night, staking out the Blend to get to Breanne, they would have seen this girl. Do you follow?"

"Yes, but—"

"Hazel Boggs was a dead ringer for my fiancée. From a distance, she fooled both of us. I think she fooled the shooter, too. I think Breanne was the target, not this poor girl from West Virginia. In fact, I don't think it. I *know* it!"

Matt's face was flushed, his eyes bright. A vein throbbed visibly in his neck. Despite the guy's physical-fitness level, I was starting to worry he might have a stroke.

"Okay, Matt, okay. I hear you. Just please calm down." I pulled a chair out from the table and shook it. "Now would you *sit* already."

For a long moment, my ex-husband stared at me (glared, really, since he could obviously tell I was skeptical of his sudden Breanne-in-peril theory). But then with a grunt he sank down beside me again, put his elbows on the table, and dropped his head in his hands.

"I think you're overwrought," I told him carefully. "You've had a lot of alcohol, then a terrible shock, then enough caffeine to jump-start a Hummer. Forget about helping me and the guys downstairs tonight, okay? You need to go upstairs and get some rest—"

"Don't talk to me like a psych patient, Clare. I'm not crazy."

"I didn't say you were."

"Just hear me out. This theory of mine didn't come out of nowhere. Something happened last Friday morning that you don't know about."

"Oh?"

"An SUV hopped the sidewalk and nearly ran Breanne down. Then it fled the scene."

"What?!"

"It happened just down the street from her apartment building."

"You were with her?"

"No." He massaged his eyes. "I'd finished my workout early, so I'd been walking toward her from the health club up the street. Bree was on her cell phone, totally distracted. But I saw the vehicle jump the curb behind her and come right for her. If I hadn't lunged for her, slammed her into a doorway, she could have been flattened."

"Did you tell the police?"

"Of course! But nothing came of it. There are thousands of black SUVs in Manhattan, and this one had mud splattered across its license plate, so I couldn't give the cops anything more than a pathetically general description. The whole thing happened in seconds, the side windows were darkly tinted, and there was a sunscreen blocking most of the front windshield. I couldn't even see whether it was a man or woman driving."

"Weren't there any other witnesses?"

Matt nodded. "An elderly couple saw the whole thing, but neither could ID the vehicle any better than I could."

"Mud on the license, huh? That does sound a bit suspicious, like someone planned it."

"Why do you think I'm bringing it up?! At the time, I thought it was a freak accident, easily forgotten, no actual harm done, you know? Just a scare. But after tonight's shooting . . ."

I got up from the table and walked to the window, out of the shadows and into them again. Thinking it over, I had plenty of doubts. But for Matt's sake, I was willing to take his theory for a test drive.

"Do you know anyone who might want to hurt Breanne? What about this Randall Knox character you mentioned earlier? Didn't you tell me he had a history with her?"

"Yeah, but . . ." Matt shook his head, "it's no big secret how Knox wants to hurt Breanne. He wants to publicly humiliate her, catch her or me in some kind of embarrassing scenario before the wedding to boost his own career. Knox's assigned stalkers have cameras, not guns."

"Is there anyone else you can think of who might be angry with her? Someone who's threatened her lately?"

"*Yes.* I can . . ."

Matt opened his laptop and struck a button to bring the computer out of hibernation.

"What are you doing?"

"I want you to see a Web site." He logged on to the Internet via the Blend's wireless connection and began typing into his browser. "Not long ago, Breanne's magazine did an exposé on a restaurant, and the chef and owner of the place has been posting some pretty disturbing things about Breanne on his blog."

"What sort of things?"

Matt slid his computer toward me and pointed at its screen. A maroon banner across the top of the Web page read, "The Prodigal Chef." Standing next to the letters was the caricature of a man with a dark brown goatee on an exaggerated chin. A tall chef's hat half covered his spiky platinum blond hair. He wore a white chef's jacket and a ridiculously broad smile. In his left hand was an open bottle of wine, in his right a meat cleaver.

Below the banner was the headline of the blog's latest entry:

10 WAYS TO SERVE BREANNE SUMMOUR

"Serve Breanne," I murmured. With a headline like that, I expected the article that followed would be about tastemaker Breanne's favorite cocktails or finger food, something along the lines of how to make the powerful *Trend* editor-in-chief happy when she visited your nightclub or restaurant.

But that's not what the Prodigal Chef meant by *serving* Breanne.

The first clue was the large picture below the headline. The chef had cut Breanne's face out of another picture and plastered it to the body of a plucked chicken. Recipes were posted below it, which included methods of frying, broiling, and roasting "the Breanne" over red-hot coals, among other things. Finally, there were instructions for cutting her up so her parts could be used when other tasty recipes called for something especially bitter. "And, don't forget," the rambling blog entry finished, "Breanne Summour makes the perfect tart."

I turned to Matt. "Who is this guy? Sweeney Todd?"

"His name's Neville Perry. Look . . ."

Matt clicked on a link that read, "About the Prodigal Chef." A brief bio popped up. "Two years ago, this guy had some sort of short-lived reality show attached to his restaurant. The place was extremely popular. Then *Trend* did an exposé. The World Wide Web spread the word, and Perry's business never recovered."

I knew—from my own daughter's recent experience—how cutthroat the New York restaurant industry could be. Still, I doubted a chef who'd publicly expressed hatred for Breanne would hire a sharpshooter to off her. How dim a bulb would you have to be to do that?

"Look, Matt, if the man was savvy enough to open a New York restaurant, I can't see him stupid enough to advertise himself as a murder suspect—"

Matt opened his mouth to argue, but I quickly added: "On the other hand, I *do* think we need to tell Soles and Bass about your suspicions. This is pretty disturbing, and we should definitely see what they think."

"Clare, I'm really freaked about this."

"I know you are, but *listen*, even if this killer was after Breanne, this person's not going to know who was shot for a while. I mean, the shooter's going to stay low for fear of being caught. And the authorities aren't going to release Hazel Boggs's name to the press until her family's been notified. That gives you a few days to work with Soles and Bass. They can pursue leads, see what turns up. And before you know it, your wedding day will be here, and you'll be getting Bree out of town. You're flying off to Barcelona for the honeymoon, right?"

"Yeah, but . . ." Matt sighed, hung his head. "I'm still freaked."

I nodded, tried to look supportive. Despite his strong feelings, however, I really doubted he was right. Matt was stressed—and paranoia was never a long trip from that state. After a good night's sleep, he was bound to see things differently.

By tomorrow, the detectives from the Sixth would probably have Hazel Boggs's shooter in custody, a murder weapon impounded, and an assistant district attorney drooling over an open-and-shut felony case. Then maybe Matt could rest easy, realize he was wrong, and finally start enjoying his last few days of bachelorhood.

In the hearth across the room, the feverish crackling had slowed. The flames that had been burning so strongly when I'd first come upstairs were now slowly dying. Rising, I gently suggested to Matt that we table this discussion and head downstairs. Then he could help Gardner behind the counter, and Dante and I could begin taking free coffees out to the New York police and fire personnel.

The long night was about to get even longer and—like I'd told my overworked baristas—morning came too early around here.

Seven

~~~~~~~~~~~~~~~~~~~~~~~~~~~~~~~~~~~~~

Ninety minutes later my body had exhausted every last molecule of caffeine, and I was ready to drop. With the lights finally out downstairs and Matt tucked into his old guest room down the hall, I pulled my chestnut hair free of its barista ponytail and changed into the softest garment I owned—no, not a pashmina nightie—an oversized Steelers football jersey.

When I was a little girl, growing up in Western Pennsylvania, my father ran an illegal sports book in back of my grandmother's grocery. Naturally, the Pittsburgh teams were his bread and butter. But that wasn't the reason I wore the shirt. My grandmother believed in signs, and she'd become convinced that Franco Harris's Immaculate Reception during the Steelers playoff with the Oakland Raiders was some kind of miracle. So she gave me the football jersey with Harris's 32 on it and said if I slept in it, I would be protected.

Yeah, I know. To the typical modern-thinking urbanite, this notion would be waved away as ridiculous, a joke, some kind of psychosis. But Nonna grew up in a remote Italian village where curses were more common than slip-and-fall lawyers, and things not seen carried at least as much validity as earth and sky. To her, the *malocchio* wasn't some quaint old-world notion. The evil eye was very real, something to be actively warded off.

Growing up in an American suburb, I didn't have nearly the same level of imagination as my grandmother, but I wore the jersey to humor her—until I grew out of it. When I was seventeen, preparing for my freshman year of fine arts studies, she bought me a brand-new one. It was the last one she gave me before leaving this life, and it's the one I still wear. Its edges are frayed now, its logo massively faded, but I wouldn't trade the threadbare talisman for a truckload of Himalayan cashmere.

Yawning like a sleepwalker, I swung my legs beneath the covers of the mahogany four-poster, but I didn't turn off the bedside lamp. Not yet. Despite the fact that my eyes were practically closed, I couldn't shut them completely until I heard one last voice.

I grabbed my cell phone off the nightstand and speed-dialed the second number on my list (the first was my daughter's). Holding my breath, I listened as the electronic pulses made the connection I'd been aching for all evening: *one ring, two—*

"Hi, Clare."

"Hi, Mike."

"Nice to hear from you, sweetheart . . ."

I closed my eyes and smiled. Mike and I had been friends for well over a year before we'd become lovers. Now his deep voice felt as familiar and protective as my timeworn nightshirt.

"Sorry I'm calling so late," I said, "but I wanted to say good night . . ."

I actually wanted to do more than that with Michael Ryan Francis Quinn, and I wanted it to start with kissing. Some men treated the act perfunctorily, as nothing more than a speedy prelude to other things. Not Mike. The man's kisses were sweet and lazy and exploratory. When we were alone, he took his time.

"You in bed?" he asked, his voice low.

"Yes."

"Really?"

"Really."

"So what are you wearing? Or *not* wearing?"

Mike's voice had slid down even further—to a provocative level of growl that seemed to touch parts of me right through the phone line. I swallowed, ready to reply, when heard a strange man chuckling suggestively in the background.

"Okay, Sullivan, just shut up and drive." Mike's voice wa muffled, his hand obviously covering the phone. Then he wa back. "Go ahead, sweetheart, I'm listening . . ."

I rolled my eyes. "Mike, I'm not giving you phone sex i you're still on duty."

"Not even a little dirty talk?"

"No. And I can't believe you'd suggest it with a colleagu in the car."

"Sullivan's not a colleague. He's a pain in my neck, not t mention a lousy driver."

"Awwww . . ." Sullivan called, presumably from behind the wheel. "Love you, too, Lieutenant."

"Eyes on the road, Sully. One more fender bender, and I'n personally revoking your license. So . . ." His voice was now talking to me. "How was *your* night?"

"Highly caffeinated."

Mike laughed. "I heard there was a shooting on Hudson Did you know about that?"

"Yes, as a matter of fact. I had a front-row seat for it."

"What?"

"I was with the girl who was killed."

Mike swore. "Christ, Clare, why didn't you call m sooner?!"

"Things got too crazy around here. You have your own work, and Lori Soles and Sue Ellen Bass were assigned to the case. They were really helpful, too. But I'd still like to talk with you about it, if that's all right?"

"Of course," Mike said. Then he fell silent a moment "You okay? Do you want me to come over?"

"I'm fine, and as far as you coming over . . . You d

remember what we discussed last night, right?" I'd already warned him about Matt's using the apartment's guest room.

"Yeah, I remember. Doesn't mean I like it any better."

"Well, he's only here until Saturday, and then he's out of my living space for good. After the wedding ceremony, he's officially handing me his key."

"Then I guess you and I better make *sure* that wedding takes place."

Mike's tone had turned hard, but I couldn't blame him. He had never trusted Matteo Allegro, and the feeling was mutual on Matt's part. Since their first meeting involved guns, handcuffs, and an interrogation (in this very apartment, come to think of it), I couldn't blame my ex-husband, either.

The thing Mike Quinn really disliked, however, was my living situation. As the owner of this multimillion-dollar West Village town house, Madame had given both me and her son the legal right to use the duplex (rent free, thank you very much).

The arrangement hadn't mattered when Quinn and I were just friends, hanging out at the espresso bar, talking about his cases. Matt had used the guest room infrequently, no more than one week a month when he wasn't traveling. But after Quinn's wife left him and we started dating, things got complicated.

Quinn refused to put up with my ex-husband barging in any time he liked, so I made the sane and logical decision to move out. Thankfully, Matt proposed marriage to Breanne and moved out first. Problem solved (apart from this week, anyway).

"Matteo's really not that bad of a guy," I said. "Once you get to know him better, you'll see."

"Uh-huh."

"No, really. He turned down a chance to go to Scores with his pals tonight. And for once he didn't attempt a pass at me. I wouldn't say he's a changed man, but I do think he's willing to make *some* adjustments in his lifestyle to see that his second marriage succeeds. I know it's important to him."

"Enough about your ex-husband. When can I see you again?"

"After Matt's wedding on Saturday."

"That's too long, Cosi. Come over to my place tomorrow night."

"I wish I could, but I have way too much to do this week. And by the way, Lieutenant, didn't you tell me the next six weeks are going to be pretty hairy for you?"

Ten days ago, Mike had been assigned to step in for a detective lieutenant on medical leave. The man had been overseeing a special experimental task force. As Mike explained it to me, prescription drug abuse along with an increased availability of heroin and opiates were resulting in a rash of overdose fatalities in the city. CompStat identified the pattern, and Mike's captain at the Sixth had proposed a special task force.

The small unit of detectives Mike was now overseeing combined his past expertise in homicide as a precinct detective and narcotics as an anticrime street cop. Nicknamed the OD Squad, these detectives were tasked with investigating any drug overdose within New York's five boroughs, lethal or not, and documenting the victim's sources, whether legit or not. It was a complicated tour of duty that involved liaising with medical professionals, DEA agents, and New York's Office of Alcohol and Substance Abuse Services.

Tonight's case had put Mike on the Upper East Side. He and another detective were just driving away from the hospital, where a wealthy young banker was taken after he'd overdosed on a mix of prescription drugs and cocaine.

"The guy was still alive when the maid found him," Mike said. "But just barely. We thought we might get a statement out of him, but he's down for the count. We'll try again in the morning."

"Oh, God. I hope he makes it."

"Yeah, so do I. He's twenty-six and already divorced. The ex-wife showed right away at the hospital, even before the mother. None of them knew anything about his habit."

I closed my eyes, the details bringing back way too many

bad memories. Suddenly, I was feeling more tired than ever—and wanting to see Mike more than ever, too. "Promise me you'll stop by the Blend when you get a chance, okay?"

"Sure, but I still don't believe you can't get away for one night this week." Mike's deep voice went low again, back to sexy growl mode. "Come on, Cosi, one night. Believe me, sweetheart, I'll make it worth your while."

I didn't doubt he could. "Let's see how the week goes."

WHEN my bedside phone rang the next morning, I rolled over and picked it up with eyes closed and a dreamy smile on my face.

Mike and I had been making love in a secluded Hawaiian cove on white sugar sand. The sweet weight of his solid body was stretched out on top of me, his caramel-brown hair lifting on the Pacific evening breeze. A banner of glittering stars flickered above us, the rhythmic crashing of the night surf the only sound.

"Hello?" I whispered, expecting to hear Mike Quinn's delicious growl again.

"Clare, dear, are you *awake*?"

"Madame?" My eyelids instantly lifted.

"You're opening in less than an hour. My goodness, aren't you out of *bed* yet?"

Except for the cotton candy pinkish crack of sunrise between the drawn drapes, the room was still dark. I reached over and clicked on the lamp. The clock radio read 6:40.

"I ended up closing last night," I told Matt's mother through a half-stifled yawn, "so Tucker agreed to open for me today."

"I woke you then? I'm so sorry, dear."

"It's okay." I yawned again and rubbed my eyes. "What do you need?"

"I was worried about you, Clare. The morning news is reporting that a woman was shot on Hudson last night. It's on Channel 1 right now, and I can see from the background that

the violence was perpetrated a block away from the Blenc
Did you know about this?"

"Yes."

"Are *you* all right?

"Yes?

"What about Joy? She's not in yet, is she?"

"No. Her flight's on Wednesday. She didn't want to mis
the luncheon you're throwing Thursday for the coffee guys.

"What about this woman who was shot? Did you know
her?"

"In a way . . ."

"She was a customer?"

"No . . ." I slowly sat up and between yawns briefly ex
plained what had happened. Needless to say, Matt's mothe
was flabbergasted.

"My goodness! What a tale! You're going to investigate
aren't you? You know you can count on me to assist!"

"I'm sure I could," I said carefully, "but there are two ver
capable female detectives *already* on the case."

"Oh," Madame replied, her disappointment obvious
"Well . . . how do you know the shooter wasn't gunning fo
Matt or you, my dear? How do you know the shooter didn'
simply miss?"

I blinked, considering the possibility for an entire five
seconds before letting it go. "There's nothing to worry
about," I said, then quickly flailed around my sleep-addlec
brain for a change of subject. "So, listen, are you all set with
your dress for the wedding?"

"The wedding . . ." Madame sighed. "Hasn't that son o
mine changed his mind yet?"

Oh, jeez, here we go . . . "No. Matt hasn't changed his
mind. So don't you think it's about time you considerec
changing yours?"

"Not until my boy opens his mouth to say, 'I do,' which I
fully expect will come out 'I don't.' "

"The wedding is in four days!"

"And the universe was created in six." Madame paused just then, and her voice went quiet, as if we were conspiring together. "Now that he's moved back in with you, I have high hopes."

For the hundredth time, I pointed out the list of reasons Madame needed to accept her son's decision to marry whomever he wanted. Matt's age for one—he was over forty now, *probably* old enough to make decisions without his mother's approval. And the proposal hadn't exactly been rash. Matt had been sleeping with Breanne Summour for quite some time. Finally, I reminded my former mother-in-law the myriad ways Matt had transformed in Breanne's shadow: wardrobe, attitude, expectations of entitlement . . .

But all of my arguments were to no avail.

"He doesn't love her," Madame declared. "And I can't accept that Matt's father and I gave birth to a son who would pledge himself in marriage to a woman he doesn't love."

I massaged my forehead, desperate for *another* change of subject, because in about two seconds the woman was going to start in again about how Matt still loved *me*.

"Listen," I said quickly, "do you know what Matt told me last night?"

"That he still loves you?"

Ack. "No! He said he thought maybe the young woman who was shot had been killed by mistake."

"What do you mean?"

I explained Matt's theory. "Given the remote possibility that Matt's right, can you think of anyone who would want to harm Breanne?"

Madame laughed, short and sharp. "That woman makes enemies on a daily basis."

"That's not helpful."

"Well, I can't very well narrow it down for you if you don't let me *assist*."

"There's nothing to assist!"

I took a breath. Then I calmly reiterated the stuff about

the two very competent detectives *already* on the case. The line fell silent after that, but I could feel Madame frowning from fifteen blocks away.

"Well," she finally said, "I *am* quite outraged that this poor girl was shot down in the street like some kind of game animal. Such a beautiful girl, too."

"Yes, you know—" I blinked. "*Wait.* How do you know she was a beautiful girl?"

"New York 1 is showing a photo of her right now. Her employer provided it, I believe. And she had such a lovely, old-fashioned first name. I haven't heard that one in years . . ."

I sat up straighter. "They're giving out her *name?*"

"Yes, do try to follow me, dear. The newspeople have it right up there on the television screen: Hazel Boggs, twenty-two, of Wheeling, West Virginia."

Crap.

"Clare? Are you still on the line?"

"I've got to go," I said, scrambling off the bed. "Talk to you later."

"But—"

I hung up the phone and grabbed my robe. I needed coffee and lots of it. Then I'd have to shower and dress fast. Matt would be waking in an hour or two, and I was going to have to break some very bad news.

I'd been wrong about the timing on Hazel's name being released to the public. I thought we'd have a few days, but clearly the detailed report on the young woman's murder was already being broadcast.

The fact was: if the shooter had wanted to kill Hazel, the release of her name wouldn't matter one whit. But what if Matt was right? What if the shooter actually meant to kill Breanne?

I still had major doubts about Matt's look-alike-stripper-shot-by-mistake theory, but the man nearly had a heart attack explaining it to me last night. As I stumbled toward the coffeepot, I knew I'd have to treat Matt with kid gloves this morning, because if he woke up *still* believing Breanne was in danger, then I was in for a heck of a lot more grief.

EIGHT

~~~~~~

You told me we had a few days! A few *days*, Clare, not *hours!*"

"I know, Matt, I know. Please calm down . . ."

We were walking north on Hudson. The air smelled springtime fresh with a hint of invigorating brine from the flowing river just a few blocks away. The morning sun was strong, and the swaying limbs of the newly budding elms were dappling the buttercup-yellow light with strokes of pearl-gray shade.

Matt didn't notice. He was too busy power striding toward the Sixth Precinct station house, a squat, concrete, narrow-windowed iteration of midcentury modern that was described by at least one architectural critic as a visual catastrophe—which from one point of view, it was.

Just not from mine.

You see, the Village's previous precinct building was located a few blocks away on Charles Street. Now *that* structure was indisputably impressive. Dedicated by Teddy Roosevelt in 1897, the thing was solid granite with a neoclassical facade. But the actions inside that grand civic monument weren't always so prized.

Before the gay rights movement gained legitimacy, homosexuals and cross-dressers in the Village were routinely rounded up and dragged through the old precinct's stately

columns. During one of these attempted roundups, the leg
endary Stonewall Riots ensued. During another, an Argen
tine student became so distressed he threw himself out th
second-floor window, impaling himself on the wrought-iro
fence below. The young man lived, but the incident was a
ugly moment in the Village's otherwise flamboyant bo
hemian history.

In 1970, the Charles Street station house was sold, and th
men and women of the precinct moved to their West Tent
address. So, okay, the Sixth's new building was a monstrosity o
pseudomodernity. But the contemporary windows no longe
looked down on a spiked fence; they looked out on Seagul
Haircutters, one of the country's very first unisex salons. Th
climate inside the building was a lot more tolerant, too.

These days, the new Sixth had a female precinct com
manding officer, employed a daring lady beat cop known a
"the pit bull," and championed the Gay & Lesbian Anti
Violence Project, the nation's largest crime-victim servic
agency for the lesbian and gay communities.

All in all, even given the abysmal architecture, I didn
see a catastrophe here.

As Matt jaywalked across Tenth between two parke
vans, skirted a couple of police scooters, and pulled open th
precinct's heavy glass front door, I trotted along behind.

The Sixth's interior had the same characteristics as a lot o
city buildings from the early seventies: an institutional floo
of high-traffic cement and walls of concrete block finishe
with a coating of shiny enamel. I could almost see some cit
official choosing a "calming earth tone" off the builder's colo
palette. But under the harsh light of fluorescent bulbs, th
gray green walls looked more like giant bricks of moldering
Gouda.

There was a booking area in the back of the ground floo
Closer to the lobby, a museum-type exhibit of police para
phernalia was displayed in glass cases. There was also a Wal
of Honor with engraved plaques of the heroic officers from
the Sixth who'd lost their lives on 9/11. (Sadly, far too man

tributes like it could be found in precincts and firehouses throughout this city.)

Unlike me, Matt didn't waste any time observing the scenery. He approached the desk sergeant, a brawny African American cop with a shaved head, a mustache, and a terminal stare.

"We're here to see Detective Lori Soles."

"And you are?" his basso voice asked.

"Matt and Clare Allegro."

"Cosi!" I corrected.

Matt turned and glanced down at me. "What?"

"You introduced us as Matt and Clare Allegro—"

"I did?"

The desk sergeant was no longer paying attention. He was already calling upstairs to the detectives' squad room. A smiling Lori Soles appeared a few minutes later. She led us up the same staircase she'd just descended, then down the hall, through the detective squad room, and into an interview room—a small space with a metal table and chairs. On the wall was a mirror that I assumed was one-way glass with closed blinds dropped most of the way down over it.

We weren't suspects being interrogated, and Lori didn't close the door after we entered. *Thank goodness*, I thought, because with no windows, the bare, airless room felt positively claustrophobic. If two detectives started questioning me in here, I'd probably confess just to get out again.

As we sat down, I was about to exchange a few pleasantries with Lori, soften her up a little, maybe find out how their investigation was going. But Matt opened his big mouth first.

"I have some information about last night's shooting. Important information."

Lori nodded with great interest and stood. "Let me get my partner."

"Oh, crap," Matt whispered.

"Too late," I said. "You're in it now."

"This Soles person is okay. But that other one . . ."

"Listen, Sue Ellen's obviously crushin' on you. Just use it to your advantage. You usually do."

"Are you *mental*? That woman's six feet tall and packing. I don't flirt with armed females."

"Too bad, Matt, because she's certainly flirting with you. Do you know what she called you after you left the crime scene last night?"

"I don't want to know."

"Mr. Tight End."

Matt groaned. "Do me a favor. Don't encourage her again."

Again? "When the heck did I encourage her?"

Before Matt could answer, we heard the quick, determined footsteps of Lori Soles and her partner approaching. More brief pleasantries were exchanged, then the two Amazons sat down across from us at the metal table.

Both women looked pretty much the same as they had the night before. Sue Ellen had her slicked-back ponytail and Lori her tight, blond cherub curls. Both were dressed similarly again, too. They each wore dark slacks and had exchanged their identical blue turtlenecks for white blouses, their nylon jackets for pressed blazers. At least their blazers were different colors, I thought. (Well, sort of . . .) Lori's was Kelly green; Sue Ellen's was hunter.

"So, Mr. Allegro," Sue Ellen Bass began, the flirtation clearly dialed way down now that we were inside the precinct. "My partner tells me you have something important to share?"

Matt immediately conveyed his suspicion that Hazel Boggs had been killed by mistake, and the single shot that ended her days had been meant for his fiancée Breanne Summour.

Sue Ellen exchanged an unhappy glance with Lori. This was obviously not the kind of "important information" they'd been expecting to hear.

Lori spoke up. "What exactly makes you think that your fiancée's life is in danger?"

Matt proceeded to lay everything out, just like he had for

me the night before. He told them about the near miss with the SUV, the Prodigal Chef Web site, and even Randall Knox's possible vendetta.

In the light of day (or at least the harsh fluorescence of Interview Room B), Matt's Breanne-in-peril theory sounded even weaker to me than it had in the shadows of last night's firelight.

"This Prodigal Chef person," Sue Ellen said. "What's his name?"

"Neville Perry." Matt leaned forward.

"I see. Well, has this Neville Perry made any *specific* threats to your fiancée?"

"What do you mean *specific*?" Matt asked.

"I mean the Web site you describe sounds like a joke," Sue Ellen replied. "Your fiancée is a public figure. If this chef sent her a threatening letter or e-mail, we should speak with her, see if she wants to lodge a formal charge. Then we can pursue it."

"There hasn't been anything specific," Matt admitted. "Not *yet* anyway."

Sue Ellen glanced at Lori then shook her head. "If the Web site is just poking fun, which it sure sounds like it is, that's a first amendment freedom. We can't arrest a guy for posting what amounts to a bad taste editorial cartoon. You *get* what I'm saying?"

"Yeah, I *get* what you're saying." Matt's body was tensing up. He laced his fingers tightly in front of him on the metal table. "Then what about the SUV? Last time I checked, *running someone down* in the street wasn't protected by the *Constitution*."

"Check that tone," Sue Ellen snapped.

"We can run the vehicle description through traffic's records," Lori quickly added, her voice obviously straining to sound helpful. "We might get a hit for reckless driving the day and time of the incident."

"But that's just it!" Matt threw up his hands. "If the driver was *trying* to run down Breanne, then that would have been the only incident. I already reported it. And the cops uptown came up with zip!"

"Take it easy," Lori said. She glanced meaningfully at me—*Can't you control this guy?*—then back to Matt. "We've got your statement, Mr. Allegro. Why don't you speak with your fiancée? Ask her if she wants to pursue a harassment charge against this man Perry, okay?"

Matt was about to speak again, but I put my hand on his arm, leaned forward, and spoke first. "I think what both of you have said is totally reasonable and logical. Matt here is still pretty upset about Ms. Boggs being shot last night, and you can understand how his worries would extend to the woman in his life."

"Oh, sure," Lori said, nodding.

Sue Ellen shrugged. "No problem."

I could feel Matt's muscles tensing under my hand. I wrapped my fingers around his arm and squeezed. *Just shut up and let me talk.*

"Anyway, the thing is, when he laid out his concerns to me, I thought you two should know about them, as well. As the detectives on the case, you want to be aware of all possible leads, right?"

Sue Ellen stared. Lori gave a weak nod.

"Now, if I were in your shoes, I'd be looking at that guy from the White Horse, the one who almost assaulted Ms. Boggs right before she was shot."

"We are," Lori said. "The bartender remembered him departing right after you, Mr. Allegro, and the victim left. He ID'd the customer from a mug shot. We have prints off a glass, too. When we get the guy in here, we'll want you two to attend a lineup and pick him out."

"The scumbag's got a history of assaulting women," Sue Ellen added. "This is the guy."

"Have you arrested him?" I asked.

Sue Ellen frowned. "We haven't caught up with him yet."

"His girlfriend kicked him out of their West Side apartment two weeks ago," Lori said. "She's got a restrainng order against him, so he's been crashing with friends, and there's no permanent residence or place of employment. But we'll get him."

"You can bet on it," Sue Ellen added. "It won't be long."

"*If* he's your guy," I said meaningfully. "See, there are a few things that keep bothering me about this man." I paused and waited.

Lori and Sue Ellen both leaned forward.

"What things?" Sue Ellen asked.

"The shooting was at night," I said. "And the shooter fired from at least a block away. The witness called you to confirm it, right? His name's Barry?"

Sue Ellen frowned. "How do you know about Barry?"

"I talked to him last night at the Blend. I'm the one who told him to call you. He said he heard the sound of the single shot right below his window, two and a half blocks from the Blend, which would put him a block and a half from where the victim was hit. Then he heard footsteps walking away right after the sound."

"That's right." Lori nodded. "We have his statement."

"Well, even if that tequila-soaked loser wasn't too *drunk* to pull a trigger and hit a target in *one* shot, at *night*, from *over* a block away, then why did he walk clear of the scene?" I wrinkled my brow as if completely perplexed. "Wouldn't a guy like that—angry and frustrated and half-drunk—wouldn't he have *run* away after a crime of passion like that?"

Lori shared a glance with Sue Ellen.

"And another thing," I said. "Hazel Boggs was done up to look exactly like Breanne Summour. Walking beside Matt with her arm wrapped around his, she could easily have fooled someone gunning for the famous editor."

Sue Ellen shifted in her chair. "Okay, Cosi. We get your point. The suspect from the tavern *may* not be our perp; although, you have to admit, he looks *real* good for it. But your conclusion that the intended victim might be some other woman . . ." She shook her head. "It's a long shot."

"But we're very glad that you let us know," Lori quickly

added. "Any information you can remember about last night is going to be helpful to us . . ."

Blah, blah, blah . . . I thought. The rehearsed patter for witness dismissal: i.e., You've been very helpful. *(Not!)* Now please go because we have to pursue a *real* lead.

I couldn't hold it against either of the detectives. Considering the attempted assault on Hazel minutes before the shooting *and* the sleazy profession she was in, I would have been pursuing other leads, too.

Sue Ellen and Lori stood up from the table. That's when I noticed someone had been leaning against the doorjamb—a very attractive someone.

He was two inches taller than my six foot ex with a lantern jaw and a street cop stare, which was currently fixed on me. The sleeves of his dress shirt were rolled up, and his service weapon was tucked into a leather holster hanging from his rock-solid shoulders. His sandy-brown hair had just been trimmed, his hard jawline closely shaved. The slightest tang of citrus aftershave slipped into the room. I could practically taste him.

My green eyes locked on his arctic-blue gaze, and for the slightest moment of time, an almost tangible spark of energy seemed to connect us.

"Hi, Mike," I said.

NINE

~~~~~~

LORI Soles and Sue Ellen Bass turned and looked toward the door. So did Matt. For a brief moment, utter stillness descended over the small space. Then my ex-husband smirked, leaned back in his metal chair, and folded his well-developed forearms.

"If it isn't Officer Quinn," he said. "What poor slob did you mistakenly arrest today?"

"You volunteering, Allegro?" Quinn's eyebrow arched a fraction. "We have room in the holding cell."

Sue Ellen laughed. "If you need help cuffing *this* guy, Lieutenant, call me." She jerked her thumb in Matt's direction, threw him a flirtatious wink, and walked toward the doorway.

"By the way," she told Quinn, passing him on her way out, "I have a bone to pick with you."

"Me?" Quinn said.

"Yeah. What's this 'banned from the building' crap I'm hearing in the squad room?"

Quinn raised his palms. "I don't have any problem with you, Bass. It's Sergeant Friar you should be bitching to."

"Did Friar call me a *bitch*?!"

"Uh-oh," Lori said.

"Don't twist my words," Quinn warned. "It's just an expression."

Sue Ellen tugged the lapels of her blazer and crossed her hunter-green arms. "It's a simple question. *Did* Rocky Friar call me a bitch or *didn't* he?"

Now Quinn looked like a doe caught on the West Side Highway. "Talk to Friar."

With a pissed-off exhale, Sue Ellen strode back into the squad room, Lori Soles on her heels.

Quinn shook his head then sauntered into the room. I liked watching the man move. His tall frame was well muscled, but he was more lanky than brawny, and he operated with the patient ease of a stalking wolf. Without making a sound, he slipped into a seat at the metal table. His dress shirt was slightly wrinkled, his bronze and maroon tie well loosened.

I met his gaze again and pointed at the doorway that Sue Ellen had just stormed through. "What was *that* about?"

Quinn exhaled. "Oh, Bass got herself involved with a detective in the Fifth's squad. They were under the radar for months. That was fine when Rocky Friar was living in Staten Island, but then he moved into my apartment building . . ."

Quinn lived in Alphabet City near the Ninth Precinct in a converted warehouse filled with divorced cops. The owner was a retired NYPD detective who believed guys on the job who got thrown out on the street by their wives should have a place to bond. A few months back, Quinn became one of those guys when his wife left him for a younger Wall Street whiz, and their jointly owned Brooklyn brownstone was put up for sale.

Quinn shook his head. "Someone spilled to poor Friar that Bass has slept with almost every man in our apartment house. He hit the ceiling."

"Did Detective Bass really do that?" I asked, eyes narrowing. "Sleep with *every* man?"

"Not every man," Quinn said. "Certainly not me. But Friar broke up with her anyway, mostly to save face. He's pretty steamed, and he announced to the guys at our weekly get-together that from now on, Sue Ellen Bass is *banned* from the building."

"That's terrible. I mean, if a man really cares for a woman, he shouldn't let her past wreck their possible future."

"Sue Ellen's been working her way through every available cop in the department, Clare. That's her past. And she should have been up-front about that with Friar." Quinn shook his head. "I'm sure *she's* got a side, but I'm not her boyfriend, so I don't have any interest in hearing it. Anyway, what are you two doing here? Helping ID the perp in last night's shooting?"

"Not exactly," I said.

Matt shifted in his seat and elbowed me lightly. "Tell him."

"Tell me *what*?" Quinn replied, spearing my ex-husband with a far less friendly cop stare than he'd bestowed on me.

"Okay, fine," Matt said. "*I'll* tell him." Then my ex-husband unfolded his arms, relaxed his bristling attitude, and leaned toward Quinn. "I'd like your advice."

Mike Quinn's still-as-stone face registered genuine surprise maybe two times a year. This was one of those times. He listened quietly as Matt laid out the whole Breanne-in-peril theory again.

Amazingly, Quinn didn't laugh. He didn't put Matt down. He didn't even "handle" him with one of those canned cop speeches reserved for city paranoids who call the NYPD about official conspiracies and UFOs.

"You know, Allegro," he said instead, "I think you might be right to worry."

"You *do*?" Now it was Matt's turn to look genuinely surprised.

Quinn nodded. "I don't like the mud on the SUV's license plate. I don't like the execution-style hit on the victim while she's dressed up like your fiancée and walking right beside you. And I don't like that your bride-to-be is a public figure who seems to make enemies of people who have something to lose."

"Thank you!" Matt cried. He turned to me. "I could kiss him."

Quinn's eyebrow arched. "Sorry, big fella. It's not the bes neighborhood for that . . . unless you mean it."

"So what do we do now?" Matt asked, palms up, brow gaze expectant.

I figured Quinn would volunteer to talk to Soles and Bass about running a side investigation on Breanne's possible en emies. But he didn't say anything close to that. What he said was, "Use Clare."

"What?!" I said.

"Clare?" Matt repeated.

"Yeah, Allegro, at the moment, you've got nothing con crete, right? The PD can't get involved with hunches. W need evidence. Have Clare stick close to Breanne this week snoop around, look for something that might warrant polic involvement."

"I don't have time for that! I have a business to run and a gourmet coffee and dessert bar to finalize before the end o the week!"

"Calm down," Quinn said.

"Mike!" I wanted to throttle him.

"Allegro has some genuine hunches here, and you know subscribe to the *Blink* theory on hunches."

"*Blink* theory?" Matt said. "What's that?"

"It means you know more than you think you do," replied before Quinn started gassing on about it. "You take in a lot of data in the blink of an eye, which is why you're supposed to trust your flashes of inspiration. Those flashe are usually right. Malcolm Gladwell researched the theory and put it in his book."

"*Blink?*" Matt nodded, looking pleased with himself "Then I am right. Breanne is in danger."

I shook my head. "That may not be true—"

"So find out," Quinn said. His tone was pushy, almos taunting, yet his eyes seemed to be laughing, as if he were having *fun*!

"What is this? A schoolyard dare?"

Quinn ignored me and leaned toward Matt. "She's good

t it, you know. Clare has all the qualities we look for when
we promote from the uniformed force, especially the four *I*s."

"The four what?" Matt said.

"Inquisitiveness, imagination, insight, and an eye for de-
ail."

"That last one starts with an *E*," I said flatly. "And what
about intelligence?"

Quinn shook his head. "We don't want intelligent cops on
he force. We want smart ones."

"There's a difference?" Matt asked.

"She might be able to turn up a lead," Quinn continued,
gnoring the question. "Unless she does, the Fish Squad's go-
ng to go after the usual suspects on the stripper."

"Fish Squad?" Matt said.

"Soles and Bass. It's what we call those two around here.
Not to their faces, of course. Lori Soles has a sense of humor,
but I wouldn't repeat the term within ten feet of Sue Ellen—
not if you value an intact skull."

"Mike, come on!" I protested. "This is ridiculous—"

"Your ex-husband's scared, sweetheart. Can't you see
hat?"

Quinn's tone was dead serious. His eyes were blue stone. I
stared for a moment in dumbfounded disbelief. Oh, I didn't
doubt his words; I knew Matt was very worried. I just never
hought I'd hear Mike Quinn express genuine concern for
my ex-husband.

"It's true. I am scared," Matt confessed. "If you could have
een the way that SUV came right for Breanne on the sidewalk . . ." He shook his head and grimaced, his expression
ntensifying for a moment into a look of almost physical
pain. "I think Quinn's right. I think you should do this,
Clare. Will you? For me? As a wedding gift?"

I couldn't believe this was happening! "I'll give it a *day*.
But if I don't turn up any leads, I'm off the case."

That seemed good enough for Matt. He thanked me. Then
he actually extended his hand across the table. "Thanks,
Quinn. You're not so bad."

The detective shook Matt's hand, declining to return th compliment. "Listen, Allegro," he said instead, "can yo give me a few minutes alone with Clare here? I'd like a wor with her."

"Yeah, sure," Matt said. "And I'll bet I know *which* word

"Matt!" I said.

He rolled his eyes. "I'll meet you downstairs."

As my ex stood and walked away, Quinn unfolded h lanky frame from the metal chair and crossed the little inte view room to shut the door.

I rose, too, and stepped right up to him. "*Why* did you se me up, Mike? I don't appreciate—"

His lips found mine before I could finish the sentenc Despite my complete and total annoyance with the man, m arms drifted north, circled his neck, and hung on. He backe me against the wall and got serious.

God, the man liked to kiss. He took his time with his lip and tongue, let my taste and smell roll over his receptor cel like a sommelier who'd finally found the time to get down t his cellar and savor the rarest vintage in his collection.

When we finally parted, he smiled down at me. Ther were stray locks of chestnut hair on my cheek. His finger brushed them aside, curled them around my ear.

"Tonight, sweetheart," he said softly. "My place."

"No way. I'm not forgiving you for this."

"For what?" He knitted his brow, a shameful attempt t appear clueless.

"Don't even *try* to play innocent with me. You're obvi ously pissed that Matteo's moved back in with me for a fe days. Hooking me up to investigate Breanne is your patheti ploy to steer me clear of the man."

"You're way too cynical, Cosi. You know that? I honestl think Allegro's theory is worth checking out."

I might have believed him, if I hadn't caught his fleetin half smile.

"You owe me, Quinn." I poked his hard shoulder. "D you *hear*?"

"Yeah, I hear. And I'll make it up to you. I promise . . . starting *tonight*."

I parted my lips to protest again, but once again Mike Quinn's mouth was faster.

Ten

~~~~~~~~~~~~~~~~~~~~~~~~~~~~~~~~~~~~

THERE are things you do for people you *don't* like because they're attached to people you *do* like. Take a sarcastic sister-in-law who drives you nuts with her barely veiled insults. She's never once thanked you for all the Christmas gifts you've sent her over the years, but you keep sending them because if you drop her off the family list, it's the brother you love who's going to get his ear chewed off about the slight.

Breanne Summour was like that for me now. She was not my favorite person. But she was about to become Matteo's wife, and since *he* cared whether she lived or died, I was stuck caring, too. I know that sounds appalling, but I found the woman barely tolerable on a charitable day.

Still, I reminded myself, *she did come through for Joy.*

Last fall, when my daughter was falsely accused of murder, Breanne had used her VIP connections to secure Joy a top criminal defense attorney. I had to give Bree credit for that. After all, Randall Knox had taken embarrassing public swipes at the woman for being connected to Matt. It must have been mortifying for her, yet she hung in there. I tried to keep that in mind as my ex began hustling me from West Tenth to Hudson.

"Where are we going, Matt?"

"Uptown. Bree's having a final fitting of her wedding gown. I got hold of her on the cell while you were with

Quinn." Matt shot me a smirking glance. "What were you two *discussing* up there, by the way?"

"Uh . . . the case . . ."

"Then why do you smell like the guy's cheap drugstore aftershave?"

"Mind your own business."

"I am," Matt said, as we racewalked the tree-lined street. "You and Quinn *are* my business now that you're going to help me figure out who wants to kill Breanne."

"I wouldn't count on Quinn this week. Not unless Breanne ODs on painkillers."

"What are you talking about?!"

I told Matt about the OD Squad that Quinn was supervising.

"Well, then, Sherlock, I guess it's up to *you* to figure this out."

We reached the corner, and Matt stepped off the curb to look for a cab. Hudson Street was one-way uptown, and the traffic was sporadic. The April breeze was mild, and the sun felt warm on my cheeks, which was lucky, because I'd failed to foresee this private investigation gig, and I hadn't worn a jacket.

At the moment, I was dressed for espresso bar work in hip-hugging Old Navy blue jeans, low-heeled boots, and a long-sleeved cream-colored jersey. I really liked the jersey ($26 at the Gap). It was super-soft cotton blended with clingy spandex; and the line of tiny cocoa buttons that marched all the way down the V-neck highlighted a somewhat sexy hint of cleavage—which, now that I think about it, was probably what provoked Mike Quinn's cop stare in the first place, not to mention the "word" we had in private.

There was nothing wrong with my outfit per se. It was cute, casual, certainly presentable, but it wasn't close to appropriate for a Fifth Avenue house of haute couture, where the least expensive item was probably a small imported silk print scarf retailing for $295. I shifted my weight from one scuffed boot to the other, anticipating the crap I was probably going to get from Breanne.

"Listen, Matt, don't push me with this investigation. Like I told you in the precinct, I'll give it a day. If I don't find any thing suspicious, you'll have to open that tight fist of you and hire a professional. *True*, you might have to give up th overpriced French cologne you've been wearing lately, bu I'm sure Quinn will tell you which drugstore you can get hi aftershave."

"Very funny," Matt said, craning his neck down the stree for a glimpse of a yellow cab. "And, by the way, it's not matter of money, Clare. It's a matter of motivation. You sa that girl gunned down in the street last night. Don't yc want to help catch who killed her?"

I closed my eyes. "Of course."

"Then stop qualifying your involvement."

Matt raised his hand to signal an approaching cab, bu the driver whizzed by us. He already had a fare.

"Okay . . ." I said with a surrendering exhale. "I'll sto bellyaching. But you can't bug out on me with the Blen this week. Double-check the schedule with the baristas an make sure our orders are coming in for the wedding on Sa urday. We'll need the extra milk and half-and-half."

"I will."

"I'm going to roast the single-origin green beans myself. brought in Janelle Babcock to handle all of the pastry an cookies, but we need to start roasting the extra house blen for the espresso drinks. You can get started on that—"

"Okay, Clare. Don't worry. Once I explain things to Bre anne, I'm coming right back down here."

"Fine."

As I took a breath, it occurred to me that my prioritie probably *were* a little skewed. In the end, showing off th Village Blend's catering abilities at a Metropolitan Museur of Art reception would be all for naught if the bride gc whacked before the wedding day.

"Taxi!" Matt whistled, at last scoring us an empty cab.

The driver swung to our side of the street. But as I bega

o open the back door, I heard a woman's voice urgently call-
ng, "Matteo! Matteo Allegro!"

Matt and I both turned to find a gorgeous young woman
triding up to us. She was model slender with large dark eyes
nd long black hair. Her smooth, mocha skin was a sharp
:ontrast to the pastel-pink minidress.

I expected her to say something sweet and charming to
ny ex. But she didn't. She spat on the ground, cursed him in
what I think was Portuguese, and then slapped him hard.

Red-faced (literally), Matt watched in stunned silence as
he woman turned on her platform sandals and stormed
way.

"Who was that?" I asked.

"An old friend," Matt said, rubbing his cheek. "Get in the
:ab."

We piled in, and Matt told the driver where to go.

"She didn't look *old*," I pointed out to Matt as the cab
ulled away. "In fact, she looked quite a bit younger than
you."

"She's an old girlfriend, okay?"

Right. No kidding. "What have you been up to, Matt?"

"Nothing! I swear. She and I were hot and heavy in Rio
for a few months, two years ago. I haven't even spoken to her
n a year."

"So why did she slap you?"

"I can't imagine." Then Matt's eyes narrowed with a
thought. "Or maybe I *can*." He glanced over at me. "Why do
I suspect my mother's up to something again?"

"You think?"

By now, Madame already had launched half a dozen
schemes to change Matt's mind about the wedding. The fake
letter from Joy begging him to remarry *me* didn't fly. The
anonymous invitation to the Playboy Mansion (mysteriously
coinciding with the week of his wedding) didn't dissuade
him, either. The pretend heart attack almost succeeded, but
Matt got wise inside of three days.

"I spoke to your mother this morning," I told him. "I think she would have let me in on any last-minute scheme. Besides, she admitted her last hope was your plan to move in with me this week."

Matt grunted. "Then she's working on the wrong ex."

"What's that supposed to mean?"

"You know what it means, Clare."

Silence descended after that statement. The cab suddenly seemed to lack oxygen. We sat motionless for a few moments, then I turned in my seat.

"Matt—"

"Don't," he said. "Don't waste your breath. You're never going to forgive me for what I put you through during our marriage. Not enough to take me back, anyway. I've finally accepted that." He looked away, cracked the window. "You moved on. And I'm *trying* to."

As nice a boost as that was to my ego, it frankly unnerved me. Matt wasn't wrong about me. It had taken years, but I'd finally gotten over my recurring, perilous infatuation with the swaggering, globe-trotting father of my child, a man who couldn't stay faithful if his life depended on it.

Maybe the eternal boy really had reached some midlife phase where he was ready to nest. But so what? The wild pirate's acute need for calm, dependable waters to drop anchor couldn't remedy the decades of rough sailing I'd endured with him. (And I remained skeptical that he'd really be able to settle for one woman for long, anyway, no matter how spectacular she was.)

What did shock me about Matt's little taxicab confession was his admission, four days before his wedding, that his impressive fiancée was essentially *sloppy seconds*—that Breanne Summour was someone with whom he was "trying" to rebound.

Despite my continual lectures to Madame about butting out of her son's love life, I suddenly wanted to ask the man *Are you sure you should be* marrying *this woman?*

Before I could open my mouth, however, we pulled up to

he corner of Fifth and Fifty-second. Matt exited the cab, lamming the door hard behind him. He paid the cabbie hrough the window and barreled straight up the sidewalk o the House of Fen.

Eleven

~~~~~~

I climbed out of the yellow taxi and paused, needing to ge
my emotional bearings as much as my geographical ones.

The low buildings and narrow streets of the Village wer
a sharp contrast to the skyscrapers around me now. Mid
town's concrete sidewalks were huge, the crowds dense an
loud, the traffic a perpetual snarl of taxis, buses, limos, trucks
and luxury cars.

People were in a much bigger hurry in this part of the cit
and generally dressed more formally. North of St. Patrick'
Cathedral (where we were now) the Avenue also boasted som
of the highest temples of haute couture: Gucci, Prada, Bul
gari, and Tiffany.

Even though my desire to stay out of debtor's prison re
stricted me to the less exclusive stores on these rarified block
(i.e., Esprit, Banana Republic, the Gap), I never failed to ap
preciate the restoration jobs some of the more exclusive es
tablishments had done on the older structures that house
them. Just across the avenue, for instance, was Cartier, whic
sold its million-dollar diamond chokers out of a converte
neo-Italian brownstone, circa 1905. It sat next to a landmar
turn-of-the-century town house with a stunning white mar
ble facade, originally erected for the family of George Van
derbilt and now occupied by Italian designer Versace, who'
spent a small fortune to restore it.

Even Henri Bendel was worth a stop now that the exclusive store had moved into the dignified old Coty Building. During that multimillion-dollar restoration, a priceless discovery was made in the upper story windows: more than two hundred panels of molded glass that formed a translucent tangle of stems and flowers. An architectural historian identified the work as that of René Lalique, the legendary French master of glass and jewelry design. (To view the only other example of this artisan's work in the United States, I'd have to fly 3,000 miles to L.A.)

"Are you coming?" Matt called, holding the heavy door open beneath Fen's arched doorway.

"Sorry!"

I hustled my dawdling butt through the boutique's entrance. Matt guided me past a strapping African American security guard and across the high-ceilinged showroom. The floor was pale-ocher marble, the walls glossy white. The display cases were beveled glass with shelves dramatically lit to look like liquid gold. Hand-tooled bags, $900 shoes, gorgeous leather belts, and silk scarves were displayed with the care of rare museum artifacts.

I respected fashion design. It was as admirable an art as any other. But my own shopping excursions were usually loud, messy hunts through the jam-packed racks of crowded outlet stores. Maybe that's why the interiors of these quiet, exclusive boutiques gave made the willies—or maybe it was just my Catholic upbringing. (Put me in a large room with a vaulted ceiling, earnest whispering, and rare Italian marble, and I started looking around for the altar so I could genuflect.)

Fighting the urge to bend a knee, I scanned the vast first floor and spotted a familiar form—a rather hefty one. Food writer Roman Brio was sitting on a white leather couch, his large head bent over the latest issue of *Gourmet*.

In his late thirties, Roman was basically an overgrown imp with dark eyes and apple cheeks in a blanched-almond complexion. His luminous, penetrating gaze in a baby face reminded me of a young Orson Welles; and, despite his girth (which reminded me of the *later* Orson), Roman was almost always stylishly dressed. Today he wore a finely tailored off-white suit with a loose, open-collared linen shirt of peacock purple and a matching kerchief stuffed in the suit's breast pocket. His loafers were polished into glossy leather mirrors; and, in a bold statement of *I'm here, I'm queer, get over it,* his purple socks matched his shirt.

Roman attributed his love of food to his family's live-in French cook. Sure, he was the youngest son in a prominent Boston tribe, but the kind and loving woman who looked after him in the family's kitchen was the one who'd effectively raised him. As he got older, Roman accompanied his parents on their travels, and by his sixteenth birthday, he'd sampled almost every major cuisine in the world.

Unfortunately for Roman, his exalted family of judges, physicians, and scientists had been appalled by his desire to make a career in restaurant work. They pressured him through four years of premed before he ditched it all and moved to New York City.

Cut off from their financial support, he couldn't afford culinary school, so he took jobs waiting tables in fine restaurants, befriended the chefs and sommeliers, and began to write chatty, flamboyant pieces on food and dining under the name Brio (a pen name made legal) for the *Village Voice*. Before long, glossy magazines like *New York Scene* and *Food & Wine* were publishing his work, and he was cowriting cookbooks and memoirs with some of the city's most talked-about chefs.

I'd first met the man last fall, during a coffee-tasting party at the Beekman Hotel, then again during my investigation of Chef Tommy Keitel's death. (Roman knew New York's foodie scene better than the back of his chubby hand, so he was a valuable informant, to say the least.)

It was a stroke of luck seeing him here, since he'd been friends with Breanne Summour for years. As I understood the story, she'd been the very first editor to give Roman a restaurant review column in a national magazine. He'd always been grateful to her for that. And their friendship had grown over the years, going beyond the professional. The way he and Breanne spoke to each other and interacted seemed more like brother and sister than professional colleagues.

I tugged Matt's apricot Polo shirt, or more precisely the snug-fitting sleeve above his bulging biceps. "I'm going to speak with Roman."

"Fine. I'm going into the fitting room area to find Breanne, explain the situation."

We parted, and I headed over to the white leather couch.

"Hello there, Roman. How've you been?"

The food writer glanced up from his magazine. "Why, Clare Cosi! Hello there, yourself." He took in my worn jeans, scuffed boots, and long-sleeved cotton jersey. "Were you looking for the Gap, sweetie? It's up the street."

"No, Roman. I'm here on purpose to . . . *help out* Breanne today."

Roman's dark eyes brightened. "Do tell?"

"Matt's going to find her and explain it all." I pointed at the departing back of my ex-husband. Roman's gaze followed the man's posterior with nearly as much appreciation as Sue Ellen Bass had the night before. Then he shut his magazine and patted the empty seat next to him on the couch.

"Sit down, Clare. *This* I've got to hear."

Roman was not unfamiliar with the history of my sleuthing, especially the cases I'd solved in the Hamptons and at the Beekman, and I knew I could trust him. I told him the basics of the situation and asked him to keep my mission to himself for now. I'd talk to Breanne after Matt came back.

"Certainly," he said. "I don't envy the job ahead of you. Breanne makes enemies on a daily basis."

"That's what Matt's mother said."

"Are you sure *she* didn't pull that trigger last night?"

"*Almost* positive."

Just then, I noticed Matt already striding back to the boutique's lobby. He was rubbing his forehead, his features displaying a look of frustration.

"What's wrong?" I asked as he approached the couch.

"Breanne won't let me into her fitting room. I told her it was important, but she barred the door." Matt shook his head. "She just kept shouting that it's terrible luck for the groom to see the bride in her gown before the wedding day."

"It is," Roman said flatly.

"It's a long-standing superstition," I agreed.

Matt frowned and met my eyes. "It wasn't with you."

Oh, for pity's sake. "I didn't have a wedding gown, just a white sundress. Don't you remember? We were married at City Hall."

With a male grunt of exasperation, Matt whipped out his cell phone and called Bree. I could hear her ringtone jingling somewhere in the back. Tensely pacing the ocher marble, Matt spilled everything to Breanne about the shooting the night before, about his worries, about Detective Mike Quinn's support of his theory that she could be in danger.

I could tell by Matt's end of the conversation that Breanne was not amused, especially when she heard about the stripper at the surprise bachelor party.

"Calm down, honey," Matt cooed into the phone. "Yes, I know what we discussed, but it was a *surprise* bachelor party . . ."

Roman glanced at me. "A look-alike stripper?" His impish eyes danced. "Soooo tacky."

I leaned toward Roman, lowered my voice. "Listen, would you mind going back there and reasoning with her?"

"Sorry, Clare. I don't see what I can do. The poor woman's been in a state for days. Bride's nerves." He shrugged.

"Just talk to her? In the interest of premarital peace? Matt's not going to give in on this. And he's not going away until she *does* give in. Try telling her that."

Roman sighed. "All right, I'll give it a *shot*—" He froze. "Ooooh, bad choice of words."

"Good God, yes."

With a grimace, he headed off. I waited for him to move through one of four archways off the lobby, then I covertly followed.

Once out of the front showroom, the ochre marble gave way to a wide corridor holding more display cases. A thirtyish, elegantly dressed boutique employee noticed me and asked, with a trenchant scan of my clothes, if I had an *appointment*.

I replied that I was a close personal *friend* of Ms. *Summour*, who was *now* being fitted.

"Oh, of course," the woman said, her censuring tone immediately turning ingratiating. "Is there anything Ms. Summour needs?"

"That's what *I'm* going to find out. If you'll *excuse* me."

"Of course!" The woman instantly backed off.

It's a doggone shame, I thought, picking up Roman's trail again, *how well naked condescension works in some corners of this city . . .*

The fitting rooms weren't far from the lobby. The corridor opened up into a spacious area, including the largest threeway mirror I'd ever seen—it practically took up an entire wall.

There were lots of closed white doors flanking the mirror. Roman had approached one. He announced himself. The door opened for him, and he disappeared inside.

I stepped up to the door, pressing my ear to the thin, lacquered wood.

"I spoke with Matteo outside," Roman began. "Your groom is very worried about you. It's sweet that he wants Clare to look out for you. Why don't you let her?"

"Sweet? Ha! Is that what you call it?" Breanne replied in tones of cultured acid. "Well, I don't think so. And I don't buy this 'danger' garbage. It sounds to me like Matt doesn't *trust* me, which is rich, given *his* reputation. How do I know he isn't boffing that little coffee-making ex-wife of his? The one he wants to sic on me for the day like a badly dressed Chihuahua?"

Chihuahua? I thought. *That's insulting. I've always thought of myself as a Jack Russell terrier.*

"Listen, honey—" (Roman again.) "Weren't you the one who kicked him out of your apartment for the week?"

"For his own comfort! I'm having the bedroom redone as part of an upcoming *Trend* design feature. The place is a complete mess."

"And you're having a few little things 'done' this week on yourself as well, right?"

"Well . . . that's true, too. The treatments do leave me rather puffy in the mornings."

"Translation: the man loves your sausage, but you'd rather he not see how it's made."

"It's not just that. This wedding has a thousand details to be overseen. The last thing I need this week is Clare Cosi pretending to be a sleuth."

"She doesn't have to pretend, honey. She's already solved more than one homicide."

"If you ask me, this is simply a ploy to ruin the wedding. That wannabe Bratz doll is not over Matt. I'll bet she's doing everything she can to seduce him back into her bed."

"I don't think that's true at all. But if you think it is, then why not make use of the situation."

"Excuse me?"

"What better way to find out how Clare Cosi really feels about her ex-husband than right now? This is your chance to spend a little time with the woman; find out the truth before you tie the proverbial knot with her ex."

Breanne huffed for a moment.

"Well?" Roman prompted.

"Fine. All right. Clare Cosi can 'investigate' this apparent threat to me. But you're the one who's going to spend time with her."

"I am?"

"Yes. I insist. *You* find out how she really feels about Matteo. Talk her up and get back to me. I can barely stand to be in the same room with that moppet."

The feeling is mutual, I assure you, I thought. But I wasn't all that annoyed. Nothing Bree said was a surprise to me—except the notion of having Roman put up to the task of "handling" me for the day, which I considered a triumph. If Bree really did have an enemy desperate enough to murder her, Roman probably had a few clues about it.

Inside of ten minutes, the bulky food writer emerged from the fitting room again. By the time he opened the door, I'd quickly slipped back to the lobby, looking expectant and clueless as he approached Matt.

"Clare can stay," he said flatly. "And you must leave."

"Okay. I'm going." Matt's puppy-dog-worried eyes met mine.

"It'll be fine," I told him. Then I gritted my teeth and added, "I'll watch out for her. I promise."

Matt nodded. "See you later, Clare. Call if you need me, okay?"

"Believe me. I will."

As I watched Matt stride through the boutique's front archway, I girded myself for an exceedingly long, excruciatingly boring day—and then my peripheral vision snagged on something. Or rather *someone.*

A Caucasian man was pacing the store's front windows. He was big, like a heavyweight boxer, but out of shape, like some of those ex-jocks and trainers my dad used to drink with—the ones who made illegal bets with insider tips.

In his midfifties at least, the man's buzz-cut hair was the color of bread crust. His prominent nose took a slight left turn as if it had been broken once and set wrong. His cheeks were florid, like he'd had one too many at lunch, yet his eyes appeared switchblade sharp as they continually peered into the showroom window.

On any given sunny day, Fifth Avenue's sidewalks were jammed with all sorts of people. Today was no different. And while there was nothing unusual about a passerby gawking at something through a store window, *this* guy just "looked wrong," as Mike might say.

His brown off-the-rack suit was snug around the belly and wincing against large shoulders. His tie was too wide and loud to be fashionable. With his military-short haircut and worn, unpolished shoes, he certainly didn't strike me as your typical customer for the steeply priced froufrou in the House of Fen.

I watched the guy for a full minute, lumbering back and forth, glancing into the exclusive boutique, then into the street, and back into the store again.

Anticipating a mug shot book, I took a step closer to the window. I wanted to see his eye color, note any scars, birthmarks, or other telling characteristics besides the ruddy cheeks and off-track nose.

But the man made me before I took a second step. He and I locked eyes for a frozen moment. His eye twitched as he looked me up and down, then he turned away, showing me his back.

I started moving toward the front door, prepared to confront him, ask if he was waiting for someone (and who that someone might be), when I heard a woman scream—and the voice sounded like Breanne's.

"Noooooooo!"

As the blood-chilling wail echoed off the House of Fen's vaulted ceiling, I raced for its fitting rooms.

Twelve

~~~~~~~~~~~~~~~~~~~~~~~~~~~~~~~~~~

"**SHE'S** fine! She's fine!"

Roman stood in the wide-open doorway of Breanne's fitting room, his substantial waistline blocking all access.

"Show's over, folks. Move along! Move along!"

The gaggle of employees and plainclothes security guards who'd come running up behind me went back to their posts. I stayed at mine, which is to say, I didn't move a muscle.

"Okay, Roman, what's going on?"

He waved me closer, dropped his voice. "Breanne's couture gown doesn't fit any longer. The bodice is too tight."

"Twiggy *gained* weight?"

Okay, that sounded so wrong I didn't know where to begin. Breanne had a vanity streak wider than Park Avenue and maintained her model thinness with a near-fascistic schedule of daily workouts. Every woman I'd ever known had tried to lose weight before her wedding pictures (except me, but I was pregnant at the time). So why would Breanne allow herself to gain—*Oh, my God.*

"She's not pregnant, is she?"

"Good Lord, no. And she's the same perfect size 0 she always was."

"I don't understand then. What's with the too-tight waistline? Has the seamstress been hitting the bottle?"

"The boutique manager just showed Breanne an e-mail

message from a few days ago. The thing sure looks like i
came from Breanne's personal mailbox at *Trend*, but sh
didn't send it."

"What did the e-mail say exactly?"

"That she lost a great deal of weight all of a sudden and
wanted her waistline taken in a full inch before her final fit
ting today."

"I am *not* a size 00!" Breanne shrieked somewhere behind
Roman's well-dressed girth, "and I did *not* send this e-mail!'

"But it's from *your* box," the boutique manager insisted
"Look!"

I stepped closer to Roman, put my hands on my hips, and
glared. "Let me in."

With a sigh of surrender, the big man stepped aside.

The fitting room was a large, plush space of white carpet
white chairs, and floor-to-ceiling mirrors. My focus immediately went to Her Royal Haughtiness, the soon-to-be Mrs
Matteo Allegro Numero Two.

Breanne looked as swanlike as ever with flawless, well-
maintained, over-forty skin, annoyingly high cheekbones
and salon sun-streaked hair weaved into a precise French
braid. By now, she was back out of her bridal gown, which
hung from a padded hanger on a high wall hook.

The custom-made garment was absolutely gorgeous. Pure
100 percent Italian silk was my guess, with a simple, classic
cut: a fitted bodice, full-length skirt, and tiny spaghetti straps
Draped next to it was an amazing-looking bridal wrap or
handmade lace that displayed an intricate pattern echoed in
both her elegant gown's short train and her opera-length
gloves. The veil was here, too, a gorgeous piece of fine tulle
dappled with tiny, hand-sewn pearls.

"Look at the printout," the boutique manager was saying
to Bree. She handed over the paper. "This came from *your*
mailbox—the same e-mail box you've used to correspond
with me for years."

Wearing only a short satin robe, nude stockings on her
endless legs, and white silk bridal heels, Breanne studied the

inted e-mail. Beneath her smoother-than-could-possibly-
-natural forehead, her eyebrows came together in clear dis-
ess.

"I did not send this. Someone *else* did. Some despicable in-
vidual is obviously trying to sabotage me—"

Just then, Breanne glanced up and in a moment of monu-
mental bad timing noticed me. Her sapphire-blue eyes nar-
owed, and I suddenly felt as if she were going to accuse me
f coming all the way from Kansas to drop a flying house on
er sister.

Everyone in the room—Roman, the boutique manager,
he head seamstress, and her two young assistants—turned
nd stared stiffly at me like a tableau of dummies at Madame
ussauds. The House of Fen had just turned into the House
f Wax.

Say something, I told myself, but I wasn't sure what, until
my mind flashed on an image of Matt's frightened-to-death
ce in Interview Room B.

"Breanne, *listen* to me," I said. "I'm here to *help.*"

The wax dummies moved. Every last head turned from
me to Breanne.

She glanced at them. "Leave us, please."

Just like that, the entourage flowed out the door.

Now her eyes were back on me. "Close it, Clare."

With a deep breath I shut the door, and we faced each
ther.

One hundred years ago, when Versace's boutique was still
town house and Teddy Roosevelt was dedicating the old
olice station down on Charles Street, the residents of Fifth
venue didn't think much about Greenwich Village. When
hey thought of it at all, it was a distant outpost, where ser-
ants lived and the lower classes did their shopping. The Vil-
age was quite the opposite these days, with its high-end real
state and chic eateries, but you wouldn't think so the way
reanne was looking *me* up and down.

"What *are* you wearing?"

"Cut the crap, Breanne. I didn't come to Fifth Avenue for

a runway cat walk. I'm here because Matt's worried to dea
about your safety. I thought he was going to stroke out la
night. When that girl was shot, he thought it was meant f
you. He believes someone wants to—"

"Stop." She held up her hand. "I know what Matt b
lieves."

"From your tone, I'm guessing you think he's overread
ing?"

"Of course."

"Well then . . ." I crossed my arms. "I guess we're *both* h
moring him today."

Breanne fell silent. One expensively waxed-and-pluck
eyebrow arched as she considered my words. "I suppo
you're right then, Clare, if that's how you feel."

"It's not that I think Matt's completely crazy," I clarifie
"There might be something to his worries. But mostly
think he's overwrought. So why don't you and I just mal
the best of it? I'll hang out with you today, and you let m
know if you see or hear anything suspicious. Deal?"

Breanne pursed her bee-stung lips. "All right. I suppo
we could *try* to get along. I mean, seeing as you're Joy
mother."

"Brilliant, Breanne. Good attitude."

"Look. I'm under a great deal of stress this week. I real
don't need your attitude, either."

Touché. "You're right . . . I'm sorry."

Breanne appeared to be readying for a retort, but my apo
ogy seemed to disarm her. She regarded me again with a pu
zled face. "You really are here to help?"

"Yes. I really am. For instance . . ." I took a step close
pointed to the printout in her hand. "Who do you know tha
would be so nasty as to send a fake e-mail to ruin your fin
fitting?"

Breanne shook her head. "My e-mail box is password
protected. No one has access, not even my assistant."

"Do you trust your assistant?"

"Yes, of course. Terri's been with me four years. She has

right future at *Trend* and knows it. I'm promoting her in a ew months—after things settle down and I can start inter-iewing for a new girl."

"Any rivalries in your office that have turned ugly lately?"

"My people are trustworthy, Clare."

She dismissively waved her French-tipped fingers. But I ound the answer far too pat. I could also see that she was etting uncomfortable.

"Let me ask you something else then. I noticed a man in ront of the boutique. He's a big guy, probably in his fifties, as an ex-boxer's sort of build. Short brown crew cut, crooked ose, wears off-the-rack suits. Do you know anyone with that escription?"

"Clare, really." Breanne folded her arms. "Does that sound ike someone I would know?"

"Well, do yourself a favor, okay? Keep an eye out for a nan like that. If you see him loitering around your apart-nent building, for instance, or shadowing your movements, lease let Matt or me know, all right?"

Breanne shifted her gaze, appearing impatient, but at east she didn't argue. "Yes. Fine. Anything else?"

"What's your schedule today?"

She checked her slim, jeweled timepiece. "Roman and I lready ate a bite of lunch. We'll be going back to the office fter I'm done here. I've got meetings all afternoon. Matt's icking me up for cocktails and dinner around seven, right fter my six o'clock meeting with Nunzio. He's my last ap-ointment at the office today."

"Nunzio? The Italian sculptor?"

"Yes, he's flying in from Rome, staying at the Mandarin." She checked her watch again. "He should have arrived last night, although I haven't heard from him yet."

"He's designing your rings, isn't he? Matt mentioned it."

Nunzio was also lending Breanne *Lover's Spring*, a gold-plated metal sculpture that actually functioned as a tiered abletop champagne fountain. The one-of-a-kind piece had een famously lent to two royal couples for their weddings.

After that, aristocrats all over Europe clamored to borrow i
As far as I knew, it had never been displayed in the Unite
States.

I still didn't know how Breanne managed to convinc
Nunzio to lend it to her, but it was going to be a spectacula
centerpiece for my coffee and dessert station. Chills ra
though me when I thought of the presentation Janelle and
had planned around that amazing piece of art.

It was also an extremely valuable opportunity for public
ity, not only for the Village Blend but for my friend Janell
Babcock, a gifted pastry chef who was just launching her nev
catering business. The entire tablescape was going to be pho
tographed and appear in a splashy *Trend* spread—apparentl
as part of a bigger profile on Nunzio—and both Janelle and
were going be credited in the caption along with our busi
nesses.

"Yes, Nunzio is a genius," Bree said. "I couldn't be mor
pleased with his wedding ring design. I've only seen sketche
and a digital photo, but he'll be bringing the actual rings t
our meeting at six today. We're featuring them in the maga
zine."

I tapped my chin, thinking Bree's day over. "If Matt's go
ing to be picking you up at your office, then I'll stay wit
you till he comes. That'll make him happy," I added quickl
before Breanne could protest. "We're *humoring* your groom
remember?"

Breanne sighed, her expression close to an aggrieved gri
mace. "So you're coming back to the office with me?"

"Yes."

Another sigh. Then she looked me up and down again
"You can't wear that to my office, Clare. We have advertiser
and VIPs coming through all the time. We have an image
you understand?"

"But I'm not part of your staff, so why would—"

Breanne wasn't listening. In three long strides, she moved
around me, opened the fitting room door. "Adele! Woul
you come in here?"

The boutique manager was a small-boned, stylish woman, head shorter than Bree and probably ten years older. Her short, cinnamon-brown hair was cut into a meticulously layered style, and her pinstriped suit, the color of raw salmon, was accessorized with a shimmering opalescent scarf that perfectly matched her sheer blouse and designer eyewear.

"Please find this woman something to wear," Bree said, then lowered her voice. "Keep it under seven."

"Thousand?" Adele asked quietly.

"Hundred," Breanne whispered.

"I can't afford that!" I interjected (neglecting to keep my voice down).

Breanne shrugged. "If you can give up a day for Matt. I can give up some petty cash."

I tried not to choke on that one. Seven hundred had been my monthly mortgage payment back in New Jersey. But if Her Highness was paying, I figured what the heck. At least I could boast to Mike Quinn that someone actually compensated me for my investigative services.

"Okay," I said, effectively green-lighting the assault on my dignity.

THIRTEEN

~~~~~~

THE humiliation began immediately. Adele looked m
body up and down with a critical eye, which included an e
ceedingly uncomfortable few moments puzzling over m
hips and buttocks. Finally, she gave me a plastic, slight
pained smile.

"Let's get you measured, shall we?"

"Fine," I said, "just give me a minute."

Skirting two tailoring dummies, I headed back down th
hall to the boutique's main floor. My gaze immediate
searched the front windows for any sign of Pacing Man. B
he was no longer on the sidewalk.

I approached Roman, who'd returned to reading *Gourm*
on the white leather couch.

"Would you do me a favor?" I asked.

"Sure, sweetie."

I explained how Breanne wanted to dress me in appropr
ate attire for her office. Then I gave Roman a description
the man I'd seen earlier. "If he comes back, I want you to l
me know right away, okay?"

Roman scratched his head. "Whatever for?"

"I want to question him."

Roman's eyes widened a bit, as if I'd piqued his inter
est. "Okay, Shirley Holmes," he said. "Consider me you
Watson."

Ten minutes later, I was back in the fitting room. As I stood there in nothing but my bra and panties, a dozen outfits were brought in for *Breanne's* approval (now who was the dummy?).

"She's got issues," Breanne said, shaking her head as she held hanger after hanger of beautifully cut cloth against my scantily clad five-two frame.

"Yes, *many*," Adele said. "She's a petite, her legs are good, her waist is fine, but those hips." She shook her head, practically tisking aloud. "A real problem area. And she's far too big on top."

I am?

"We could put her in a wrap dress, even an empire waist," Breanne mused, "but we're going to my offices, not a tea party. And the fitted suits won't work without alterations. We have no time for that. Let's try some separates."

Adele nodded. Then she regarded me again. "Who did your work, by the way?"

"My work?"

She tipped her head toward my chest. "Your augmentation?"

Oh, for pity's sake. "These are real."

Adele frowned. "Aren't they a burden?"

"They weren't when I was nursing my daughter."

"You've never considered a reduction?"

"No!"

"Well, you should if you want to wear quality designers."

Okay, maybe it was my early exposure to Renaissance art and all those plump, buxom Madonnas with breasts and bellies looking like lovely ripe peaches; or maybe it was simply my disgust with reading about yet another runway model who died from ingesting nothing but lettuce leaves and Diet Cokes, but I could never understand this requirement that women starve themselves until they no longer had their God-given hips, breasts, and buttocks.

My gig here might be attempted murder, but I found it a crime how some women shamed others when it came to something as beautiful and natural as a healthy female form. Just what the hell were we teaching our daughters, anyway?

"Not everyone's a slave to high fashion," I pointed out to Adele.

"Clearly," she replied, her eyebrow arching at the Old Navy jeans she'd gleefully impaled on Fen's fitting room hook.

"I do have designer outfits in my wardrobe," I said, "and they fit my body just fine the way it is."

"Is that so? And where did you purchase these clothes?"

"The discount outlets."

The woman actually winced. "Let's move along, shall we?"

"Yes, *let's*."

When all was said and done, Breanne had bought me a classic black pencil-style skirt that allowed room for my "problem" hips but narrowed on my "good" legs. Atop the skirt was a sheer silk blouse of chartreuse, a color I never would have selected for myself but didn't look half-bad against my light-olive skin and green eyes. A bolero jacket matched the blouse exactly, and its black piping tied the garment back to the black skirt. The finely made fabrics were soft as kitten fur, the tailoring very flattering. With the wide black belt cinching my waist, the ensemble evoked a sort of retro forties hourglass silhouette. I had to give it to her. Breanne certainly did know her business.

"Not bad," she said, observing me.

High praise indeed from someone who'd referred to me as a Chihuahua thirty minutes ago.

As I stepped into a pair of modest pumps and took possession of a small bag of quilted-style leather (we were getting perilously close to $1200 now), someone knocked on the fitting room door.

"Ms. Summour?" a woman called in a loud, impatient voice

"Come in."

The door flew open, and a pair of thigh-high black leather

boots strode into the room. The woman wearing them was in her late twenties, about five-seven, and very slender with pale skin and blue-black hair cut so bluntly it drew a sharp line from the back of her head to the edge of her angular jaw. Her features were more handsome than delicate: a straight nose, darkly glossed lips, and dramatically made-up eyes that darted around the room only long enough to find the reason she'd come through the door in the first place.

Ignoring Adele and me, she strode right up to Breanne and began a loud monologue. Above the bold boots were layers of offbeat high fashion: a lilac plaid miniskirt, sheer black blouse over a deep blue minitee and violet tank. Long beads around her neck and bangles on her wrists as well as a diamond stud in her nose gave the impression of a funky, club-loving girl.

With her loud, strident voice and agitated gestures, she reminded me of the kind of girls I sometimes saw in Manhattan. Intelligent, well-educated, with backgrounds of privilege and plenty, they tended to think very well of themselves and believe that things would be just great in their lives if only the damn world, and everyone in it, could revolve a little faster around them.

". . . and Terri told me that you called. So, of course, I picked them up from Petra and grabbed a cab to bring them over to you *myself*, as you can *see*."

Club Girl had been carrying a leather portfolio under her arm. Now she forcefully unzipped it and held it out for Breanne to take.

Breanne frowned down at the portfolio. Instead of reaching for it, she moved slowly to her handbag. Taking her time, she removed a pair of rimless reading glasses from their case and perched them on the end of her long, thin nose.

"Privacy please," she announced to the room.

I filed out with Adele. Before the door was shut, I glimpsed Breanne first settling herself into a chair and then waving Club Girl over to present whatever she'd just carted across town.

"I expected to review these pages an hour ago at lunch Monica," Breanne sharply began. "What happened?"

"It was Petra. The woman's way behind in her work. She wasn't finished with them . . ."

I wanted to remain by the fitting room and eavesdrop some more, but Adele was right there, watching. Figuring the boutique manager would object to my pressing an ear against the closed door, I threw in the towel and returned to the boutique's showroom.

Roman was there, still on his couch. His dark eyes danced approvingly when he saw the new outfit.

"Well, well . . . didn't you go all Judy Garland on me."

Ack. "I remind you of Dorothy in the *Wizard of Oz*?"

"No, sweetie, Esther Blodgett in *A Star Is Born*."

"Oh." *Not bad.* "Thanks."

"You need a *much* bolder lipstick, though."

"I'm not wearing *any* lipstick, Roman."

"My point exactly."

I sat down next to the food writer. "Listen, did you, by any chance, notice a young woman in cranberry bog boots tramping through here?"

"One can't help *but* notice that girl. It's her main goal in life."

"Who is she?"

"Monica Purcell aka Breanne 2.0."

"Excuse me?"

"That's what they call her at the office. She's a lot like Breanne—intelligent, audacious, driven—only she's a newer version of the old model."

"So you'd call her ambitious?"

"I'd call Vladimir Putin ambitious, sweetie. Monica I'd call something less flattering."

"You don't like her."

"It's a sticky situation for Breanne. Monica was a golden girl for years, but several months ago her work started slipping—too much partying, that sort of thing. Monica, already a full editor now, climbed right over her colleagues to make it up the masthead, but she's been bucking for senior editor lately, and Breanne won't promote her again until she gets back on the ball."

"How bad are things between them? I mean . . . could she have been the one who sabotaged Breanne's fitting with that counterfeit e-mail?"

Roman shrugged. "Your guess is as good as mine."

"Do you know what exactly she brought to Breanne?"

"Pages from the magazine. Royally mucked-up pages."

"I need more."

Roman sighed. "*Trend*'s doing this huge piece on Nunzio in the magazine's next issue—"

"I know about that. It's going to include a photo of his *Lover's Spring* sculpture. Janelle and I are turning it into a Prosecco Bellini fountain for the wedding."

"Believe me, honey, I know all about that already. Bree consulted with me on every detail. *Especially* the food. Who do you think gave the thumbs-up to your friend Janelle Babcock in the first place?"

"Janelle's not exactly a slouch. She was the pâtissier under Tommy Keitel."

Roman hung his head, giving a moment of silence to the death of one of his favorite American chefs. "I do miss the king. And I well remember Janelle's desserts under his reign at Solange. *Ambrosia*. I can't wait to taste her confections on Saturday."

"So, *anyway*, about Monica Purcell?"

"Oh, yes, well . . . Monica's in charge of the pages on Nunzio. And there have been all sorts of problems getting them composed. Bree's in a state because Nunzio has final approval of the profile *Trend* is publishing on him. He's dropping by this evening to review it."

"Why wouldn't he approve it?"

"Nunzio's known for his artistic temperament. In a fit of pique, if he doesn't like the pages, he just might put the kibosh on the entire piece. And, from what Bree told me at lunch, there are all sorts of reasons the pages might give him heartburn: bad typefaces, clashing colors, blurred photos, and typos galore. Last week, Breanne gave Monica all of her notes for corrections, but none of the changes were made. Monica claims she handed the notes over, and it's the art department's fault."

"Is that a common thing? For the art department to ignore the chief editor's notes for changes?"

Roman pursed his lips. "Let's say it's rare. If you want to keep your job under Breanne Summour, you *do* your job and do it right."

"So what really happened? Did Monica *not* give them Breanne's changes?"

"She claims she did. And Petra, the art director, claims she didn't. So Breanne isn't blaming anyone. But she is making Monica jump through hoops to get the pages in shape before Nunzio sees them this evening."

I might have let all of this go as typical office politics— if it hadn't been for that nasty e-mail sent from Breanne's own box. Someone obviously had an ax to grind inside her office.

Leaving Roman again, I slipped back to the fitting room area. By now, Adele was busy with another customer, and I was able to casually move back to Breanne's fitting room door.

". . . and I *still* see typos, Monica, even in the pull quotes, for God's sake. Get every last one of them fixed, do you hear me? Nunzio's mother's name is *Rose* not *Pose*."

"Yes, Ms. Summour. What about the TK areas?"

"Nunzio knows there'll be photos to come. He's more concerned with checking over his biographical information and approving the cropping and layout of the photos taken at his workshop in Florence. *Lover's Spring* will be shot on Saturday at the wedding reception along with my rings."

"Your wedding rings!" Monica exclaimed. "They still haven't been photographed yet? But I thought they were already sent to you? Terri told me a package came a few days ago from Florence."

"Nunzio's bringing the rings from Italy personally. He should have them for me today."

"Ooooh," Monica gushed, "I'd die to see them!"

"I'm sure everyone will see them once they're photographed."

"I meant I'd die to see the *actual* rings."

"I know what you meant. Just get those pages fixed and on my desk no later than four this afternoon. Got that?"

"Yes, Ms. Summour."

I heard scuffling inside and quickly stood back. The fitting room door flew open again, and Monica's thigh-high boots were off and running. I quietly followed her down the corridor, across the showroom, and through the boutique entrance. I intended to announce myself once we were outside, far enough away from Breanne that Monica wouldn't have to worry about the woman overhearing. Then I'd ask her a few questions and gauge her reactions.

But the moment Monica hit the sidewalk, she pulled out her cell phone and made a call. I hustled along behind her through the crowds as she walked and talked, nearly colliding into her when she stopped on the edge of the curb and raised her hand to hail a cab.

The traffic was a snarl of buses, delivery vans, and SUVs. I bided my time, waiting for her to finish her call, when I realized the call itself was actually worth listening to: ". . . yes, Her Royal Bitchiness finally gave it up," Monica told the person on the other end of the phone line. "Nunzio's bringing the rings in to Breanne at six o'clock this evening . . . No. I don't know yet . . . You were? . . . I'm sorry I missed you then. I would have arrived earlier, but I'm running behind today . . . Yes, she's still at Fen's, and they have *tons* of security there. I told you that already. But she's going back to the office for her afternoon meetings . . . I already told you! I have no idea! I *said* I'll get *back* to you about the damn rings!"

As a cab pulled up and Monica climbed in, I quickly backed off, checking my wristwatch to note the exact time.

Given what I'd just heard, I decided to postpone my dire
questioning of Monica Purcell. Since Breanne was taking m
back to her offices anyway, I figured a bit of subtle snoopir
would be a whole lot smarter.

LESS than an hour later, Breanne, Roman, and I piled in
a cab and drove across town to Columbus Circle, an uptow
traffic loop at the southwest corner of Central Park. In tl
center of this famous hub was a seventy-foot granite colum
holding a marble statue of Christopher Columbus.

A century ago, the monument had been erected to hon
the intrepid Italian mariner, but these days Christopher w
an afterthought. Columbus Circle was all about the Tin
Warner Center, a two billion dollar complex of twin eight
story towers soaring above a seven-story base with an inge
ious design that curved halfway around Christopher's circl

On a sunny spring day like this one, the reflection of Cer
tral Park's budding trees off the glass-wrapped skyscrape
made the whole complex glimmer like Emerald City. Ar
when you got right down to it, the Time Warner Center w
its own little city, with 198 condominiums, the largest foo
market in Manhattan, rental offices, a luxury hotel, resta
rants, and a concert hall.

The complex also housed the offices of Breanne's bab
Trend magazine.

We exited the cab, walked through the Center's main er
trance, and took the escalator up through the arcade of uj
scale shops. Hanging a right, we moved through a pair (
transparent doors tucked between the Samsung Experien
and the Aveda hair care boutique. Inside this small, seclude
lobby was a special bank of elevators that went directly up
the floors in the towers above.

We ascended over twenty levels and entered *Trend*'s o
fices, which were as sleek and sun-drenched as the arcade b
low: all glass and chrome and lacquered cherry wood.

Roman and I trailed Breanne's statuesque form as she a

proached the receptionist. "Any messages for me while Terri was at lunch?"

"Yes, Ms. Summour."

The pretty young blond in the retro fluffy cashmere sweater handed over two slips of paper. "The first one's from the Sinamon Urban Design people," she said. "They confirmed their meeting with you at three. The second one's Nunzio. He said his plane was delayed. It got into JFK at noon today instead of last night, so he's totally jet-lagged, and he wants to meet with you at two o'clock instead of six so he can get some sleep before an important dinner meeting he has tonight. I tried to talk him out of the time change, but he was really snappish with me. Anyway, he said he's coming at two, whether you like it or not."

I glanced at my watch. The time was ten minutes to two.

"What?!" Breanne cried.

The receptionist blinked. "I *said* that Nunzio—"

"Oh, shut up!"

Instantly Her Haughtiness was on the move again, the clock in her head already ticking: *Countdown to Nunzio.*

Fourteen

~~~~~~

For the second time in two hours, the unflappable Breanne Summour was well and truly flapped. Like a gazelle on the veldt, she sprinted out of the magazine's reception area, her treadmill-toned legs dashing across the carpeted hallway. My short limbs struggled to keep up while Roman huffed behind us like an overweight rhino trailing a Serengeti stampede.

Bree made a right turn, then a left, and poked her head into one of the many offices lining the corridor.

"Have those final fixes been made yet?" Bree demanded.

"Which fixes?"

"Wake up, Monica! The ones I gave you at Fen's less than an hour ago!"

"Petra's staff is working on the Sinamon fixes *first*, since her people are arriving at *three*."

"Well, *Nunzio* is *now* arriving at *two* instead of six!" Bree cried. "Tell Petra I'm giving her fifteen minutes to make the final changes on his pages."

"Only fifteen? Do you really think that's enough—"

"I can stall the man for a little while, but he'll want to see those pages. You *stay* with the art department, do you hear me? *Make sure* every single correction is made. I'm holding *you* personally responsible this time!"

"Yes, Ms. Summour."

Monica Purcell's thigh-high boots raced out the door like her pirate ship was on fire. She zipped down the hall, nearly knocking over an older editor, and disappeared around a corner.

Breanne let out a moan, shook her head, and began massaging her temples.

I stepped up to her. "Is there anything I can do?"

The chief editor shuddered, obviously startled to be reminded of my existence. "I don't know, Clare, what *can* you do?" She looked down her long nose at me. "Are you a whiz at Photoshop?"

"Not lately."

"Then why don't you just . . ." Her voice trailed off, and she squeezed her eyes shut. A moment later, she sighed. "Why don't you just go make us some coffee. Okay?"

"Coffee? You're kidding."

"There's a coffeemaker in the break room—*that* way." She pointed, then waved her hand, shooing me away.

"But—"

She turned to Roman. "Come on. Let's go to my office."

Office, I thought, watching Bree and Roman disappear down the hall. *Now there's a better idea . . .*

Monica's office was right in front of me. And Monica would be out of it for at least the next fifteen minutes. *What if I take a look around?* I checked the hallway. No one was paying attention to me, so I slipped inside and shut the door.

At over twenty stories up, the view was breathtaking, all cerulean sky and shimmering cityscape. But I wasn't in here for the heavenly vision. Regrettably, my business was somewhat lower. Turning my gaze downward, I scanned Monica's desktop and immediately spotted her cell phone. It sat next to a stack of mail and an overflowing in-box on the glossy, fine-grained wood.

I dropped my new Fen bag on the edge of her desk, sank into her ergonomically designed chair, and opened the sleek device. I didn't like invading her privacy, but this was about one woman's life—and another's death. I took a breath and figured out how to read the call logs.

Using a pen and a piece of memo pad paper from Monica's desktop, I wrote down the last five numbers I found—outgoing and incoming—along with any names listed. I put an asterisk beside the call she'd made on the sidewalk outside of Fen's. It was easy enough to figure out, since I'd already made a mental note of the exact time she'd placed it. Unfortunately for me, there was no name listed next to the number.

This is going to take a bit of research. I could use the reverse directory on the Internet, but if the number was unlisted, I'd have to ask Mike for help.

I closed the phone, folded the paper, and slipped it into a handy interior pocket of my new little Fen jacket. Then I tried the desk drawers. Nothing looked out of the ordinary, until I carefully lifted up a plastic tray of paper clips, pencils, and erasers. Hidden beneath was a lacquered black box.

Hello . . .

I lifted the box's lid and spied a collection of amber-colored prescription bottles. There was a business card there, too, facedown. I was about to reach for it when I heard, "Has anyone seen a woman named Clare Cosi? I can't find her!"

Damn.

I closed the black box, dropped the tray of paper clips and pencils back on top, closed the drawer, and hurried to open the door.

A fairylike waif of a girl was hurrying down the hall. She had long, super-straight auburn hair, delicate features, clearly glossed lips, and in her small hand she held a Who Loves Kitty? mug with a tea bag string hanging over the side.

"I'm Clare," I said, walking up to her. "And you are?"

"Terri."

"Breanne's assistant?"

She nodded. "Ms. Summour sent me to find you. She wants to know if you need any help making your coffee."

"My God, Breanne was actually serious about that?"

"She says if Nunzio's jet-lagged, then he's probably going to need a few cups when he gets here, and she could use some, too. Sorry, but I don't know the first thing about making coffee." She lifted her mug. "I only drink green tea."

"Right . . ." *What now?* I couldn't very well bug out on this girl with an excuse of needing to invade her coworker's privacy. So I shrugged and said: "You better show me where your break room is."

As Breanne's assistant took me through an open area of cubicles, I decided to make the most of this detour.

"Terri, what can you tell me about Monica Purcell?"

"Monica?" She laughed—a little nervously, I thought. "What do you mean?"

"I mean, has Monica been very angry with Breanne lately?"

"Not that I know of. They've always been pretty tight. Before Monica was promoted, she used to be Ms. Summour's assistant."

"You mean like you are now?"

Terri nodded.

"So you trust Monica?"

The young woman laughed nervously again. "I didn't say that—and why do you care, anyway?"

We arrived in a room with a fridge, cupboards, and some vending machines. The space was empty. I closed the door and lowered my voice.

"I'm trying to help your boss right now, Terri. You can trust me on this: my questions are important. So tell me the truth. Why wouldn't you trust Monica?"

"It's just that . . ." Terri shrugged. "Monica can be slippery sometimes."

"What do you mean by slippery?"

Terri looked away. "She'll say one thing to someone's face—like she thinks an idea for an article is really good, you know?—and then she'll turn around and deny it in a big meeting." She shook her head a little, like she was getting agitated. "I heard that when Monica was Breanne's assistant, she undermined some older editors with that sort of thing, going to Ms. Summour before a meeting, telling her about this or that idea she'd overheard and spinning it badly, totally dissing the thing before the editor got the chance to present things her way. One editor felt so demoralized with the pattern, she just quit. That's when Ms. Summour promoted Monica over other junior people into the woman's job."

"How long ago was that?"

"Before I started here. About four years."

"Has that older editor been in touch lately? Maybe threatened your boss?"

Terri shook her head. "The woman got married and moved to Australia with her new husband. I hear she's doing really well, started her own e-book publishing company." She checked her watch. "Listen, we better get that coffee started. Ms. Summour's going to be pissed."

Oh, God forbid Ms. Summour should be pissed. "Okay, fine, let's see what we've got to work with here."

I rummaged around the cupboards and fridge, satisfied with what I found (at first). There was a small grinder and a bag of whole coffee beans beside the microwave. I found milk in the fridge and a few lemons, no doubt for the many tea drinkers on staff (one entire cupboard was filled with herbal, green, and "weight-loss" varieties). Unfortunately for me, the situation deteriorated from there.

The drip coffeemaker stank of mildew. It probably hadn't been cleaned since the Carter administration. And the beans on the counter were nearly as old. The French roast was a quality Arabica, purchased from the Whole Foods Market in the basement. The beans might have been okay if the vacuum bag hadn't been left wide open (air and light being the enemies of freshness). I sniffed the shrunken black gravel and gagged at the level of bitterness.

Great.

Nunzio was an Italian artist, born and raised in a country with over 200,000 espresso bars and a century-old tradition of serious java making. If I served him this swill, he'd probably spit it out right in front of me.

I considered my options and had a thought.

"Terri, you have a product closet here, don't you?" (I remembered Matt scoring a few choice items when Breanne invited him to peruse the thing.)

"That's right," Terri said. "It's down the hall."

"Show me."

It took me all of three minutes to dig among the straightening wands, kitchen appliances, shower attachments, and exercise devices to find a home espresso maker, sent gratis to the magazine in hopes of getting a mention in *Trend*'s Hot Products page. As a bonus, I even found a set of espresso cups and a serving tray. Terri helped me carry everything to the break room, where I hurriedly set it up.

"Do you know where Bouchon Bakery is, Terri?"

"You're kidding, right? Everyone in this *building* knows where it is: right downstairs in the lobby shops, follow the smell of warm croissants."

I fished out some cash (after all, if Bree could buy me a $1200 outfit, the least I could do was spring for some decent joe). "Go down to the bakery's take-out counter and buy a package of their whole bean coffee—"

"Their what?"

"Bouchon doesn't just peddle éclairs and tartlets. They sell freshly roasted coffee beans in small bags. Ask for whole bean. *Not* preground and not decaffeinated."

"Whole bean. Not decaf. Got it," Terri said, giving me a team-player thumbs-up.

Bouchon Bakery was run by Thomas Keller, one of the greatest American chefs alive. And the coffee beans I'd just sprung for weren't only served at the man's bakery twenty-two floors below me, they were artisan roasted by the same woman-owned company that provided the coffees for Keller's French Laundry in California and his Per Se in New York, two of the finest restaurants in the country.

No home espresso unit could summon the level of heat and pressure of a professional machine. But the premium Bouchon beans would help overcome the limitations of the method. Even if the home machine extracted *half* of what was present, I figured I'd get some magnificent, mood-altering cups for Nunzio.

Terri was gone and back in under ten minutes. "Nunzio's arrived, Clare. He's been escorted to Breanne's office already. I better get back there."

As Terri raced off, I opened the bag of magic beans and went to work.

The Bouchon House Blend smelled heavenly: woody and sweetly dark, like caramelized nuts with traces of cocoa and spice. It was primarily a Sumatra Golden Pawani mixed with African and Latin American beans. I ground them fine, packed them into the portafilter, secured the handle, and started the pull.

While the test cup was extracting, I grabbed a lemon from the fridge and used a small knife from a cupboard to artfully corkscrew the rind. Then I reached for the first cup and tasted it.

The roast method was Viennese, which brought out the tropical wood nuances in the beans while preserving a wallop of caffeine punch. The taste profile included a hint of citrus and berry with a heavy spice finish.

Not bad!

I drew four new espressos, placed a tiny, perfect lemon rind curl on the saucer of each demitasse, and set the small cups and saucers on the serving tray. Then I hoisted the tray onto my shoulder and headed down the hall.

I found Terri pacing in front of Breanne's office. The double doors were closed, but I could hear muffled voices from the other side.

"Careful," she whispered. "Nunzio's in a really foul mood, and Monica hasn't come back from the art department. The profile pages should have been here five minutes ago. See, I told you Monica can't be trusted."

"Open the door for me, Terri."

She did and stood aside. Then I strode in.

FIFTEEN

WALKING into Breanne's corner office was like stepping into a giant magic carpet floating high above Manhattan. Two of the four walls consisted of unbreakable glass. Far below me, traffic looped Christopher Columbus's statue in a diorama of matchbox cars. Stretching out before me, the tops of Central Park's trees sprouted newly green buds all the way to the horizon line.

If this were my office, no work would ever get done. I'd just stare out the floor-to-ceiling windows all day with a sketch pad in my lap, continually reframing the views—uptown and downtown and crosstown.

Breanne wasn't looking at any of these sights. She was sitting tensely behind her massive glass desk, having obvious issues with the brooding sculptor, who was sprawled across the geometric lines of the art deco chair in front of her.

In his late thirties, Nunzio was clad in black Armani with a plain white T-shirt beneath. He'd chosen a fitted size, I noticed, snug enough to reveal his well-developed body. His long, wavy ebony hair was tied into an ink-black ponytail.

"Ah, at last," Breanne said, her smile tense, her blue eyes almost pleading as she waved me in.

Holding the tray with one hand, I set my first shot in front of the editor-in-chief then turned to her jet-lagged guest. Nunzio had a broad, forceful face, not unlike the chiseled

marble monument to the intrepid Italian mariner twenty-tw
floors below. His dark eyes were half-closed, and he barel
glanced at me as I handed him one of the three remainin
espresso cups.

When I'd first come through the door, Breanne had bee
telling him all about her wedding plans. Nunzio didn't ap
pear to be listening. As she resumed her chattering, th
man's large hand lifted my tiny cup to his Roman nose. H
sniffed once, grunted, and downed the shot in a single gulp

His heavy, half-closed eyelids lifted a fraction. "Mm
mmm."

While Bree continued talking, I took the empty demi
tasse and saucer, placed them on my tray, and handed him
second espresso. He glanced at me briefly, then one corner o
his frowning mouth lifted slightly.

"*Grazie,*" he said.

"*Prego,*" I whispered.

He sipped this one slowly until it was finished. While h
did, I found myself studying his hands. The man was a hard
working artisan on the rise, and his hands were amazingl
muscular. I noticed thick calluses on the pads of his finger
and thumbs, wondered what his workshop looked like, wha
he was molding these days.

He noticed me noticing him, and his head tilted slightly
Then his artist's gaze moved subtly down my body and u
again. "Very nice," he murmured in Italian. He drained hi
second cup and held it out to me.

"You'd like to offer me something more, *signorina?*"

Again he'd used Italian. The tone was suggestive. I ig
nored it. Averting my focus downward, I placed his empty
demitasse back on my tray and held out the final espresso
Nunzio intentionally overreached, moving his hand beyond
the cup. His long, callused fingers lightly brushed my wris
then moved down, tickling the outside edge of my hand be
fore taking possession of the saucer.

The contact was not subtle. The caress was deliberate an
a little bit shocking. When I glanced up, his liquid-brow

yes locked on to my startled green ones. Then his lips lifted a private amusement. Obviously, the sculptor had caught me admiring his hands, so he'd decided to let me feel them, too.

I said nothing, simply swallowed and turned to leave the room. There was a palpable intensity in the man that became more apparent as he became more awake. I was glad, frankly, to get myself clear of it.

As I approached the double doors, they swung open, and Monica strode in.

"Ah!" Breanne halted her nonstop monologue when she noticed the younger editor. "I see the layout is here!"

"Bene!" Nunzio said.

He was sitting up straight now. The dark storm in his olive-skinned face had dissipated; his mood had visibly improved.

As I turned around to close the double doors, Breanne stood, met my eyes, and nodded—probably the closest thing to a thank-you I'd ever get from the woman.

I slipped away as the three of them—Bree, Nunzio, and Monica—began to examine the layout. Back in the break room, I brewed up four more espressos, attracting attention from some of the magazine staff. Drawn by the heavenly aroma of the Bouchon House Blend, the assistants clustered around me at the counter. They were all young women. Like Terri, they were very slender with an ethereal beauty that reminded me of pixies in the forest.

I gave them a quick lesson in how to work the machine for themselves, taking the opportunity to casually question them about Breanne and Monica and office politics. I didn't get much beyond what I already knew. Breanne was a tough, demanding boss, who had little patience for screwups and sometimes belittled employees. (Telling the receptionist to shut up was apparently par for the course.) And Monica had been a very trusted, well-liked golden girl for years, which she cunningly used to advance herself.

A few minutes later, I was off again with a tray full of

espressos. Returning to the corner office, I found Nunzio ar
Bree talking animatedly—but not unhappily—about h
profile pages. By now, Roman Brio had also joined them.

I served the sculptor, Monica, and Roman. This time Br
anne passed, so I took the last espresso for myself and backe
away. Sipping the shot near the office doorway, I quietly ol
served the scene, paying special attention to Monica. Sh
seemed agitated and tense, just as she had at the House
Fen. There was a notepad in her hand, and she was furious
scribbling in it as Nunzio made comments on the pages.

"The layout is good," he finally declared, his Italian a
cent strong. "Make the changes I desire, and I will review h
again before she prints, *si*?"

"Of course!" Breanne said. "Your instructions will be fo
lowed to the letter, Nunzio. I assure you."

"And now I have something for you . . ."

The sculptor's powerful hand reached into his Arma
jacket and came out holding a small blue ring box. H
flipped open the lid and, with a little bow, presented it t
Breanne. Nestled in the blue velvet were two wedding ring

"Oh. Oh God. They're magnificent . . ."

Bree's voice had gone soft, as if she were actually envisior
ing the moment the rings would be exchanged with he
groom—instead of the moment they'd be photographed fe
her magazine.

Everyone in the room fell silent, aware of Breanne's emo
tional shift. I stepped a little closer to see the rings, too
Then Monica, Roman, and Breanne began gushing abou
the intricate design. Hundreds of micro-thin strands of th
finest white, yellow, and rose gold had been woven into
patterned circle. The design was inspired, with the meta
lic threads reflecting light as if shimmering stars were hic
den within.

"I worked with the finest goldsmith on the Ponte Vecchi
to realize this vision," Nunzio said. "There are no other ring
like these on earth—" He paused and smiled. "At this time.

"Yes, of course. They're the perfect prototype to launc

our international jewelry line," Breanne said, her tone all business again. "And your profile in *Trend* will be your introduction to a lucrative market in the United States."

Nunzio set his empty espresso cup aside and rose from his chair. With a little smile he said, "May your marriage be blessed."

Breanne thanked the sculptor and turned to Roman. "Take these," she said, handing him the blue velvet box. "You're as good as my best man, Roman, and I'd like you to watch over the rings until the ceremony."

Roman smiled, obviously touched. He tucked the box into his lapel pocket. Like Puck making promises to his fairy queen, he crossed his heart with his pudgy hand.

"I'll keep them with me at all times, my dear. I'll guard them with my life."

"I believe him," Nunzio said with a laugh. Then he checked his watch. "Now I must go. *Scusa*, please."

Breanne air kissed the artist. "Monica, show Nunzio to the elevators."

"Yes, Ms. Summour."

Before the young woman left, Bree caught Monica's eye and smiled. "Good job on the pages."

Monica's tense expression registered relief. "Thank you." She returned her boss's smile then led Nunzio toward the door.

On his way out, the sculptor noticed me. "*Arrivederci, signorina.*"

"*Buona permaneza,*" I replied, telling him to enjoy his stay.

Monica continued into the hallway, but Nunzio slowed his steps until he'd stopped dead in front of me. Using two long fingers, he reached into his jacket's breast pocket and brought out a cream-colored card. He held it out to me, his gaze holding mine until I took it. Then a half smile broke his intense mask, and he continued out the door.

Breanne didn't miss the gesture. "What's that he gave you?"

I shrugged. "Just his business card."

Her eyebrow arched. "Let me see that."

I handed her the small, flat rectangle. She examined it, flipped it over and laughed.

"What?" I asked.

"He asked me your name after you left the room. Then watched him write something on one of his cards. It's his hotel room number, Clare."

"What?"

"At the Mandarin Oriental, about thirty floors up."

"Good Lord. You keep it then. I have no intention of visiting the man in his hotel room. What does he think I am?"

She laughed again, slumping down in her chair as if the air had been let out of her. "You should be flattered. He obviously liked you as much as your espressos. Why not give him a whirl?"

Give him a whirl? Then and there I decided that Breanne Summour was the perfect mate for my ex-husband. Neither of them viewed sex as anything more meaningful than a carnival ride.

"I'm not going to the man's hotel room," I said, "because I'm in a relationship, and I don't cheat."

Breanne rolled her eyes. Clearly my morals, like my clothes, were far too bourgeoisie for her taste.

"Ms. Summour?" Terri was at the door, holding a package. "This was just delivered by courier. There's no return address, but it's marked 'Wedding gift, open immediately.'"

"Bring it in," she said. "Terri, would you like to see my rings?"

Terri nodded vigorously. Roman brought them out again.

"*Ohmigod,* they're so beautiful!"

Bree and Terri talked for a minute about the rings, then her schedule, then some phone calls that had come in during her meeting with Nunzio.

"Terri, I don't know what I'd do without you. You're a gem! I'm just sorry your promotion will have to wait a little longer."

"Oh, I don't mind," she said. "I'm already making lists for

rticle ideas. I'll be ready to help out any of the section editors
ho want to work with me . . ."

As the two continued to talk, Roman examined the label
n Breanne's new gift. "Bree, sweetie, this gift says to open
mediately. You might want to do that. What if it's perish-
ble? I mean, for heaven's sake, it could be *edible*."

"You open it then. I don't want to break a nail."

As Breanne sent Terri off to run an errand on another
oor, Roman cut the tape with a letter opener and opened
he cardboard box. Inside he found a long, slim package
rapped in glossy black paper. He pulled the gift card free
nd handed it to Breanne.

"It's heavy," he announced, tearing away the black paper.
oman opened the gift box and stared at the contents with
uzzlement. "Odd gift for you," he said, "seeing as how you
eldom set foot in your own kitchen."

I stepped forward and peered into the gift box. Nestled
nside a blizzard of packing peanuts was a brand-new, stain-
ss steel meat cleaver with a great big bow attached to its
olished wooden handle. Like the wrapping paper, the bow's
olor was not bridal white but funereal black.

The sight of it alone chilled my blood. "Who gave you
his?" I asked Breanne sharply.

Her blue eyes squinted at the gift card. "It's from Neville
erry. 'A special gift to express my feelings for the bride.'
igned, Neville. Oh, and he includes his ridiculous Prodigal
hef Web site address."

Bree rolled her eyes and tossed the card into the garbage.

"Don't do that!" I fished it out. "The gift is a threat. The
ard is evidence."

"It's a *joke*," Breanne said. "And not a very clever one."

I stepped up to her desk. "Let me use your computer."

"No, Clare. I'm sorry, but I don't have time to indulge
ou with this." She checked her watch. "I have a call to make
nd e-mails to return. If you really need a computer, use
erri's. She's doing some research for me, so she'll be away
rom her desk for a little while."

"Fine."

I left Breanne's office and went straight to Terri's cherry wood desk, sat down, and examined the computer screen to find an icon that would bring up her link to the Internet. Roman trailed behind me, looking over my shoulder.

"Roman, tell me something. You must have met Neville Perry once or twice, right?"

"I know him quite well, actually."

"You do? How does he strike you?"

"He's a fairly eccentric individual, actually."

"Eccentric? Or *crazy*? Could he be dangerous?"

A woman laughed. I turned to find Monica Purcell standing there watching us in her thigh-high boots, arms folded. "Neville Perry's not dangerous, for heaven's sake. He's hilarious. I read his blog all the time."

"Really?" I said. "He's got a real hate on for your boss. That doesn't bother you?"

Monica shrugged. "I just read his site for the restaurant and bar reviews."

I glanced back at Roman. "Does Perry strike *you* as the kind of person who could do physical harm to someone?"

"That I couldn't tell you," Roman said. "But if you're curious, you can meet him tonight and judge for yourself."

"Tonight? Really? Where? When?"

"I've been invited to dinner at an underground restaurant in Flushing, Queens. Neville is going to be there, too. He mentioned it in his blog posts already. You're welcome to accompany me, Clare."

"Underground restaurant?" Monica said. "I've heard of those but I've never been to one."

"It's quite clandestine, because it's also quite illegal," Roman said. "At eight thirty this evening, I'm to stand in front of the Friends Meeting House on Northern Boulevard. A man will approach me and take me to the secret location. Doesn't it sound intriguing?"

Monica shuddered. "It sounds weird. Plus it's in *Queens*. Ugh."

"Neville Perry will be there?" I pressed. "You're sure?"

Roman nodded. "I'll introduce you. Then you can ask the chef any questions you like."

"All right, Roman. You've got a date."

"You two have fun," Monica said, shaking her head. "I'd rather go clubbing."

"Well, before you go, Monica, I'd like to ask you a few questions." I stood up to confront her.

"Who *are* you, anyway? I mean, you work for Fen, right? I saw you at the boutique."

"My name's Clare Cosi. I'm a friend of Breanne's. I'm helping her with the wedding."

"I see," Monica said, stifling a yawn.

"And I was wondering if you had an opinion on something that happened at Fen's."

"What's that?"

"Breanne's fitting was sabotaged."

Monica folded her arms. "What do you mean *sabotaged*?"

"I mean someone sent an e-mail from Breanne's mailbox, telling the boutique manager to have her gown altered a certain way. Do you know about that?"

"Why would I?"

"It's just that Terri told me you used to be Breanne's assistant. I thought maybe you'd have an idea who would have access to her passwords."

Monica glanced around, stepped closer, and lowered her voice. "If you ask me, Terri's the one who probably did it."

"Really?"

"She's slippery, that girl. She'll tell you one thing to your face then turn around and undermine you in a meeting. She got an editor fired over it, you know, and she's royally pissed she didn't get the woman's job. She's also angry it's taken her four long years to get promoted when she knows I did it in two. So I'd be careful believing what that little waif tells you."

A moment later, the door to Breanne's office swung open. The editor-in-chief strode out, barely glancing at us as she raced away.

"Where are you going now?" Roman called.

"The art department, darling! The Sinamon feature article's still got issues, and her people are due here in fifteen! Monica! Tell Belinda to make sure the conference room's ready. And Clare! We'll need more of your coffee! *Lots* more!"

As Breanne's long legs swept her away, I noticed she'd left her door wide open. Terri was still off on her errand. And except for us, the area was deserted.

"See?" Monica whispered, pointing to Breanne's office. "If you go in there, you'll probably find Ms. Summour's e-mail box still wide open. She did that all the time when I was her assistant, just walked away from her computer, sometimes for hours at a time. I warned her about it. What good is password protection if you don't close your e-mail box?"

With a shake of her blue-black hair, Monica turned and walked away. I watched her disappear down the hall and wondered whether her comments were trustworthy. Was *Terri* really the slippery one? Or was Monica lying to my face?

Well, one of her claims was easy enough to check out. I got up from Terri's desk and walked inside Breanne's spacious corner office.

"What are you doing?" Roman called.

"Checking Monica's story."

I moved around the huge glass desk. Breanne's computer screen was lit up and active; her e-mail box was still open, just as Monica had warned. Anyone could have slipped into her office and sabotaged Breanne. A password wouldn't have been needed. And who better to know when and how long her boss would be away than her *current* assistant?

"Clare!" Roman called from Terri's desk. "Look at this."

Neville's Web site was now up on Terri's computer screen. Today the former chef was blogging about wanting to chop his critics into little pieces. There was even an animation loop showing a meat cleaver swinging at a woman's neck. Recipes followed for seasonal stews and soups.

"That meat cleaver looks exactly like the one he sent to

reanne," Roman said, "complete with the death-black bow.
y, he really is getting morbid."

"Oh, God . . ."

Feeling sick to my stomach, I told Roman to give me a
inute. Then I stepped back into Breanne's office, shut the
oor, pulled out my cell phone, and called Mike Quinn.

I ran down everything: the suspicious man hanging
round Fen's while Breanne was inside; Monica's phone call
) an unknown number concerning her boss's schedule and
ne arrival of some one-of-a-kind wedding rings; the coun-
erfeit e-mail that mucked up the bride's fitting. Finally, I
old him about the rivalries that seemed to be bubbling in-
ide *Trend*'s cauldron of an office.

"You've got a lot of observations, Cosi. What's your con-
lusion?"

"When you get right down to it, this place is filled with
he typical bitchy backbiting of office politics. It's not pretty,
ut I don't see anyone here with a grand vendetta to threaten
Breanne's life . . ." *Then* I described Neville Perry's black-
vrapped wedding gift.

"The meat cleaver goes beyond prankish, Mike. It feels like
real threat to her life, which is why I'm calling you now."

"Does Breanne want to pursue charges?" he asked.

"No." I closed my eyes. "She still thinks it's a joke."

"Well, no ADA I know would waste time on a case like
hat. Unless this guy Perry makes an actual threat to Breanne
r attempts to harm her, you're stuck. You need to get more
n him, Clare. Can you find a way to do that without break-
ng the law?"

"Yeah, Mike. I think so. Otherwise, I'm relying on you to
ail me out."

"Bail you out?" Mike laughed. "With *what*? Since I lent
ou my checkbook to furnish my apartment, I'm broke."

"Sorry, buddy, but a girl can eat only so many 'picnics' on
bare living room floor before it gets old—not to mention
old."

"Honeymoon's over, huh?"

"Not if you consider cuddling up on a new sofa romantic.

"I do. What's more, Cosi, I expect to see you on that ver sofa tonight. When are you coming over?"

"I'll get back to you, Quinn. I'm on the job!"

I closed the phone on Mike's sputtering (I *was* still a litt pissed at him for getting me into this) and left Bree's office

Roman was still at Terri's desk.

"Okay," I told him, "tonight's more important than ever

"You mean the underground restaurant?"

"I'm going with you to Flushing, and I'm going to inter view Neville Perry, try to press a few of his buttons. You ca be a witness to any threats he makes or confessions of violer intentions toward Breanne. Whatever we hear, we'll bot convey to her. Then maybe she'll finally press charges, an we can get a police interrogation, maybe even a warrant t search his residence. What do you think?"

"Sounds like a plan, Shirley Holmes." Roman's impis eyes danced. "It seems I really am going to be your D Watson—your big, gay, epicurean Watson."

"Right."

"But, listen, honey, before you start solving crime again . . ." Roman tapped his watch. "You'd better get tha coffee made."

Damn. The coffee . . .

I took off down the hall. On the way to the break room, rang Matt and gave him the update on the cleaver, quietl warning him to keep Breanne out of public places.

"Talk her into eating takeout at her place tonight, okay And for heaven's sake, use a private car service. Don't *wal* anywhere. Between that SUV last Friday and the look-alik shooting last night, the last place that woman should be i on a New York sidewalk."

"You believe me now, Clare, don't you?" Matt asked.

"I believe Breanne has at least one serious enemy Whether or not that person is serious enough to commi murder, the jury's still out."

Sixteen

~~~~~~

I met Roman at precisely seven thirty on the Times Square platform of the Number 7 line. We grabbed the last two seats aboard the first car, and the train took off, rumbling toward the East River and the borough of Queens.

On subway lines that ran through the touristy parts of Manhattan, laughter and conversation were common. On this line, at this hour, the quiet weariness was palpable, like an oppressive fog. The riders around us were recent immigrants, their tired eyes scanning foreign-language newspapers, staring into space, or closed altogether, grabbing a few minutes' peace before tackling a second job or the next chore on life's endless list.

Roman Brio failed to notice. His demeanor was giddy, anticipating a magical night in gastronomy land. "These underground restaurants provide quite a thrill. A few have been disappointing, but most are full of delights."

I nodded silently. At the moment, I felt more simpatico with the other passengers. Matt's wedding was four days away. I'd already worked hard on the advance prep, but there was still more to be done. I certainly didn't want to be schlepping out to Flushing to talk to a disgruntled chef who could very well have the bride-to-be in his crosshairs.

Our train made two more stops under Manhattan's avenues, then it rolled beneath the East River, emerging minutes later

out of its subterranean tunnel like a giant steel snake. We as
cended four stories to a wide-ranging system of elevated track
and sped farther into the low-rise borough, leaving Manhat
tan's glittering skyscrapers far behind.

Roman leaned close. "We've slipped the bonds of civiliza
tion and plunged into the untamed frontier of the metropo
lis. The culinary adventure begins!"

"We're on our way to Flushing, Roman. Not Calcutta. O
are you testing the opening line of your next column?"

"I'm simply making an observation. To most residents o
Manhattan, Queens is an undiscovered country. Sure, they
come here to use the airports, but that's it."

"Not so true anymore." (Having employed part-time
workers who didn't have Roman's bank account, I knew As
toria and Long Island City were getting hotter by the year.
"Even young white-collar professionals are having trouble af
fording Manhattan rents. Queens is a close alternative."

"I suppose you're right."

"No supposing about it." I checked my watch. "Listen
we have a good forty-minute ride in front of us. Why don't
you fill me in on this Chef Perry feud with Breanne. How
personal is it, anyway? Do they have any kind of history?"

"No history. Those two only met in passing—parties
openings, that sort of thing."

"Then the *Trend* exposé on Perry's restaurant started it?"

"I told Breanne not to bother, that Perry would sink un
der his own substandard practices. But Bree has a mind of
her own on such things." Roman shrugged. "You know the
story, right?"

"Only broad strokes; I need details."

As I gazed through the scuffed Plexiglas windows at passing
shops, churches, and row houses, Roman explained how Bre
anne sent a bright, young Latino writer to work undercover in
Chef Perry's popular new eatery in Tribeca (the chic *tri*angular
shaped area *be*low *Ca*nal Street, hence the name). Apparently,
the writer took extensive notes and hundreds of secret photos
of what really went on in Perry's kitchen, including the use of

xpired meat and dairy products as well as frozen pre-prepared
eafood (not unusual for some restaurants but blasphemy for a
hef who loudly professed his brilliance on his short-lived realty television show and later in the press).

"And let's not forget the frantic preplanned hiding of ex-
ired foodstuffs on days the health inspector came calling."
Roman sighed. "It's an ugly thing, what Chef Perry did. So-
histicated diners expect the freshest and finest when they
and over Benjamins for what's supposed to be gourmet cui-
ine, not garbage that's past its prime. It's a violation of
rust. And it gets worse."

"What could be worse than serving expired product?"

"Tip pooling."

"No."

Tip pooling was frowned upon in the restaurant biz. Typ-
cally a waiter kept all of his or her own tips. In a restaurant
hat pooled, the waitstaff was forced to place all gratuities
nto a common kitty to be divided at the end of the day.

"It stinks," I said, "but technically it's not illegal."

"You're correct. It's not, as long as the owner doesn't take
 cut. But Chef Perry did take a cut. A big one."

"Wow. The man really is an idiot."

"The whole matter ended up before a Department of La-
or arbitration board." Roman shook his head. "It was a
moot point by then. The New York City Health Department
had already shut down his restaurant for a slew of violations,
ll stemming from Breanne's exposé, which embarrassed the
neck out of them. The place never reopened."

"Chef Perry was the owner, wasn't he? Between the start-
up costs and the annual lease, he must have lost a fortune."

"Actually, it was his *mother* who lost the fortune. But Mrs.
Perry is the queen of downtown real estate, so she can afford
t. Anyway, she's the one who got him the prime location for
his restaurant, and her networking is what got her son *on* a
network in the first place."

"Real estate and reality television? I don't get the connection."

"You would if you were an up-and-coming producer fo
one of the big four, and you wanted a particular loft in a pa
ticularly hot building in Soho, along with some prime spac
to tape your shows. Mrs. Perry delivered on both, barterin
the reality TV deal for her son in the process."

"I see. So Perry's mother was the key to his success?"

"Oh, yes." Roman's head bobbed like a bird at a fountain
"Mommy's lawyers helped him squirm out of trouble wit
the arbitration board, too, when those poor, unemployed wait
ers tried to recoup their losses. All the spoiled brat got fo
his questionable business practices and culinary transgres
sions was a bruised ego."

"What a creep." I was beginning to see Breanne in
whole new light—as a crusading journalist. It didn't mak
me like the woman any more, but it did help me dislike he
a little less. "So the young chef is blaming Breanne for hi
restaurant's collapse, even though he was the architect of it?

"Those blogs of his are adolescent. That should give yo
your first clue to the man himself."

I sat back in my plastic orange seat, thinking that over
and smiled. Now I had more than enough info to ambus
the little twerp. It gave me a thrill, I had to admit. Not tha
this was fun and games—I hadn't forgotten about that poo
girl from West Virginia, lying in a cold morgue drawer—bu
at least my weariness was cured. Now I could hardly wait t
confront Chef Perry.

I peered through the Plexiglas windows, trying to mak
out landmarks, to determine how close we were to our stop
At the moment we were passing over the huge expanse o
Flushing Meadows Park. Against the purple twilight sky
the dark sprawl of budding trees was interrupted by the bril
liant illumination of the Mets baseball stadium. I pointed i
out to Roman.

"Looks like there's a night game."

Across from the enormous baseball stadium was a cluste
of much smaller stadiums. None of their lights were burning
The train shuddered to a stop just then, and the conducto

arbled something over the speaker about delays ahead. I huddered myself, finally realizing what those little, dark tadiums were.

Roman must have seen the expression on my face, because he asked if anything was wrong.

"Just a bad memory."

"Do tell?"

"Not much to tell, really."

"Oh, come on. We're stuck here anyway."

I pointed out the window again. "You see that shadowy complex over there?"

Roman nodded.

"That's the Billy Jean King Tennis Center. Back when I was still married to Matt, he took Joy and me to the U.S. Open. I think she was seven or eight at that time."

"Sounds like a happy memory so far."

"It gets unhappy fast. After we settled into our seats, Matt went off to buy a cold drink, and he never came back."

"What?"

"There was a British couple with us, friends of his mother's that he'd invited along. They wondered aloud if we should look for him, but I told them not to bother. An hour turned into two, and Matt never returned."

"My God, did you contact the police?"

"That's what the Brits suggested, but I explained that my husband had done this a few times before, and I knew from experience that I had to wait forty-eight hours to file a missing persons report. I went home with Joy alone. Thirty-six hours later, Matt showed up at the Blend."

Roman blinked. "Why didn't you call him?"

I almost laughed. "This was before cell phones."

"So where was he?"

"He'd run into 'a friend' at the concession stand, and the two of them took off on a cocaine-fueled bender." I met Roman's eyes. "I suspected the 'friend' was female, but he never admitted it."

Roman shook his head. "So what did you do?"

"I divorced him—eventually. It took a few more years."

"Good heavens, why?"

"Because even though Matt acted like a grade-A jerk during our marriage, most of the time he'd been supportive and caring, a passionate lover, and a besotted father; he loved Joy more than anything. But finally, I got tired of forgiving the eternal boy crap and found the strength to leave." I gestured to the lighted baseball stadium. " 'The great beginning has seen a final inning,' you know?"

Roman smiled. "Who can argue with an Ira Gershwin lyric? 'The Man That Got Away,' right?"

I laughed. "You're the one who said I reminded you of Garland in *A Star Is Born*."

"It's the outfit, sweetie. Retro-adorable. So what happened to you and Matt after that?"

"I moved to Jersey, and he hit bottom. He went into rehab, straightened out, relapsed, straightened out again." I touched Roman's arm. "Don't get the wrong idea, okay? Matt's worked hard since then to turn his life around, and I honestly think he's going to be fine. He has no interest in becoming an addict again."

"I understand." Roman folded his hands over his belly. "But, you know, Clare, there's something else on my mind now that you've brought up your marriage to Matt."

"What's that?"

"It's clear that you and he are still close—two snow peas in a tenderly steamed pod, if you will. When I see you two together, it's as if your marriage never ended."

"It ended, Roman, trust me on that."

"So the last inning's played then? The game's over? There's nothing between you?"

Roman's phrasing made me shift on my plastic seat. *Nothing* between me and Matt? That wasn't true. There was a living, breathing daughter between us; a vital coffee business; an important family relationship with his mother; a long-standing friendship; and the residual affection that didn't just evaporate after years of sharing a life. But that answer

as far too nuanced for what Roman wanted to hear. So I adjusted the $300 skirt that Breanne was nice enough to buy
me and cleared my throat.

"There's *no* chance of our marrying again," I said firmly.
"And Matt wants to move on with his life, you understand?"

"Yes. But, sweetie, here's the million dollar question: Do
you?"

"Yes, of course. I have only one reservation about Matt
getting married again."

Roman sat up a little straighter. "Do tell."

"Matt strayed during his ten-year marriage to me. And he
led a pretty wild life in the decade after we parted. If he starts
to feel restless, he may stray on Breanne, too. Does she understand that possibility is more likely than not?"

Roman actually laughed. "Breanne's no fool. Matt's been a
playboy for years, and she's ready to endure his extracurricu-
lar activities. Unlike you, Clare, Breanne understands that
there are at least as many types of marriages in the world as
cultural cuisines."

"Meaning?"

"Meaning . . ." He shrugged. "Not everyone believes one
should marry for love."

I raised an eyebrow. "And what do you believe?"

The Puckish smile returned. " 'What fools these mortals
be . . . ' "

"Excuse me?"

"Lovers deceive and are deceived, Clare. It's been that way
for centuries. Look at you and Matt. You imagined your love
to be firm and constant, but it wasn't. He strayed, and you
lost faith in him."

Oh, God. "I never really thought of it *that* way."

"Injured parties never do. They've been injured, after all.
But your ex-husband still wants you back, doesn't he?"

I sat motionless for a moment. It was true: Matt did want
me back. The man's taxicab confession outside of Fen's had
implied exactly that. But I didn't like the way Roman asked
the question, and I hadn't forgotten bridezilla's fitting room

fit. Breanne specifically ordered Roman to find out wheth
or not I wanted Matt back.

Well, the food critic was a good interrogator, I had to giv
him that. But I was no slouch, either, so I simply replie
"Matt and I are over. He knows it as well as I do. That's wh
he proposed to Breanne in the first place."

Roman nodded, appearing pleased with that answer. "Br
anne's getting up in years. She doesn't want to remain si
gle for a lot of reasons. She and Matt have been linked in th
public eye, and their nuptials will silence the gossips in th
tabloids. I sense Matteo has his own reasons for wanting t
link himself with Breanne, as well, reasons that have nothin
to do with the sentimentalities to which you still subscribe

"Don't be condescending, Roman. Just because I believ
in the virtue of fidelity doesn't make me a fool."

"Forgive me, Clare. I don't mean to be rude."

"So what are you saying? Breanne and Matt are marryin
for convenience, both of them?"

"You of all people should know why. Love is fleeting. Bu
a *partnership* where two people thoroughly understand eac
other? Well, that can last forever."

We sat in silence after that, and I considered Roman
words. The train lurched suddenly and then began to mov
With mixed feelings, I watched the dark tennis center fac
from view. My past with Matt was fading, as well. And yet–
if I wanted to admit the truth to myself—something mor
than friendship did still quietly burn between us.

I considered that reality as the train rolled out of Flushin
Meadows Park and into Willets Point, land of auto grave
yards. Stacks of dead cars had been dumped here for years. I
the evening shadows, the sprawling heaps of smashed-u
chassis looked like a depressing installation of modern art.

It was hard to remember that the rusted, twisted met
had once been shiny and new. I thought about the peopl
who'd ridden around in those vehicles: the first dates an
shopping trips, Sunday drives and passionate kisses. Bu
now every last one was junked, useful to the scrap ma

maybe, but of little value to the people who'd once cherished them.

For years I'd treasured the old, applauded the preservation of the historic. Now I thought about the history between Matt and me. Up to now, I'd been treating his wedding as just another party to cater. Sure, I'd been telling myself it would be okay, but the mind and the heart were two very different organs.

I didn't want Matt back—that wasn't the issue. But the man had been my first lover, my passionate bridegroom, the father of my only child. Would I really be able to see him commit to another woman without feeling an emotional impact?

I had no answer to that question, and there was no more time to consider it. The train plunged us underground once more, and a short black tunnel blotted out my elevated view. A few moments later, steel wheels squealed to a halt in the station, and the conductor put the brakes on my musings.

"Main Street, Flushing. End of the line."

Seventeen

THE subway doors opened, and the mob shuffled out. Ro‑
man took my arm and led me onto the concrete platform
The newly renovated Queens station had a high ceiling an
walls overlaid with tiles of radiant white, interrupted b
black mosaics spelling out Main Street.

"Okay, Roman, this whole underground restaurant thin
is new to me. What do we do next?"

He waggled his black eyebrows. "Now the intrigue begins.

"I don't need intrigue. I just want to nail Neville Perry t
the wall."

"Come on then, sweetie. Follow me." Roman led me to
forty‑foot escalator. We boarded with the other commuter
and slowly rode up.

"Don't be nervous about the area, Clare," Roman whis‑
pered. "Just pretend we're on a clandestine rendezvous in a
exotic foreign city. Someplace really strange. Istanbul, per‑
haps. Or Cleveland. And speaking of strange—"

Roman pulled a baseball cap out of his pocket and place
it over his thick black hair.

"We have to blend in with the populace," he said when
gave him the fish eye. He pointed to my clothes. "In that Fe
original, you resemble the elegant Asian businesswome
you'll see up on the avenues. In this hat, I look like one of th
wastrels who roam the side streets."

"I doubt very much the street wastrels around here wear
[A]bercrombie & Fitch safari jackets, powder-pink chinos, or
[th]e hot new line of Hush Puppy casuals—never mind the Yan-
[ke]es cap. I guess you didn't notice: Queens is Mets country."

Roman threw up his pudgy hands. "Mets? Yankees?
[W]hat's the difference? A bunch of sweaty men hitting little
[wh]ite balls with sticks. Or is that golf? Well, never mind,
[m]y wardrobe will have to suffice."

We exited the escalator beside Macy's Flushing store on
[Ro]ppman Plaza and walked right into a fog of noxious fumes
[em]itted by a parade of idling MTA buses. The stench was
[pu]nctuated by the roar of a passenger jet descending over-
[he]ad, and I remembered LaGuardia's tarmac was only a few
[mi]les away.

We turned onto Main Street next, and I understood why
[R]oman regarded Flushing as some sort of exotic frontier. The
[in]tersection of Roosevelt and Main, once a Dutch neighbor-
[ho]od, had become the city's center for Chinese culture and
[sm]all businesses. This Chinatown had a size and scope that
[d]warfed the Manhattan original. English was not a common
[la]nguage on the street. Even the billboards and neon signs
[th]at advertised American products—Verizon, Crest tooth-
[pa]ste, and Chase Manhattan Bank—were printed in Chinese
[ch]aracters.

"A few years ago, this whole area was dominated by Ko-
[re]an businesses," Roman told me. "But most of the Koreans
[ha]ve moved on by now, and Chinese concerns have taken
[th]eir place."

We strolled past shops catering to an Asian clientele, with
[n]ames like Singapore Optical, Tai Pan Bakery, Hong Kong
[Cl]othing, and Lucky Bamboo Flower Shop. A dealer of gin-
[se]ng and herbs displayed outdoor stalls stocked with mush-
[ro]oms of every shape, size, and color. One clear cellophane
[ba]g contained black flakes identified as Fungus from the
[M]ountains.

"Are these medicinal herbs or culinary ingredients?" I
[as]ked Roman.

"Both."

Roman pointed down the block. "Along here, you c dine on a marvelous selection of Chinese, Japanese, Kore or Malaysian fare, and end the night swilling warm sake an authentic Japanese-style karaoke bar. I know, because I done it, although I prefer to come to Flushing for the und ground restaurants. They're so much more interesting."

"If these restaurants are underground, how do you ev find out about them?"

"Oh, there are lots of ways. Foodie networking most chefs and friends of chefs; amateur reviewers; and, of cour the local blogs. If you throw a little money around, waitsta will usually clue you in on their neighborhoods' culinary crets."

"Is that how you got in tonight? Throwing mon around?"

"Tonight's meal is a bargain, believe me," Roman said. ' hot young chef named Moon Pac wants to open a restaura and needs financial backers. If he dazzles the right people, might get his sugar daddy, so he's been throwing this din once a week for the last two months. I was invited by e-ma Other influential New York foodies and restaurateurs ceived the same invitation."

We hiked past St. George's Episcopal Church and fina reached a mixed residential block that paralleled Northe Boulevard. We stopped under the glow of an orna Victorian-style streetlight.

"According to my e-mail," Roman said, "we're to wait he at the Friends Meeting House for our connection to arrive."

With its simple lines and dowdy appearance, the lan mark Quaker building more resembled a colonial farmhou than a place of worship. The structure was separated fro the sidewalk by an old stone wall. I turned to watch the tr fic flow along Northern in a slow but steady pace.

"I don't see why we couldn't have taken a cab he What's the point of the long subway ride and a rendezvo on a darkened street?"

"Cabs bring attention and unwanted scrutiny. Too much ffic can be the death of an underground eatery. It's happened fore. For instance . . ." Roman pointed to a gas station down e block. "Once upon a time you could park in front of that ation, make a cell phone call to an unlisted number, and in a w minutes an order from the famous dumpling speakeasy uld be delivered to your car or cab—"

"Excuse me, did you say 'dumpling speakeasy'?"

"Best dumplings I've ever eaten outside of Shanghai. dly, the cab and car traffic caused too much attention. ord leaked to the local supermarket sheets. It hit the big- r papers, then New York 1, and that was that!"

"What happened? Did the Department of Health de- nd?"

"More like the tax man. An underground restaurant is an licensed business. That's one reason for the secrecy."

It certainly felt secretive enough loitering there, I de- ded. At eight thirty in the evening, the traffic on Northern as heavy. There were a lot of police cars around, too, but the dewalks were pretty empty, except for a trio of men hang- g out just like us at the end of the block, in front of the iwan Cultural Center. One of the youths wore a black cket with an elaborate dragon design on the back. He no- ed me looking and glanced away.

I wondered if they were coming to the secret dinner party, o. I considered asking them when I felt someone grab my bow. I whirled to find black eyes staring at me from under e shadows of a dark hooded jacket. I broke away from the ranger, ready to scream, when the man pulled back his od and said, "Are you with Roman Brio?"

"Right here! Party of two!" Roman waved his chubby nd as if we'd been waiting for our table at Babbo's bar.

"So nice to meet you, Mr. Brio," the young man said with slight accent. He had dark, almond-shaped eyes and a shy nile, which he flashed as he gestured us forward. "Please al- w me to seat you."

I noticed a waiter's black pants and white apron under the

young man's jacket. "So he's our waiter?" I whispered to R
man. "This is his job?"

"I'm sure he's a waiter at a real restaurant," Rom
replied. "Tonight's probably his night off, and he's getti
paid cash to moonlight for this event."

The young man led us across Northern. We passed t
huge redbrick Town Hall and turned onto a residential blo
filled with newly built two- and three-family town hous
But we weren't going to those houses. We turned abrup
instead into a narrow alley that ran behind the Town Hall

Tiny weathered clapboard houses lined both sides of t
short, shadowy block. The buildings were so close to ea
other, they muffled the noise of the traffic on Northern. Fo
moment, given the age of the structures and the abru
quiet, I felt as though I were back in my own Village neig
borhood.

Roman sniffed the air. "Charcoal."

The smell tickled my nose, too, along with the scent
hot sesame oil, garlic, and ginger.

"I think we're getting warm," Roman said with a quav
in his voice.

Halfway down the block we stopped in front of a sma
gray-shingled house with a gambrel roof like an old barn.
single, tiny window covered with scarlet curtains faced t
alley.

While the youth opened the unlocked front door,
glanced up the block and spied the men who'd been loite
ing in front of the Taiwan Center. Were they fellow dinn
guests?

I was about to ask our waiter but never got the chance. F
hustled us into a foyer, and a wave of cooking scents wash
over us: Indian and Asian spices, seared meat, and a peppe
smell that woke up my tear ducts.

"Positively delightful!" Roman closed his eyes and wav
his hands like a *parfumeur* experiencing a riot of new scents

We were ushered into a cozy living room with powde
blue walls covered with family photos. Floor lamps gave t

...pace a soft glow. At the far end of the room was a nook of dining space. A long, narrow table started in that small room and flowed out of it, reaching well into the living room. It was set for ten. Three couples were already seated, sipping wine and speaking with a stocky man who stood over them. As we entered, the well-dressed group turned in their seats to greet Roman, who seemed to know them all.

"This is Clare Cosi, everyone. She's the manager of the Village Blend."

In a rush, everyone shouted their names. They were all Caucasian and appeared to be prosperous professionals in their thirties and forties. One man stood out, however. Younger than the rest, I recognized him from the uncannily accurate caricature on his Web site.

"Chef Perry!" Roman said, "Clare's been *dying* to meet you."

Ack. So much for subtlety.

Neville Perry stood up. I quickly stepped forward and offered my hand. He shook it firmly.

"I'm flattered to meet a fan."

Wearing a Levi's jacket over a loose Hawaiian shirt, the chef was no older than thirty. His spiky hair was platinum blond (obviously bleached, since his goatee was dark brown), and I noticed the glint of a silver loop in his ear. The striking contrast of perfectly even white teeth against a salon-perfect tan screamed Hollywood. So did the way his shirt was open at the neck to flaunt as much bronzed flesh as possible.

His eyes were the pale-green color of honeydew melon, and they checked me out so quickly from head to toe I would have missed it if I hadn't been watching.

"So, Clare . . ." He smiled. "Were you a fan of my *canceled* reality show, my *defunct* restaurant, or my Prodigal Chef blog?"

"Oh, all three," I said, surprised by the dry humor in the man's tone. Self-deprecation was the last thing I expected from this guy.

"Well, that's really nice of you to say. Have any favorite episodes? Or dishes?"

"It's really your Web site that's got my attention lately."

"That's great, too." Neville glanced at Roman. "I'm happy you're socializing with someone *besides* your gossip mongering, yellow journalist buddies." Neville slapped his forehead. "Wait a minute! I forgot. You're *one* of those gossip mongering, yellow journalists, aren't you?"

"Oh, Neville. You're jealous because I actually get *paid* for my writing. By the way, I've been wondering. What *do* you do for a living?"

Chef Perry winked at me. "I wonder if our food critic gets paid by the word or by the pound?"

Roman rolled his eyes. "Ersatz cheese is sold by the pound, Neville. That would be *your* department."

Our escort reappeared, minus his hooded jacket, bearing a tray of wine. Roman accepted a glass, sniffed it with theatrical trepidation, then took a sip and made a face.

Perry lifted his chin in my direction. "I'll bet Clare doesn't think my blogs are crap."

Roman raised a finger. "I didn't say crap. I said *ersatz cheese*. There is a minor difference. Considering your reputation, it's one you should recognize."

Though the men were throwing comments as prickly as cactus leaves, I didn't get the impression Neville Perry actually disliked Roman.

"Man, I hope we eat soon." Perry glanced at his bling-heavy watch. "These aromas are making me ravenous."

"Anything to clean my palate of this subpar wine," Roman said, plopping his glass on the table.

"We're still waiting for someone to arrive," said one of the other guests.

Just then a loud voice boomed from the foyer. "I'm here all! Start ringing the dinner bell!"

Roman looked as though he'd just sampled something more displeasing than the "subpar" wine. He turned to Neville. "Well, Perry, it appears you're not the only show biz chef to taint us with his presence this evening."

"Oh my God. Rafe Chastain is here," burbled a woman at ₑ table.

I knew Chastain by reputation, but I never expected the ₔdventure Channel's infamous *Exotic Food Hunter at Large* to ₔow up at a place like this. The man looked much the same ₔ he did on my TV: a leanly muscled charmer with a face ₑll lined from years spent under the harsh sun (not to men-ₒn his decades of hard living, if the man's reputation for ₔinking, drugging, and daring was accurate). He wore his ₔyptian cotton shirt open at the collar and rolled up at the ₑeves, and his long legs sported tight black denims over ₔinted snakeskin boots.

Chastain's television travels had taken him all over the ₒrld in search of new culinary experiences, which often in-ₔlved eating the kind of stuff I'd run away from, not put in ₔ mouth. We're talking bugs, snakes, lizards, rats, along ₔith the occasional feast of entrails, gizzards, and other ques-ₒnable parts of animals, domesticated and wild.

I'd seen the show once or twice but was more familiar ₔith the serious culinary articles he'd written for the *New ₔrker*, *GQ*, and *Food & Wine*.

Intimidated by the celebrity's entrance, no one rose to ₑeet him. Mostly they just gawked, as if the man were still ₔ display behind their high-def screens. Out of politeness I ₑpped forward.

"Hello, Mr. Chastain, my name's Clare—"

"Nice to meet you, honey." He gripped my hand, glanced ₔwn my blouse, and looked right past me. "Where's the ₔoze?"

Eighteen

Ihe waiter with the wine tray approached, and Rafe Chastain snagged two glasses for himself. He downed one immediately and set the empty glass back on the tray. That's wh[en] he noticed two familiar faces in the room.

"Roman. Neville," he said, nodding in their general d[i]rections. Then he ran his fingers through his short, iron-gr[ay] hair, showing off the tattoos on his gangly forearms. Final[ly] he sniffed the air.

"Yum-yum. Something smells good."

Frowning, Neville Perry glanced at his watch again. "[I] hope the food hasn't gone cold. It's been *so* long."

Chastain smirked at the dig but held back his reply wh[en] he saw an older Asian woman bowing graciously before us[.]

"I'm Mrs. Weng. Welcome to my house."

"Quiet, kids. The show's starting," Chastain loudly wh[is]pered.

"Tonight you will experience the cuisine of Chef Mo[on] Pac," Mrs. Weng continued. "Born in Chonju, South Kore[a,] Moon Pac first learned to cook beside his Malaysian moth[er.] The chef moved from there to some of the finest kitchens [in] Asia. He apprenticed at Jeolla Hoigwan, then went to Ho[ng] Kong and cooked at the Hoi Tin Garden—"

"I'm impressed," Chastain interrupted before draining h[is] second glass.

"Now he's here," the woman added, "and Chef Pac is [r]eady to bring his unique fusion of Eastern cuisines to Amer-[ic]a. Please be seated."

Chastain snatched another glass of wine from the waiter's [tr]ay and suddenly hooked my arm. "Clare, wasn't it? Come [si]t beside me, honey."

"But I was speaking with Neville—"

"Yeah, Rafe, hands off," Perry said. "I saw her first."

"Gentlemen," Roman interrupted. "Clare accompanied [m]e to the ball."

Chastain shrugged but failed to release me. "Fine. Then [yo]u two Flying Monkeys can sit next to us."

Roman sniffed. "That's *Mr.* Flying Monkey to you!"

Chastain took the seat at the far end of the table, near the [ho]use's back patio door, and plopped me down beside him. I [qu]ickly offered Neville Perry the seat to my right. Roman [se]ttled into the chair across the table. Then the waiters [st]reamed in with the first course.

"Malaysian hotcakes with curry dipping sauce," our host-[es]s announced.

A platter with a pile of hot, sticky dough, thin as tissue [p]aper, sat beside a bowl containing a breast portion of [ch]icken in a curry-colored sauce.

"Do they have to serve it with the bones?" asked a woman [at] the other end of the table.

Chef Chastain smirked. "The bones are where the flavor [is], baby. They make the sauce rich and savory." He tore into [th]e thin pancake and plunged it into the bowl of hot sauce.

"This roti is the best Malaysian flatbread I've ever tasted," [P]erry declared, his mouth still full.

"The sauce is piquant," Roman noted. "It's reminiscent of *[m]urgh makhani*—classic Indian butter chicken—but without [th]e tomato base."

"Mmmmm. Besides the ginger, I taste garlic, coriander, [c]umin, and white pepper," Chastain said. "Too much white [p]epper."

"A few too many sprigs of lemongrass, as well," Roman said.

Neville Perry caught my eye. "And a few too many critic
Don't you think, Clare?"

I couldn't argue. The crepelike pancake was so moist an
delicious it almost tasted fried. And the dipping sauce w
luxuriously succulent—buttery smooth yet spicy with th
faintest kiss of heat. But I wasn't here for the food. As
chewed and swallowed, I considered my next step wit
Perry.

*Just go for it, Clare. Reel him in, pull the rug out, and see ho
he reacts.*

I waited for the next course to come, *ipol poh piah*,
steamed Malaysian spring roll stuffed with white turni
egg, onions, minced dried shrimp, and a salty fish paste. R
man and Chastain began discussing the benefits of dried ve
sus fresh herbs and spices, and I laid my hand on Neville's.

Time to get down to business.

"You're a pretty popular guy among my employees,"
said, summoning a warm (hopefully trustworthy) smile. "I
fact, one of my baristas swore you were near our coffeehous
the other night. Or maybe it was last night?"

"The Village Blend?" Neville shrugged. "Could be.
hang in the Village a lot, when I'm not downtown."

"Is that where you live?" I leaned toward him. "Dowr
town?"

He smiled flirtatiously. "I can give you my number if yo
like. See, I'm transitioning. I had to move out of my ol
place; now I'm checking different neighborhoods to see wha
suits me."

"You should try the Village," I said. "Someplace historic
Or are you more interested in the modern amenities? Th
apartments in the Time Warner Center are luxurious. I wa
there today, at *Trend*'s offices, visiting my friend *Breann
Summour* . . ."

That did it. Neville had been fine conversing with Roma
earlier. At the first mention of Breanne's name, the freshnes
of Neville's smile expired. I saw his reaction and decided t
up the pressure.

"I read that piece on your site. You know, the one about :rving' Breanne? A little too Hannibal Lecter, don't you ink? Or is it just that you don't like my friend very uch?"

Neville dropped his flat bread. "What I don't like, Clare, e *bullies*. Especially so-called trendsetters who wield their ige circulation and massive advertising base like a sword ver everyone's head. A sword that's always ready to chop iu off at the knees."

Head? Knees? Brother, this guy was into chopping body parts. ow he just needs to say the right words, threaten Breanne with irm, violence, something specific. Come on, Neville . . .

Reaching for his napkin, Neville sat back in his chair. Anyway, your friend Breanne is big enough to take my in- ilts. Believe me, she has them coming. That's why I started iy blog. Thanks to the Internet, magazines and newspapers longer have a lock on taste or opinion. In my blog, every- ie out there can hear what I have to say. The *other* side of the ory—"

"Wow," Roman interrupted. "There's *another* side to serv- ig up expired poultry, seafood, and produce to your cus- imers? Please, Neville. Let's hear it."

Neville narrowed his pale-green eyes. "For one thing, rio, those products weren't expired. They were frozen and iawed, not that I'd expect Ms. Summour to tell the truth. ikay, not the freshest ingredients, maybe. But at that point ie restaurant was in trouble. I had to cut corners to keep the ream alive and protect the livelihood of my employees."

"If you cared so much for your staff, why did you gouge ieir tips?" Roman demanded, all playfulness gone from is tone. (I'd almost forgotten how he'd started out in this iwn—as a lowly waiter, dependent on tips to make the :nt.)

Neville met Roman's accusing gaze, leaned forward, and iunded his fist on the table hard enough to shake the wine- lasses. Conversations stopped, and the other diners looked is way.

"Just because *your* boss published that *crap*, doesn't mak
it *true*. I was *cleared* by the arbitration board. I'm still waitin
for Summour to print a retraction—"

Okay, here we go. Threaten Breanne now, buddy, get it out . .

"And I'll tell you one more thing—"

"Jesus Christ!" Chef Chastain spat. "Will you give it
rest. Some of us are here for a relaxing evening!" He lowere
his voice. "I'd like to digest."

Perry's flushed face glanced around. "Sorry," he said an
sat back in his chair.

Damn! Chastain's outburst effectively doused Perry's rag
I was annoyed at first—he'd been *so close* to a real threat—bi
then I thought it over.

*Would an adolescent mind close to homicidal rage really be ab
to control his temper so fast?*

"*Ikan bakar*," the hostess announced.

"How delightful," Roman said, his own fury dissipatin
in the tempting aromatics of the newly arrived dish.

"What is it?" I asked quietly.

He leaned toward me. "It's a Malaysian dish of seafoo
grilled using fragrant charcoal."

"Is that all you've got for her, Brio?" Chastain drained an
other glass of wine and turned toward me. "*Ikan bakar* mean
'burnt fish' in Malay, honey. The seafood is marinated in
slew of spices and a chili and fermented shrimp paste calle
sambal belacan."

The tight space filled with a charcoal aroma as the plate
were served. Each dish contained three strips of seared whit
flesh with blackened edges and visible grill marks, served o
a banana leaf.

"Man, Chef Moon Pac really went all out on the presenta
tion." Perry's genial mask was obviously back in place (if i
was a mask).

Chastain signaled to his waiter. "Is this *sotong*?"

"That's squid for you civilians," Roman said.

The waiter shook his head. "Stingray."

As I considered my next line of questioning, I watched
he waiters place three large white bowls on the table. Each
ontained a mashed chili paste that resembled a thick salsa.
eside each was a plate of bamboo skewers.

"This is *sambal belacan*, very hot," the hostess said. "It con-
ains a chili pepper called *bhut jolokia*—"

"Christ, are you kidding me?" Chastain squawked. "That
uff's like an 800,000 on the Scoville scale!"

"The what scale?" asked a man at the end of the table.

Roman rolled his eyes. "The Scoville heat unit is used to
ssess the chemical heat given off by capsaicin, the active in-
redient in chili peppers."

"Please use the skewers to dip the seafood into the sauce.
on't get any on your hands, or touch your eyes," the hostess
arned. "When we handle these peppers in the kitchen, we
ear rubber gloves."

As an added precaution, the waitstaff set small plates of
lack-speckled salt beside the volcanic sauce. Curious, I tasted
ome with my finger. It was salty, of course, but with the
dded licorice taste of five-spice powder. (I didn't know a lot
bout Asian cooking, but I did know five-spice powder was
sed extensively in Chinese dishes and consisted of equal
arts cinnamon, cloves, fennel seeds, star anise, and Szechuan
eppercorns.)

"If the fire is too much, use the salt to cleanse your
alate," the hostess warned. "Wine, water, or tea will only
ake the peppers burn longer."

Rafe Chastain boldly skewered a strip of stingray and
ipped it into the sauce. As he chewed, we all waited to see
he'd keel over or run screaming from the room.

"Wow," he said, face flushed. "That's a real mouth peeler.
ut *tasty*."

Intrigued, I followed his lead, touching the corner of my
sh into the potent sauce. When I bit into the stingray,
othing happened at first. Then the inside of my nose began
 burn, and I blinked back tears. When the heat reached my

throat, I was certain I'd swallowed fire. But as the burn sub
sided, other layers of flavor surfaced. I coughed, tasting
sweet and tangy smokiness.

Unable to stand the burn, I took a quick spoonful of sal
which made me cough some more. I felt a bead of perspira
tion roll down my back. The experience was capped by
rush of pleasure that must have resembled a drug high.

"Whoa . . ." I croaked. "That clears your sinuses."

"Feeling good, Clare?" Chastain grinned big as he too
another look down my blouse. "Pleasure chemicals are releas
ing now in that hot and tasty little body of yours to counter
act the capsaicin. Endorphins are a real aphrodisiac, by th
way. It ain't opium, but it's legal."

*Good Lord, Chastain's getting drunker by the dish. But I'm n
cutting him any slack. One more look down my blouse, and I'
pouring that hot sauce down his pants!*

Neville Perry opened his mouth and waved air into i
"I'd serve this—if I still *had* a restaurant."

The tone was dry again. Perry was back to sel
deprecation. He even shot me a wink. Clearly, my friendshi
with the hated Breanne wasn't that serious of an issue to hin

Maybe if I poke the wound a little . . .

"But, Neville, your restaurant was *ruined*. Your reputatio
shredded. Don't you miss running your own business?"

Perry shook his head. "Truthfully, Clare, I have no regret
In the end, having the Wicked Witch of Style criticize m
restaurant was a stroke of luck."

"Luck?" I blinked. "You're being ironic, right?"

I was waiting for the rage, the obscenities, the verba
threats to Breanne that he'd naturally want me to convey t
her. But Perry remained relaxed, authentically, it appeared.

"Honestly, running that place was wearing me down. Nov
that it's closed, I've launched a new career as a food write
My blogs about Breanne have opened up some surprising op
portunities. Her rival publications are lining up to offer m
assignments in *their* magazines, a publisher's just bought m
cookbook, and two newspaper syndicates are in a biddin

r to put me under contract for a national column on food
l wine."

"Wait . . . you're saying that you're *happy* with how
ngs turned out?"

Neville shrugged. "In a way, I owe Breanne a thank-
—not that she's ever going to get one from me. Skewer-
; *Trend's* trendsetter is just too damn much fun. She's
rned a lot of people over the years, and they're my most
al readers."

Neville Perry was glowing now, and it was more than the
ct of the *bhut jolokia.* The culinary school graduate was
viously a mama's boy who wanted fame and fortune but
ln't want to work very hard or long to get it. Writing blog
ries and restaurant reviews was apparently a lot easier for
rry than running a restaurant, so he'd found a happier ca-
r path. He looked pretty proud of himself, too, and the
th is, the man really was turning his devastating failure
o success. I couldn't condemn him for that. More to the
int, I was beginning to conclude that Matt's bride-to-be
d been right all along.

This man was a joker (or a *joke,* depending on your view of
past). But a killer? *No, I don't think so.* Sure, his feelings
vard Breanne weren't charitable, but then neither were
ne.

I began to get irritated with myself for going on this
ld-goose chase. The day felt totally wasted. What I'd wit-
ssed at Breanne's magazine was classic office politics. *Big
l. Alert the media.* Neville Perry's black-wrapped meat
aver was my strongest lead—and it had led me to a dead
d. I was sure of it.

I forcefully speared another piece of stingray and dipped
in the hotter-than-hell sauce. But before I could take the
st bite, there was a loud crash in the foyer, and a woman
ed out.

I stared in horror, the skewer hanging between my plate
d my mouth, as our gentle hostess was pushed through the
chen doorway so hard she bounced off the wall. Then the

waiters and two men in kitchen smocks marched into t
room single file, their hands behind their heads.

Finally, three men charged into the room. They were
in dark clothes, and their heads and faces were covered w
black ski masks. The tallest of the three waved a big, nas
looking handgun.

"If nobody moves, nobody gets hurt," said the tall m
with the gun, his voice muffled by the ski mask.

"What's going on here?" One of the well-heeled gue
rose from his chair. "What do you men want?"

You idiot, I thought. *Sit down and shut up.*

Too late. One of the two shorter bandits stepped forwa
snatched a bottle of wine from the table, and clubbed t
man with it. The woman beside him screamed as the ot
raged diner dropped back into his seat, clutching his head

"Didn't you hear me?! I said nobody move!" the arm
man cried, dark eyes wild behind the mask.

The shorter bandit stepped around the gunman.

"Your wallets, jewelry, watches, and money in this bag
He tossed a red pillowcase at the woman. "Fill it now, la
Before *jefe* decides to pop someone!"

NINETEEN

∽∾∽∾∽∾∽∾∽∾∽∾∽∾∽∾∽∾∽∾∽∾∽

THE room was silent as the trembling woman stripped off her earrings and dropped them into the thief's red pillow-case. Beside her, the less-than-brilliant diner who'd protested the invasion clutched a bloodstained napkin to his head.

"Where's the purse, lady?" the man with the pillowcase demanded.

"It's on the f-floor," the woman said, her voice breaking.

The thief placed his gloved fist against the side of her head and mock-punched her. "Yo, bitch, pick it up!"

Silently sobbing, she lifted her Christian Dior clutch and dumped its contents into the cloth sack.

"The purse, too."

With a sniff, she released the Dior into the sack.

Oh, God. My mouth was dry, my skin clammy. The shock of the robbery was making everything move in slow motion. *Stay calm, Clare. Hold it together.*

Quinn once told me the best thing I could do in a situa-tion like this was to stay cool and give the robbers what they wanted. *"No money or piece of jewelry is more valuable than your life, sweetheart. Just give it up and get away . . ."* I couldn't agree more. I certainly wasn't going to put up a fight for my stupid bun bag or the money inside it.

Waiting for my turn to be fleeced, I placed my hands on

the table, in plain sight. A soft whimpering came from
side me. I glanced to my right and saw it was Neville Per
The man looked ill, sweat was slick on his brow, and he w
quivering like a mass of panna cotta.

*Wow, what do you know. Under pressure, the crazy, cleav
wielding Prodigal Chef is no different from the rest of us.*

Then I heard another sound, one I couldn't believe. (
the other side of me, Rafe Chastain was softly chuckling
glanced in his direction and saw the bemused smile on l
well-lined face.

"Son of a bitch," he muttered with a glance my way. "Th
is the third time this year I've been robbed."

Okay, I thought, *maybe all of us aren't quivering masses
panna cotta.*

"Shut up, you!" the gunman cried, hearing Chastain's l
tle laugh. "Or you can eat this." He gestured to the gun ba
rel.

Chastain lifted his hands. "You're the boss, kimosabe."

Thank goodness Chastain's being smart. No stupid heroics.

The red pillowcase was passed to the next dinner gue
the bleeding man. He dropped a Rolex and very nice leath
wallet into it.

While the tall man held the gun and the other gathere
up the loot, the third robber held back, letting the others (
the work. That's when I noticed his back reflected in a wa
mirror and saw the familiar dragon design on his jacket.

A chill ran through me. These were the same guys I
spotted loitering in front of the Taiwan Center on Northe
Boulevard. I'd thought they were fellow diners. Now I wo
dered. Had the men been shadowing Roman and me, speci
ically? Or had they heard about this dinner from anoth
source?

I jumped when someone nudged my foot. It was Roma
I looked across the table at his panicked expression. I
mouthed *Breanne* to me, and with a sick jolt I remember
the wedding rings.

Oh, God. Oh, no. Roman had promised Breanne that he

ep the rings until the wedding day, and guard them with
: *life*. I could tell from the look on his face that those one-
a-kind Nunzio rings were on him right now.

I grimaced, watching the fleecing continue around the
ble. Finally, they got to Roman.

"Give it up," the thief snarled, holding the red pillowcase
t.

Roman pulled up his sleeve and fumbled with the clasp
his expensive watch. He dropped it into the sack, fol-
wed by his wallet and a polished titanium money clip
affed with bills.

The thief was ready to move along, but the man in the
agon jacket pointed directly at Roman. "He didn't give it
up," Dragon Man calmly said. "We need those rings."

Rings? How does this guy know Roman's carrying rings?

"Come on, man! Give 'em up," the thief with the bag de-
anded.

Roman held up his hands and wiggled his pinkies. "No
ngs," he said. "And my navel isn't pierced, either." The
an cuffed Roman with his free hand, and he nearly tum-
ed off his chair. "See here!" Roman cried. "That's not sport-
g!"

"Let me convince the little shithead," the tall man with
e gun said.

"No, wait! Keep everybody covered," Dragon Man com-
anded.

But the gunman pushed past his partner and placed
e barrel of the gun against Roman's temple. Brio's eyes
idened as the armed man leaned down to speak right into
s ear.

"He's says you got those rings. Give 'em up now, or I'll *pop
u dead.*"

The armed man's face was two feet away from mine, just
ross the narrow strip of white tablecloth. I saw the robber's
ld eyes under the ski mask, and I knew he meant business.

Okay, Roman, I wanted to shout, *you've done enough for Bre-
ne. Give them what they want before they take it off your corpse!*

Roman's lip quivered, but he shook his head. "I do[n't] know what you're talking about."

There was a scuffling movement to my right. I turned [to] find Neville Perry out of his chair. *My God.* The chef was a[t]tempting to bolt for the back door. But he wasn't going [to] make it. The gunman was already shifting his weapon aw[ay] from Roman's head. He took aim at the chef's back. Nevil[le] was about to be gunned down in cold blood.

Not in front of me, you son of a bitch!

In less than a second I'd chosen my weapon: the bowl [of] *sambal belacan.* I grabbed the blazing hot chili paste a[nd] threw it straight into the gunman's mask.

"Eat that, asshole!"

The man screamed as liquid fire hit his eyes. He dropp[ed] his gun, clutched his face, and went down howling.

"Aaaaaaaaah! I can't see! I can't see!"

"Nice move, honey!" Rafe Chastain was already lungi[ng] at the robber holding the loot. I heard the solid smack o[f his] right hook connecting. The bag went flying, and the pu[nk] went down. So did Chastain, whose tattooed arms began d[e]livering nonstop rabbit punches.

A floor lamp crashed to the carpet, sparked, and we[nt] black. With shouts and screams, the waiters bolted for t[he] front door, knocking another lamp to the floor and plungi[ng] the room into semidarkness. Dragon Man tried to stop t[he] horde, but without a weapon he couldn't scare anyone.

His screaming partner was still trying to rip the drench[ed] ski mask off. But his movements only put more capsaicin [in] his eyes, nose, and mouth. He flailed around, grabbing h[is] partner's legs.

"Help me, man! Help me!"

Dragon Man was dragged to the floor, where he starte[d] groping through the shadows for the lost gun.

Amid the chaos, I leaped over the top of the table a[nd] grabbed Roman's collar. "Come on!"

Chubby as he was, Roman still beat me out the fro[nt] door. We saw the diners fleeing up the dark alley toward t[he] brightly illuminated new town houses. I pulled Roman in he opposite direction, deeper into the gloom.

"Where are we going?" he whined.

"Those guys were after *you*, Roman, and I don't think hey'll give up easily."

"Huh?"

"They *knew* about Breanne's rings!"

"Oh, really, Clare? Think so?"

"This is no time for sarcasm! Come on, duck."

I pulled Roman behind a ten-year-old Honda. Through ts windows, we watched the house we'd just fled. One of the obbers burst through the front door a moment later, followed by Chef Chastain, who was yelling obscenities and waving the steel shaft of a broken lamp like he was back in he Australian bush, scaring dingoes away from his cameraman with a campsite tent pole (one of the *Exotic Food Hunter*'s better episodes).

Both Chastain and his game ran down the alley and around the corner.

Roman began to rise. "It's all clear."

"Not yet." I pulled him down again.

Less than thirty seconds later, Dragon Man appeared at he door. I watched him tuck the gun into his belt and step cautiously into the alley.

"I have to pee," Roman whispered.

I shushed him and watched Dragon Man take off in the opposite direction, following the noise of the fleeing dinner guests.

"Come on, let's get out of here."

We took to the side streets, which were deserted at this ime of night. Even so, I imagined eyes watching us at every urn, feared an ambush any second. Dragon Man could be anywhere, which made me want to get out of Flushing ASAP.

"Let's head back to Northern Boulevard and hail a cab."

Roman snorted. "It's easier to get a cab during a hailstorm n Manhattan than it is to find one in Flushing on a sunny afernoon. And it's not the afternoon. It's after ten."

"How much after?"

"I don't know, precisely. The brigands stole my Cartier Divan watch. And they took all my money, too, so I can even pay for a cab."

"I have plenty of cash in my—Oh, no! I left my bag back at the underground restaurant!"

I felt a weight in the pocket of my tailored jacket and breathed a little easier. At least I still had the keys to the Blend.

Roman frowned. "Poor Clare. A Fen original."

"I didn't like it that much anyway. Fortunately, I took your suggestion and left my credit cards and IDs with Matt when he came by to pick up Breanne. But all the cash I had was in there, some of my favorite makeup, and my Metro card, too."

"Don't worry, I still have mine. We can take the subway at least."

"I can't believe you didn't give up those wedding rings, Roman. You almost died to protect them. And after all that crap on the train out here about not believing in sentimentality."

"Sentiment has nothing to do with it, sweetie. If I lost those rings, Breanne would never forgive me. In the world of New York style, a real suicide is preferable to *career* suicide."

Oh jeez. "Thank God I live on planet earth."

When we reached Northern Boulevard, we stuck to the shadows, of which there were plenty. Still convinced Dragon Man was stalking us, I kept checking our backs.

Then I spied an odd-looking building set back from the wide boulevard. The brick structure resembled an old castle, complete with turrets at each of its corners. Though no one was in sight, light streamed through the first-floor windows and illuminated the long sidewalk to the entrance. When I got close enough to read the large block letters over the institutional green front door, I figured our troubles were over.

QUEENS TASK FORCE NORTH

"We're saved, Roman! This is a police station!"

I reached for the big man's arm, but he pulled away. "I'm ot going to the police!"

"What! Why not? We just got robbed, assaulted, and one f the bad guys is still out there looking for us."

Roman dismissed my concern with a wave of his hand. You're paranoid, Clare. Those banditos are long gone by ow."

"We can file a theft report. You want your watch back, on't you?"

Roman folded his arms. "Not *that* badly. If word ever got ut that I went to the law, I'd never get invited to another underground restaurant, ever again!"

"I can't believe what I'm hearing."

Roman turned his back on me and walked away. I was so ngry I was tempted to let him go it alone. But as I watched he stubborn food critic huff and puff up Northern, I realized e was oblivious to the danger and utterly incapable of taking care of himself. If anything happened to Roman, I'd feel errible. So I followed him.

By the time we reached Main Street, it was so late the place was nearly deserted. The click of my heels on the racked concrete was the only sound as we passed darkened torefronts, shuttered magazine kiosks, and empty bus helters. We were the only two people riding the long escalator down to the train. Except for the sleepy MTA clerk n the service booth, I saw no one in the subway station, either.

Because Main Street was the end of the line, there was a train already idling on the tracks. We walked the length of he last car and entered the next to the last, both of which vere empty. Breathless, we dropped into the plastic orange eats.

"Men like Rafe Chastain may relish a life of adventure on he wild frontier," Roman said, "but after a night like this, I an't wait to get back to civilization."

The announcer's voice crackled over the speaker.

"Number 7 to Manhattan. This train is running expres
Express train! First stop Junction Boulevard!"

The doors closed and opened again—something that ha
pens when a passenger tries to board the train at the la
minute and gets hung up in the door instead.

"Please let go of the doors in the rear of the train," th
conductor warned.

The doors closed again (all the way this time) and th
train rolled into the dark tunnel.

"Wait a minute!" I said. "We're at the rear of the trai
aren't we?"

Roman saw my alarmed expression and turned pal
"What's the matter?"

"I don't think our adventure is over yet."

I rose to my feet. The floor lurched under my heels, and
stumbled to the door at one end of the train car. Through i
window I saw Dragon Man in the middle of the last ca
walking down the aisle in our direction. His mask was of
and he appeared to be part-Hispanic, part-Asian, with angu
lar features, a shaved head, and the hard, catlike gaze of
predator.

I turned. "Run, Roman!"

"Run? Run where?"

"To the next car!"

I grabbed his wrist and pulled him up the aisle. When w
reached the end, I slid aside the heavy steel door. The roar o
the tunnel filled the car, along with a whooshing blast o
musty underground air.

The Metropolitan Transportation Authority doesn't lik
riders crossing between the subway cars. On every line i
Manhattan, the doors between the cars are locked. But fo
some reason—tradition, maybe, or because it's an elevate
train—the doors between the cars on the 7 line are neve
locked.

*That deviation in transit system procedure might just save ou
lives,* I thought, but it wasn't over yet. Roman and I had t
cross a gap between one car and another while the rockin

rain flew across the ancient track at forty miles per hour.
There was plenty of incentive to risk the move. Dragon Man
had just entered the car we were about to vacate.

I turned to Roman. "Go!"

The heavy man stepped through the door and over the
frightening gap. The thundering rumble was deafening, and
the wind whipped through his thick hair as he moved to the
door of the next car. He took hold of the latch, muscled the
door open, and stepped through.

Now I moved onto the small, open platform, closing the
door behind me. Through its Plexiglas window, I saw
Dragon Man in the middle of the aisle. He paused to reach
into his jacket, pull a gun from his belt, and take off the
safety.

I moved quickly to the next car, realizing something aw-
ful. Even if we ran full out to the other end of this car,
Dragon Man's bullets would be faster.

"He's coming!" I yelled to Roman over the roar of the
train. "And he's got a gun. We can't outrun him. We'll have
to fight!"

I felt the temperature changing and realized the train had
emerged from the underground tunnel. A blast of chilly
nighttime wind ripped through my hair, and I saw we were
racing up an incline to an elevated position, heading for the
sprawling auto junkyards of Willets Point.

Dragon Man was stepping out now onto the ledge between the two train cars. Grinning at me, the punk waved
the gun in the air, making sure I saw it.

He stepped forward, and I suddenly remembered that
scumbag from the White Horse Tavern, the one who'd
jammed his motorcycle boot into the back room's doorway.
Only this time, the door in my hand wasn't flimsy wood, it
was heavy steel on a sliding track. I reached up to release the
overhead safety latch. As Dragon Man's foot moved into the
car, I slammed the door on the gunman's instep.

The man's bellow of surprise and pain was loud enough to
be heard over the clatter of the metal wheels on the track.

Cursing, the man slammed the butt of his weapon agains the window. The Plexiglas cracked but didn't shatter. H repositioned the gun in his hand.

"He's going to shoot us through the window!"

Roman's eyes narrowed. "The hell he is!"

The big man yanked the door back open, stepped aroun it, and with a shriek of pure fury lunged at the gunma arms flailing like windmills.

Dragon Man's weapon discharged, but the bullet wen wild, ricocheting off the train's metal framework. Roma kept flailing, and the gun was knocked free. It dropped dow between the cars, swallowed up by the night and the ancien tracks.

The train kept rolling, and Roman continued fighting Dragon Man lunged backward, desperate now to get awa but the door behind him was shut, and Roman kept coming using his girth to slam the man like an angry bull.

With a string of raging curses, the robber was knocked o his feet. He tumbled over the chain-link guardrail, his scream diminishing in the shadows of the junkyards below. grabbed the hem of Roman's safari jacket and pulled with a my might to keep him from following the man over the side

Panting, the two of us moved back into the car and col lapsed on the orange seats. Then we stared speechlessly ou the open subway door, watching for long minutes until ou train was clear of the rusting graveyard.

Twenty

MIDNIGHT came and went, and the Blend had long since closed its doors to paying customers. But lights still blazed behind the coffee bar and the cozy, caramelized aroma of freshly pulled espressos was still going strong.

Roman Brio balanced on a tall stool, his heavy legs curled under him. Beside him, my laptop was open and connected to the Internet. I stood behind the counter, watching the food writer mainline his third espresso.

"I'll need another one," he said, dabbing his lips. Roman set the napkin on the blueberry marble beside the demitasse. I noticed his hand tremble. I wasn't sure if it was the result of too much caffeine or the aftershock of tonight's events. Either way, I knew it wasn't a good sign.

"Maybe you'd like a cappuccino instead," I suggested. "I have one almost ready to go."

"No, thanks, Clare. I haven't lapped warm milk since my nanny force-fed me the stuff in the nursery. Make it a *doppio*, please. *Rapidamente*."

I shrugged and went back to work at the machine. Twenty-five seconds later, the beautiful caramel-colored *crema* had oozed into the cream-colored cup, and I heard a knock on the front door. I glanced over my shoulder and saw a familiar silhouette through the beveled-glass window. I

handed Roman his freshly pulled shot, stepped around th
counter, and unlocked the front door.

"Hi, Mike."

"Hi, Clare."

Quinn stared down at me, blew out air. "You okay?"

"I'm fine, but it was pretty scary. I could really use a—"

Mike pulled me against his chest. I closed my eyes and
held on, soaking up his strength. He stroked my hair for
quiet minute, then broke our embrace and held me at arm'
length to look me over.

"Relax. Nothing's damaged. Not even bruised. You know
I can take care of myself."

Mike didn't agree or disagree. What he said was, "Wha
the hell were you doing in Flushing?"

I didn't care for his tone. "I was investigating the threa
against Breanne. Just like *you* thought I should."

He folded his arms. "And you were attacked and nearly
robbed?"

"Not *nearly*. I was robbed. I lost my brand-new purse
And we have another *I* word to add to your list, by the way.'

"Sorry? Another what?"

"You remember that little list of attributes you look for in
a detective? Well you can add *incredulous* to it, because that'
your expression right now. You're surprised, and do you
know why, Lieutenant? Because you never believed there was
any threat to Breanne, did you?"

"Slow down, Clare!" Mike unfolded his arms and put his
hands on my shoulders. "Listen," he said, "I know you're
tired and upset, and it's true, I *am* surprised—you're right
about that—but only that you were ever in any physical danger. Now, start from the beginning and tell me everything
that happened."

We moved to the counter. I made us a couple of lattes.
The rote routine calmed my nerves (it always had), then I sat
down beside Mike on a barstool and told him the whole
story, starting with Neville Perry's feud with Breanne and

·nding with the incident aboard the Number 7 line. Roman ›rovided a few details here and there, but he wasn't his usual .oquacious self. When I mentioned that we'd both seen the ·obber's face, Mike directed his next question to Roman.

"Did the man seem familiar to you?"

Roman shook his head.

"Someone you might have seen at the office, maybe?" Mike pressed. "A delivery guy? Someone from the mail room? The local deli? Or someone from your neighborhood? Someone you met in a bar? A club? *Think*."

"No, no, no, and no, Detective. But I'm sure I could iden-tify that rough beast if I saw him again. He had the face of a stone-cold criminal."

"I'll set you up at a terminal tomorrow," Mike said. "But you might end up looking at mug shots all day. The files on armed robbers are extensive."

"These were more than armed robbers," I insisted. "These guys targeted us, Mike. They knew about the rings, they knew Roman had them. They even knew precisely where and when to find us."

Mike nodded. "They probably would have hit you in front of the Friends Meeting House on Northern if there hadn't been so much traffic and a strong police presence nearby."

I plopped my elbows on the counter, pulled my hair back. "I wonder why they didn't wait for us to leave the dinner and rob us in the alley?"

"The punks got greedy, that's why. They probably saw how many whales were inside that illegal restaurant and fig-ured they'd just take it all."

"Of course!" Roman said.

"It doesn't matter." Mike rubbed his jaw. "Figuring that out gets us exactly nowhere. We need to know who provided the inside information to the robbers."

"I've been thinking about that, and I have a theory." I told Mike about Breanne's ambitious underling, Monica Purcell. "I overheard her talking about the rings with someone on her cell phone. It sounded suspicious at the time, so I snooped around her office."

I reached into the inside pocket of my little Fen jacket and pulled out the folded paper of Monica's cell phone numbers.

Mike's expression was priceless—somewhere between amazed and amused. "Nice work, sweetheart."

"There were five numbers on Monica's call log," I said. "Two of them had names attached, and Roman recognized them both. The first was Mrs. Muriel Purcell, in New Haven, Connecticut."

"That's Monica's mother," Roman piped up. "A divorced beauty queen on a Botox bender. Someone should really stop that woman."

"The other call was to Petra, *Trend*'s art director. The final three didn't have names in her log. I was going to run them through the Internet's reverse directory."

Mike nodded, and I went to work. The first two of the three numbers had Manhattan area codes, and the search engine revealed that one was for the Fitness Plus Day Spa on Eighth Avenue and Seventy-first Street; the second was a health food store on Amsterdam.

"The local numbers are a bust," I said, disappointed.

I'd scribbled a star beside the final telephone number, because that was the call Monica had made outside of Fen's boutique, when she informed *someone* not only where Breanne was but also that Breanne's rings hadn't arrived yet and weren't scheduled to until Nunzio brought them personally.

I typed the number into the search engine.

"Information not available?"

"It's unlisted," Mike said. He scribbled the digits down in his notebook and pulled out his cell phone.

"Are you calling your precinct to have someone trace the number?" I asked.

He shook his head. "I'm calling the *number*."

Mike listened for a moment then disconnected the call.

"What did you get?" I asked.

"An answering machine. No name or business. Just a
canned mechanical voice telling me to leave a message." He
dialed another number. "Put me through to the one-oh-
seven."

While Mike spoke with the precinct's night commander,
I pulled yet another espresso for Roman—at his request.
Then I dug up the Manhattan phone book. Monica Purcell
was listed; her apartment was on the Upper West Side, not
very far from the health club and veggie deli stored on her
cell phone log. I wrote down the address and finished my
own latte.

"Thanks for your help," Quinn said, ending the call.

I set the cup down. "Well?"

"Captain Blunt *strongly* suggests you both return to
Queens tomorrow to file crime reports with his detectives.
It's the 107th Precinct on Parsons Boulevard."

"A police report? With *my* name on it!" Roman's eyes
bugged. "I'll be ruined. No one will ever invite me to an underground restaurant again."

Mike's glance at Roman wasn't amused. "Word about
your little secret garden in Flushing is already out. The detectives of the one-oh-seven are all over the crime scene as we
speak. It was the woman who owned the house, a Mrs.
Weng, who called the robbery in. Several other diners have
also filed reports, so I think you'll be forgiven."

Quinn turned to me. "No arrests have been made, Clare.
Even the man you assaulted with hot sauce recovered enough
to flee the scene. They did recover some of the stolen property. Maybe you'll get your purse back." He folded his arms.
"And maybe Roman can identify the perp you dumped off
the 7 train, or maybe the punk will turn up in the hospital or
the morgue. Otherwise . . ."

"We're not out of leads yet, Mike. We still have Monica
Purcell. She lives near Sixty-ninth Street, on Amsterdam Avenue. I say we go see her right now."

Quinn glanced at his watch. "Okay, Clare. But first we'll
drop Mr. Brio here and those one-of-a-kind rings he's holding

at his home, before something else happens that jeopardize the wedding"—he met my eyes—"and any chance of ejectin Allegro from your living space."

Ten minutes later, Quinn had double-parked in front of Roman's Soho building, and we both escorted the ma through the lobby and all the way up to the front door of h loft apartment.

"Are you sure you won't come in?" Roman asked. "There a passable port and an exquisite Stilton in the larder, and I al ways have Dom Perignon well-chilled for just such an occa sion."

"What occasion?" Quinn asked.

"Surviving New York. What else?"

Quinn's eyebrow arched (which, in my experience wit the man, was as good as a hearty guffaw). "Maybe some othe time," he told Roman. "Just be sure to get a good night sleep. I'm going to dispatch a sector car to check up on yo at ten AM. *Answer* the door, okay? Or I'll have them break down."

I half expected a sarcastic retort from the acerbic foodie but none came. Roman simply nodded. "Thank you, Lieu tenant, for all of your help. Good night to you both."

Fifteen minutes after that, Quinn double-parked again this time on the West Side. (I did love parking with the man since he essentially had a license to ignore New York's dra conian regulations.)

Monica Purcell lived in a nineteen-story apartment build ing on Amsterdam, a few blocks away from Lincoln Cente The ground floor was dominated by a national clothing out let and a Go Mobile phone store. A door between the tw storefronts led to the lobby and the apartments above. Mik showed the sleepy doorman his gold shield, and the man ad mitted us.

"Monica Purcell?" I asked.

"Twelve D."

We rode the mirrored elevator to the twelfth floor. Quinn knuckles politely knocked on the woman's door several times

hen the meat of his fist took over. He pounded for a while,
ut no one answered. A small dog began yapping in another
partment. A middle-aged man opened the door; a tiny furry
ead poked out and back in again.

"Can I help you?" he said.

Mike flashed his gold shield. "Do you know if Ms. Purcell
s home?"

"Sorry. I don't know anything. I mind my own business."

The door shut in our faces, and the little dog resumed its
nnoying yapping. I smirked, remembering Breanne's comment to Roman, calling me a badly dressed Chihuahua.

"Mike, if I were a dog, what breed would I be?"

"Huh?"

"Forget it." I checked my watch. "Monica really should be
nome. It's almost two in the morning on a Tuesday night.
The girl said something about clubbing. But tomorrow's a
workday for her."

"She could be sleeping at a boyfriend's house—or with a
guy she picked up. Either way, there's no way to find her
now. Why don't we go to *Trend*'s offices in the morning and
question her there?"

I stifled a yawn. "Okay."

"All right then, Cosi, let's get going." Mike's long strides
were already halfway down the carpeted hall.

I had to move double the speed to keep up. "Slow down,
Mike. Where are we going?"

Mike shook his head. "How quickly she forgets."

"Forgets? Forgets what? Seriously, Mike, where are we going?"

Mike jabbed his thumb into the elevator button. He
braced his legs, folded his arms, and looked down at me.
'Don't you remember our little conversation this morning in
Interview Room B?"

I folded my own arms. "I remember blaming you for getting me into this case."

"And did I or did I not promise I'd make it up to you?"

"Your point?" My hands moved to my hips.

Mike's blue gaze followed my hands. Then it dropped lower and traveled back up my body, taking its time moving over my new little Fen outfit. Ever so slightly, the edges of his mouth lifted.

"Simple, Cosi. A promise is a promise."

With a *bing*, the elevator arrived. Seeing it was empty, Mike gave me a full-on smile. "C'mon," he said, "we're going to my place." Then he reached for my wrist and pulled me inside.

WHEN I opened my eyes the next morning, I felt something heavy draped across my bare midriff. Confused for a moment, I glanced around. Mike was lying beside me on his stomach, his arm curled possessively around my torso.

I relaxed and sighed. It was a good sound, a happy one—for the moment anyway.

Mike and I hadn't been on a sugar sand beach last night, just the king-size mattress of his Alphabet City bedroom. There was no rhythmic pounding of Pacific surf, either, just smooth FM jazz and the occasional whine of an ambulance siren. None of it mattered, because the man made love like a dream.

I stirred, and he groaned, his arm pulling me closer in what felt like an autonomic response. Now my naked flesh was flush against his warm skin.

"Mike?" I called, glancing at the clock in the weak yellow splash of rising sun. "We should get up."

"Mmmmmm . . ."

"Mike?"

The man's hand moved as if it were independent of his heavy, sacked-out body. His fingers lightly brushed my curves, his hand seeking and finding.

"Mike!"

The strong hand began to play, determined fingers teasing, caressing.

"Oh, God. Don't do that. We have to——"

"Sweetheart, we don't *have to* do anything *yet*," Mike murmured on the pillow, his eyes still closed. "But there are a few things we might *want* to do . . ."

The rest of Mike finally stirred; his head came up off the pillow, his mouth moved where his hand had been. After that, I made sounds that resembled speech, but my brain was already scrambled. For at least an hour more, nothing that came out of my mouth made anything close to sense.

Twenty-One

〜〜〜〜〜〜〜〜〜〜〜〜〜〜〜〜

HOURS later, my body was still humming, but my patience was getting thin. I was more than ready to interrogate Monica Purcell, but Quinn had an early meeting at the Sixth then another one crosstown with a DEA agent, so he dropped me off at the Blend.

I changed into another skirt and blouse (pretty enough, although nowhere near as high-end as Fen). I checked in with the Blend staff and found out I'd just missed Matt, who'd opened that morning but was now off to meet Koa Waipuna for breakfast, along with a small group of coffee guys who hadn't been able to make Monday's bachelor party.

Then I headed uptown to meet Quinn at the Time Warner Center. He said he'd be there at ten, but it was nearly ten twenty, and there was still no sign of him. Rather than loiter in the main lobby, I left a voice mail message for him to meet me in *Trend*'s offices on the twenty-second floor.

After exiting the elevator, I found the reception area crowded with half a dozen male and female models, each accompanied by an agent with an oversize portfolio in a lap or under an arm. Young, buffed, and beautiful, they all seemed interchangeable. I moved through the gaggle, found a seat on a leather couch near the receptionist's desk, and picked up *Trend*'s latest issue off the coffee table.

The blond receptionist had been on a call when I'd arrived.

Now she hung up the phone and lifted a shallow cardboard box with the words 4 Your Health printed on its side. She checked the slip taped to it.

"Yuck," she muttered. "I can't believe she eats this same thing every morning."

I lowered the magazine and cocked my head. The receptionist held the box aloft. "Anyone here have any interest in a wheat grass shake and a soy-protein muffin?"

The models and agents shook their heads, and I privately shuddered, longing for another Clover-brewed cup of my Rwandan Butambamo Blend (and one of Thomas Keller's buttery Bouchon Bakery croissants wouldn't have hurt, either).

The receptionist punched a button on her phone. "Terri, Ms. Summour hasn't picked up her breakfast yet. Is there a reason for that? . . . Oh. Okay. You should have let me know she was working from her apartment this morning. Will you send an intern to get her breakfast off my counter? Frankly, it's disgusting. I don't know. Put it in the break room. Maybe someone else will want it."

I stifled a laugh, listening to that exchange, but I was happy to overhear that Breanne was working at home. *Maybe Matt's finally convinced her to keep a low profile. I certainly hope so.*

A minute later, a young intern with shaggy brown hair walked down the hall and up to the reception desk. He looked like he weighed ninety-five pounds, wore earrings on both ears and black lipstick. Without a word, the terminally hip dude snapped the breakfast box off the counter, then his polished crocodile cowboy boots moseyed away.

The glass front doors opened, and I looked up, expecting Quinn. But it was another man who snagged my attention. Tall and heavyset like an athlete gone to seed, he crossed the crowded reception area. His steps were cautious, as if he feared breaking one of the living, breathing Barbie and Ken dolls that surrounded him.

I know this guy, I thought as he approached. He was the same man who'd been loitering outside of Fen's Fifth Avenue boutique the day before—at the very time Breanne was having her final fitting.

Now, as then, his appearance seemed wrong. Today he wore a too-tight wool suit of chocolate brown, black shoes with thick rubber soles, a white shirt so tight his neck bulged around the collar, and a tie the color of overcooked oatmeal. When he addressed the receptionist, his fingers tapped the counter impatiently.

"Ms. Summour, please."

"I'm sorry. Ms. Summour isn't in this morning. Perhaps you'd care to leave a message, or your card, and we'll call you to set up an appointment for a later date?"

"I'll come back."

When the man turned around, his worn rubber heels squeaked. He strode past me, and I stood up, caught the receptionist's eye. "Who is that man?"

She shrugged. "Never saw him before."

"Thanks," I said, bolting for the elevator. I made it just as the doors were closing. The car was crowded, but I squeezed inside. I used the close quarters as an excuse to get nearer to the big man. I smiled up at him once, but he looked away.

Damn. I waited until we reached the lobby before I tried again. As he stepped out of the elevator, I blocked his path. "You wanted to see Ms. Summour, right? I heard you talk to the receptionist. Maybe I can help. I know Breanne very well."

His surprise turned to recognition, and I knew he remembered seeing me at the House of Fen, right before Monica Purcell showed up. Monica's phone conversation came back to me in a rush. She'd said something about the rings, of course, but she'd also made another comment: *"I'm sorry I missed you,"* she'd told the person on the other end of the cell call. *"I would have arrived earlier, but I'm running behind today . . ."*

This must have been the man that Monica missed. He certainly looked alarmed to see me. Suspicious now, he easily moved around my much smaller form and hurried away.

"Wait a minute!" I demanded.

But the man wasn't waiting, and a tide of office workers as already pushing me back inside the elevator car. I ripped the door and searched for the big man, but he was one.

"In or out, miss!" the man beside me barked as another gure stepped into the crowded elevator. His broad shoulers, sandy hair, and square jaw attracted an openly admiring glance from a leggy young thing in a micro-miniskirt.

"In," I said, tugging Quinn's arm.

"Sorry I'm late, sweetheart," he whispered as we rode up. There's been a development. I'll tell you about it later."

I didn't want to spill my racing thoughts in a crowded elevator, so I held my tongue, too. Unfortunately, there wasn't any privacy in the reception area, either. So we approached ae receptionist together, ready to ask for Monica, when the oung man with the black lipstick hurried up to the front esk.

"Call 911!"

The receptionist's eyes bugged. "What! Why?"

"It's Monica. Petra just found her on the floor in the adies' room. She's not moving, and we can't tell if she's reathing—"

"Where is she?" Mike demanded.

The young man pointed down a carpeted hallway, and Mike took off.

"You can't go back there!" the receptionist called.

"He's a cop," I told her.

"Call 911. Now!" Mike shouted over his shoulder.

The receptionist dialed while I grabbed the hysterical intern. "What happened?"

"Like I said, Petra found her. She's still with her. I took a peek, and I think she might be dead. She's blue, and her ongue's, like, hanging out."

"Okay, take it easy," I told him. "Take a breath and sit own."

I was about to follow Mike but decided against it. I knew

where Monica's office was, and that's where I went instead.
The door was open, and the computer was on when I got
there. Monica's purse was on the desk, but I went right for
the drawers. I lifted up that pencil tray and found the black
lacquered box. The array of plastic, sepia-colored prescription bottles was still inside.

Using a tissue from a container on her desk, I carefully
picked up each one and lined them up on the glossy, fine-
grained wood. I examined the labels of each bottle. There
was no pharmacy name or phone number printed, only the
word Rxglobal and a Web address.

Still keeping the tissue between Monica's things and my
own fingerprints, I lifted the business card inside the box.
The card was for a "Mr. Benjamin Tower, freelance photographer." There was a telephone number and e-mail address. On
the back someone—presumably Mr. Tower—had written a
note:

Great lunch, Monica! Looking forward to working with you!

I placed the card on the table beside the bottles and
touched the computer mouse. The Runway New York
screen saver vanished, and Monica's Internet start page appeared. I scanned the list of Web sites the woman had book-
marked. Most were fashion designer home pages, the sites of
competitors' magazines, or news pages. One address jumped
out at me: Rxglobal.

I hit the button, and the computer connected to the Rxglobal home page. There were lists of vitamins for sale, along
with dietary additives, herbal supplements, and homeo-
pathic remedies—in short, nothing Monica or anyone else
would require a prescription to purchase. I cruised the site a
bit to make certain I wasn't missing something and came up
empty.

Someone touched my shoulder, and I jumped in the chair.
Mike was frowning down at me. "This is a crime scene,
Clare. You shouldn't be here."

"How's Monica?"

"Ms. Purcell is dead." His tone was suddenly cold. "It's
not official, but that's only because the medical examiner
isn't here yet. I've seen enough overdoses to know she's
gone."

"Look at this." I pointed to the bottles on the desk.

Mike snapped on a latex glove and read one of the labels.
"Amphetamines."

"There are at least nine vials here, Mike. She must have
been abusing speed for months, probably to control her
weight."

He placed the bottle on top of the desk, examined several
others. "A cocktail of these other drugs with the speed may
have caused her death. We won't know for sure until the tox-
icology report comes in. But I know one thing."

"What?"

"These prescriptions are counterfeit. There's a doctor
name, sure—probably also bogus. But there's no DEA number. Every legit prescription sold has a valid DEA number
that consists of two letters, six numbers, and one check digit
that's too complicated to explain right now. There should
also be a pharmacy name and address on the label, but all
we've got is—"

"Rxglobal. I know. I was looking at their Web site."

Mike peered over my shoulder at the terminal. "Yeah,
that might be their site. Or they might have another site
that can only be accessed with a special password. We're going to have to look into this."

"You said there were other developments. That's why you
were late, remember?"

Mike nodded. "This morning I traced that unlisted number you got from Monica's cell phone. The call was made to a
man named Stuart Allerton Winslow, a chemist who lives on
the West Side, not too far from Monica's apartment. This
guy once owned a small pharmaceutical research company
that went out of business because of multimillion-dollar law-
suits filed against it in civil court."

"Why would this Winslow be interested in Breanne' wedding rings? What's he going to do? Break down thei chemical composition? It doesn't make sense."

"Things always make sense, Clare, once all the facts are in.'

Out of the corner of my eye, I saw a bright-orange colo coming toward us, a cheerful hue, like freshly peeled carrots A wiry man, attached to the conspicuous shade, entered th room. He was a head shorter than Quinn, his perfectl pitched tenor trumped by a heavy Queens accent.

"Is this the office of the deceased?"

Quinn turned to me. "Clare, meet one of the detective I'm working with, Sergeant Sullivan. That's *Finbar* Sullivan so you can see why we call him Sully."

Sullivan's face was open and friendly. I met his eyes an smiled. "I think Finbar is a perfectly fine name. Very Celtic.'

"Yeah, well, it's not so hot when you're growing up i Ozone Park. That's John Gotti country, land of Tonys an Vinnies. But thanks," he said, then leaned toward me an cupped a hand over his mouth. "I can see why the big guy here's fallen for you. You say the sweetest things."

"Don't flirt with my girl, Sully."

Sully threw me a wink anyway, then turned to Quinn. " saw the victim, Mike. She was thin. *Real* thin. You thin drunkorexia?"

"Drunk-a-what-ia?" I asked.

Quinn glanced at me. "It's not an official medical term just shorthand for a relatively new condition: a combinatio of addiction like binge drinking, and eating disorders lik anorexia. We usually see it in younger women, college age The girls starve themselves to be thin, often abuse drugs and consume alcohol as pretty much their only sustenance Once they start, they have a life expectancy of about fiv years."

"It's crazy, all right." Sully shook his head. "These girl won't put an olive in their mouth, but they got no proble sucking down the martini it came with." He turned to hi partner. "You want me to secure the scene. Right, Mike?"

"Bag up Ms. Purcell's personal effects and all the prescription bottles you can find. We'll check them for residue. Prints. I'll get back to you soon. I'm going to get Ms. Cosi out of here and swing by the Sixth for notification."

"I hate that part." Sully's light mood suddenly vanished. "Okay, Mike, I'll cover things here."

As we left Monica's office and walked down the hall, I touched Quinn's arm. "What's notification?"

Quinn stared straight ahead. "When I tell the next of kin what happened to their loved one, that's notification."

"Oh."

The reception room was nearly empty now and eerily still. Two uniformed police officers stood at the front desk. The magazine's art director was sitting behind it. The tall East Indian woman with long dark hair was sobbing into a handkerchief.

As we moved to exit through the glass doors, one of the uniforms called out, "Lieutenant? A word."

Quinn looked at me. "I need a few minutes."

"Go. I'll wait."

The glass doors opened a moment later, and Matt walked in. "Hey! Clare! What a morning I had! You won't believe it!"

I blinked.

"Just look at me," he said. "I'm dripping wet."

Dark stains marred his white cotton button-down.

"It happened right outside, at Columbus Circle." Matt threw up his hands. "Thea Van Harben walked up to me and assaulted me with her Starbucks—insult to injury, huh? I'm lucky I didn't get second-degree burns."

I closed my eyes. "What did you do *now*, Matt?"

"Nothing! I swear! Thea just said, 'You threw your wedding plans in my face, so I'm throwing this into yours.' And she let me have it. But, Clare, I swear I never mentioned my wedding plans to her. I haven't even seen the woman since . . ." he shrugged. "You know? I can't even remember."

"Matt, something's happened here—"

Before I could finish, he'd already looked past me and seen the policemen. His face went from perplexed amusement to stricken in less than a second.

"What's going on? Why is Petra crying? Is Breanne all right?"

He moved to get around me, but I caught his arm. "It's Monica Purcell, Breanne's former assistant. She overdosed on prescription medication, Matt. She's dead."

"My God, what about Bree? Is she okay? Where is she?"

"She's not here. She's working at home this morning. Didn't she tell you?"

"No. She told me she had a dermatology appointment."

Dermatology? That sounded odd to me until the light went on. Breanne had said something to Roman in Fen's fitting room about having "work done" before the wedding.

"I've got to find Breanne," Matt said.

I noticed Quinn walking toward us. He nodded stiffly. "Allegro."

Matt's greeting was about as warm. "Quinn."

"Matt," I said, "before you bolt to find your bride, we all need to talk."

"About what?"

I gestured to the uniformed police and the sobbing Petra. "Not out here."

Matt nodded. "There's a conference room we can use. I know where it is. Come on . . ."

As Matt led Quinn and me past a line of cubicles to a glass door, he pulled out his cell phone and rang Breanne to make sure she was okay. It was a short call, and he quickly signed off. I noticed he hadn't informed her about Monica. Before I could ask, he volunteered, "I'm not telling Bree over the phone. After we're done here, I'll head straight for her place."

I nodded, pleased to hear Matteo Allegro was going to take care of the woman he was about to marry—but then my ex always had been a very loving man. (That was his problem, really, he loved women a little too much.)

"She's bound to be pretty upset," I said.

"I know."

The meeting room was large, with buff leather executive chairs, a huge conference table, and a panoramic view of the city skyline. Quinn put his back to the view. I sat down across from him, and Matt shut the door.

"Okay. What's going on?" Matt demanded.

He crossed to take the chair at the head of the conference table, and I brought him up to speed, telling him about the attempted theft of Nunzio's rings and the suspicious-looking man who'd popped up two times in two days, looking out of place, the second time shortly before Monica Purcell's body was found. I told him about Winslow and the possible connections between Monica's drug habit, her interest in the wedding rings, and the questionable timing of her death.

Matt rubbed the back of his neck. He looked confused. "What do you mean, 'questionable' timing? I thought you said she died from an overdose of prescription medication."

"She could have. But the prescriptions are bogus and appear to be illegal. And given the kind of people she's gotten herself involved with, I'm betting the drugs she took this morning were purposely tainted."

"Hmmm." Quinn's eyebrows lifted. "That actually makes sense, Clare."

"Then don't look so surprised."

Quinn folded his arms. "You're on a roll. Go on."

"Okay. So the key to this whole mess really comes down to this chemist, this Stuart Winslow."

Matt closed his eyes. "Wait a minute! What chemist?"

"I'll lay it out again, Matt, slower this time. But you have to pay attention and try to keep up."

Quinn cleared his throat—or stifled a laugh—or both. I couldn't tell which. I cleared my own throat and turned to Matt again.

"We know that Monica phoned a chemist named Stuart Winslow. I overheard the call. So we know that Winslow cared very much about when Nunzio's rings were arriving and what was going to happen to them. We know Monica witnessed Breanne giving the rings to Roman, who vowed to keep them with him at all times until the wedding. Then robbers targeted Roman that very night, and they knew he was holding valuable rings. But the robbery went bad, they didn't get the rings, and Monica conveniently died right before we were going to interrogate her about what she knew."

Matt leaned back in his chair. "Jeez."

"I don't know who this Stuart Winslow is, or how he's connected to Monica—or even Breanne for that matter—but I'm almost positive he had something to do with the robbery attempt and maybe even Monica's death." I glanced at Quinn, relieved to see him nodding in agreement.

Matt scratched the back of his head. "But if this Winslow guy is the one who tried to run Breanne over, and he also tried to gun her down on Monday night, then what was the point? Why does he want my fiancée dead?"

I drummed my fingers on the table then stilled when it hit me. "Maybe it was *Monica* who wanted Breanne dead. Maybe she and Winslow were working together, even sleeping together—"

"*Maybe* isn't going to solve this, Clare," Quinn interrupted.

"No," I said. "It's up to us to get to the bottom of it."

"How?" Matt asked.

I met Quinn's eyes. "I have an idea . . ."

Twenty-Two

~~~~~~

STUART Allerton Winslow lived in The Residential, a massive, prewar apartment building along Seventy-second Street. It was the kind of place that featured all the amenities: solid construction, firewalls and soundproofing, working fireplaces, a twenty-four-hour doorman, a laundry room, and a health club in the basement.

The Residential sat between Broadway and Central Park West, just a few blocks away from the steepled facade of The Dakota, the Gothic-Victorian landmark building where John Lennon was shot to death, and a pebble's throw from Strawberry Fields, a quiet area of Central Park dedicated to the memory of the murdered recording artist.

We couldn't see Strawberry Fields from our current location. We couldn't even see outside. In the stairwell of The Residential, between the ninth and tenth floors, the windowpanes were glazed to admit only light. The thick walls and steel-frame construction muted the city sounds, too, so the stairwell was eerily quiet, except for the insistent voice of Detective Mike Quinn.

"This is a bad idea, Clare. I can have a female detective here inside of twenty minutes. Let her do the heavy lifting. That's what she's trained for."

I shook my head so vigorously I got a warning from Sergeant Sullivan.

"Don't move or you'll mess me up here," Sully said. "And lift your blouse a little higher, please."

He was kneeling beside me, taping a long wire to my bare midriff. Sullivan's hands were warm, but the tape was cold, and there was a draft, too. I shivered.

"Listen, Mike," I said. "No stranger can walk in there and pull this off. This Winslow has to believe that I'm a friend of Monica's for the plan to work. He saw me in Fen's during Breanne's fitting and again today, at *Trend*'s office. He'll believe my story, because he's seen me around Monica, and *Trend*."

"You've told me this already. The only trouble is, we don't know if this big guy you've seen is actually Winslow—"

"Excuse me, there, Ms. Cosi, but this microphone part has to go a little, er, higher." Sully looked up at his partner. "Maybe you should do it, Mike."

Sully stood up and turned around while Mike ran the thin wire through my bra and tucked the tiny microphone between my breasts. I shivered again, only this time it wasn't the cold. I tried to catch Mike's eye, but he avoided my gaze.

"Cover up, Cosi," he murmured.

I dropped my blouse, and Sully faced us again. The sergeant was wearing headphones, and he handed another headset to Quinn. Then he touched a button on the digital recorder. "Say something, Ms. Cosi."

I locked eyes with Quinn. "This will work. I know it."

"Loud and clear." Sully grinned.

Quinn crossed his arms. "What if you're wrong, Clare? What if Winslow's *not* the man you saw outside of Fen's and again this morning? You couldn't ID the guy from the driver's license photo I pulled up from the state's database."

"It was an eighteen-year-old photo and blurry." The man in the picture was a lot thinner than the one I'd seen, and his hair was a lot longer, but he was the right age, had the same color hair and eyes. His nose was wrong, too, but he could have broken it sometime after the photo was taken.

Quinn exhaled. He still wasn't happy.

"Listen to me, Mike, even if Winslow isn't the man I saw, he might be one of the men who robbed the underground restaurant last night. If that's the case, then he saw me with Roman, and he knows I'm not a cop."

"And what if he's not one of the robbers, either?"

I shrugged. "I'll just have to work a little harder to be convincing."

"Can't fault her spirit," Sergeant Sullivan said.

"Shut up, Sully."

"Hey, Mike," Sully replied, "I'm just saying that if this guy is selling deadly drugs without a prescription, then it's our job to stop him. Ms. Cosi is just doing her civic duty to help keep the streets of our fair city safe from predators."

Quinn rolled his eyes. "Enough with the public service announcement. Let's get this over with."

I took a deep breath. I guess I should have felt nervous, but what I mainly felt was exhilarated. I couldn't wait to get in there and nail this jerk.

"We'll be right outside, and we can hear everything you say," Quinn told me. "If something happens, we'll be through that door and into the apartment in seconds, no matter how many locks and dead bolts are on it. If Winslow makes a move, stay out of his reach until we can get to you."

I nodded.

"Apartment ten-sixteen, through the fire doors and to the left," Sully said, the headphones squeezed his carrot head. "Nail him, Cosi. You can do it."

"Thanks, Sully."

Thirty seconds later I knocked on the door. There was no response after a ten count, so I knocked again. Finally, I spied movement behind the peephole.

"What do you want?" The voice was male.

"Mr. Winslow. My name's Clare. I'm a friend of Monica's. *Monica Purcell.*"

I heard a click, then the rattle of a security chain. I recalled the size of the man I'd seen at *Trend* this morning and lifted my chin. But when the door opened, I was in for a surprise. The man who answered was tall, but he wasn't the big man I was expecting. I'd never seen this guy.

Okay, Clare, don't panic. You'll just have to talk faster.

"Mr. Winslow—"

"*Dr.* Winslow. They haven't taken the Ph.D. away from me. Not yet."

The man appeared much older than fifty-seven, the age we'd come up with based on the birth date of his old driver's license. He had a head too large for his scrawny body. His painfully thin frame was clad in gray sweatpants, and his matching sweatshirt was frayed at the neckline. Winslow's facial features had been hard to make out on the old New York State license, but in person they appeared patrician. A thick head of brown hair crowned his chiseled WASPish features, but it was dirty, tangled, and thoroughly shot with gray. In short, the man was a sight, but his complexion was what truly unnerved me. Pale as a ghost, Winslow's skin seemed almost powdered with the dust of ages past.

As he regarded me through slightly bulging eyes, I realized something was wrong with his pupils. They were too wide and dark, as if he were intoxicated, but I couldn't smell alcohol on him, and (given my own difficult years with Matt) I'd bet the farm that he was on drugs right now.

"Well, *Doctor*," I said, "I'm a friend of Monica's, and I'm here to inform you that she's out of the picture."

The man gave me no reaction to the news. Winslow just stared, expressionless.

"Monica has been hospitalized with an overdose," I continued. "She can't help you anymore. But I can."

"I don't understand," he finally said. "What do you mean?"

"I can help you get Breanne Summour's *wedding rings.* That's what I mean. The one-of-a-kind Nunzio creations? You want them, don't you?"

One of the man's bulging eyes began to twitch, but he said nothing. We just stood there, staring at one another.

"Look," I finally said. "I don't want to talk out here where

meone can eavesdrop. Can't I come inside so we can speak
private?"

This was the moment of truth. Stuart Allerton Winslow
uld close the door in my face right now, and he would
obably walk away from this mess clean. The police had no
oof that he had anything to do with the home invasion in
ueens. And there was nothing to tie him to the attempts
Breanne's life (if that's what they were). The only people
ho could implicate him were the robbers, who were still at
rge, and Monica, who was dead.

I waited for his decision. Finally, Dr. Winslow opened the
or and ushered me in. I stepped across the threshold, and
e door closed behind me. I heard the dead bolt click and
oped that if something went terribly wrong, Quinn would
e able to keep his promise and break down the heavy-
oking door.

I felt Winslow's touch and winced.

"This way."

Everything in the bone-spare apartment was coated with
e same dust that clung to its occupant. What furniture
ere was looked like it came from a thrift shop. But there
ere fleeting signs of former prosperity, too. A marble floor
the foyer gave way to parquet overlaid with plush but
irty Persian rugs. The doorknobs and light fixtures were
ade of dulled but costly looking brass, and a loudly ticking
randfather clock with an intricately carved relief appeared
o be at least a century old.

In the living room, the couch and chairs were shabby, the
aint peeling and faded. The windows were closed and the
eavy curtains drawn. The only light came from the dull
low of a Tiffany lamp. There was a fireplace, but it was
lled with soot, its marble mantel scorched. Worst of all, the
ingy, airless room stank of creosote, a smell I'd loathed
nce I was nine years old, and our neighbors' house had
urned to the ground.

Dr. Winslow gestured me to a chair. I sat down and folded
y hands on my lap. He dropped onto the threadbare couch.

Then he glanced at me and said, "You were saying som
thing about my ex-wife's wedding rings?"

"Yes, I—" *Wait a minute!* "Did you say your ex-wife? Yo
were *married* to Breanne Summour?"

The man smirked. "Monica didn't tell you?"

"No, she never mentioned it."

My God, I hope Quinn and Sully are hearing this . . .

"You said your name was Clare." Winslow was starin
hard at me now. "Monica never mentioned you. How is
you found me?"

"I was in Monica's office last week, and I saw her prescrip
tions." I rattled off the exact names of her little cache so he'
know I really had seen the bottles. "I asked her to help me g
some pills, too, and she mentioned you. Of course, Monic
never told me how you two hooked up. How did it happe
anyway? I mean, I'd like to know who I'm dealing with."

Winslow was silent, still staring at me. "Tell me wh
you're here."

Focus, man. "Breanne's rings," I told him again. "I kno
you want them. Are you planning to sell the jewelry proto
types to Nunzio's rivals? I'm sure they'd pay a pretty penn
to—"

"What I do with the rings is not your concern."

Okay, this is a start. He's engaging. "You *do* want Breanne
rings, then, right? I can still get them. It will be easy."

Winslow crossed to the heavy curtains and pulled the
back to look out the window. "That's what Monica said. '
will be easy.' She's the one who proposed the deal in the fir
place. I only took it because Breanne still owes me for thos
lost years, my lost life."

"What do you mean, exactly?"

He didn't reply. "About the rings—you can get them?"

"Yes," I said, "but if I get you the rings, what do I get i
return?"

"The same deal I offered Monica. Free drugs. Anythin
you like, for as long as you like, without a prescription. N
more doctor shopping. No more risk. How does that sound?

"I have a bad back. It hurts right now."

For the first time since I entered, Winslow's grim mood lightened. With the semblance of a friendly expression, he lowered the curtain and turned to me.

"Come this way," he said.

Twenty-Three

~~~~~~

WINSLOW crossed to a dark hallway. I followed warily. Stepping through the shadows, I entered another dimly lit space with peeling paint and a soiled rug. Like the front room, this one was sparsely furnished: one bookshelf, a cracked-leather chair, and a large computer on a desk of scuffed mahogany. The computer was the newest, most expensive item in the large, gray room. Its flat-screen monitor emitted more color than the Land of Oz.

"Is that your Web site's home page?" I pointed to the screen, where the primary shades of Rxglobal tempted like the storefront of a candy shop. "I think Monica mentioned something about it."

"It's my business, yes."

"I clicked around the site, but I didn't see anything that could control my pain."

"That's because the vitamin and herb supplement pages aren't where I do my important business. The other pages have a special password."

"Oh, so that's why!" I laughed. The joke was on me, right? I wasn't in the know. "Do you have a local carrier?"

He shook his head. "My server is set up outside the country. That's where I get the prescription drugs, too."

Winslow moved a standing dresser aside to reveal a hidden closet. He drew a key from his sweatpants and unlocked he door. There were several boxes sitting on a shelf; all had abels with foreign script. He reached into a carton and ulled out a clear plastic bag of pink pills. G164 was em-ossed on each one.

"OxyContin is quite effective for the control of back pain. 'll start you off with a hundred and fifty tabs."

He sat down at his desk, quickly counted out the tablets, using a plastic pill sorter. Then he poured them into a sepia-olored bottle like the ones I'd seen hidden in Monica's desk.

"You have a medical degree, too, right?" I said with a hrug, as if it really didn't matter either way. "I mean, in ad-lition to your doctorate. You seem so knowledgeable about ll this."

"If you could get these from a licensed physician, you wouldn't be here, would you?"

"So that's a *no*?" I looked around the room as if searching or his degrees. "You're just a Ph.D. then, and not an M.D.?"

He capped the bottle. "Does this look like your gynecolo-gist's office, miss?"

He leered, and I shivered. *God, what a creep.*

"This is just a down payment," he promised, holding the bottle out to me. "You get me the rings, and I'll get you all the OxyContin you want."

"Thank you, Dr. Winslow, for giving me the pills," I said, oud and clear.

Got that, Mike? I hope you heard me!

I took the bottle, and Winslow ushered me back into the living room. As he headed for the front door, I hesitated.

I didn't have enough on this guy yet. The man had been married to Breanne Summour. I figured there must be a mo-tive for his wanting her dead (other than the woman's per-sonality, of course). He was in league with Monica Purcell to steal Breanne's rings. The two were probably working on an elaborate revenge plan, too. I just had to get him to say so.

Think, Clare. Do something!

"Excuse me, Doctor?" I called as he unlocked the heavy door.

He turned. "Yes?"

"May I trouble you for a glass of water? I'd *really* like to take a few of these now . . ." I shook the bottle. "Please? My pain is bad."

The man paused for a moment then nodded. He left the room. When he came back with a half-empty glass, I was sitting, uninvited, on his shabby sofa.

"Here you are," he said.

The glass wasn't the cleanest, but I had to make it look good. I put on a show of shaking a few pills into my hand. I knocked back the imaginary hit and took a drink of the stale water. Then I leaned my head against the couch back and pretended to close my eyes—the junkie getting her fix.

Winslow was still standing over me. His unkempt odor combined with the smell of creosote was making me queasy; the loudly ticking grandfather clock was close to maddening.

Through the bottom of my lashes, I watched the cadaverous drug dealer watching me. Winslow stood motionless, his dilated pupils sweeping my body up and down. For long minutes, my breathing stopped altogether and my heartbeat pulsated like something out of Poe.

Mike's out there listening, I reminded myself. The ticklish wire between my breasts was my lifeline, the only rope that could save me if this scarecrow in sweats decided to slip me something other than narcotics.

Winslow's skinny limbs began to move. Every muscle in my own limbs stiffened, ready to fight him off if I had to.

But I didn't have to.

The gamble was working. The man moved away. When he finally settled into a nearby chair, I released my held breath. He misunderstood the reason for my sigh.

"Good, isn't it?" he whispered.

"It always takes a little while to kick in for me." I opened my eyes. "You don't mind if I hang until it does, do you? Like I said, my pain is bad."

Winslow gave me a little smile—one junkie to another. "I understand."

I scanned the dreary space, deciding the best way to prod more information out of Winslow was to goad him.

"You know, it's hard for me to believe you and Breanne were a couple. She's so dynamic. A woman with exquisite taste in fashion, art, wine—"

Winslow laughed. "She didn't start out that way. When I met Breanne, she was a struggling journalist. She could barely afford the rent on her East Village walk-up."

"That must have been a long time ago."

"She was in her twenties. I was considerably older."

"The first marriage for both of you?"

Winslow shook his head. "I'd been married for over a decade to a proper wife. I had two proper children, as well, and operated a proper pharmaceutical company."

"So . . . how did the two of you meet?"

"Breanne interviewed me for a piece in *New York Trends*—"

"You mean *Trend*, right?"

"*New York Trends* doesn't exist anymore. Breanne saw to that."

"Oh, I see . . . so what did Breanne interview you about, exactly?"

"An antiwrinkle pill my drug company had developed. It was quite effective, in some ways revolutionary."

"Wow. Sounds lucrative. So what happened? Did you two fall in love during the interview?"

"Love . . ." Winslow laughed. The sound was harsh and hollow. He leaned back in his chair and closed his eyes as if envisioning the past. "Breanne was stunning back then, dazzling, even more of a beauty than she is now. It was hard for me to concentrate with her sitting across from me. She seemed impressed by my background, my academic records at Haverford and Princeton, my 'patina of refinement' as she called it. She was flirtatious and seductive. And so we had sex, lots of it."

"And you married her."

Winslow opened his eyes. "I didn't want to, but Breanne wasn't content with being a mistress. She found a way to inform my wife about our relationship."

"Was that really such a big deal? I mean, you probably weren't happy in your first marriage, right?"

Winslow shifted his wasted frame. "The breakup of my marriage caused me problems. My family was unhappy They settled the Winslow fortune on my ungrateful off spring. At the time, I didn't care. I still had my company and I had Breanne. It was enough for me. It was not enough for her . . ."

The man sighed, fished a vial of pills out of his pocket and dumped a few into his mouth, swallowing them dry Then he stared off into space.

Come on, Clare. Find another button to press . . .

"So why did you and Breanne break up exactly? It sounds like you had a pretty good thing going." (*If you can call a torrid extramarital affair capped by a heartbreaking revelation for th wife and kids a "pretty good" thing.*)

"Breanne wanted more than just a marriage. She always wanted more. It's her defining characteristic."

"I don't understand."

"She worked at *New York Trends*, but she wanted her *own* magazine. So she convinced me to give her $250,000."

"For what?"

"A pitch. That's what she called it. A prototype and multimedia demonstration for Reston-Miller Publications."

"So your money helped start her magazine. That was really nice of you."

"Nice? I was a dim-witted *dupe*. Within a year the bitch dropped me like an out-of-season handbag. She started an affair with the photographer who shot her magazine's first cover. Then she filed for divorce, the greedy little lying tart . . ."

Winslow's mood was getting uglier by the minute, and I wondered what he was on right now. While I needed to push him off balance emotionally, the drugs were heightening his agitation, and I was starting to worry about physical safety.

I wasn't ready to give up yet. I wanted badly to nail this creep for Hazel Boggs's murder. To do that, I had to get him

o admit he wanted his ex-wife dead. Of course, I didn't
want to end up dead in the process. Quinn would never forgive me for being that stupid.

"So, was the divorce messy?" I asked, pressing on.

"*Expensive* is what it was. Bloodsucking lawyers, all of
hem. Of course, I still had plenty of money *then* so I didn't
pursue a percentage of her magazine. I wanted to be rid of her,
nd I assumed *Trend* would fail in its first year, anyway. Then
hose bureaucratic *bastards* at the FDA forced me into bank-
uptcy."

"The FDA?"

Quinn had said something about Winslow's company go-
ng out of business because of a multimillion-dollar lawsuit.
I made a leap.

"Was it the antiwrinkle drug? The one Breanne inter-
iewed you about?"

"There was nothing wrong with it!" Blue veins throbbed
visibly on the man's forehead. "The FDA trumped up false
data about life-threatening side effects and forced a recall!"

"I can see they robbed you blind." I gestured to the crum-
bling paint, the soiled rugs, the empty spaces where posses-
ions once existed. "I guess that's why Monica's deal sounded
pretty sweet then, huh? How did you two hook up, anyway?"

"Oh, that . . ." He waved his hand. "Monica overheard me
arguing with my ex-wife in her office. I only wanted the
money the woman rightfully owed me."

"You mean that $250,000? The money you lent her to
start *Trend*?"

"I demanded every penny back *with* interest. She said no.
I stormed out, and Monica followed me. We had lunch, and
she asked me about my past with Breanne—just like you're
doing now. Stealing the rings was her idea."

"Yeah, Monica never could stand her boss. And Breanne
made a complete fool of you, right? I'll bet you wouldn't
mind seeing her get what's coming to her."

"Oh, the bitch will get what's coming to her. I'm sure
of it."

"Are you? How? I mean . . . Do you need any help with that? I'm no fan of the woman, either. I wouldn't mind seeing something happen to her. It could look like an accident. It'll be easy."

Winslow froze for a moment after I'd said those words. He stared at me for a long, silent minute, then he stood and said, "You have to leave now. I'm going out."

"Out where? Maybe we can take a taxi together?"

Winslow shook his head. "Come, miss. Time to go."

Dammit. I stood up slowly and followed him to the door, my mind racing. But I couldn't think of what else to say. Abruptly, he turned to me.

"When will I hear from you? About the rings?"

"Soon," I said.

Before I could think of another ploy, Winslow unlocked the apartment door and opened it. Lieutenant Quinn and Sergeant Sullivan stood there, badges in hand, two men in uniforms behind them. In one fast motion, Quinn grabbed Winslow's wrist and twisted his arm behind his back.

"Stuart Allerton Winslow, you're under arrest for the distribution of a controlled substance without the consent of licensed and authorized physician."

Quinn slipped a handcuff around one wrist. From under his tangled hair, Winslow's eyes caught mine. "You set me up?"

I backed away from the enraged man.

"You little bitch!" he shouted. "You set me up!"

"Quiet," Quinn said, twisting his arm a little more.

Winslow howled and spat at me. "You'll die for this bitch! I'll kill you myself, with my own—owww!"

"*Listen* to me, *asshole*," Quinn said as he cuffed Winslow's other wrist, none too gently. "You have the right to remain silent . . ."

When he finished rattling off the man's Miranda rights, he handed the prisoner over to Sullivan and the two young cops in uniform. Winslow continued to shout obscenities and threats until the elevator doors closed in his face.

"Sorry, Mike," I said, "I couldn't get him to admit to
planning the robbery or trying to kill Breanne."

"It's okay, Cosi. You did good. Better than good. You got
us a lot of material to use for interrogation. We should be
able to soften Winslow up, get him to admit conspiracy in
the robbery. A confession to murder might be harder to get,
but he could slip up, admit he wanted his wife dead. Then
we'll go from there, try to get him to admit to the SUV incident and the shooting of the stripper by mistake. We've got
a search warrant on the way, too. Who knows?" He glanced
inside the musty apartment. "We might find the murder
weapon in this dump."

I shook my head. Quinn had wanted to use a policewoman, but I convinced him I could do the job. "Still—"

Quinn lifted my chin. "Lighten up, sweetheart. You did
what you came to do. With Winslow in custody, your ex-
husband can rest easy. Breanne Summour is no longer in danger."

Twenty-Four

"I'D like us all to raise a glass . . ."

Matt lifted his goblet of sangria *blanco* to begin a toast, but Machu Picchu's dining room was currently displaying the noise level of a Times Square subway platform. When he realized few people had heard him, he climbed onto a chair, pulled a pen out of his pocket, and began loudly knocking it against his half-filled goblet.

"Attention! *Atención!*"

It was Thursday afternoon, and all of Matt's coffee colleagues had shown for Madame's special luncheon. They were having a grand old time, laughing, singing, and loudly conversing over cocktails and Peruvian-style tapas.

The restaurant itself was a charmer, with terra-cotta walls, Incan art, and an impressive display of handmade clay pots. But Madame hadn't chosen the hot, new Soho eatery for its food or decor. The place's name was what attracted her, reminding her of a sweet memory long past: ascending the actual Machu Picchu with Matt's late father decades ago.

"Hello! Your attention, please!"

Conversations diminished and heads turned. Matt cleared his throat and began again.

"I'd like to start today's toasts with one to a very special woman. A woman to whom I'll always be indebted . . ."

Standing next to her groom, Breanne looked sleek and

rgeous in a form-fitting white sheath. A stunning silver
d turquoise necklace circled that swanlike neck, matching
rings hung from her delicate pink lobes. Her royal blue
es were shining, her ivory skin (even more wrinkle-free
an I remembered) appeared radiant, her alluring smile
ore bee-stung than I remembered, too) widened with
ery new word of praise Matt lavished on her.

"So please raise your glasses to someone I've always been
le to depend on," Matt finished, "a woman who really
me through for me, my business partner, Clare Cosi!"

What?!

Breanne's perfectly made-up face fell like an eggless souf-
, and I felt like an absolute heel. As sweet as Matt was to
ant to thank me publicly for saving his bride's life, I
uldn't believe he was stupid enough to do it before toast-
g the bride herself!

"Clare Cosi!" Everyone cried, lifting their glasses.

Matt climbed down from the chair and grinned at me.
eanne curled her lips, too; it was the kind of smile the old
one gave Hansel and Gretel the morning she wanted to
op them in her oven.

Matt turned to his bride. "Go ahead, Breanne. Don't be
y. You can propose a toast to Clare, too."

Bree's Beaujolais Red lips froze so stiffly I thought they
ere going to crack off and fall into her *antichuchos*. She set
r small plate of diced, marinated, and grilled cow heart
wn on the room's long bar, took a substantial hit off her
hite sangria, and said, "I'll pass."

"You'll pass?" Matt echoed.

"You've said it so eloquently already, darling. Why would
want to *gild* the lily?"

A vision of Breanne lowering me into a vat of molten gold
me to mind. I shuddered—while maintaining my own
astic smile.

"My mom's the greatest, isn't she?" Joy gushed beside us.

I turned to my daughter and thanked her with a smile
ns synthetics). Matt and I had picked her up at Kennedy

Airport the night before, and it was honest-to-God heave having her home again. We ordered a fully loaded New Yo pie from Village Pizza, opened some ice-cold beer, an talked for hours (all three of us).

I couldn't get over Joy's transformation. Her health w back, for one thing. She'd lost a great deal of weight a fe months ago. After her false arrest, the murder of her frien and her degrading expulsion from culinary school, she spent two solid weeks doing nothing but crying. Her sk had gone sallow, her bright eyes had dulled.

The magnificent city of Paris had recharged her spirit and tempted her with its cuisine. Her too-thin figure ha filled out again, her cheeks were rosy, her skin a warm peac She said she and her roommate had gone down to Nice for few days to catch a tan, not to mention the attention of a fe cute-looking French boys from the cell phone pictures she showed me.

She looked cute herself at the moment in a sundress t color of lemon pie. She'd arranged her glossy chestnut hair a French twist as sleek as Breanne's golden do. But she st had my green eyes, and they looked as bright and lively this sunny spring Thursday—a huge change from the ho low, red-rimmed look she'd sported a few months back.

It had been hard as hell, sending my broken daught away. But seeing her so happy now recharged my own spirit I was proud of the way she'd pulled herself together and d into the demanding job she'd secured (with a little help fro her grandmother's connections). Working as a line cook any restaurant had its challenges: long hours, low pay, dif cult bosses. Joy was apprenticing under a demanding bo now, and the chef de cuisine and his executive staff werer cutting her any breaks. On her third beer last night she r cited for us the long list of French obscenities she'd learne courtesy of her superiors on the Michelin-starred kitche staff.

"I learned so much from my mom," Joy told Breann (which I certainly hoped *didn't* include a long list

bscenities—in French or any other language). She glanced
at me then and raised her glass once more. "And I owe her a
ot, too."

I almost pinched myself. Given the rough ride I'd endured with my child over the past few years (which mainly
consisted of Joy telling me—with a great deal of attitude—
o butt out of her business), I often wondered whether we'd
ever again be as close as we were when she'd been a little girl.
Her maturing outlook gave me hope.

"Despite what your lovely daughter implied," Breanne
told me in private a few minutes later, "I don't feel that I owe
you anything."

"*You* don't owe me," I said. "That's true." We were standing alone at one end of the bar. Matt had taken Joy by the
arm to proudly introduce her around the room, leaving Breanne and me to talk alone. "What I did, I did for the father
of my child, as a wedding gift. And I hope you know the
only reason Matt thanked me was because I saved the thing
he most wanted in his life right now: you."

"*Right now.*" Bree rolled her eyes. "You're so transparent,
Clare."

"I am?"

"You want him back."

I nearly choked on my sparkling water. After last night's
beers, I'd declined any alcohol. I suddenly changed my
mind.

"Pisco Sour," I told the bartender.

Hoping to shake Breanne's interrogation, I gave her my
back, turning my attention instead to the bartender. With
swift, efficient movements the young man mixed the Pisco (a
brandy made from grapes grown in Peru's coastal valley)
with lemon juice, sugar, and ice, garnished it with Angos-
tura bitters, and handed me the tumbler. (It was Matt who'd
introduced me to the cocktail. He'd sampled it in Lima during one of his Andes buying trips.)

"Answer me, Clare," Breanne hissed in my ear. "You
won't deny it? You want him back?"

Oh, for pity's sake. Can't this woman take a hint? I turned to face Breanne (since she gave me no choice) and took a nice long, unhealthy hit of my cocktail. The flavor was sweet yet tart; and though the drink itself seemed mild at first, the ninety-proof Pisco carried a kick you had to respect. I mainlined it into my quiet reply: "All right, Breanne, listen to me, and listen good. You've got the Tiffany's engagement ring and the big, lavish wedding. On Saturday, you're even acquiring the optional accessory to your grand event—a worthy groom. So why don't you focus on that instead of what I do or don't want in my life because, frankly, I'm sick to death of your superior attitude."

"And I'm sick to death of your meddling."

Meddling?! Unbelievable! I risk my life for this woman, and this is what I get?

"You know what, Bree? You're a big girl. I think it's time you heard the unvarnished truth: I *don't* want Matt back, and do you know how I can prove that to you for once and for all? If I *had* wanted him back, you wouldn't be planning this wedding."

Breanne's royal-blue eyes narrowed. "Don't you *dare* imply that I'm sloppy seconds," she hissed, her ivory cheeks turning the color of her lipstick.

"I'm not implying anything that crass. I'm trying to get you to *remember* that Matt's going to put Nunzio's ring on *your* finger a few days from now. Not mine."

"Hey, kids . . ." Matt walked over, a big, clueless grin on his handsome face. "How are two of my best girls doing?"

Breanne turned on him. "What's that supposed to mean?" The man's puppy-dog smile fell.

Congratulations, Matt, you finally picked up on your bride's mood. What did it for you? The acid tone or the murderous scowl?

"What?" He scratched his head. "What did I say?"

Breanne rolled her eyes. "*Two* of your best girls?"

"That's right." Matt shrugged. "I've got my daughter here today, too. And my mother. I have a lot of important girls in my life, Breanne, you know that."

*God, Matt, just open your mouth and put your Bruno Magli
oe in already.*

Breanne took another drink of her sangria. "I need some-
ing stronger than this."

"Allow me." I turned to the bartender and ordered Bree
er very own Pisco Sour.

"Everything's okay, isn't it?" Matt said, his gaze darting
om Breanne to me and back again.

"Ask *her*," I said.

Breanne waved her French tips. "I was just telling Clare
at although her concern was appreciated, I really don't
ink my ex-husband was anything more than a nuisance.
he entire episode was blown way out of proportion."

Matt's eyes found mine. "I don't feel that way." He turned
o his bride, took hold of her arms. "I was worried about you,
ree. And Clare helped me out. She helped us both out, as
r as I'm concerned."

Breanne broke away, took her drink from the bartender,
nd began nursing it.

"Clare, dear! Over here!" From across the crowd, an older
oman with sleek silver hair, a softly wrinkled face, and
mused blue eyes waved at me.

Saved by the ex-mother-in-law!

"Excuse me," I said to the unhappy couple. "Madame is
alling." Then I moved with all speed to the opposite end of
he party room.

Twenty-Five

~~~~~~

"Having a good time, dear?" Madame asked in a cheerful tone. Then she lowered her voice. "You looked like you needed someone to throw you a rope."

"Yes," I said, my stiff smile still in place, "and, as you can see, I grabbed it."

"Well, you're out of the hole now, Clare." She raised a silver eyebrow. "For the moment."

The remark was pregnant with meaning, but I wasn't up for pursuing it. "I'd just like to get my appetite back."

"Well, have another cocktail, dear, and you'll be feeling far less pain. In the meantime—" She took my arm. "Let's work the room together, shall we?"

I drained my cocktail and set it on a passing waiter's tray. "Lay on, McDuff."

Together we began to move around the room. I'd already said hello to many of the men who'd been at Monday's bachelor party: Koa, the big Hawaiian Kona grower; Dexter, the Rasta-haired Caribbean coffee merchant; and Roger Mbele of Kenya's Nairobi Coffee Exchange.

But there were lots of others here as well, men who hadn't been able to make Matt's bachelor party, and some women too, although none of us could hold a candle to Madame, whose impeccable taste had her looking as elegant as ever in shimmering V-neck double-tiered sage dress with a matching scarf thrown over one shoulder and a long, stunning necklace of pearls threaded through delicately entwined chains of white gold.

"Who have we here . . ." Madame began, introducing me to a number of people from her son's long, globe-trotting life that I'd never had the chance to meet.

First was Joao, a stout, apple-cheeked, middle-aged grower from Brazil whose teenage granddaughter was thrilled to be making her first trip to New York. Then I met a well-spoken young Costa Rican man and his bubbly sister, both with hazel eyes and beaming smiles.

Matt wandered over when he noticed us speaking with Pierre Audran, a striking Belgian blond who used to be an officer in the French Foreign Legion, and who now grew coffee in Africa. With a mental roll of the eyes, I excused myself when he and Matt started reminiscing about some wild nights they'd had a long time ago with a half-dozen half-drunk Parisian girls.

Finally, Madame presented me to a sweet Indonesian couple, who'd been providing the Village Blend with their earthy, full-bodied Sumatra for the last five years.

"We're so happy your country is recovering after the tsunami," I told them both.

"Yes, it was like a bad dream, a terrible dream," Mr. Raja said. "Many were lost. We ourselves lost friends."

"But we were lucky, too," his wife added, touching his arm. "Our farm is on a mountain near Lake Tawar in northern Sumatra, so it was not damaged."

"Matt tells me your farm is very beautiful. And it produces beautifully, too. That last crop was incredible—wild herbal notes, amazing complexity. Delicious."

The couple smiled shyly and exchanged proud glances. "Thank you," they said.

A new round of tapas was served, and my appetite was finally back—with a vengeance, unfortunately. I pretty much inhaled my small plate of *ceviche de camarones* (shrimp marinated in freshly squeezed lime juice served with toasted Peruvian corn and sweet potato).

The dish was stupendously refreshing but not filling enough, so I reached for the next offering: *quinoa paella*, a delectable version of the Spanish seafood dish. I dug in with gusto, and the rich, spicy flavors tangoed on my tongue. The real surprise, however, was the texture.

In a clever swap, the Machu Picchu chef had replaced the traditional Spanish rice with quinoa (aka Inca rice, a supernutritious grain that the people of Peru had been eating continuously for, oh, about 5,000 years). Like an al dente Italian risotto with a Spanish-Peruvian flair, the combination of crushed saffron, garlic, onion, chorizo sausage, tomatoes, green peas, and *piquillo* chilies steeped in fresh chicken stock suffused the clams, shrimp, and mussels with bright and piquant flavor.

"Yum-yum," I said, absently parroting Chef Rafe Chastain's trademark phrase. I couldn't help thinking of the man himself, throwing punches with his tattooed arms and chasing a home invader down a Queens back street with a broken floor lamp.

Madame noticed my reverie. "Now what's that private little smile about?"

"Nothing, really, I was just thinking that I'll never watch *Exotic Food Hunter at Large* the same way again."

"I take it you're referring to your most recent sleuthing adventure. Matt clued me in on some of the more colorful details. You know, dear, I'm still a little peeved at you for not including me."

Uh-oh. I'd just found the hole I was apparently not out of yet.

"I *distinctly* remember what you told me, Clare. There were two female detectives *already* on the case."

"I certainly would have included you, Madame, but once the train started moving, there was just no turning back—"

"Excuse me," a deep voice interrupted. "I would like to thank Matt's mother for the very lovely lunch."

"Javier! So nice to see you could make it to the wedding after all."

A tall, stiffly formal man about Matt's age took Madame's hands and kissed her on both cheeks. His face was bronzed, and sun wrinkles framed his dark eyes. He wore his jet-black hair slicked back, and his mustache was thick and long—a very retro south of the border machismo look, which the man carried extremely well.

"Thank you for coming, Javier." Madame turned to me. "Javier Lozado, this is my daughter-in—excuse me, my *manager* at the Village Blend, Clare Cosi."

Good try, Madame, I thought. *You'll get it down sooner or later.*

(Several months ago, during the planning stages of the wedding, Madame introduced me as her daughter-in-law, right in front of her *future* daughter-in-law, Breanne. It was a fairly awkward faux pas and did little to improve my relationship with the next Mrs. Allegro.)

Javier's smile widened. "Ah, Ms. Cosi! You are the woman we toasted."

"That was very nice of Matt. How do you know him, Mr. Lozado?"

"Please, call me Javier, if I may call you Clare?" he said, his crow's feet crinkling attractively. "Matt and I met years ago. In those days, I was a coffee buyer, too."

"You're not a buyer any longer?" Madame said, surprised.

He shook his head. "It was too much like my career in the army. It sounds exciting and glamorous, and I confess I enjoyed it for a while. 'A woman in every port,' as my American friends used to say. But I soon discovered that I did so much traveling I didn't have a home. That's why I *grow* coffee now, in Colombia, the land where I was born."

His eyes caught mine, and Javier smiled slyly. "When I long to travel or lack for feminine companionship, I explore the nightlife in a nearby city, or—excuse me, one moment—"

Javier hailed someone and gestured him forward. The short, sad-eyed man approached us. "Madame Dubois. Clare

Cosi," Javier said with great formality. "I am pleased to introduce you to my manager, Hector Pena."

Like Javier, Pena had clearly spent hours in the scorching sun. But the older man's deep tan didn't appear glowing and healthy like Javier's. His flesh almost seemed to sag, and there were dark circles under his eyes. There was an air of heaviness about the man, as if he were bearing the weight of Job on his slouching shoulders.

"I was just telling Clare it is good to get away sometimes. To travel, eh, Hector?"

Still unsmiling, Hector nodded. "I very much needed to make this journey."

A waiter appeared with a tray of *lomo saltado*, a hearty meat dish that's a favorite in Peru. Marinated strips of sirloin are sautéed with hot and sweet peppers, cilantro, garlic, and oregano. Usually served over rice and garnished with crispy French fries, the chef made the dish "hand-friendly" by skewering the beef, along with chunks of succulent pepper and a fried potato square. I took a bite of the marinated meat and slipped into a food trance. When I came out again, Hector Pena had drifted away.

"Why is your friend so sullen?" Madame asked.

"A recent personal tragedy," Javier replied in a lowered voice. "His young daughter was a beautiful and talented singer. She moved to Bogotá to pursue her career. About a month ago she died quite suddenly, by gunshot." Javier frowned and shook his head. "I have never seen Hector so desolate, and I have known him for fifteen years, since we were both with the *Lanceros*—"

"My, that sounds dashing."

"There is little dash to be found in the Colombian army," Javier replied. "Only an endless battle against drug cartels and terrorists."

"It's appalling, the tragedy in the world," Madame said, shaking her head. "Roger Mbele was telling me about Kenya's troubles not long ago. The post election violence left over a thousand dead in his country."

"Yes, yes, there is much sadness in the world. That is why I encouraged Hector to come with me to the wedding. He knows Matteo, of course, and is very happy for him, but I am personally grateful for this opportunity to get Hector away from home, away from his troubles, and cheer him up. I am afraid, however, that I am not doing a very good job. Perhaps a lady's touch?"

"Let's you and I try together," Madame said with a wink. She took Javier's arm and led him off in the direction of his sad friend.

"That's what happens when you come to the party late," a deep voice said to me a moment later, "you lose your best girl to a younger man."

I turned to find Otto Visser standing beside me—Madame's latest love interest. He was a tall, dapper fellow, leanly built with thinning but still-golden hair. In his late sixties, Madame had met her "younger man" a few months ago, while we were having dinner uptown. They "eye flirted" across the room at each other (Madame's version anyway), and then Otto approached her, and they'd been dating ever since.

I smiled up at him. "Madame wondered why you hadn't showed."

"Work, as usual," he said, his voice carrying a slight Dutch accent.

An art dealer now, Otto had originally studied to become a Roman Catholic priest, but he left the seminary and became an art historian instead, working for years at the Vatican museums. Now he ran the Otto Visser Gallery in Chelsea and performed private consulting work for several of the city's most prestigious museums and auction houses.

"I know all about working too many hours, but one of these should cheer you up." I snagged the waiter.

Otto sampled a bite of the new tapas offering: *chicharron de calamar*, a crispy fried squid served with *crema de recoto*, a kind of Peruvian creole sauce.

"Mmmm, delicious," Otto said. "I'll have one of *these*,

too." He snatched a glass of the flowing sangria *blanco* from passing tray. After a long drink, he sighed. "I was caught i the middle of another dispute between a buyer who's willing to spend the moon, and an artist who refuses to sell."

"Anyone I know?"

"I doubt it. The artist in question is Spanish, famous i some circles, but not yet widely known—"

Apparently, Breanne was near enough to overhear our con versation, because she walked right up to Otto and withou even a polite greeting asked, "Do you know Nunzio?"

"The Italian sculptor?" Otto shook his head. "Only by reputation."

Breanne shot me a sidelong glance. "A shame, because just got a text message with some very bad news for *you* Clare."

"Me?" I blinked.

"Yes, it seems Nunzio has had second thoughts abou loaning us his fountain."

My breath caught. The fountain was to be the *centerpiece* o the wedding's coffee and dessert station. Janelle Babcock and I had worked like dogs planning the details of the tablescape around it.

"That fountain was part of Nunzio's profile in the maga zine," Breanne said. "Without it, your little display won't be included in that section. I don't think our photo editor will even bother including it in the magazine's wedding spreads.'

I gritted my teeth. The Village Blend certainly didn't need *Trend* to make it popular. If I it were up to me, I'd drop the whole damn thing, but it wasn't just me involved here. I'd be letting Janelle Babcock down big time. She'd just started Pastries by Janelle and she'd worked on the wedding presentation for over a month. Janelle was counting on this national exposure to showcase her dessert catering.

I faced Breanne. "*Why* is Nunzio backing out?"

"I don't know for sure." Her eyebrow arched. "But I have an idea."

"Well?"

"From the wording he used, I believe it has something to do with spending the last few nights alone."

"Excuse me?"

"Don't you remember that card he slipped you?"

Matt appeared just then. "Card? What's this about a card?"

Breanne glanced over her shoulder at Matt. "It seems our favorite Italian sculptor took a shine to our little barista here. I told her she should give the man a whirl, and now she has a second chance. The text message said Nunzio will talk only with you, Clare. He's expecting you to 'discuss the situation' with him in his hotel room *tonight*."

Matt's jaw dropped. So did mine.

"It's your coffee and dessert station," Breanne added blithely. "If you want it featured in the magazine, then you have to find *some* way to change Nunzio's mind. I have enough to do. Oh, look who's here! Come, darling." She crossed the room, a slightly stunned Matt in tow.

"Unbelievable," I whispered. Otto was still standing beside me. I noticed he was wearing a half smile. "Otto, did you just hear what she implied?"

"I heard."

I closed my eyes, massaged the bridge of my nose. "How in the hell am I supposed to handle this?"

Otto softy chuckled. "I may not know Nunzio personally, Clare, but I'm sure he's like almost every other artist I've dealt with. Their most vulnerable organs aren't their hearts or their brains but their egos."

"Their egos?"

He nodded. "A tortured artist wrestles with a negative self-image. A confident artist brandishes an arrogance that can undo him. Paint it bold or shade it shy, on either end of the spectrum, it's the artist's ego that's in play."

Otto drained his glass and set it aside. "Believe me, Clare, I deal with it regularly. Today, for instance, my travails were with Tio, that rising Spanish sculptor I was telling you about. An important collector wanted to purchase the man's most famous work. It's called *The Trellis*. Oh, you should see it. I'll have it on display in my gallery for at least another week. It's a stylized garden trellis with a pair of lovers wrapped around each other like vines. Tio was reluctant to part with it, until I pointed out that the buyer would soon be lending his collection to the Museum of Modern Art for an exhibition, and so . . ." Otto paused and smiled. "Tio relented."

I nodded, happy for Otto's triumph, even though I frankly didn't see how his advice was going to help me in my current situation. My problem was with Nunzio's *libido*, not his ego.

"There you are, you rotter!"

A British voice was shouting over the party noise. I turned to see a redheaded woman knocking a server aside. The young man's tray of *choros a la chalaca* went flying, and I gasped, heartbroken at the sight of a mountain of mouthwatering mussels sent clattering across the floor.

The woman who'd done the dirty deed didn't appear to care. She looked to be in her late thirties, and she hadn't dressed for a party. Her bulky wool pinstripes and sensible heels looked more like she was on a break from a bank office or legal firm. The dreary gray outfit didn't take away from her flawless, peaches-and-cream complexion, however, and I watched with growing interest as the woman made a beeline for Matt, her angelic face flushing angrier by the second.

"Bugger!" she cried. "You're 'not the marrying kind'! That's what you told me! Then I get *this* in the post!"

The woman waved a gold-embossed card and threw it in Matt's face.

"Bridget, I—"

"Oh, shut up, you git."

I thought the woman was going to slap Matt. Instead, tears came to her long-lashed brown eyes, and she fled the room.

In the silence that followed the confrontation, Matt stooped down and picked up the engraved card she'd flung. I moved closer and saw that it was a wedding announcement.

knew what Matt and Breanne's wedding invitations looked ike, and this wasn't it. This was just a simple engraved announcement card declaring that Matteo Allegro would be marrying Breanne Summour in New York City. It gave the date of the nuptials but no other information.

Seriously odd.

From the expression on Matt's face I could tell he was as dumbfounded as I was. Then a conclusion appeared to dawn in his eyes, and he whirled to face his mother.

"Someone's been sending out wedding announcements to my old flames—which explains *why* these women have been confronting me all week. This was *your* doing, Mother, wasn't it?"

Madame, who was still visiting with Javier Lozado and trying to cheer up Hector Pena, blinked in complete shock. "I swear to you, Matteo, I did no such thing."

Matt turned to face his fiancée. As soon as he saw her expression, he knew the truth. "*You* did this. Didn't you, Breanne?"

"Yes, it's true," she said, not a trace of contrition in her tone. "I had my assistant download your PDA for the addresses and phone numbers stored inside. I just wanted all of your friends and acquaintances to know that you were getting married, that's all."

"When?" Matt demanded. "When did you do this?"

Breanne shrugged. "Maybe a month ago."

I shook my head. The woman's expression appeared to be all surprised innocence, but her action had been coldly calculated. She'd effectively notified every last woman in Matt's little black PDA book that he was no longer available.

"Son of a—" He shook his head. "You invaded my privacy, went into my PDA without telling me. You contacted people from my past, with your own agenda, without even *warning* me. You humiliated me, Breanne. You, you—"

Breanne reached for her groom, but he pulled away.

"Get away from me," he rasped.

"Matt, please—"

But he wasn't listening. Before anyone could stop him, Matt stormed out.

"Please, someone, follow him," Madame said with worried eyes.

Flanking Matt's mother, Javier and Hector instantly nodded and chased after Matt. Koa Waipuna took off after them.

As soon as they were gone, all heads turned to Breanne. By the time she finished a swallow of her Pisco Sour, her calmly superior mask had slipped back over her stunned expression. But I'd gotten to know the woman well enough in these last few weeks to see the little cracks around her edges. Matt's violent reaction to her brazen stunt had rocked her. Up to now, he'd been patient and accommodating. She was probably expecting him to roll over and accept this little prank without a peep. Clearly, she'd miscalculated.

On the one hand, I was appalled that Breanne had violated Matt's privacy. But I had to admit I was pretty impressed with the move. It was shrewd, a way to keep Matt from straying—with all the old flames, at least. Her actions also made me wonder just how well Roman knew his best friend. Sure, Breanne gave lip service to being free of middle-class morals, but this little trick made it clear that she actually did care about fidelity—or at least sharing Matt with other women.

I felt myself smiling. If anything, this was a good sign. In my opinion, Breanne was starting to act like a wife.

For a good twenty minutes, the bride-to-be put on a good face for her luncheon guests, chatting with the Rayos, an Ecuadorean couple, before finally retreating to the ladies' room.

I felt a touch of pity for the woman. After what just happened, I assumed she must be feeling terrible. I glanced at Madame, hoping the mother of the groom would take it upon herself to comfort her future daughter-in-law. But when I saw the expression on her face, I knew she wasn't unhappy with

e conflagration. Clearly, Madame continued to hold out
pe that her son would say, "I don't."

But somebody *should really check on Breanne* . . .

When it was obvious that no one else was going to step
, I sighed, set my glass down, and followed Ms. Wonderful
the women's room.

Twenty-Six

~~~~~~~~~~~~~~~~~~~~~~~~~~~~~~~~~~~~~

"**Breanne?**" I called. "Are you okay?"

There were three stalls in Machu Picchu's ladies' facilit only one of them appeared to be in use. Behind its close door, I sensed movement then heard a muffled sound.

Was that a sob?

"Breanne, please answer me."

No response, just more movement inside the stall.

With a sigh, I glanced around. The floor space in th restroom was bigger than some of my baristas' studio apar ments. The decor wasn't half bad, either. An array of prim tive masks continued the pseudo-Inca theme of the dinin room. Andean wood flutes warbled from hidden speaker and sweet-smelling incense burned in clay pots. Three sand stone sinks lined one mirrored wall. Three stalls stood oppo site, their rustic wooden doors reaching almost to th terra-cotta floor.

I approached the only stall door that was closed and hea a choking gasp. "Breanne, are you *crying?*"

I didn't relish playing girlfriend to the grand bitch Trend. But the woman did sound like she was suffering; an if anyone knew what it was like to choke on tears over Ma teo Allegro, it was yours truly.

"Come on now, Bree. It'll be all right. Come out and we' talk about it—"

But the fashion maven didn't want to talk. Instead, one of her thousand-dollar double-strapped Fen pumps flew through the small space between the bottom of the stall door and the floor, narrowly missing my ankle.

Great! First she dismisses my detective work, now she's throwing shoes at me. Forget this! I was about to turn and leave when the stall door rattled and cracked open.

"What? Did you change your mind? You want me to come in now?"

I cautiously pushed the door wider—and froze.

Matt's fiancée was choking all right, but not on prewedding tears. A man was standing behind her in the stall. I couldn't see his face or much else to define him. He wore a black ski mask, a long black coat, and his thick black gloves were literally squeezing the life out of Breanne's slender white throat.

"Help!" I cried at the top of my lungs. "Heeeeelp!"

I could see Breanne's French-tipped fingernails were digging into her attacker's black gloves, but it was no use, the strangling grip was firm.

"Helpppp!"

My voice echoed hollowly in the tiled space, and I feared the remote bathroom was too far away from the loud party for anyone to hear. Bree's eyelids were fluttering; her long, lithe limbs were going limp; she was losing consciousness!

I feared leaving her to get help so I lunged into the stall myself, pulled on the man's gloved fingers, tried to break his merciless grip. It began to work, until the attacker's body turned enough to kick out and slam me backward.

"Dammit!"

I landed on the floor, my whole side throbbing. The sloppy fall had dispersed the contents of Breanne's handbag. Makeup, credit cards, a red leather wallet with hundreds of dollars falling out—my gaze quickly scanned the scattered items. Finally, I spied something useful: a small can of Mace.

Yes!

I grabbed the pepper spray, aimed the nozzle, and pressed

the trigger. The burning stream struck the man point-blank in his ski mask. The attacker howled, and his gloved hands released Bree's neck. I grabbed Matt's half-conscious fiancée around her waist, yanked her backward with all my strength, and we tumbled together onto the floor.

Coughing, the man stumbled out after us. Breanne was thinner than I was, but she was also much taller, and I was trapped for a minute under her large, limp form. I squirmed, trying to turn my head, get a decent look at her attacker. I glimpsed brown pants and shoes under the long black coat. He wasn't a giant, but he wasn't small, either. From the floor, I had trouble estimating his height; and with the ski mask on his head and the gloves on his hands, I couldn't even be sure of his race!

I only had a second to make an ID, and I couldn't do it. Howling and clawing at his saturated mask, the man bolted for the exit. I heard the door swing shut, then an eerie silence.

With a groan of pain, I rolled over to check on Breanne. She was already sitting up and clutching at her long white neck, now bruised with angry red marks. Her necklace snapped off, the silver and turquoise tumbling from her throat like a dead serpent.

I faced Breanne, my heart still racing. "Are you okay?"

Breanne was gasping for air. "No," she rasped. "Dizzy. Sick. Need a minute."

"I'll be back," I said.

One of my wedge platform sandals was half off my foot. I quickly fixed it, ran out the door, and madly scanned the corridor. But no one was there. The ladies' room was in the very back of the restaurant, beyond the kitchen entrance and even remote from the men's room, which was off the building's front bar. I noticed the fire exit door was hanging open, and I guessed the man had escaped through the back alley.

I could have risked running after him into that alley, but it wouldn't have been smart. I was small, unarmed, and I didn't want to leave Breanne alone for long. Since I'd left my

l phone in my bag, which was still sitting in the dining
om, I hurried toward it. On the way, a waitress nearly col-
ed with me coming out of the busy kitchen. I grabbed her
n.

"Call 911," I said. "Be quiet about it. Don't cause a panic,
t a woman was just attacked in your ladies' room. When
e police and paramedics arrive, tell your manager, okay?"

I went back to the restroom and found Breanne still on
e floor. There was a lingering smell of burning pepper
m the Mace, and I hit the switch on the room's powerful
is. The air cleared quickly.

"You're bleeding." I pointed to the hollow of Breanne's
oulder.

She looked down. "My necklace . . . while he was choking
. The metal dug into my skin . . ."

Her voice was still raspy, and I worried about damage to
r vocal chords. I pulled a wad of paper towels from the dis-
nser and dampened them in the sink. Then I sat back
wn on the bathroom floor and gently pressed her bleeding
und. She winced.

"Just hold that on there, okay?"

With an exhale, she nodded. Then she regarded me. "Are
u okay, Clare?"

"Oh, sure . . . the scumbag kicked me pretty good." I
bbed my aching hip where the jerk had slammed me. "But
l survive. I've got pretty good padding down there, as you
eady know."

I gave her a little smile, glanced down at myself, and
owned. I'd worn a new dress of pearl-pink silk to the party
name designer at outlet prices, thank you very much). But
rt of the wrap dress had unwrapped during the struggle. I
od up to secure my dress back around my body and
ghten the matching belt.

"So what the hell happened?" Breanne's voice was a lot
ss raspy now.

"What do you mean?"

In record time, the woman's expression went from human

and caring to cold and accusatory. "I *thought* you told M
that I was *out* of danger."

Wow, I thought. *The bitch is back.*

I folded my arms. "I thought you didn't believe you we
in danger."

"Apparently, I was wrong."

"Well, apparently, so was I."

I crossed to the stall where we'd struggled and studi
the floor, hoping to see something the attacker may ha
dropped, but all I could make out were some of the conten
of Breanne's purse. I stooped down and began to clean up t
mess.

"Did this guy say anything to you?" I asked. "Dema
anything? Threaten you?"

Still on the floor, Breanne shook her head. "I came in
the bathroom, and he attacked from behind. I guess he w
hiding in one of the stalls. When he saw me, he sprang ou
dragged me in, and slammed the door shut. I tried to fig
him off, but then his hands were around my neck, and
couldn't breathe."

I nodded, processing the tale, trying to make sense of it
was still picking up scattered items. I found her PDA behir
the toilet and returned it to her.

"I wonder how it got way back there?" I said.

"I was trying to call Matt." Breanne studied the floor. "
was in my hand when that man grabbed me."

I continued picking up her things. When I got to t
Mace can, I held it up. "Coffee notwithstanding, chili pepp
is getting to be my new favorite ingredient." I smiled, ho
ing to lighten her mood a fraction.

It didn't.

"I guess this is all pretty funny to you, too, huh, Clare?'

"*Funny?* Are you mental?"

"Before I came in here, I saw you getting your jollies ov
my distress. When Matt pitched a fit and stormed out, I sa
the smile cross your face."

"Oh, for the love of . . . I'll tell you why I smiled, Breann

nd it had nothing to do with relishing your pain. I was ad-
niring what you did. I was happy to see you finally act like a
vife!"

The stunned look on the woman's face was nearly price-
ess. Of all the responses I could have given her, she'd never
ambled on that one. But then she never wanted to think of
ne as anything more than the ex-wife, the enemy.

"You're not kidding, are you?" she said.

"Roman told me that your marriage was just one of con-
enience, that you really didn't care about Matt's playboy
ifestyle; and it made me sad to think you weren't going to
lemand what any real wife should: faithfulness. When I saw
vhat you did with those announcements, I realized you did
are."

Breanne glanced away, massaged her forehead. She'd obvi-
usly cast me as the villain in this little play, someone who
vas only set on sabotaging her. My words now and my ac-
ions three minutes earlier flew directly in the face of those
ssumptions.

"Okay," she said softly. "Okay . . ."

I wasn't sure what *okay* meant, but her tone sounded a lot
ess accusatory and a whole lot friendlier. I took that as a good
irst step.

"Breanne, can I give you some advice—ex-wife to hope-
ully *not* future ex-wife?"

Breanne gritted her teeth, but she nodded.

I crouched down, back to her level. "Stop trying so hard
o cut Matt off from his past."

"But you just said you admired what I did with the old
lames."

"The old flames are one thing; his family and his life's
vork are another."

Breanne frowned, shook her head.

"Listen, Madame is hostile to you for a pretty basic reason.
he's picked up on your animosity vibe, your jealousy. She's
eard you say things that imply Matt would be better off not
vorking for the Blend. Madame is afraid you're going to pull

her son away from the family business that she's kept going for half a century, a business that started with Matt's great grandfather. She's afraid you're going to cut the strings that attach her son to her life."

Breanne met my eyes. "You're afraid, too, aren't you, Clare?"

"Maybe I am. We all have threads in our lives, continuous strands that reach back years, decades, entire lifetimes. Those threads are what help define who we are. Matt has always meant a lot to his mother, to his daughter, and to me. My advice to you is pretty simple: instead of trying to cut Matt off from what's defined him over a lifetime, try harder to entwine yourself with it. Like those gorgeous wedding rings Nunzio created for you. Three different types of gold—white, yellow, rose—all weaved together into one band. Past, present, and future, right? Isn't that why he chose the design?"

Breanne looked away again, began to chew the gloss off her bee-stung lips. "Okay, Clare. I've heard everything you said, and I'll think about it—"

"They're in here!"

The shout came from just outside the bathroom door. The waitress was back with her manager and a half-dozen others. The door flew open, and I heard sirens in the street.

"Sounds like the cavalry's here," I said. Then I took Breanne's arm and helped her to her feet.

ⓢⓢⓢⓢⓢⓢⓢⓢⓢⓢⓢⓢⓢⓢⓢⓢ

mugging! Come on, you can't be serious!"

"Do I look like I'm kidding, Ms. Cosi?"

I stood in the middle of Machu Picchu's dining room, facing off with the senior detective assigned to the case. Rocky Friar was in his early thirties and built like a granite statue. Trying to talk with Friar, I soon discovered, was like trying to reason with a granite statue, too.

"I was there, remember? I saw it. That man was trying to kill Breanne Summour, not rob her. It was attempted murder."

"What would lead you to this conclusion?" Friar asked, his skepticism thinly veiled and infuriating.

"The man was choking her," I said. "His hands were wrapped around her throat—"

"The perpetrator was trying to steal Ms. Summour's valuable necklace."

"If this was just a simple robbery, then why did the man ignore a wallet, credit cards, and hundreds of dollars in cash spilled all over the floor?"

"Generally speaking, Ms. Cosi, your average criminal type isn't the brightest bulb on the Christmas tree."

"A five-year-old knows how to pick up money."

"I'm not going to waste time trying to fathom the stupidity of the criminal mind."

"Oh, is that so? Silly me. And I thought that's what co[
did for a living!"

Oops. Friar's expression just went from strained patience t[
openly annoyed in under a second. *Okay, so maybe that la[
quip was a little over the top . . .*

"I'm sorry, Detective. I'm still a little upset about wha[
happened. But I need you to hear what I'm saying: this isn[
the first time there's been an attack . . ."

I told the man about the SUV jumping the sidewalk o[
the Upper East Side, and the murder of Breanne's look-alik[
stripper, Hazel Boggs, in the West Village. Finally, I tol[
him about Breanne's ex-husband, Stuart Allerton Winslow.[
explained that he was under arrest now for illegal distribu[
tion of medication and conspiracy to rob his wife.

Before I even finished, Friar raised his hand. "I might b[
missing something, seeing as I'm not delving into the crim[
inal mind like I *ought* to be. But with Winslow sitting in a[
interrogation room on Tenth Street, I don't see how he ca[
possibly be implicated for today's mugging in a Soho bath[
room."

"But he could have hired someone to attack her—"

"And I *really* don't see any connection between a dead strip[
per and the attempted robbery of a socialite in a restaurant—[
beyond the fact that both victims have blond hair and nic[
legs."

"What about the attempt to run Breanne down on th[
street?"

"Gas guzzlers run amok all the time in this burg. You'[
have to do better than that."

I stared at the man. Broad and angular, the detective's jav[
jutted like a concrete window ledge; his neck resembled [
Greek column. His hair was the color of toasted walnuts, hi[
eyes were the color of warm rum, but his mind had all th[
flexibility of a stale baguette.

"Why don't you talk to the detectives at the Sixt[
Precinct involved with the cases I mentioned. You can ca[

Mike Quinn or the investigating officers in the Hazel Boggs murder case, Lori Soles and Sue Ellen Bass."

At the mention of Sue Ellen's name, Rocky Friar's eyes bugged. And then it hit me. When Friar first arrived, his name sounded familiar, but I was still rattled by the attack and hadn't made the connection. Now I remembered.

Rocky Friar worked out of the Ninth Precinct and lived in Mike Quinn's Alphabet City apartment building (Divorced Badges 'R' Us). He was also Sue Ellen's old boyfriend, the one who'd declared her banned from the building.

"Frankly, Ms. Cosi, I don't buy your theory of the case. Sounds like a tangled mess to me. I think you're overwrought from the attack." He jerked his thumb at the bar. "Do yourself a favor: have a good stiff drink and find a seat."

"But Lori Soles and Sue Ellen Bass might have a new lead on the—"

"Forget it. I'm not talking to Sue Ellen Bass about *this* case, or any other."

Friar turned his broad back to me and gestured to a young Hispanic detective. Like Friar, the younger man was dressed in a sport coat and dark slacks. He wore his gun on his hip and his gold shield on his belt. The man nodded to Friar, ended his conversation with a waiter, and hurried to Friar's side. I willed myself invisible and stepped closer to the pair.

"What d'ya got, Victor?"

"Nobody from the kitchen staff saw anything out of the ordinary. The party guests are still being interviewed, but no one's come forward with an eyewitness account other than the woman you were interviewing. And I got the victim's statement before the ambulance took off—"

"Did the perp make any sexual advances? Fondle the victim?"

Victor shook his head. "She claims he didn't even demand money or valuables, just started choking her—"

"You mean he grabbed her *necklace*," Friar said.

Victor glanced at his notes. "The victim called it *choking*."

Friar noticed me lurking, just then.

"I've taken your statement, Ms. Cosi, so I'm *done* with you. Move along."

Gritting my teeth, I walked away, fumbled in my bag for my cell phone, and hit the second number on my speed-dial list. Mike Quinn's voice mail picked up.

Damn.

Okay, *next*. I fished out the card Detective Soles had given me. She said to call if I uncovered any new developments in Hazel Boggs's murder. In my opinion, *this* was a new development, so I pulled out my cell phone and punched in the number, half expecting to get her voice mail, too. But I got an answer on the second ring.

"Detective Lori Soles."

I identified myself, and the woman's tone instantly turned friendly. "Clare Cosi, my favorite PI."

"Anything new in the Hazel Boggs case? It's important I know, or I wouldn't be bothering you."

"The bullet was recovered at the autopsy," Lori said. "We're expecting a ballistics report this afternoon, tomorrow morning at the latest. Anything new on your end?"

"I'm at Machu Picchu in Soho, and Breanne Summour was attacked here about thirty minutes ago. The senior detective on the scene thinks it's a mugging."

"Who is it?"

"Rocky Friar."

"Oh, brother."

"But Friar is wrong," I quickly added. "I was there, an eyewitness to the attack, and I say it was a hit. I'm more convinced than ever that the death of Breanne's look-alike and this murder attempt on the real thing are connected."

"I don't know what you've got," Lori said. "But it certainly sounds interesting. I'll run it by my partner. If she's good to go, we'll be there in fifteen."

I closed the phone and returned to Madame and the luncheon.

Breanne was gone by now. The ambulance was taking her

Beth Israel's ER. The paramedics didn't think her vocal cords were damaged, but they suspected a hairline fracture of her collarbone. For that she needed X-rays.

By now, my daughter had returned to the Village Blend to visit with some of the baristas she hadn't seen since leaving for Paris. Frankly, I was glad to get Joy clear of this mess. A dozen or so guests remained. They were speaking in hushed whispers by the bar. Two uniformed officers were taking final statements. Seated at a corner table, I saw Madame nursing a glass of sangria *blanco*. I sat down beside her.

She glanced at me and sullenly shook her silver white head. "The groom stormed off, and the bride-to-be was strangled within an inch of her life. I'd say the luncheon was a stunning success, wouldn't you?" She drained her wineglass and asked her boyfriend, Otto, to fetch another: *tout de suite.*

"There's a silver lining, though," she added. "This ill-advised marriage will very likely be canceled."

"Not so loud."

Madame waved me off. Otto came back with her fresh glass of sangria, and she downed it nearly as fast as her son had chugged beers at the White Horse.

"Are you grieving or celebrating?" I asked.

"Both." She shook her head again. "Neither. Oh, Clare . . . I just want my son to be happy. Matteo won't be. Not with that woman."

"Well, don't be so sure the marriage is off. Breanne Summour generally gets what she wants."

"That's what I'm afraid of."

Suddenly, a bright flash of light shot through the room. Everyone froze. Then I heard Rocky Friar's voice boom, "Grab that guy, *now!*"

Near the entrance to the restaurant's front bar, a uniformed officer caught the arm of a middle-aged, balding man. I saw an expensive-looking camera in the man's hand, a khaki photographer's vest around his paunchy torso, and shook my head.

"The paparazzi are here—or at least one paparazzo."

"I said no reporters," Friar barked. "Who let this vultur in?"

The uniform shrugged. "He *was* in, Detective. Liqui lunch up front."

"I'm only alone because my date was delayed," the pho tographer said.

"I'll do the talking," Friar shot back. "What's your name and who do you work for? And for the love of God, don't te me you're a tourist."

"I'm not a tourist, Detective. I'm a *freelance* photographe So I don't work for anyone, specifically—"

"That's a load of bull!" shouted a familiar female voice.

Sue Ellen Bass's never-ending legs strode boldly into th restaurant and right up to Friar. Hustling up behind he were the blond cherub curls of Lori Soles. I was relieved t see both women.

"That mook's name is Ben Tower," Sue Ellen said, "and h works for that sleazebag Randall Knox at the *Journal*."

Ben Tower?

I blinked, suddenly seeing the black courier type on th white card that I'd found hidden away in Monica Purcell secret drug box. So *this* was the freelance photographer who' given Monica his card.

When I first read the man's handwritten note, I though Tower was a fashion photographer seeking work from *Trend* somebody who was young and hot that Monica might hav been interested in personally. But the bald man in the rum pled plaid pants and bulky vest was not young, and he wa obviously a newshound, not a fashion photographer.

Meanwhile, Rocky Friar was already starting in on his ol girlfriend. "Oh, man . . ." He grabbed his head. "My freakir migraine headache just got a whole lot worse."

Sue Ellen flipped her sleek black ponytail over her shoul der. "I'm not the cause of your headache, barrel neck. It those muscles of yours. They constrict and squeeze the bloo outta your pea-size brain."

I realized there was something different about Sue Ellen today: makeup and earrings, delicate pearl studs. She'd applied fresh lipstick and gloss, too.

Friar glared at the smoldering Amazon. "What do you know about biceps and triceps? From your reputation, your interest lies in *another* muscle on the male anatomy."

"What? *Yours?*" Sue Ellen rolled her eyes. "Speaking of pea-size."

"Listen up, Bass. You're not only banned from my apartment building, you're banned from my crime scene." Rocky jerked his thumb in the direction of the exit. "Hit the road."

"Banning me from the building is a load of crap, and you know it."

"Listen, honey, it's for your own good," Friar said, his voice theatrically softening. "The building's full of guys on the job. All single. All virile. All teeming with testosterone. I wouldn't take an alkie out drinking, or a junkie to a crack house—"

"You son of a—" Sue Ellen lunged forward.

Lori snared her waist. "Whoa, partner! Hold up, there!"

Friar laughed. "That's right, Annie Oakley. Simmer that filly down!"

"You're not helping, Rocky," Lori shot back. "And you can't ban us from this crime scene. We're here at the behest of one of the witnesses to investigate possible links to another crime."

"Which witness?"

"Right here!" I said, waving my hand like Roman Brio signaling a waiter.

"Oh, jeez," Rocky groaned, his hands mashing down his toasted-walnut hair. "Victor!"

"Yeah, Rock."

"Liaise with these—"

"Watch it," Sue Ellen warned.

"—*detectives* from the Sixth. And look out for the big brunette. She's a freakin' man-eater."

"Hey, shutterbug!" Friar shouted at Ben Tower, who wa
trying to slip away. "Where the hell do you think you're go
ing?"

"I'm not breaking any laws."

"No?" Friar said. "Let's see how the management of thi
chic eatery feels about paparazzi hanging around and bother
ing their celebrity customers. Then let's see how Ms. Sum
mour feels about having her party photographed on privat
property. Maybe she has a restraining order out on you. O
maybe she'll want to take one out. Either way, I'll have t
check downtown. That may take a *long* time."

"Okay, okay!" Tower held up his hand.

I stifled a smile. Friar was a long way from winning m
over, but I couldn't help being impressed with his turn-the
perp dance step. He was almost as good as Mike Quinn.

"I do work for the *Journal*," Tower admitted. "The lady
cop was right, okay. But I was just having a few drinks and
bite at the bar. Then you guys showed, and I figured ther
was a story—"

"A story? It's a lousy mugging. Big deal. Why should you
and Randall Knox care about something so small-time?"
Friar leaned close to the man, his face inches from Tower's
"Unless you had *another* reason to be here besides the gour
met tacos."

Tower dropped his voice. "Knox sent me here to watch Ms
Summour, okay? Maybe shoot some interesting pictures."

Friar folded his arms. "And did you get anything interest
ing?"

"Some dame waving a wedding announcement. The groom
storming out. A lover's spat, I guess. Not exactly JFK, Jr."

"I hope not. The man's been dead quite a few years now."

"But those photographs of him fighting in public with hi
fiancée were worth a fortune."

Friar shook his head. "Breanne Summour's not nearly tha
famous. Why bother?"

I stepped up to the men. "Excuse me, Detective, but
have a few questions for Mr. Tower."

Friar rolled his eyes, but he didn't stop me.

"Mr. Tower, were you at your boss's birthday party a few onths ago?" I asked pointedly. "The one that featured a ripper dressed up like Breanne Summour? Did you shoot y interesting photos there?"

Tower frowned down at me. "I must have missed that sh."

"What about Monica Purcell?" I asked. "What can you ll me about her?"

"Who?" Friar asked.

"Monica Purcell overdosed on prescription medication," I id, "presumably from the painkillers and uppers I found in r desk. There was a business card hidden with those drugs, r. Tower, *your* card."

"I had nothing to do with Monica overdosing," Tower id, his bald head vehemently shaking now. "I had nothing do with any of that!"

"Why did she have your card then?" I asked. "And why d you write that you enjoyed your lunch with her and were oking forward to working with her?"

Tower held up his hand again. "I didn't set up that lunch. andy Knox did. If you want to know about Monica's deal ith Randy, you ask *him*."

"All right, that's enough questions from you, Ms. Cosi," iar said. "I have my own questions for this guy." The uscle-bound detective grabbed the collar of the photogra-er's vest and pulled him away.

I approached Lori Soles. "You're going to interview Ran-ll Knox, right? He's obviously fixated on Breanne Sum-our."

"We already interviewed Knox," Lori said. "We came up npty."

"What if it wasn't a coincidence that Tower was here?" I id. "What if Knox knew Breanne would be attacked, aybe killed, and he wanted his photographer on hand to pture images of the crime scene?"

"Look, I know Tower is a shark. I caught him sneaking

into the apartment of that TV actress who OD'd last year, s
he could shoot pictures of her body. But I can't see Tower
a party to murder."

"But you can question Knox again, right?"

Lori frowned. "I don't see the point. There's nothing su
picious about paparazzi hanging around celebrities."

"But there's a connection to Monica Purcell. You kno
about that case, right?"

"Drug distro and conspiracy to commit robbery of M
Summour's rings. Yeah, Quinn talked to Sue Ellen and m
about it already. But I don't see how Tower is involved."

"I found Tower's card hidden in Monica's desk."

"That's pretty thin, Cosi. Even for you."

Suddenly Sue Ellen Bass took off, chasing after Detectiv
Friar—presumably for another round of verbal sparring.

Lori blanched. "Sorry, got to go!" she said, hurrying aft
her partner.

"But somebody's got to talk to Randall Knox," I calle
Then I felt a warm hand on my shoulder. I turned to fir
Madame standing there. "How long have you been liste
ing?"

"Long enough," Madame said. "I learned a thing or tw
watching you, my dear." She threw me a wink. "And I a
ready have a solution to your problem."

"Which is?"

"You and I will talk to Randall Knox *together*."

I nodded. "You're on."

"You know," Madame said, as we headed for the street, "a
ter surviving the Indonesian tsunami, drug violence and te
rorism in Colombia, and the post election chaos in Kenya
Rift Valley, our guests probably didn't blink an eye at th
disaster of a luncheon, but *I'm* certainly relieved to be walk
ing away from it."

Twenty-Eight

~~~~~~~~~~~~~~~~~~~~~~~~~~~~~~

THE receptionist was hardly out of her teens. Hispanic, with dark hair and hot-pink lips, she was filing her moon-and-stars fingernail design when we approached her desk.

"Madame Dreyfus Allegro Dubois to see Mr. Randall Knox," Matt's mother declared with the aplomb of Queen Elizabeth.

From her doe-eyed expression, I could tell the elaborate name had bewildered the poor girl.

Madame cleared her throat. "Simply inform your boss that Matt Allegro's mother is here to dish dirt on mutual foe, Breanne Summour."

While the receptionist dialed her boss, I looked around. The *Journal's* run-down digs were a far cry from *Trend's* ultra-modern headquarters. There was no Columbus Circle view here, no ready access to Central Park, either. The *Journal's* offices were on a dingy stretch of Eighth Avenue, a few blocks south of Penn Station, and the building's other occupants weren't Time Warner Inc., CNN, and Thomas Keller's Bouchon Bakery, but Manny Kinn Enterprises, a "manufacturer of vinyl outerwear," and the Circle Jay Group, publishers of *Wag* and *Live Nude Girls.*

"Mr. Knox will see you now," the girl said, waving a tiny night sky on her long fingernails. "Down that hall, make a right. You'll find Mr. Knox in the corner office."

The hallway's avocado walls were dingy, the beige carpet threadbare, and a fluorescent light fixture buzzed somewhere above our heads. The short hall ended in a large room divided into cramped cubicles and offices along the wall. As we approached the corner office, a man stepped forward and extended his hand.

"I'm Randall Knox. Come in, please."

Most of the view in Knox's office was of another building's brick wall. The wooden desk was small and the steel shelves cluttered with magazines, file folders, and back issues of the *Journal*. Knox himself stood in sharp contrast to his shabby office. Pressed and polished, the slight, bald gossip columnist wore a London-tailored suit of blue pinstripes with a silk tie of bright scarlet.

He gestured to two battered wooden chairs opposite his desk then moved to occupy his own worn leather chair. While he silently regarded us through little, round Joseph Goebbels–style glasses, I read the large plaque hanging off one shelf:

PUBLIC OPINION IS A SHIP ADRIFT.
OUR JOB IS TO TAKE THE HELM!

Reading that, I suspected Knox's resemblance to the Nazi propaganda minister wasn't limited to his eyewear.

"Mr. Knox," Madame began, "my name is—"

"No need for introductions, you're the mother of Matteo Allegro, costar in the wedding of the week."

Randall Knox leaned across his desk and spoke in a conspiratorial whisper. "I also know you're not particularly happy that your son is marrying Breanne Summour. By the way, that heart attack you staged was masterful. My kudos. We had a nice photo of Matt partying at Le Shellac, and we were all set to go with the headline 'Boy Toy Clubs While Mom Has Coronary,' but our reporter found out you were faking it."

Madame looked down her nose at the gossipmonger. "And how in the world did he accomplish that?"

"I don't usually give up a source, Madame, so I'll just say
was a hospital aide who clued us in. You see, I have feelers
erywhere." He smiled. It wasn't warm.

"Not everywhere," Madame said. "Surely, you exaggerate."

"Oh, you'd be surprised. I know many things about many
ople in this town—the sort of things one *thinks* are com-
etely private. For instance, I know that you covered the
avel and hotel costs for many of your son's Third World
iums so they could attend his wedding. Despite some valu-
le assets—your Fifth Avenue penthouse, the West Village
wn house, an impressive collection of jewelry, and a
useum-quality wardrobe of vintage designer clothes—you
e not a very wealthy woman when it comes to liquidity.
our expenses are covered by your late husband's annuity, so
come up with that quick chunk of change for your son's
lebration, you sold off a valuable painting in the collection
ierre Dubois left you—"

"That shows how little you *do* know, Mr. Knox. *Portrait of
Vintner* by Marcel Brule was *not* valuable. It was only mar-
etable because the descendants of the vintner who was the
bject of the painting coveted the work, hence my agent at
isser Gallery was able to secure a premium price."

"And your agent was Otto Visser, your current beau." He
niled again. "Still, Madame, to part with a cherished objet
art—"

"*Not* cherished, Mr. Knox. My late husband, Pierre, was
nd of old masters–style portraiture. My tastes are more
iodern."

"The luncheon earlier today was also hosted by you, and
ou footed the bill, too, I understand."

Madame pursed her lips, clearly annoyed by the man's re-
entless one-upmanship game. "I've been humoring my son,"
he admitted. "The lunch was a pleasure—apart from the
vedding. There were many old friends I wanted to see."

"I'm sure," Knox said. "But it seems to me these are not
he actions of a woman who really wants to *sabotage* her future
iaughter-in-law's wedding plans, which is why I sincerely

doubt you're here to 'dish dirt' on Breanne Summour, despi[te]
the story you gave my receptionist."

Madame narrowed her eyes on the gossip king. "I ju[st]
want my son to be happy."

"And if Breanne Summour makes him happy?" he sai[d.]
"What then?"

Madame stared speechless at the man. He'd painted he[r]
into a rhetorical corner.

Great.

This guy was a whole lot smarter than Stuart Winslow (o[r]
maybe he just seemed that way because he wasn't blasted ou[t]
on pills). Either way, I could see I had my work cut out fo[r]
me. He'd already stunned Madame into silence. Now it wa[s]
my turn to step up.

"Excuse me, Mr. Knox, but I have a question for you." [I]
leaned forward in my chair. "I'd like to know why you sen[t]
Ben Tower to Machu Picchu today."

Knox shifted his gaze. "Ah, Ms. Cosi. I was wonderin[g]
when you were actually going to speak—"

Bite me, gossip boy.

"It was rude of you not to introduce yourself as Matte[o]
Allegro's ex-wife."

"Actually, I didn't introduce myself at all, but what doe[s]
it matter? You seem to know everything already."

Knox simply stared at me. Apparently, I'd rendered hi[m]
as speechless as he'd rendered Madame.

Score one for the Chihuahua.

"I asked you a question, Mr. Knox. Why did you sen[d]
Ben Tower to the restaurant? A fortunate coincidence for [a]
gossipmonger, wouldn't you say? There's your photographe[r]
all ready to snap pictures moments after Breanne is brutall[y]
attacked. It's almost as if you knew something was going t[o]
happen. Maybe something you engineered."

Knox chuckled hollowly. "Sorry, Mrs. Allegro—"

"It's Ms. Cosi, which you already know."

"Look, I don't need to have Breanne Summour mugge[d]
to take her down. Truthfully, I just heard the news of th[e]

ttempted robbery a few minutes before you arrived—Ben ower phoned me—which means this must be one of your leuthing adventures. Am I right?"

Now I felt my lips pursing in annoyance. *Okay, score an-ther one for gossip boy.*

"And what do you know, Mr. Knox, or *think* you know?"

Knox's pale-blue eyes gleamed behind his little round glasses. "Let's see, where to begin . . . how about last fall? When your daughter was briefly held for the murder of Tommy Keitel, you were the one who cleared that case, not New York's finest. Before that, you were mixed up with a most unfortunate international incident near the UN, at the Beekman Tower. Then there was that shooting at David Mintzer's East Hampton beach house." Knox shook his head in mock wonderment. "Yes, Ms. Cosi, it seems wherever you go, trouble follows. Or is it the other way round?"

I studied the small man's smirking face, thought of something Matt had mentioned to me right before his bachelor party. "I know things, too, Mr. Knox. My ex-husband told me that your animosity toward his fiancée reaches back years. Is that true?"

Knox glanced away. "Breanne Summour is just another flighty celebrity. More fodder for my gossip page—"

"That's crap, and you know it. You have some kind of his-tory with her. So what was it? Were the two of you lovers once upon a time?"

"Lovers? Me and Breanne?" Knox snorted. "I could hardly stand the woman, even back then."

"Then I'm betting Breanne undermined your career."

Knox raised an eyebrow. "You're guessing."

I was, but I figured—given Monica Purcell's sleazy office tactics—career sabotage had to be it. After all, Breanne Sum-mour had been Monica's first boss. Who better to teach the girl techniques for undermining colleagues? Even Roman had called her Breanne 2.0.

"What else could it be?" I said. "That's it, isn't it? Breanne ruined your career."

"She certainly gave it her best shot."

Bingo! Got his motive. But I still need more. I need specifics . .

"I never heard that particular story, Mr. Knox. Of course Breanne would never tell me something like that, because it wouldn't make her look good. And you and I know that Breanne likes to look good."

Knox smiled—a little warmer this time. "You know, Ms. Cosi, you're very good at this. What you do for free you could do for me at a handsome profit."

"Excuse me?"

"I'm sure you have stories to tell." He leaned toward me, lowered his voice. "You know, secrets. Things you've uncovered while you were hanging around with the likes of Chef Keitel, David Mintzer, and his society cronies. Even Ms. Summour. The *Journal* is willing to pay for the smut you dig up. We have a number of people, just like you, all over this town."

I decided Knox was worse than Hitler's propaganda minister, he was more like the head of the Gestapo, with secret agents ensconced all over the city. I had no intention of becoming one of Randall Knox's goose-stepping stool pigeons, but pretending I *might* take the offer would certainly get me farther with him.

"What you're proposing is . . . intriguing," I finally replied.

"So you'll consider it?"

"Yes, Mr. Knox, I will consider it—"

"Clare! How could you?!" Madame turned on me, looking appropriately outraged, but I could tell from the sparkle in her eye that she was in on it, too.

"Don't worry, Madame," I said, patting her arm. "I'd never, ever reveal a thing about you or our family."

"Oh, well, I guess it will be all right then. There *are* a few people in my social circles I wouldn't mind seeing taken down a peg or two."

Knox laughed—genuinely this time. "Sounds like I'm getting two muck diggers for the price of one!"

I pretended to laugh and elbowed Madame to chuckle ght along with him.

"But, first, Mr. Knox, I'd really like to know more about e woman marrying my child's father. You understand? Vhy don't you tell me about *New York Trends*. Breanne's x-husband mentioned that she started out there. And she lso saw to it that the magazine was closed down. Is that ue?"

"Not only is it true, you may be surprised to know that I ave Breanne Summour her first big break when I put her on e staff of my magazine."

"Your magazine?"

"Aha! Something else you don't know. Yes, *New York rends* was mine. I started it. I built my own staff up from cratch. It took ten hard years."

Knox slid his bottom drawer open and pulled out a bottle f Jack Daniel's. He splashed a shot into an empty paper cof-e cup. Held the bottle up as an offering. Madame and I oth shook it off.

"For a while Breanne worked out fine. Then one day she sked for a short leave of absence. 'Just a few weeks to get my ead together,' she said. I gave her the time off."

Knox lifted the cup to his lips, paused. "The next thing I new, Breanne had started *Trend* by stealing most of my staff ut from under me." He knocked back the whiskey. "Bre-nne became a raving success, the talk of the town. I was not o fortunate. *New York Trends* tanked soon after she pillaged ny staff."

"You must have been enraged." *Maybe even homicidal.*

"I was pissed, all right, Ms. Cosi. And I was out of work. I vrote freelance for a long time, spent some time working in lorida, and then I landed this very glamorous position." He mirked. "The digs are sleazy, I grant you, but the pay is sweet. And you know what's even sweeter? I'll bet you can guess."

"Yes, Mr. Knox, I can guess: the chance to have a little re-enge."

"Just look at it from my point of view. Breanne humili
ated me, and now it's her turn."

"See, now you're making me wonder . . ." I leaned for
ward. "Is that why you hired her look-alike to strip for you a
your birthday party? To humiliate Breanne, if only b
proxy?"

Knox shifted in his desk chair. "Honestly, Ms. Cosi.
don't know if you're serious about working for me, but yo
should be. It can be quite lucrative. As I said, I have feeler
everywhere—"

"Monica Purcell was one of your *feelers*, wasn't she? Wha
do you know about her death?"

"Nothing." Knox met my eyes. "It was a tragedy wha
happened. But I certainly can't shed any light on that mat
ter."

"But you were paying her—to give you dirt on Breanne?

"My arrangement with the late Monica Purcell is a pri
vate matter. Just as our arrangement would be, should yo
decide to work for me."

"Tell me about the stripper then, because she ended u
dead, too."

"Hazel Boggs wasn't the only celebrity look-alike at m
birthday party—although I have to admit she was certainl
the most interesting. She was also willing to learn a thing o
two from me."

"What's that supposed to mean?"

"I gave her a few pointers for her act, that's all, ways to
improve her impression of the grand dame of New York fash
ion. After all, I'd known Breanne for years. Ms. Boggs wa
quite sharp, a quick study."

Randall Knox's obsession with Breanne had to be partly
sexual, I decided. The whole stripper scenario only under
lined that, and it made me wonder something else.

"So, how well did you get to know Ms. Boggs?"

"Very well. I treated her to a few shots of some very goo
scotch, and I discovered that the late exotic dancer and th
fashionista actually shared more than a physical resemblance.'

The man met my eyes, his eyebrow arching suggestively, nd I thought immediately about my philandering ex-usband.

Oh, God, Matt . . . what did you do?

My mind raced back to that night on Hudson Street. I never got the impression that he and Hazel had met before, but then she was a professional, and Matt was well-practiced n denial where one-night stands were concerned.

I stood up, placed my hands on his desk. "I'm getting ired of this game, Mr. Knox. What exactly are you trying to ay? Put your cards on the table."

"I intend to—in Monday's edition of the *Journal*. Two days after Breanne's society wedding, you'll have all the answers you like in headlines, photos, and newsprint. Until then, this file stays closed."

"You're bluffing."

"Hardly. And feel free to pass that on to Ms. Summour. Tell that designer-draped python that a near-fatal mugging is a walk in the park compared to what I have in store for her." Knox stood, too, held my eyes. "I promise you, Ms. Cosi, when the *Journal* goes to press in the wee hours of Monday morning, Breanne Summour will *wish* she were dead."

The intercom buzzed, cutting the tension in the room. Knox punched the button. "Yes!"

"Your five o'clock appointment's arrived."

Knox straightened his bright-red tie, and I blanched, thinking of the fresh blood I'd seen dripping down Breanne's ivory shoulder.

"Duty calls," Knox said. "You can find your own way out."

Dismissed, we left the man's office. But the visit wasn't over yet. As we walked toward the reception area, I noticed a heavyset, middle-aged woman approaching from the opposite direction. She had a rosy complexion, wore attractive auburn highlights in her short cocoa-brown hair, and was stylishly dressed in a loose black pantsuit.

Her mood seemed buoyant, but when she spied Madame,

her face fell. As the two women passed each other, they nodded a curt greeting. Then the heavier woman hastily moved on.

"Madame, do you know that woman?" I whispered. "Because she sure seems to know you."

Madame nodded. "That's Miriam Perry of Perry Realty."

"Chef Neville Perry's mother? The woman who lost a small fortune when Breanne published an exposé on Neville's restaurant?"

"Yes."

"Okay, spill. How do you know her?"

"Miriam set her sights on the Blend a few years ago. She was trying to broker a deal in the name of a corporate giant who coveted our Hudson Street address."

"She was trying to buy the Blend out from under you?"

Madame nodded. "She wanted to turn my beloved coffee-house into a fast-food franchise."

"Which one?"

"Funky Town Fried Chicken." Madame shuddered. "I rebuffed her, of course, told Mrs. Perry that she was destroying the character of the neighborhood with her real estate deals. I told her that I wasn't going to stand by and let her turn Greenwich Village's historic district into a cheap facsimile of a suburban strip mall."

I blew out air, my gaze returning to the heavyset Mrs. Perry. She walked right to the corner office where Randall Knox stood waiting for her. They greeted each other like old friends.

"Thank you, Randy, for *everything*," Miriam Perry gushed, air kissing the diminutive Knox.

"The pleasure's mine." Knox led the woman into his den. While Mrs. Perry settled in, they talked and laughed. Then the two lifted paper cups—presumably filled with whiskey shots.

"I'll drink to that," Mrs. Perry said before Knox moved to close his office door.

I turned to Madame. "Don't you find it suspicious that

Mrs. Perry and her buddy Randy are toasting each other the same afternoon Breanne was attacked and nearly killed?"

"I do, indeed, my dear."

We took the elevator down to Eighth Avenue. The sidewalks were jammed with commuters, traffic was snarled, car horns were honking. The sun had disappeared, taking the day's brightness with it, and above the skyscrapers, storm clouds were painting my city the color of cemetery stone.

Madame flagged down a cab, and we climbed into the backseat. As the driver took off, she turned to me.

"It seems there's much more to this case than one angry ex-husband."

I nodded. "Neville Perry and his mother, Randall Knox and his vendetta, Monica Purcell and her deal to dish dirt on her own boss. And who knows what else is out there . . ."

"Lots of threads," Madame said.

"And they're tangled together worse than the Gordian knot."

"Maybe there's a single strand you can pull that will unravel the whole thing."

"Maybe," I said, channeling Mike Quinn. "But *maybe* isn't going to solve this case."

Twenty-Nine

WHILE the evening rush washed over Manhattan, the postwork crush swept through the Village Blend. Today the crowd was literally spilling out the front door. Feeling depleted and defeated, I waded through the mob, the rich earthy scents of freshly roasted coffee beans leading me toward the espresso bar like a lurching zombie.

"Caffeine . . . must have caffeine."

"Hey, Clare!" Tucker Burton called. "What's up?"

"Hit me twice, Tuck. I need it bad."

"You got it, sweetie."

It was my day off, but I stepped around the marble counter anyway to check on the state of the shop. Tucker—my lanky floppy-haired assistant manager—was in charge today, and we briefly chatted about the employees, the stock, and the machinery. The normalcy of it all felt reassuring, along with the news that everything in my house was under control.

Since my people were veterans at dealing with a postwork rush, I let Tuck shoo me away. Picking up my double espresso, I headed across the crowded room to a just-vacated café table near the fireplace.

The Pisco Sour or Randall Knox (or both) had given me a slight headache, but the warmth of my double espresso was starting to cut through the bewildering fog of alcohol and vitriol. As my taste buds soaked up the nutty, caramelized flavors, my wedged platform sandals began tapping to the electronic drum machines of Tucker's retro eighties mix.

Tuck must be psychic, I decided, because the titles playing over the Blend's speakers were like a sound track to the events of my week: New Order's "Blue Monday" followed by Boy George's "Do You Really Want to Hurt Me," the Eurythmics' "Would I Lie to You," and Billy Idol's "White Wedding."

"Okay," I muttered, "if Cher comes on next with her eighties retread of 'Bang, Bang, My Baby Shot Me Down,' I'm going to lose it."

But the next song I heard didn't come from the Blend's audio speakers. It came from my handbag. I pulled out my cell and silenced the ringtone, then checked the display and smiled.

"Hi, Mike. I knew you'd call when you had the chance."

"Are you okay, sweetheart? Lori Soles just told me you witnessed a mugging today—in a restaurant bathroom. Is that right?"

"I'm fine, but it was an attempted murder not a mugging . . ."

I filled Quinn in on the details, along with my conversation at the *Journal* with Randall Knox and the little toast I spotted him sharing with Neville Perry's mother. When I finished, Quinn remained silent for a few seconds.

"Knox sounds wrong, Clare. He has a strong motive to be involved with a revenge scheme. So does Mrs. Perry. But you need—"

"Evidence—I know! Have you gotten anything out of Stuart Winslow yet? Maybe they're all working together."

"Sorry, sweetheart. I don't have good news for you on Winslow."

I groaned, forecasting the need for another *doppio* espresso. *Rapidamente.* "Tell me."

"When we got him down to the Sixth, he started talking without a lawyer—ranting, mostly. But he wouldn't admit to anything. After a few hours of questioning, he finally lawyered up and clammed up."

"Where does that leave us?"

"I can tell you where it leaves him. Free as a bird. He's on his way to being arraigned right now. He should be out on bail very soon."

"Oh no, Mike. Isn't there any way to hold him? Charge him with attempted murder?"

"We searched his apartment, but that single bottle of Oxy-Contin that he handed you was the only narcotic we found."

"What about the other pills he had? I saw them!"

"Other than a little more OxyContin, we found zip. We raided his closet, but the only items in there were the kinds of supplements and herbal products you'd find in any health food store. He must have his dirty stash somewhere else, most likely under another name. We couldn't find it in his residence, and he wouldn't talk. So the only charge that stuck to him was one count of intent to distribute an illegal substance."

"No murder weapon, either? No gun."

"No weapons of any kind in his apartment."

"What about all the other things he's guilty of?"

"The DA's office can't charge Winslow for the robbery in Queens, or Monica Purcell's overdose, or attempted murder of his ex-wife, because he wouldn't admit to any of those things, and there's no evidence that directly connects him."

"And the Rxglobal Web site?"

"That's an angle we're working with the DEA, but that will take time. No judge will hold him without bail based on the evidence against him right now. And your testimony against him is just about the only thing we've got to even make the first charge stick. The prosecutor's office wasn't even comfortable charging him with conspiracy to commit robbery."

"But he agreed on the wire! We have it on tape!"

"The rings were never actually stolen, and he never accepted them from you, just agreed to let you steal them. The defense will cry entrapment. It's not enough for the prosecutor to go forward, Clare."

I rubbed my forehead, tried to figure out a next step.

Winslow couldn't have been the mugger at the restaurant," reasoned aloud, "because he was still in custody then. But if e's going to be free soon, he might try to hurt Breanne him-elf."

"Yeah, I know."

"I'll try to reach Breanne and warn her. I'll try Matt again, oo, but he's been unreachable for hours."

"Why?"

I sighed. "It's too long a story to explain now."

"Fine, but you better suggest to Breanne that she hire a odyguard."

"I will."

We signed off, and I rang Breanne. By now, she was out of he ER and back in her Sutton Place apartment—no hairline racture, no damage to her vocal chords. She was just bruised, ore, and shaken. Before I could ask her about Randall Knox, he asked me about Matt.

"Have you heard from him yet, Clare?"

Bree's typical cool, clipped tone was gone. Her voice ounded vulnerable and human. For the first time since Matt ad announced their engagement, Breanne Summour sounded ike a woman in love.

"I'm sorry," I said gently, "he hasn't come back yet. I can't each him on his cell, either."

"Neither can I. You'll let me know when he shows, won't ou?"

"Of course."

I told Breanne about my visit to Knox's office, including he Miriam Perry appearance. I also warned her about gossip oy's declaration that he'd be publishing a scandalous story n Monday, something that included an angle on the strip-er Hazel Boggs.

"Whatever this story is, he promises it's going to upset ou a great deal. So brace yourself."

Breanne had little to say after that, just thanked me for nforming her. Finally, I told her about her ex-husband being eleased on bail.

". . . and since Matt isn't there with you, Mike Quinn strongly suggests you hire a bodyguard."

"I already have," she said. "He's outside my apartment door right now."

It's about time. "Okay, Breanne, just make sure you show him a photo of your ex-husband, so he can stop the man the moment he comes near you. Would you do that?"

"Good idea, Clare. I'll do that right now."

I hung up, went back to the bar for another double shot and sat back down near the fireplace to continue thinking things through. When the bell jangled over the door a few minutes later, I glance up and noticed an African American woman walking in.

"Janelle!" I waved her over.

Janelle Babcock waved back and crossed the wood plank floor, her ample hips smoothly negotiating the crowded café tables.

"Espresso?" I asked as she sat down across from me. "Latte?"

"No, thanks, Clare." She smiled.

Like the city she hailed from, Janelle had a smile that was warm and easy. Her flawless skin was the shade of a lightly creamed cup of Sumatra, and her features were Creole, not surprising since she'd grown up in New Orleans. She'd learned French there, too, along with the building blocks of French cooking, which is what led her to her first professional bakery job and eventually to a plane ticket to Paris, where she'd studied at the Cordon Bleu.

"I've got to get back to my kitchen," she said. "I just came to drop off some more samples . . ."

Beaming with pride, she pulled three white bakery boxes out of her large tote bag and set them on the marble-topped café table between us. We glanced at each other in silence, then I peeked into the first box with nearly infantile excitement.

"The *anginetti*! Oh my God, Janelle, they look spectacular! What did you do with them since the last batch?"

"I adjusted the ingredients slightly, and instead of making the ring with a small rope of dough, I used a pastry bag. Now each cookie ring is made out of eight little mounds that touch. See . . ." She pointed to the delicate cookie. "During the baking, the small mounds create a single ring that looks just like a miniature coffee cake."

"The white glaze and nonpareils really complete the effect." I picked up one of the tiny cookies and examined it. "Amazing. It's like a miniature work of art, but then all of your samples have been."

"Thanks, Clare. You always say the sweetest things. You know, for fun, I pulled out my food coloring and made a few *anginetti* with purple, green, and gold glaze. See . . ."

She handed me one of the alternate samples.

"Oh my God! It looks just like a tiny king cake! You could sell these for Mardis Gras parties next year!"

"That's what I was thinking. If I can figure out a few more novelty cookies, I could even set up a mail-order business online. But I really need more catering clients in New York first." She squeezed my arm. "I can't thank you enough for getting me this job on your ex-husband's wedding. My whole family's waiting for *Trend* to come out so they can see my name in the caption under our tablescape." She sighed and smiled. "Imagine, my little pastries showcased around Nunzio's *Lover's Spring*, in the Metropolitan Museum of Art!"

My phone rang again. "Excuse me, Janelle. This shouldn't take long." I pulled out the cell, hoping it was Matt. (I'd left him five messages by now.) But I didn't recognize the number.

"Hello?"

"Clare? Clare Cosi?"

The voice was deep and male, betrayed an Italian accent, and was (regrettably) recognizable.

"Yes. This is Nunzio, right?"

Janelle's big brown eyes widened. "Nunzio!" she whispered. "He's on the phone with you now?"

I nodded.

"Omigawd!" Janelle bounced up and down. "Nunzio! Omigawd!"

"*Si, bella . . .*" The Italian sculptor's voice was low and silky, like my cat Java's purr. Unfortunately, a few hits of Pounce treats weren't going to satisfy this smooth-coated predator. "Breanne, she tells me you are coming to see me this evening? She says you are willing to discuss my concerns about my *Lover's Spring*. You do still wish for me to lend you my beautiful fountain, *si*, Clare?"

"Yes." I cleared my throat. "Breanne told me about your, uh . . . situation." (I'd almost said *proposition*—only it wouldn't have been much of a slip.)

Glancing at Janelle, I tried to decide what to do. She was grinning at me, but that was only because she hadn't heard that Nunzio was balking on his deal to lend us his fountain, and unless I could find "some way" to change the man's mind (in his hotel room, no less), Breanne was dumping our tablescape out of *Trend*.

"I was wondering, *bella*, what you are drinking when you come to see me. Is champagne to your liking?"

"I, uh—"

God, it was so humiliating being put in this position, but if I hung up on the guy now, without even trying to persuade him, I'd feel far worse. The Village Blend didn't need a *Trend* splash page, but Janelle did. I had to do this, I had to try to persuade the man to change his mind, or I couldn't live with myself.

"Yes," I told Nunzio through gritted teeth, "I like champagne."

"*Bene*. My room number is 5301. See you soon, *bella*, eh?"

I checked my watch. "Right. Soon."

"*Ciao.*"

He hung up, and I hung my head.

"Hey, girlfriend, you look upset? Anything wrong?"

I massaged my eyes. "Let's just say this has been a very long day—and it's about to get a whole lot longer."

~~~~~~~~~~~~~~~~~~~~~~~~~~~~~~~~~~~~~~

THIRTY

THE five-star Mandarin Oriental Hotel occupied 248 rooms
in nearly twenty floors of the Time Warner Center's north
tower. Nunzio's two-room suite featured Italian-made bed
linens, a fully stocked private bar, a marble bath with a flat-
panel TV, and a soaking tub with a picture-window view.

If I hadn't been in a relationship, I *might* have considered
ending the night with the sculpted Italian sculptor (if only
to have the transcendent experience of soaking in a tub with a
bird's-eye view of Central Park). But I was in a relationship—
with a man I cared very much about—so sleeping with Nunzio was out of the question, which meant I had to outwit this
guy or I was screwed (a vulgar term, I grant you, but all too
apropos, considering Nunzio's implied agenda).

The moment I stepped out of my cab, the skies opened
up. Everything the storm clouds had been carrying for the
past few hours sloshed out like an overfilled fountain—and
came down all over me.

Perfect.

I hurried the few steps from the curb to the entrance of
the glass-wrapped tower's West Sixtieth Street entrance, but
I got plenty wet anyway. I headed directly to the elevators,
ascended to the fifty-third floor, took a resolute breath, and
knocked on the door of Nunzio's hotel suite.

"*Ciao, bella.*"

His broad features were as forceful as I remembered, h
dark eyes as bedroomy, too, like twin bottomless pools o
spiked cocoa. His wavy hair was still caught in its rakish blac
ponytail, but he'd exchanged his Armani suit for brown slack
and a form-fitting sweater the subdued yellow shade of Ita
ian polenta.

"Hello," I said after an unfortunate moment in which m
tongue failed to work. "I'm here . . . as you can see."

Nunzio must have taken the "see" part as some kind of ir
vitation, because he leaned against the doorjamb and studie
me, his artist's gaze sweeping my body a lot less subtly tha
it had in Breanne's office. I wasn't dripping wet, but m
pearl-pink wrap dress wasn't exactly dry, either. His gaze ap
peared to smolder as it lingered on certain areas. I felt m
cheeks warming, but I refused to look down at the state o
my thin, silk, embarrassingly damp garment.

"Come," he finally said, waving me in.

The suite was tastefully appointed: an odd blend of 1940
Hong Kong and sleek, efficient, generic modern hotel. Th
sitting room held delicate fine-grained tables of Asian cherr
wood, original Chinese artwork, plush sofas in forest green
and a state-of-the-art entertainment system. The rug an
walls were a neutral cream, but the decor wasn't really th
point. Nothing in the room could hold a candle to the expan
sive floor-to-ceiling views of Central Park and the Manhatta
skyline, its million golden windows shining through the ur
ban night like earth-anchored stars.

Through an open door, I glimpsed the suite's bedroom
The view was just as spectacular in there. With the tabl
lamps turned low, the drapes fully opened, and the Fili D'or
linens crisply waiting, I knew sleeping with a man in a plac
like this would feel like making love on a cloud in heaver
But then I thought of all those mortal girls pursued b
Greek deities and shivered; few of them came to good ends.

Nunzio closed the front door and locked it, then crosse
to a bucket of icing champagne. "Go into my bedroom, *bella*
and take off your clothes."

Every muscle in my body froze. I'd expected to have at least a little wiggle room to talk this man out of his feudal bargain. But if he was going to take that attitude, I had no choice. With a sigh, I turned around and headed for the front door.

"Where are you going?!"

"I'm not here to take demands, Nunzio."

He threw up his hands. "Your clothes and shoes are wet. There is a robe in the bath. Hang your dress over the towel warmer, and it will dry." Nunzio popped the champagne and began to pour. "I will not touch you, Clare, unless you wish it." He met my eyes. "Cross my heart."

I gritted my teeth, my hand on the doorknob, and glanced down at my wet dress. It wasn't obscene or anything, but the clinging silk wasn't exactly modest, either.

"Fine."

I moved into the bathroom, ignored the damn marble tub with its damn Central Park view, and removed my damn damp dress. The towel warmer was on, and I hung the silk garment over the dry towel already on it. I took off my platform sandals, too, and wrapped the long, fluffy terry robe round me. My hair was wet, so I used the blow dryer on the counter to fluff it up. With another fortifying breath, I moved back out into the sitting room.

Nunzio was waiting with the poured champagne. He handed me a flute. "To Breanne and her groom," he said, raising his glass to mine.

I drank to that (hoping the groom had at least *called* his bride by now) and tried not to enjoy the dry tickle of costly bubbles on my palate. Then I started my rehearsed speech.

"Nunzio, listen to me, okay? Despite what this looks like—" I gesture to my robe and bare feet. "I'm not here to trade my body for your fountain."

He laughed. "*Lover's Spring* is not on the auction block, *ella*. I was going to *lend* it to Breanne for her wedding, not give it away."

"Well, I'm not on the auction block, either. If you have

legitimate concerns, I'm willing to discuss them, allay any worries about the way it will be displayed—"

"It's not that," he said, moving to sit on one of the overstuffed sofas. "I have never shown the piece here in America." He shook his head, gesturing to the muted flat-panel TV where an Italian channel was playing highlights of a soccer match. "I don't know if Americans will be able to appreciate my art."

"Why? Because we play baseball instead of soccer?"

"Your culture is . . ." He shook his head. "Loud. Violent *Scusa*, but I find it . . . how you say? *Volgare*."

"Vulgar? Americans are vulgar? Oh, really? The country that gave birth to Ben Franklin, Mark Twain, Billie Holiday, Ira Gershwin, the Wright brothers, Frank Lloyd Wright, F. Scott Fitzgerald, Jackson Pollock, and Jacqueline Onassis is vulgar? I see. Then I suppose you're not expecting to distribute your new jewelry line here—one of the most lucrative markets on the planet? If we're too vulgar to appreciate your genius sculpture, then I guess we're too vulgar to pay for your amazing rings and necklaces, too, is that right?"

He frowned. "How do you know about my new jewelry line?"

"I was in Breanne's office during most of your meeting. overheard her mention it."

Nunzio nodded, stretched his free arm across the back of the sofa. "I remember that meeting, too, *bella*. I remember the look on your face when I touched your hand. Come sit beside me."

Nope, not gonna work. "I'm only here to persuade you to go through with your promise."

"*Si*. That is why you are here. I agree." He sipped his champagne and smiled. "To persuade me."

"Good!" I crossed to where I'd dropped my tote bag. "Then try these . . ."

I pulled Janelle's three bakery boxes out of the damp bag. Luckily, the thick tote had shielded the boxes from getting the least bit wet. "You heard about Hurricane Katrina's damage to New Orleans, right?"

"Katrina?" His dark eyebrows came together in confusion. "*Si.* I heard of this tragedy. But why—"

"The woman who made these amazing confections came to New York after she lost her job in a restaurant that was destroyed by Katrina. For a few years, she worked as the pastry chef at Solange, a highly acclaimed New York restaurant. But the place closed last fall after the owner died, so she took a job with a specialty cake baker. She worked two shifts a day to earn the money to quit after a few months and start her own company. These pastries, for Breanne's wedding, were baked by her new little company. Here, try an *anginetti* . . ."

"This is an *anginetti*?" He examined the tiny work of art.

"Amazing isn't it?"

Typically, Italian desserts were delicious to eat but presented in unassuming forms, unlike the polished precision of French cuisine. Italian bakers favored simple presentations, using things like candied fruit and nuts, powdered sugar, or a light glaze to finish a cake or tart. "The perfect is the enemy of the good." That's how my grandmother used to put it. (And she probably would have pointed out: *"What good is Monica's perfect body doing her in the morgue?"*)

I did understand wanting to be perfect. I used to strive for perfection in everything—my coffee, my marriage, myself. But life was naturally messy, and perfection required far too much ruthlessness. Being human was better. Humans made mistakes and moved on. Like Nonna tried to tell me years ago: being good was better than being perfect.

Still . . . looking at Janelle's beautifully shaped and decorated *anginetti*, I had to admit that she'd done a near-perfect job on reinventing the rustic Italian cookie, getting it all dressed up for its Manhattan debut.

"I enjoyed these cookies at family weddings when I was a little girl. The ring shape represents the wedding bands. But Janelle recast the idea of a single rope of dough. See how she sculpted each tiny cookie to look like a coffee cake ring?"

"*Si.* Very clever."

I sampled a bite for myself. The texture was tender and buttery, the glaze of icing a sophisticated kiss of lemon flavor.

"Janelle's using Meyer lemons. They have less acidity than other varieties. And the sculpting of the *anginetti* into a tiny coffee cake shape goes with our primary theme for the dessert display: Saloma Sunrise."

"Saloma?" Nunzio smiled. "My little hometown?"

"And Ovid's, too, right?"

He nodded, clearly happy that I'd done my research.

"We worked with the metric volume of liquid that your fountain holds and determined the perfect amounts of peach nectar and cherry juice to be added to the Prosecco in order to create a Bellini that will mimic the romantic golden orange color of a Saloma dawn. The wedding is at sunset, but the coffee and dessert station is looking to our bride and groom's future, to their first sunrise as a married couple. So the primary pastry theme is breakfast."

"Breakfast?" Nunzio frowned. "What? Eggs and bread?"

"No, no, no . . . it's just a *theme*. Look . . ." I opened the second box. It was filled with samples of cookies shaped and baked with a slight egg wash to look exactly like miniature croissants. "Each cookie carries a different flavor experience. The Grand Marnier croissant cookie is accentuated with orange rind, the Frangelico with finely powdered hazelnuts and the Kahlua with a premium coffee infusion from Panama Esmeralda Especial geisha coffee trees—what we call the champagne of the coffee world."

Nunzio sampled each one, sipping champagne between bites of the tiny, sculpted pastries. *"Delizioso!"*

"Now try Janelle's version of *orange à l'orange*."

Nunzio nodded, picked up one of the delicate confections that resembled a tiny half orange.

"Janelle dyes and shapes marzipan, fashioning it to resemble the shell of an orange rind. She then cooks oranges in a simple syrup, incorporates slivers of their own candied skin, and fills the marzipan shell."

"Mmmmmm. *Buonissimo.*"

"Because it's marzipan, you'll taste a creamy hint of sweet almond to counterbalance the tangy-sweet yet slightly tart citrus filling. She's imported blood oranges from Sicily just for the wedding. She's doing the same thing with Key limes, which have a milder level of acidity.

"Our secondary theme is tied directly to your *Lover's Spring* fountain. Since each tier in the gold-plated fountain is sculpted with reliefs that tell the stories of great lovers through time, we attached pastries to each tier.

"For Adam and Eve, we have Forbidden Fruit Cakes, which are not actually fruitcake but mini–sponge cakes soaked with the grapefruit-orange-honey flavors of the cognac-based Forbidden Fruit liqueur.

"For Antony and Cleopatra, we have stuffed caramel walnuts, a recipe translated from hieroglyphics and said to have been used by Cleopatra to fortify her lovers."

"Ah!" Nunzio perked right up on that story. "Do you have any of those?" He began looking in all three boxes.

"Sorry, no sale."

"Oh, too bad." He threw me a wink.

I cleared my throat. "I'll bet you can guess what we're doing for Romeo and Juliet."

Nunzio laughed. *"Baci di Romeo e Baci di Giulietta!"*

I smiled and nodded. Romeo's Kisses were small almond-flavored cookies, sandwiched together in pairs with chocolate filling. Juliet's Kisses were the same, only the cookies were chocolate.

"For Romeo's Kisses, Janelle is replacing the almonds with pistachios, and for the filling, using her favorite recipe for chocolate ganache. For Juliet's Kisses, she's staying with the chocolate-flavored cookie, but for the filling she's using vanilla pastry cream infused with raspberry—since, of course, chocolate and raspberry are a wonderful pairing. We have a latte that uses that same flavor profile at my coffeehouse."

Nunzio tasted Janelle's twists on the old Verona favorites. He nodded and smiled. "She is very good, Clare. An *artista*."

"I was hoping you'd say that. But as good as she is, her

field is highly competitive. Breaking out of the pack and getting noticed is very difficult in this town—in any profession. That's why Breanne's wedding is so important for Pastries by Janelle, and that's why your fountain is so important. Without it as the centerpiece of our display, *Trend* magazine won't photograph it. Janelle Babcock will have lost a great opportunity for exposure."

"Your friend, she is quite talented. And these treats are *delizioso*. But I think . . . listening to you speak so passionately for her, it makes me want a taste of something else even more . . ."

He stepped closer. I stepped back.

"I'd like you to agree to lending us the fountain."

"We both want something then? I think we can both get it, don't you? A nice little transaction?"

"My virtue's not on the bargaining table."

He snorted, genuinely amused. "Keep your virtue, by all means. I only desire your company for the evening. Is that so terrible?"

I closed my eyes. *It would be easy to give in, so easy . . .*

My attraction to Nunzio wasn't some fantasy on his part. I was in awe of his talent, and the artist himself was magnetic. But if the situation were reversed, if Mike slept with some woman in a casual one-night stand, I'd be devastated, and I'd begin to doubt him, especially after what I'd been through with my ex-husband.

Mike's own broken marriage was still a fresh wound. The pain of his wife's cheating had tortured him for years. I cared too much about the man to risk damaging what we had for a fleeting few hours of fantasy love; and that's what it would be: the facsimile of something real.

Nunzio certainly had a girlfriend or even a wife back in Italy. I was a momentary trifle, an *amuse-gueule* during a brief business trip. What I had with Mike wasn't an illusion. The view was closer to earth in Alphabet City, but so was the affection: real, well-rooted, and just starting to grow. I wasn't willing to trade that for anything.

So what *else* did I have to trade that Nunzio wanted? *Nothing.* But I could trade on something. His reputation. *That's what Otto Visser was trying to tell me today; the key to Nunzio was his ego!*

I walked to the floor-to-ceiling windows and pointed down fifty-plus floors. "Tell me something, Nunzio; you've seen the monument of Christopher Columbus at the center of the traffic circle, right?"

The sculptor smirked. "That is why they call it Columbus Circle, no?"

"Yes, but did you know that statue of your countryman is the point at which all distances to and from New York City are geographically measured?"

Nunzio's eyebrows rose. "Is that so?"

He stepped up behind me. He wasn't touching me, but he was standing so close I could feel the heat of his body. I swallowed uneasily, continued my little speech.

"The Metropolitan Museum is like that for America—the place from which art is measured—the most important museum of art in the country. For your work to be seen and photographed inside the Met, among the other great masters, that would really be something, wouldn't it?"

"I have considered this. But I have also decided that it is still not a good enough bargain. I have had second thoughts on what was agreed to."

"What are you taking about?"

"My deal with Breanne Summour. She is publishing the big profile on me and my work and my new jewelry line. And I give her the wedding rings in trade. Lending *Lover's Spring* was part of this deal. But now I think this is too much to allow without further payment. I think I am owed something more . . ."

"Wait, back up. You're telling me that Breanne bartered editorial space in her magazine in exchange for *free* wedding bands from you?"

Nunzio sighed. "I thought you knew this. I am soon opening boutiques in Rome, Paris, London, Tokyo, Beverly

Hills, and on New York's Fifth Avenue. *Trend* will feature me
and my work and also showcase the rings I designed for Bre
anne's wedding. Next season, I will be selling that same ring
design in my stores." He glanced down at me and smirked
"Place your orders now."

"Oh, my God."

"*Volagare, si?* But I need the income. As you can see . . ."
He laughed. "I do enjoy living high."

"Yeah . . ." I felt a little dizzy all of a sudden. "Fifty-three
floors is awfully high, all right."

But it was this revelation that had thrown me off balance
Matt often told me about wonderful items Breanne received
from her designer or artist friends. But he—and I—assumed
these were gifts, freely given. I had no idea the woman was
making backroom deals. Now I wondered: Could one of
those deals have backfired on her? Could someone have felt
cheated? Cheated enough to want her dead?

"She is doing this with others, Clare," Nunzio went on. "I
am surprised you did not know. The flowers, the cake, her
gown—Breanne told me all of this. I was part of a group
part of her grand plan. She is using her position to get many
goods and services gratis for her wedding."

"I didn't know."

"That woman dresses like aristocracy, but she acts like a
peasant in the way she wheels and deals and threatens. You
know, my grandfather had a saying: 'For the quiet falcon, her
feathers are enough. It is the braying donkey who needs the
silk shawl.'"

"The braying donkey . . ."

A cartoon animal image entered my mind and fixed itself
there. I saw Breanne as a donkey, Stuart Winslow riding her
ranting about how she'd struggled financially when she'd
started out in New York. I hadn't thought much about that
stuff when Winslow had spewed it. He was high at the time,
and Breanne's public bio, online and elsewhere, clearly stated
that she'd come from money. It even included a long list
of her upper-class associations. But now I wondered . . .

Nunzio's revelation about backroom deals certainly didn't add up to a woman with a typical patrician upbringing.

"My sweet one, let's you and I not speak of these things any longer . . ." Nunzio had switched languages. He was now cooing to me entirely in Italian. "You are here. I am here. I know you will enjoy my touch."

He'd been standing close; now he stepped even closer. I felt the front of his legs brushing the back of my robe, and then his muscular forearm was snaking around my waist, his lips were pressing against my neck.

"Don't do that," I said in plain English.

"Perhaps we can make a simple little trade of our own, *bella*? You enjoyed my touch the other day. You would enjoy feeling my hands on more of your body, no?"

"No!" I broke away, stepped clear.

Nunzio folded his arms, looked down at me, his patience obviously wearing thin. "But you want the fountain, *si*? And what would I get in return?"

"The satisfaction of knowing you were displayed at the Met!"

"I'd like something a little more satisfying tonight, and I think you would, too?"

He stepped toward me again. I backed away—a lot farther this time. I strode all the way to the bathroom, locked the door, got dressed in my dried-out clothes and shoes, and headed for the suite's front door.

I paused in the sitting room to collect my tote bag. Nunzio was back on his sofa. I met the man's eyes.

"I'm sorry you won't change your mind."

He shrugged. "Likewise."

I was about to turn and go when I realized I had one last card to play, a piece of information Otto had given me.

"I'm sorry, Nunzio. Then you leave me no choice. I'll have to go to Tio."

"Tio?"

"Yes, the up-and-coming Spanish sculptor. You've heard of him, right? Well, his famous *Trellis* is in town, an amazing work. He begged Breanne to use it for her wedding, but she'd already committed to displaying your sculpture. Janelle will be disappointed. But I think we can make adjustments in our tablescape to highlight his piece instead." I turned and headed for the door. "He'll certainly be thrilled to see his sculpture displayed at the Met—and prominently featured in the same issue of *Trend* where you're profiled—"

"No!"

"Sorry." I reached for the door handle. "I really have to get going."

"Wait!" Nunzio was on his feet. "Wait, *signorina*! Wait, wait, wait!"

Ten minutes later, I was downstairs, waiting for the doorman to hail me a taxi. *Lover's Spring* wasn't very large—just a tabletop fountain—but it was gold-plated and heavy. The sculpture was disassembled into a single base with nesting bowls, all packed expertly into an easy-to-handle wheeled suitcase.

Afraid the sculptor would change his mind, I insisted on taking it right up to the Metropolitan. I invited Nunzio to come with me, but he waved me off.

"My sculpture is well insured," he said as we stood on the sidewalk, watching the doorman and taxi driver load the Pullman into the trunk. "Of course, Clare, should you lose it, you *will* owe me something. And then, *bella*, I *won't* take no for an answer."

Nunzio bent to kiss me on the lips. I turned my head, giving him my cheek instead. He laughed then kissed the other cheek, as well.

Ciao, bella.

"Yeah, pal," I muttered as I firmly shut my cab door. "*Arrivederci* to you, too."

should have been relieved the second my cab door closed,
ut I held my breath all the way along Central Park South.
When we reached the horse-drawn carriages across the street
rom the Plaza, I finally exhaled. The glittering glass towers
f the Time Warner Center had faded from view at last, and
was home free.

Well, almost. Given Nunzio's warning, my virtue wouldn't
e fully secure until I delivered his priceless fountain to the
Met.

I massaged my temples, trying to release the built-up
ension. After everything I'd gone through, I certainly hoped
here'd still *be* a wedding Saturday. I had no doubt Breanne
vould show, wearing her gorgeous Fen gown. The only wild
ard now was the groom.

A sweet tune played in the cab as we turned uptown on
Madison: "Edelweiss," my favorite song from my favorite
nusical. I answered my cell, but the melodic ringtone was a
ar cry from the state of the voice on the other end of the line:
Mom! Thank goodness! You've got to help!"

"Joy! Are you all right?"

"It's Dad. He's back, and—wait a minute." I heard a
truggle, and Joy cried out. "No, Dad, don't—"

A loud crash sounded, followed by Joy getting back on

the line. "I hope you weren't too fond of that Chippendale end table."

"What the heck is going on down there?!"

"Dad's back, and he's crazy drunk. He's yelling about canceling the wedding and cursing in, like, six languages."

"Are you alone?"

"Koa's here, but he has to leave soon. So do I, Mom. I'm meeting some old friends from culinary school. I have to be in the East Village in, like, ten minutes—"

"Joy, can't you stick around a little longer? I have to drop Nunzio's fountain off at the Met. I can be home in an hour."

I heard another crash.

"Chill out, dude!" Koa cried.

Matt replied with a particularly vile Italian obscenity.

"Please, Mom! Come *now*! You're the only person who can handle Dad!"

I gritted my teeth. "On my way."

I redirected the cabdriver, who made a right on Sixty-fifth, shot over to Park, and raced downtown. Traffic wasn't too bad, and I was back at the Blend in under twenty minutes. The cabdriver lifted the heavy fountain out of the trunk, and I pulled the wheeled suitcase into the back stairwell, made sure the doorway was firmly locked, and climbed the steps to the apartment above the Blend.

There was no sign of Matt or Joy. I found Koa Waipuna alone, slumped on the couch in a rumpled jacket. The collar of his shirt was open, and his face was flushed, the odors of beer and Jägermeister wafting around him like a fog of hops and black licorice.

"Koa? Where is everybody?"

"Joy headed out to meet her friends," Koa said. "Matt's in the bathroom. I finally convinced him to take a shower. Sober up a little."

"You look like you could use a bit of sobering, too." I sat down beside the big Hawaiian.

"I couldn't let the dude drink alone. That's like . . . pathetic."

Koa sat up and pulled the cord off his ponytail. He shook his head until his long black hair flowed like an obsidian waterfall around his huge shoulders.

"What happened?"

"After the scene in the restaurant, me, Javier Lozado, and his buddy Hector—"

"Hector Pena?" I asked, recalling the sad-faced man who was mourning his daughter.

"That's him. We took off after Matt, but he was long gone by the time we hit the sidewalk. We all split up." Koa rubbed his bleary eyes. "I found Matt about an hour later, at a bar he took me to the last time I was in town. We started drinking, and he told me his troubles. I called Javier's cell, and he met us, helped me get Matt back here."

I'd only just met Javier. But I remembered him well (most women probably would). The retro south-of-the-border machismo thing was hard to forget, but it was his dashing, good-natured aura that impressed me most.

"Where's Javier now?" I asked. "I should thank him, too."

"He went off to find Hector, who's still missing," Koa replied. "Javier was worried about finding the man, the state he's in. But until he left, he was great. He spoke to Matt a long time in Spanish, as if they were brothers. It was like all that crap over Louisa never happened."

"Louisa? That one's a new name. Who's Louisa?"

From his expression, I could tell Koa regretted his schnapps-loosened tongue. "Oh, just some girl down in Colombia. I don't even know her last name. Javier was dating her—or was he engaged to her? I forget. Anyway, the way Matt tells the story, she and Javier had a big fight, and he stormed off, leaving the girl hanging for weeks. Louisa didn't know whether Javier was ever coming back, so Matt tried to comfort her, and they ended up in bed."

I rolled my eyes. "Matt's a cad, but at least he's true to form."

"What do you mean?"

"He loves women, that's what I mean. With Matt, sex

never implied love or commitment, just a way to express a fleeting feeling. Did Javier ever want his girl back?"

"You know men." Koa grunted. "Women, too, for that matter. Louisa threw it up in Javier's face that she slept with his friend, and Javier dropped a rock. He and Matt ended up rolling around in the street." Koa shrugged. "But they got over it. They're pretty close now, those two. You should have seen them tonight."

Koa glanced at his watch. "I've got to go, Clare. I'm sorry—"

"No, don't worry. I don't hear any breaking glass upstairs. Matt's probably in bed already, sleeping it off."

I said good night to Koa, then went to check on Matt. Unfortunately for me, the bed was empty, except for my little coffee bean–colored cat, who looked quite happy, her paws extended, her white belly showing.

"Don't get too comfortable, Java, another occupant's on his way."

I went to the bathroom and knocked on the door. I didn't hear the shower, and I didn't get an answer.

"Matt?"

Still no answer.

I pushed my way in. Matt was on the floor, curled up on (and regrettably not *in*) his black silk kimono. I dropped a towel over his toned flanks and knelt down beside my buck-naked first love.

"Let's go. Time for bed," I said, taking his arm.

Matt was still damp from his shower, and just about as slippery as Randall Knox, but I managed to get him on his feet and into the guest room, ignoring his mumbled demands.

"I want some black coffee," he said as I forced him onto the bed.

(He wanted some other things from me, too, a list of things, actually. All of them would have been stimulating. None had anything to do with caffeine.)

"Forget it," I firmly told him. "You have to get some rest. You don't want your eyes to look bloodshot for your wedding pictures, do you?"

"There's not gonna be any damn wedding," Matt said.

(Okay, I'm *paraphrasing* what he said. But what's the point of filling half a page with obscenities?)

While Matt ranted, I stripped away the towel, nudged my little cat over, and forced Matt to lie back on the pile of pillows. Then I covered his hard body with a soft blanket.

"Look, Matt, I know you're still furious about what Breanne did. It was wrong for her to send every person in your little black PDA book a wedding announcement. But, come on, wouldn't these women have found out anyway?"

"Maybe. Maybe not. A lot of them live in other countries. I doubt they read New York gossip columns or American magazines."

"You mean you were actually planning to *date* some of these women after your wedding?"

"You know how I am, Clare. I like to keep my options open."

I sighed, nudged his leg over, and sat down on the edge of the bed. "It's going to be hard for you to hear this, but as much as I can't stand Breanne personally, I have to confess I *admire* what the woman did."

Matt's bloodshot eyes widened in outrage. "What?"

"It's smart. She obviously wants you to give fidelity a try."

Matt frowned. "That wasn't part of our deal."

"What *deal*? This is supposed to be a *marriage*."

"Monogamy's retro. Breanne's said it herself, more than once."

"Yeah, well, I don't care what she said. I think, deep down, Breanne feels the same emotions I used to about you: jealousy, possessiveness, anger——"

He waved me off. "You don't know Breanne like I do."

"No. *You* don't know women as well as you think you do."

Matt and I could usually communicate with very few words. At the moment, I felt as though we were talking two different languages. I sat in silence for a moment.

"Tell me, truthfully," I finally said. "What is it that you love about Breanne?"

This question seemed to baffle the groom. (Not a good sign.) I waited as he searched the bedroom ceiling, finally he met my eyes.

"I . . . I guess I love my life with her," he said quietly. "It's always fun to be with Bree, you know, exciting. She can always find a party, no matter what city she's in. Man, that woman loves to party. And seeing Rome, Paris, Tokyo with her . . . it was great. It's always the best with her: limos, top hotels, the finest restaurants."

"So it's her money you love?"

"No . . ." Matt frowned. "Honestly, it's what we enjoy together, Clare. I mean, Bree loves that life—the traveling, the networking with new people—and when I'm with her, she arranges everything, makes life easy. I don't have to sweat the small stuff. It's kind of a relief. She doesn't mind taking care of things and taking care of me, too—like she did when I broke my arm last fall."

Like a mom, I thought. It made sense, their relationship. With Breanne in control, Matt was free to extend his eternal boy status all the way to the retirement home.

"Breanne likes adventure, too," he went on. "After fashion week was over last year in Milan, we took off, ate and drank our way across Italy from behind the wheel of a Lamborghini that some designer loaned her. We skinny-dipped in the Mediterranean at five in the morning, and then we went paragliding. Oh, man, that was such a blast."

Matt's expression softened. "I guess I love her for things like that, too." A hint of a smile moved across his features. "And I guess . . . I guess I do love Breanne."

"Then, uh, maybe you should *marry* her. But I mean really

marry her, Matt. Try being a real husband for a change. That might just be an adventure, too."

Matt studied my face. "You and I weren't a total disaster, were we?"

"One look at our daughter will answer how I feel about that."

Matt sighed. "Okay, Clare. I heard everything you said, and I'll think about it . . ."

It was the exact same response Breanne had given me at the restaurant earlier today. I returned Matt's smile, holding out hope that this was a sign the two really were simpatico.

"So the wedding's on?" I pressed. "You'll marry Breanne?"

Before Matt could answer, the phone on the nightstand warbled. I picked it up.

"Hello?"

"Clare?" It was the harsh, clipped tone of a woman who wasted no time with pleasantries.

"Yes," I said.

"I gather things didn't go well with Nunzio, or you wouldn't be home alone right now."

Here we go: the return of bridezilla. "Actually, Breanne, I secured the fountain. And I'm not alone. Matt's here."

I heard a sharp breath on the other end of the line. She began speaking again, but I put my hand over the receiver and turned to my ex-husband.

"Listen to me, Matt, I have something important to tell you . . ."

I spilled the beans about Breanne being attacked in Machu Picchu's bathroom. Before I could get to Randall Knox or my Gordian knot of conspiracy theories, he snatched the phone from my fingers.

"Breanne, are you all right, honey? You're not in any pain, are you? Do you want me to come over?"

I listened to Matt's end of the conversation for the next few minutes. I heard more than one "I'm sorry" and "Your forgiven" before things got really mushy. Then I slipped out of the room, deciding to table my discussion of the Breanne-in-peril case until after I got back.

The way Matt was cooing to his fiancée, I was certain of one thing: Saturday's wedding was definitely back on, which meant I had to get Nunzio's fountain to the Met!

╢KIRTY-TWO

ⓥⓥⓥⓥⓥⓥⓥⓥⓥⓥⓥⓥⓥⓥⓥⓥⓥⓥ

On most evenings, taxis ran fairly regularly up Hudson Street. Chic residents of uptown neighborhoods knew downtown was the hottest Manhattan scene, so cabbies routinely spent the night transporting the clubbing set to bars and restaurants in Soho and Tribeca, then reversing course to go back uptown for a new load of trendily clothed forms to carry.

I'd just missed one yellow cab. It swerved for the fare across the road. In the glow of the streetlamp, the silhouette of a man in a trench coat and ball cap climbed into its backseat. But another cab rolled up a moment later, and I snagged the ride.

Traffic was still pretty light, and we traveled from Greenwich Village to the Upper East Side without any major snarls. As the cab circled the block at Eighty-sixth Street and doubled back down Fifth, another taxi hugged its bumper. I saw the flash of annoyance on my driver's face in the rearview mirror.

"Damn tailgater," he muttered.

Soon the floodlit walls of the Metropolitan Museum of Art loomed into view. Bordering Central Park, the massive museum occupied five full city blocks, its interior crammed with a stultifying array of irreplaceable artifacts. The paintings included many of the world's masterpieces; the sculptures dated

back to ancient Greece and Rome. There were historical di
plays of furniture, jewelry, arms and armor, vases, tapestrie
photographs, ancient mummies, and even an entire Egyptia
temple, removed from the banks of the Nile River and trans
ported to the New World. Soon one more treasure would b
added to that list, albeit temporarily: the Italian sculpto
Nunzio's *Lover's Spring*.

By now, the museum's visiting hours were over. But fo
Breanne's wedding, I'd been given an events pass by th
trustees of the museum, a pass which gave me twenty-fou
hour access to a locked storage space filled with the thing
we'd need to cater Saturday's reception.

I exited the taxi at the corner of Eighty-fourth Stree
right in front of the manned security booth. One of th
guards hurried across the broad sidewalk and helped me li
the fountain out of the trunk. While we fumbled to deplo
the handle on the heavy Pullman, the cab that had bee
trailing mine sped around us and zoomed away.

The guard helped me roll the heavy suitcase down th
steep concrete ramp and through the employees' entrance t
the second security checkpoint inside the museum. I showe
the guard my pass, and he admitted me to the museur
proper.

Pulling the fountain behind me, I crossed a wide loadin
dock and followed a gloomy hallway to the holding area.
unlocked the storage unit, rolled the fountain inside, an
locked it up again. Mission accomplished!

Too bad, Nunzio. Better luck with the next barista . . .

My virtue secured, along with the fountain, I headed ou

It was after eleven when I left the museum and trudge
up the shadowy ramp back to the street. The storm ha
passed, but the air was still damp, and the temperature wa
dropping, too. I shivered under my flimsy sweater. The wra
dress was starting to chafe, and I'd been wearing the sam
wedge platform sandals for ten hours now. They'd been com
fortable most of the day, but by now my feet were throbbin
with each step.

I waved good-bye to the guards inside the booth and walked uptown. There was an M3 East Village bus stop at the corner of Eighty-fifth Street, right in front of a fenced-in children's playground that was part of Central Park. There was a streetlight nearby, but much of its glow was blocked by tree branches. Traffic was light on Fifth, and there wasn't a cab in sight, so I was relieved to see a bus rolling toward me, though it was still several blocks away.

Standing in the shadows, I groped around in my purse for a Metrocard. That's when I heard the scuff of a shoe and sensed movement behind me. Before I could react, a skeletal arm wrapped around my throat, and something hard pressed against the small of my back.

"I have a gun. Don't make a sound, or I'll shoot you right here."

I recognized the rasping voice: Stuart Allerton Winslow. He stank of sweat and desperation. I glanced over my shoulder and spied unkempt hair sticking out from around the rim of a baseball cap. Though he'd ditched the trench coat, I realized now that he was the man in the cab, the one who followed me from the Blend to the museum. My mind was racing. Quinn had warned me the man was going to be released.

"Back up. Into the park," Winslow said.

His hot breath hit my face, and I flinched at the whiff of onions and refried beans. *Jose's Burritos,* I thought; the place was just up the block from the Blend. He must have gone straight to Hudson Street the second he regained his freedom, waiting outside my coffeehouse until I showed.

I risked a sidelong glance in the direction of the security booth, about fifty feet away. I could barely see the glow of its lights behind a screen of tree branches.

"Don't even think about it," he warned, his grip around my throat tightening.

With the gun still pressed against my spine, Winslow pulled me into the dark playground. He dragged me backward, past a slide and a set of swings, to an elaborate jungle gym standing in the middle of the yard.

"Little bitch," he rasped.

Swinging me around, he shoved me face-first against the metal bars. He used his body to pin me there, then his arm tightened around my neck again, like a smothering snake.

I struggled against the scumbag, but the man held firm. He'd seemed puny and weak in his dungeonlike apartment. But he wasn't weak now. He was furious, his grip cruel. I tried to ignore the pain, stay calm, search my mind for a strategy of escape.

You're not helpless, Clare. You outwitted him once. You can do it again.

"I could have killed you on the sidewalk," he rasped against my ear. "But that would be too quick."

"You don't have to kill me at all," I whispered. It was hard to do more than that with his arm so tightly around my throat.

"You're suggesting I should let you live? To testify against me in court? No, no, little bitch. That will never do. We can't have the law looking any further at my business."

I tried again to break free, but he tightened his grip. Once again, I felt the hard poke of a gun barrel against my back.

"Why are you doing this? You don't even have any drugs. You lied to me."

"Is that what you think? My word, you are stupid. And your cop friends are even stupider. They searched my apartment, came up with nothing."

"Because you were lying."

"Because my real office is in Jersey. The dump's not in my name, but I assure you the cabinets are full of my product. So you see, little bitch, your stupid cops are to blame. They couldn't keep me in custody, so you can thank them for the pain I'm about to inflict."

I struggled harder.

"Ssshhh, shhh, now. Accept your fate, and it will be easy . . ."

Winslow laughed again, and the pressure of the gun

against my spine vanished. With one arm still wrapped around my throat, he raised the other. I struggled to turn my head—it wasn't much, just a fraction—but out of the corner of my eye, I saw a glint of silver in the shadowy light. A long knife was clutched in his hand.

He doesn't have a gun! He used the handle of the knife to trick me!

The blade was descending toward my right shoulder. And my move was almost instinctual. Winslow himself had given me the idea: *Accept your fate.*

Instead of resisting, I gave up. My knees sagged, and I let every pound of my small form go limp. I began to slip underneath his curled arm. On my way down, I opened my mouth and sank my teeth into the man's stringy flesh. The blade came down, striking sparks off the metal bars he'd been pressing me against.

Winslow cursed me with every word ever invented to degrade a woman.

I bit down harder, a pissed-off pit bull.

Winslow cried out. Using the weight of his body, he slammed me against the jungle gym bars. I kicked at his knee with my big platform wedge and jammed my elbow into his belly. Finally, the man released me, stumbling backwards with a howl. He fell to the ground, and I ran toward Fifth Avenue.

I heard a clang, saw the flash of the hurled knife as it bounced off the slide. I stumbled and nearly fell, but I kicked off my shoes and kept going, right into the headlights of an NYPD sector car.

Tires squealed, and a uniform jumped out.

"A man dragged me inside that playground! He had a knife! Tried to stab me!"

The cop drew his gun and raced into the shadows. His partner leaped out of the vehicle and followed, barking into his radio for backup as he ran. I sagged against the police car, knees weak, bare feet scuffed, hands trembling.

The night seemed suddenly darker. I doubled over at the waist, feeling like I couldn't get enough oxygen. Another sector car rolled up behind the first, and a policewoman hurried to my side. She helped me into the backseat of her vehicle then leaned against the roof.

"Ma'am, we're going to get you to an ER. Is there anyone you want me to notify?"

I nodded. My neck was sore, my voice shaky, but it didn't matter. I only had to speak four words: "Mike Quinn, Sixth Precinct."

Thirty-Three

~~~~~~

"**Clare?** Are you all right? I heard you screaming."

Mike stood in the bedroom doorway, a steaming mug of hot coffee in each hand. Shirtless, he wore navy-blue pajama bottoms, and his dark-blond hair was still mussed from sleep.

I blinked, rubbed my eyes, tried to banish the phantom images. Then the real memories rushed back, and they were no less nightmarish—Stuart Winslow's attack outside the Metropolitan Museum, the fight for my life in the dark playground, my escape and rescue by patrolmen from the Twenty-second Precinct. I remembered my trip to the busy ER, then the chilly old horse stables, a renovated building that now housed the Central Park precinct, where I'd answered a series of questions.

Mike had been there for me, every step of the way. The moment he'd heard I'd been attacked, he had rushed to the hospital; and when all the examining and questioning was over, he'd brought me back to his apartment in Alphabet City, where I'd accepted a good hard shot of his Irish whiskey and passed out.

Now he crossed the bedroom in three strides, set the coffee mugs on the nightstand and took me in his arms.

"What scared you, Clare? What did you dream?"

"I was chasing Joy through a playground," I murmured

against his bare shoulder. "She transformed right in front of me, into this beautiful falcon. I tried to catch her, but a photographer jumped in front of me, snapped a flash. I couldn't see, just heard a gunshot. A woman screamed, and then—oh, God, Mike—I was facedown on a white marble floor, and there was blood, so much blood . . ."

"Hold on to me, Clare. Hold on as long you need to."

For a few minutes, I did. Then my nose twitched. "Mike?"

"Mmmm?"

"Do I smell fresh coffee?"

He reached over to the nightstand, pushed a warm mug into my hands. I lay back on the bed pillows, took a test sip, and sighed. The man had come a long way from when I'd first met him. Back then, he'd been swilling stale robusta bean crap by the gallon. The hot, fresh java he'd made for me this morning was my own Breakfast Blend roast, brewed nearly to perfection (which, for me, was better than perfect).

"You know, Mike, you're getting pretty good at this. You should seriously consider barista work."

"Thanks. I'll get back to you if the whole law enforcement thing doesn't pan out."

I finished my cup and placed it next to his on the faux-mahogany nightstand—part of a set from the Crate and Barrel catalog that I'd helped him pick out. I thought the dark, sober finish suited his rugged personality. Mike thought the faux part made it easy on his public servant–size wallet.

"Anyway, sweetheart, as far as your future nightmares, I think I can ease your worries. I *had* called the precinct to arrange for a plainclothes officer to watch your back—"

"That's not necessary—"

"You're right. But not for the reason you think. The Jersey state police arrested Stuart Winslow at three fifty-five this morning."

I closed my eyes. "Thank God."

"And guess what? He had rental papers on him, and keys to a storage space in Wayne, New Jersey. They opened it up soon as a judge issued the warrant, found the man's stash f illegally imported narcotics." Mike smiled like an alley cat ho'd just snagged his rat. "Winslow won't be getting out of il for a long time. Congratulations, sweetheart, you did it."

"We did it." I hugged Mike again, and then we were do-ng more than hugging. I was wearing the matching top to is navy-blue pajama bottoms, and I seriously considered re-oving both.

"Damn," he murmured against my lips. "Some of us have report to work."

I sighed. "I have work, too. Matt's wedding's tomorrow, nd I have so much to do, including a final batch of beans to oast—the trickiest ones yet, and the most expensive. Kopi uwak sells for three to five hundred a pound—"

"Dollars? You're kidding?"

"Drop by early this evening, say eight o'clock? I'm brew-ng samples for my baristas on the Clover."

"Free coffee? I'm there."

He rose up off the bed and crossed to his new faux-ahogany bureau. As my eyes watched him dress, my mind trayed back to the Breanne-in-peril case.

"Mike?"

"Yeah?"

"With Winslow in custody, do you think Breanne's safe ow?"

Mike glanced up from buttoning his shirt. "She hired a odyguard. You know that, right?"

"Right. I spoke with her yesterday."

"And I spoke with your ex-husband while I was making ur coffee, filled him in on everything."

"Thanks. I appreciate it."

He shrugged. "Well, like him or not, I guess we're all in his together."

"Yeah, that's basically what I told Breanne on the bath-oom floor of Machu Picchu. So you think it was Winslow who hired the hit man? Arranged for that bathroom attack?"

Mike pulled on his pants, tucked in his dress shirt. "It's

the angle that makes the most sense, doesn't it? Winslow'
scum. He paid off Monica Purcell in drugs to commit
crime. He probably did the same with the man who attacked
Breanne in the bathroom. Whether or not Winslow was i
custody is beside the point if he already paid the guy to take
her out."

"I'd have to come to the same conclusion—at least based
on what we know. I've been thinking about Randall Knox
and I can't make him as a murderer."

"The gossip guy?" Mike grabbed his wallet, cell phone
and gold shield off the dresser. "You think he's innocent?"

"I wouldn't call him innocent, but after sleeping on it, I'm
willing to bet his hits are limited to the pen, not the sword."

"Good bet. After I spoke to you, I ran a background
check. No felonies. No outstanding warrants or restraining
orders. Just a lot of unpaid parking tickets. Whereas you can
see what kind of nut job Winslow is."

"Exactly. If I had to guess, I'd say Knox and Miriam Perry
were toasting something other than Breanne's demise. Prob
ably whatever smut story Knox is planning to publish or
Monday."

"The one on Breanne?"

I nodded. "He claims Breanne and the dead stripper
shared more than a physical resemblance."

"And what does that mean?"

"It *might* mean they shared Matt, in which case the gossip
column will be about a particularly embarrassing episode in
my ex-husband's playboy past."

Mike tightened the knot on his tie. "Will something like
that hurt his new marriage?"

"I don't know. Breanne's one tough fashionista. Some
thing tells me she'll be able to handle whatever Knox throws
at her. As for Matt, I think he may actually care for the
woman he's about to make his new wife."

"Then maybe they'll just get their first lesson in making a
marriage work."

I met Mike's eyes. "Forgiveness?"

He winked. "Got it in one."

I smiled. "The thing is . . . I found something else out last night, something that makes me think the story has nothing to do with Matt."

He slipped on his shoulder holster. "I'm listening."

I climbed out of bed, crossed to the new computer desk, and opened his old laptop.

"What are you doing?"

"You'll see."

I logged onto my Internet account and called up Breanne's official biography on the *Trend* Web site. "It says here that Breanne Summour is a pen name she legally uses to shield her aristocratic family from publicity. They reside in Europe, and Breanne grew up all over the world, studying at the Sorbonne with sons and daughters of royalty. She has an impeccable sense of fashion that she acquired at the knee of an older family friend, a stunning beauty who once modeled for world-renowned Parisian designer Coco Chanel."

"So?" Mike said.

"So it doesn't add up. Breanne was well educated and well connected. It doesn't exactly fit with what Winslow implied. Or what Nunzio told me last night."

"Wait. Who's Nunzio?"

"An Italian sculptor—he's not important, but what he said is. Breanne's been wheeling and dealing behind the scenes, making bargains to get herself freebies. It doesn't sound like the woman in her bio."

Mike leaned over my shoulder to read the computer screen. "Yeah. There's a lot of spongy language here." He pointed. " 'Studied at the Sorbonne.' When? Doesn't say she actually graduated. And who's this 'family friend'? No hard dates, names, facts. She admits in the bio that she's legally changed her name, which would discourage any cursory background checks; someone would have to spend money and a whole lot of time to dig up a story, if there even is one, on her past. You're right. Sounds like a scam job. Why don't you ask Breanne about it?"

"If it's just résumé enhancement, it's no big deal, right?"

Mike laughed. "If that were a crime, I'd have to arrest half the city—and *all* the politicians."

"Maybe it's nothing," I said. "But with Knox threatening an exposé, and my own investigation turning up facts about Breanne that don't add up, I'd really like to know what Matt is marrying into."

Mike began to massage my shoulders. "Joy's about to get a stepmother. Is that it?"

"I'd just like to know what Breanne is hiding, what's behind the cashmere curtain."

"Will she tell you if you ask?"

"Doubtful. She's got the brick wall thing down pretty well."

"You know, Cosi, whenever I hit a brick wall, I go the other direction."

"What do you mean?"

"You said Randall Knox implied there was some kind of link between Breanne and the stripper Hazel Boggs. They shared more than a physical resemblance, right?"

"Right."

"So look at *Hazel* to find out what they shared. Call the Fish Squad. Ask them what they dug up on the girl. Maybe you'll find a connection to Breanne."

A horn honked outside, and Mike glanced at his watch. "Sorry, sweetheart. I've got to go. Sully's picking me up down on the—"

The horn honked again. Mike poked his head out the window. "Knock if off, Sully!"

"You're late!"

"I'm coming! Stop disturbing the peace!"

He brought his head back in. "Don't forget, you have a change of clothes here in the top drawer. Your sneakers are in my closet. Now kiss me good-bye."

I did (and for a lot longer than was probably prudent, given Sully's third horn blast). Mike slipped out the door,

d I sighed. It was hard to see my man go. I hung out the
indow, waited for him to hit the street—one last look.

"Bye, honey!" I shouted.

"See you tonight!" he shouted back.

He threw me a kiss and climbed into Sully's car. I drew
y head inside the window, went to the kitchen, and poured
other cup of Mike's coffee. Then I called the Sixth
ecinct.

"Detective Lori Soles."

"This is Clare Cosi, Detective. I'd like to talk to you one
ore time about Hazel Boggs . . ."

didn't dress for *Trend*'s offices. The sneakers, jeans, and
weater that I'd stashed at Mike's apartment would have
do.

"Breanne, I need to speak with you."

"What?" Breanne glanced up from her massive glass desk,
er delicate eyewear perched on the end of her nose. "Clare?
What are you doing here?"

I walked into her office, shut the door, and threw the lock.
'm here to get your side of the story."

"What story? I don't understand?"

"I just spoke with Hazel Boggs's mother. She's down-
wn, collecting Hazel's remains and personal items. Like
er daughter, Rhonda Boggs looks just like you."

Breanne blanched for a moment. Then the mask was back.
don't know what you *think* you've uncovered, Clare, but—"

"There's no *thinking* about it." I strode up to her desk and
owed her my cell phone photos of Hazel, Rhonda, and a
napshot among Hazel's possessions that linked both women
Breanne. "I blew up the image of the snapshot on my
omputer and printed it out."

I reached into the back pocket of my jeans and unfolded
e paper. The enlarged photo showed a young Breanne,
anding in front of a run-down trailer, arm in arm with a

young Rhonda Boggs, who was pointing proudly to an iss▪
of *Vogue*.

"I couldn't read the smaller type on the magazine cover,
I looked up this issue on the library's database. And gue▪
what the cover story was titled: 'Architect of Fashion,' ▪
Breanne Summour."

Breanne sat back in her chair. "Okay, so you *are* a dece▪
sleuth. Why are you here?"

"Randall Knox claims he knows what you and Hazel Bog▪
shared besides a physical resemblance. He obviously kno▪
what I know, and on Monday he's going to publish it."

Breanne shook her head, took off her glasses. "I doubt th▪
little twerp knows the *whole* story. No one knows the who▪
story. Not even my ex-husband knew the truth. No o▪
knows but me."

"Well, I certainly know a lot of it based on my intervie▪
with your younger sister. You were born Rita Boggs in ▪
trailer park outside of Wheeling, West Virginia, the oldest ▪
four children. After high school, you attended communi▪
college, but you were forced to drop out of school after on▪
one year when your father, an ex-con who did time for arme▪
robbery and attempted murder, got on his hog and rode awa▪
Am I warm?"

"Okay, Clare. What do you want?"

"What do you mean, what do I want?"

"Everyone who comes to me with that story wants som▪
thing. What do *you* want?"

"Breanne, I don't understand you. Hazel Boggs was yo▪
niece, for God's sake. You never even admitted to Matt th▪
it was your niece who was murdered!"

"I never met the girl, Clare. It's been twenty years sin▪
I've even seen my sister. Now, what do you *want* to kee▪
this quiet?"

"I don't want anything! Clearly, you've cut all ties to you▪
past. That's the way you want it—and I can see now that ▪
why you expected Matt to cut his ties, too."

"I don't expect it anymore."

"I'm glad to hear it. But, look, even though your background is your own private business, Matt should know the
truth before you marry him."

"No."

"Why? You have nothing to be ashamed of. Your sister
told me that you send her and your younger brothers money
on a regular basis—"

"And I only ever asked them for one thing in return: to
never speak of my background. Rhonda obviously forgot
that bargain."

"Don't blame her for opening up to me. She believed I
was working with the detectives who were investigating her
daughter's death—which I was, frankly. She had no idea I
had a connection back to you."

"She shouldn't have talked to you, Clare. And she *should*
have told me that Hazel was living in New York." Breanne
glanced away; her clipped tone softened. "I never met my
niece, but I would have helped her if I'd known she was here."

"Hazel didn't want you to know. She knew you wanted
your privacy. And she had her own pride, too. That's how
Rhonda put it. She said her daughter came to New York to
make it on her own like her aunt did. Maybe Hazel never
met you, Breanne, but she greatly admired you."

"Is that so? And is that why she dressed like me to *strip*?"

"She only did it twice. The look-alike agency regularly
booked her out as other celebrities. It was Randall Knox who
saw the resemblance and paid her to imitate you. Your sister
had no idea Hazel was hiring herself out as an exotic dancer
to make ends meet."

Breanne paused, the steel in her eyes softening. "How is
she? My sister. Is she holding up okay?"

"She was very sad, of course. But she seemed okay, a sur-
vivor. Her husband came with her. She said she has two
younger daughters and a son back home." I stepped up to
Bree's desk and put down a piece of paper. "This is her hotel
and phone number. She'll be in New York until tomorrow
morning if you want to see her before she leaves."

Breanne bit her lip. "Rhonda's daughter was shot instea of me." She closed her eye, shook her head. "It's my faul the girl's dead . . ."

"That's ridiculous. *You* didn't gun her down. And your lif was in just as much danger."

"But if I had known that Hazel needed money, sh wouldn't have had to do the exotic dancing. I could hav helped her—"

"Like I said, according to your sister, Hazel didn't wan your help. She was proud of her looks, her talent. She wante to make it on her own." I raised an eyebrow. "Sounds a lo like you, from what Rhonda told me."

Breanne met my eyes. "And what else did Rhonda tel you?"

"That you were barely out of your teens, yet you quit col lege to take care of your younger sister and brothers on noth ing but food stamps and welfare checks. What you did wa admirable, Breanne. I don't understand why you're trying s hard to hide it."

"My father was a criminal, and my mother was an alco holic who ended up in a mental hospital. Not a very pretty past, Clare. I also did things, illegal things, for extra money Did Rhonda mention that?"

"No."

"Well, what's the difference? In for a penny in for a pound, right? I didn't have to do it for long. A family frienc helped me get a legitimate job at a local department store."

"Rhonda said you were very smart, you made friends with the store buyers."

Breanne nodded. "I wrote articles for local publication: about new products. But there was one story that broke me out."

"The one on the *Vogue* cover? How did you manage tha from a trailer park in West Virginia?"

Breanne's hard blue gaze softened again. "There was a clothing buyer at the department store, a very nice man. He told me about a famous architect who was collaborating with fashion designer to create a new line of women's clothes. So took a bus to Pittsburgh, where the architect lived, interviewed him extensively, and put a slick piece together with the help of one of my old community college teachers. Before she retired, she'd worked in New York as a reporter. She was the one who made a few calls, found out which editor at *Vogue* would be receptive to the piece."

"And *Vogue* bought it? Just like that?"

"Fortune favors the foolish, I guess. The circumstances were unusual."

"What do you mean?"

"The architect was no spring chicken. The man suffered a heart attack and died right before fall fashion week. The clothing line he helped create was a huge hit, and I had the only interview."

"So your article ran as a *Vogue* cover story under a pen name you invented: Breanne Summour."

She nodded. "By then Rhonda was old enough to take care of my brothers. So I moved to New York and, with a completely fabricated résumé, landed a job at *New York Trends*."

"But I still don't understand. Why did you have to hide your past?"

Breanne's laugh was sharp and cynical. "I didn't have an Ivy League degree—or any degree. I talked my way into the job with the single *Vogue* piece."

"Didn't anyone look into your background?"

"*New York Trends* wasn't exactly high on the food chain. Randall Knox was just a horny little editor-in-chief. I fluttered my eyes, flipped my blond hair, crossed my legs, and he didn't bother checking out my fake credentials. He just hired me on the spot. The creep hit on me regularly, by the way, along with every other woman under thirty in his office, which is one reason I *vowed* from day one to create my own magazine. Taking most of Knox's staff with me was just the cherry on top."

I regarded Breanne, looking as polished as ever in her

thousand-dollar Fen business suit, her million-dollar vie
around her. "It was your ex-husband who did the polish jo
on you, wasn't it?"

Breanne's glossed lips twisted into a smirk. "I considere
it a fair trade at the time. Stuart Winslow was a bluebloo
Back then he was riding high with money and connections. I
the ten years we were together, I did a lot of catching up. H
taught me how to dress, how to speak, what to praise, what t
disdain. And I taught him how to screw."

"I don't doubt it."

"His *Mayflower* name was a huge help on my pitch t
Reston-Miller to start *Trend*. I'd been a Winslow for so lon
by marriage, I'd created a whole new me, a whole new lif
No one in my new social circle ever questioned my right t
be there."

I looked at Breanne once more, but I didn't see Nunzio
braying donkey. I saw the Esmeralda geisha, a spindly coffe
tree that no one noticed until she was planted at a higher al
titude, cultivated, and brought to market, where biddin
could drive up her value.

I'd once read a breeder's notes on the varietal. The geish
he'd written, was an undesirable type of bean, long and thin
which, under neglectful conditions, produced a liquor of poo
quality; yet it almost always displayed resistance to leaf rus
Breanne carried innate resistance, too, and she'd been force
to become hearty in the big, bad city. She'd not only learne
how to adapt and survive but flourish. Still, Breanne
choices had exacted a price. Women with real patrician back
grounds had nothing to prove. They floated through socia
circles on lilting breezes of carefree laughter. For Breanne
the facade of taste and class had to be scrupulously main
tained. Without the silk shawl of Nunzio's little proverb, th
world might just label her a pack mule.

"If Knox knows what I know, he can ruin you. Can't he?"

"He *can't* take away *Trend*'s phenomenal circulation," Bre
anne said. "But he can embarrass the hell out me."

"So what are you going to do?"

"Don't you worry about Knox. I'll swat that little pest *myself*. This isn't the first time I've had to deal with this sort of thing, and I doubt it will be the last." She exhaled and met my eyes. "Okay, Clare, you know everything about me now, the ugly truth."

"It's your private business, Breanne. I just need to know one more thing. *Why* are you marrying Matt? What's the real reason? Is he some part of an elaborate game plan, like your first husband was?"

"Not even close."

"You really love him?"

Breanne glanced away, which I didn't take for a good sign. I waited in silence as she studied the view beyond her floor-to-ceiling windows. Finally, she answered. "More than any other man I ever met, Matt makes me feel the way I used to feel about myself."

"I'm not sure I understand."

She faced me again, met my eyes. "I'm a fighter, Clare. I did what I had to for my family and for myself—to succeed. Here at the magazine, I'm the bitch boss. It's a role that gets the job done, gets the magazine out on time, keeps my people employed and my bank account healthy. But when I'm with Matteo . . ."

"Go on."

"He's like no other man I've ever known . . ." The woman's brassy voice had become a whisper, and her gaze drifted back to the clouds, the park, her dreamy view. "When he takes me in his arms at night, I feel vulnerable again, innocent and sweet and beautiful. When he kisses me, he makes all the bad days . . . all the bad *years* . . . disappear . . ."

I never, not in a million years, expected an answer like that from the grand bitch of fashion. It was exactly how Mike Quinn made me feel; and in that moment I realized, beneath all of her Machiavellian scheming and bridezilla-on-steroids demands, Breanne Summour really did love her groom.

"Thank you for being honest with me," I said.

Breanne nodded, then her gaze fell on the piece of pape
on her desk, the one with her sister's contact information.

"She misses you," I said. "And she still admires and love
you."

"She said that?"

"She didn't have to. The way she talked about you—i
was clear as sunlight through plate glass."

Breanne sighed. "I know what you must be thinking
Clare, but seeing my sister again, making contact . . . I don'
know if I can do it." She shook her head. "When you travel s
far from who you were, it's like living in a new world. Yo
can't go back again. I decided that long ago. My famil
would never understand my life, my choices."

"Maybe . . . or maybe you just never gave them a chanc
to understand."

Breanne picked up the piece of paper. "Maybe. I'll thin
about it . . ."

I nodded and turned, heading for the door. Before throw
ing the lock and departing, however, I turned back to say on
last thing.

"Breanne, I really will keep your past a secret, but only o
one condition. You have to tell Matt the whole truth abou
your life before you take your vows."

"I can't do that," she whispered. "He'll never want m
then . . ."

"If that's how little you think of Matteo Allegro, then yo
really should call the wedding off."

Thirty-Four

OKAY, guys, what's the verdict?"

"Pretty amazing, Clare," Gardner said, paper cup in hand.

Dante nodded. "Good job on the roast!"

"Superb," Tucker said.

"Thanks." *Three down one to go.* "What do you think, Esther?"

Esther Best pushed up her black rectangular glasses and peered at me with her big, brown, hypercritical eyes. "I think I can't get my mind around where these beans have been."

It was eight o'clock in the evening. Matt, Joy, and Madame were all at the wedding rehearsal dinner. Here at the Blend, I'd just finished roasting the final batch of green beans for tomorrow's reception. My top baristas and I were now sampling the freshly roasted Kopi Luwak.

Mike elbowed me. "What does she mean by that? Where have the coffee beans been?"

"You can ask me directly, you know?" Esther told Mike flatly. "I won't bite your head off. I generally don't bite people's heads off unless the moon is full."

Mike raised a sandy eyebrow. "Okay, Esther. What do you mean by that?"

I stifled a smile as she explained that *kopi* was the Indonesian word for "coffee," and *luwak* referred to the small catlike animal from which the coffee beans were collected.

"I don't understand," Mike said, taking another heart quaff from his paper cup. He looked down at me. "Coffee beans come from trees, don't they?"

I bit my lip, met Esther's eyes.

"He has no idea, does he?" Esther asked.

I shook my head, and she looked about ready to lose it. Then she did, literally doubling over with laughter.

"What?" Now Mike's blue gaze was spearing me.

"The *luwak* is a feral, forest animal," I explained. "It eats coffee cherries and voids them whole. The Indonesian farmers collect them, process them, and sell them as the most expensive coffee on earth: Kopi Luwak."

Mike stared into the ten-dollar cup he'd previously been enjoying and blanched. But there was nothing wrong with the coffee! Kopi Luwak had the cup characteristics of a really good Sumatran, heavy and earthy with hints of caramel and chocolate, as well as a superlative smoothness and a unique lingering mustiness.

His eyes met mine again. "You're telling me this coffee came out of a cat's—"

"The digestive tract changes the chemical composition of the bean," I said. "See, a coffee bean's proteins contribute to its bitterness. The *luwak*'s digestive process breaks down some of the proteins, making the coffee extremely smooth."

"Kopi Luwak is its official name," Esther said, "but some people refer to it as something else."

"Don't tell me," Mike muttered.

"Cat-poop coffee!" Esther cried then cracked up again.

Now Dante, Gardner, and Tucker were laughing, too.

Mike put down his cup.

Oh, God. I should have warned him.

"You look a little green, Detective," Dante said. "What's wrong?"

He glanced back at me. "Too much information."

I bit my cheek. "Didn't you once tell me that you can never give a detective too much information?"

"Yeah, but in this *one* case, I would have made an exception."

"Its okay, Mike." I patted his shoulder. "I'll get your usual."

As I prepared an extra special make-it-up-to-him latte, the bell over our door jangled. A few minutes later, Mike was introducing me to the customer who'd walked in. He was a cerebral-looking, middle-aged man with a receding blond hairline, fair complexion, and a bit of a paunch under a tweedy blazer.

"This is Dr. Mel Billings, Clare. He's a pathologist who works with the OD Squad."

I greeted the man, made him a cappuccino, and joined both men at a café table. Mike turned to me. "Dr. Billings is the man who performed the autopsy on Monica Purcell."

"Oh?"

Billings nodded, took off the half-glasses he wore on a black cord around his neck. "Mike asked me to drop by and speak with you. He thought maybe you'd have some ideas for us."

"Okay, I'll do my best."

"The victim I examined didn't die of an overdose of conventional medication. She was *poisoned*—and not by anything usual. An exotic batrachotoxin was used to kill her. It's perplexed us all."

"Me included," Mike said. "I thought maybe you'd have a theory, Clare."

"*Me?* On what? What exactly is batrachotoxin?"

"It's a poison extracted from the skin of toxic frogs," Billings said. "Very rare. In Colombia, natives use it against predators. An expert I spoke to in Colombia tells me that many rural farmers dose thorny trees around their land with the batrachotoxin to scare away marauding bands of FARC."

"FARC," I repeated. "That definitely rings a bell. Matt's mentioned FARC to me, usually with an expletive attached. As far as I know, they're a revolutionary group that stands opposed to Colombia's current government. They terrorize farmers and land owners."

"You should also know that the items in Ms. Purcell
stomach were barely digested," Billings said. "There wa
some kind of bread or muffin product made primarily of so
protein and a pulpy beverage made of wheatgrass."

"I'm thinking Monica Purcell saw Winslow that morn
ing," Mike said. "The robbery went bad the night before
I'm thinking he poisoned her breakfast."

"Her breakfast . . . soy and wheatgrass . . ."

My mind went back to the morning that Monica was po
soned. I'd been sitting in the reception area when the inter
came out in a panic, telling us about finding Monica's body
But shortly before that, Breanne's breakfast was taken fror
the front desk to the company's break room.

"Mike, the food items you're describing in her stomac
are exactly the breakfast I turned down the day Monica wa
found dead: a soy-protein muffin and a wheatgrass shake
The receptionist couldn't give those items away, so she ha
them moved to the company's break room. She said th
breakfast was a regular daily delivery to *Trend*'s offices."

"A delivery for Monica?" Billings asked.

"No." I met Mike's eyes. "That breakfast was meant fo
Breanne Summour. She didn't come to the office that day."

"You witnessed the delivery?" Mike asked, leaning for
ward. "In the reception area?"

"I didn't see who delivered the food. But I witnesse
it taken to the break room. And I can't believe it wa
Winslow who poisoned it, either. He had access to so man
conventional drugs. Why would he use something so ob
scure?"

"The connection to Colombia is clear," Dr. Billings note

"Which means we'd need to find a man from Colombi
with a motive for murder," Mike said. "Clare, what do yo
think? You've been working this case all week. Does anyon
come to mind?"

Oh, my God. "Javier."

"Who?"

"Javier Lozado. I met him at Madame's luncheon. He's

ry dashing Colombian man, operates several coffee planta-
ons down there. He also had a terrible past experience with
att over a woman he loved named Louisa. Matt slept with
e woman behind his back. They came to blows over it."

"Is Javier's grudge strong enough to commit murder?"

"He's a proud Latin American man." I closed my eyes.
And he told me he used to be a commando in the Colom-
an army! He'd know how to stalk someone, how to shoot a
an and hit a target. My God, it was *Matt's* past all along
d not Breanne's that was the key to the danger. Why didn't
ee it?"

I leaned forward in my chair, laid out the facts. "The
ght Hazel Boggs was murdered, Javier *wasn't* at the bache-
r party, which means he could have been staking out the
llage Blend, waiting for Breanne to appear. When he saw
e look-alike with Matt, he could have shot her for
venge—by mistake."

Mike nodded. "Go on."

"Javier would have discovered the next day that Breanne
as still alive. So he changed tactics and used the poison.
hen that didn't work, he got more brazen and simply at-
cked her in the restaurant's bathroom. He certainly had the
pportunity for the bathroom attack. He was at Madame's
pas luncheon, but he *left* before Breanne went into the
throom! We all thought he ran after Matt, but he could
ve doubled back to attack Breanne. Koa Waipuna said
ey all split up to find Matt, and he didn't see Javier again
r almost an hour!"

Mike nodded again, pulled out his notebook. "We need
ore on this man. Write down his name for me, Clare. I
ant his description and anything else that can ID him. Do
u know where he's staying?"

"No, but I can find out."

I rang Matt to warn him about Javier. Matt had trouble
lieving it, but not after I told him about the poison.

"Is Javier there now?" I asked. "At the rehearsal dinner?"

"No," Matt said. "He's not a member of the wedding

party. I haven't seen much of the man all week. I don't ev
know where he's staying!"

"Take it easy, okay? Mike Quinn's on the phone with I
precinct now. He's going to have a BOLO issued. We'll fi
him."

We spoke a few more minutes, and then I had to as
"Matt, did Breanne have a talk with you? Did she tell y
about her past?"

After a pause, Matt lowered his voice. "She told me ever
thing, Clare. Where she was born, how she grew up, her re
name, everything."

"The wedding's still on, isn't it?"

"Of course! I don't give a crap about her past. It's n
body's business but her own. All that matters to me now
our future."

I couldn't stop the smile. For the first time in a lo
while, I was actually proud of my ex-husband. "Now tha
the Matt *I* married."

"What?"

"Forget it. I just hope you'll both be very happy."

A minute later, Mike finished his own call. "If we ca
pick up Javier before tomorrow's wedding, we're going
the wedding in plain clothes."

"It's a big crowd, Mike. How many cops are coming?"

"Soles and Bass, some of the guys in my building. The d
tectives on the Machu Picchu attack."

I shook my head. It was hard to believe, but Breann
white wedding was about to become an NYPD stakeout.

⚬⚭⚬⚭⚬⚭⚬⚭⚬⚭⚬⚭⚬⚭⚬⚭⚬⚭⚬

Thirty-Five

"Everything looks perfect, Clare! Just *perfect*!"

Janelle Babcock folded her arms and stepped back from our coffee and dessert station. Her delicate confections were arranged on serving trees, surrounded by hand-blown Venetian glass, each jewel-toned piece filled with samples of my rare, roasted coffee beans.

"*Perfect* isn't my favorite word," I said. "But it does look spectacular."

Esther Best strolled up to us, her wild dark hair tied neatly back, her blue Village Blend apron covering a plain white blouse and black slacks. "Nice bling," she said, pointing to Nunzio's fountain at the center of the display.

"Priceless bling," I said. "Go ahead and take a closer look."

The tabletop fountain consisted of three golden catch basins. Around the rim of each bowl, finely detailed reliefs depicted scenes from the stories of history's most famous lovers. The entire sculpture was capped by the stylized nudes of a man and woman. Sparkling Prosecco—kissed with the sweetness of peach nectar—poured out of the apple in the woman's hand and flowed like golden rain from one bowl to the next, through hundreds of holes in each basin's bottom.

"Okay, let's see what we've got here," Esther said. "Adam

and Eve at the top, and I can see the snake, too, with real ruby eyes. Nice. And what's on the middle tier?"

"That's Antony and Cleopatra," I said. "You can follow the story in pictures around the bowl. See the poison asp biting the queen of the Nile? The snake has real emeralds for eyes."

"The base is Romeo and Juliet," Janelle noted.

Esther studied the entire piece for a moment then scratched her head. "Ah, kids? Weren't these lovers sort of screwed by the end of their stories? I mean, I don't see any happily-ever-after here."

I froze for a second then glanced at Janelle. We'd been working with photos and dimensions and metric volumes. We'd never considered the sculpture's overall meaning.

"I think she's right," Janelle said, stifling a laugh.

I folded my arms and sighed, recalling my evening with Nunzio. The man was sexy as hell, but he'd displayed all the sentiment of a soccer ball. "You know what? I think the artist knew exactly what he was doing, and the joke's on us."

I checked my watch. At this very moment, beneath a rose bower on the Met's Roof Garden, Matt and Breanne were exchanging vows, surrounded by a half-dozen NYPD detectives, including Mike Quinn, Sully, Soles and Bass, and Rocky Friar. I felt confident they would snatch Javier Lozado the moment he showed his mustachioed face.

Everything was good to go on our end of the European Sculpture Court. The espresso machines at the Blend's station were up and running, the Clovers were in place, the cups and glass mugs ready, and my baristas were eager to begin serving the moment the guests arrived.

"Tell me again about the first toast?" Janelle asked.

"As soon as the bride and groom come down from the roof, we're going to become the center of attention. The newlyweds will walk right over to us and toast each other with shots of espresso."

I showed Janelle the heavy, sterling silver tray Madame was going to use to serve the couple the first cups of their married life.

Janelle shook her head. "I still don't get it. Why toast with coffee when there's all this great champagne around?"

"The guests will be drinking champagne, but not the wedding party. Toasting with coffee is a family tradition started by Matt's great-grandfather. It's based on an old Turkish custom. The bridegroom made a promise to always provide coffee for his wife. If he failed to deliver, it was grounds for divorce."

"Coffee is *grounds* for divorce?" Janelle groaned. "There's a joke in there somewhere."

Another man with a camera approached our coffee and dessert display, which the *Trend* photographer had already snapped dozens of times.

"Clare, look at the man's ID. That photographer's from the *New York Times*!" Janelle whispered. "Come on, let's talk our way into his pictures."

"You go, girl." I smiled. "It's your night."

I checked my watch again. Once the tidal wave hit, I wouldn't have a moment's peace for at least four solid hours. With my servers chatting around the coffee station, and Janelle speaking with the *Times* photographer, I decided to circle the vast sculpture court before the crowd came at us.

Across the expanse of white marble, a string quartet had begun tuning up. Their perfect prolonged notes rose hauntingly in the airy space, but the blush of the setting sun, suffusing everything with burnished light, was what made the last room absolutely magical. The glowing rays streamed through the glass panels of the pitched roof, giving the fifteen-foot stone sculptures the patina of antique brass. More light streamed from the west through the transparent wall that faced Central Park. Below the endless blue of a cloudless sky, newly budding trees swayed in the mild spring breeze.

I paused inside the Sculpture Court to watch a photographer rearrange his subject under the marble likeness of Perseus. More pixielike models in designer gowns posed amid the statuary, the artfully arranged raw bar and hors

d'oeuvres, and the mountain of tastefully wrapped weddin
gifts piled like pirate booty.

The photographers were hustling now, trying to finish be
fore the 350 guests descended from witnessing the weddin
ceremony. As I moved to the far end of the quiet atrium t
study a fifteenth-century Venetian sculpture of Adam, a ta
man in a tuxedo approached me. He was clean-shaven wit
spiky hair and a rugged, handsome face. I didn't realize wh
the man was until he stopped right in front of me.

"Good evening, Ms. Cosi. Are you prepared for the bi
event?"

In shock, I stared at Javier Lozado. I took a breath
glanced around. There was no one close to help. The mu
seum guards were all clustered out of sight, at the entranc
to the event. The waitstaff was busy at their stations at th
other end of the vast room, and Mike and his detectives wer
on the roof with the bride and groom.

Fat lot of good that does me now!

"You seem surprised," Javier said, stroking his smoot
chin. "Is it my new look?"

I wanted to run, scream, call for help. But I couldn't tak
the chance that Javier was armed. The police upstairs ha
guns, but I knew the Met security staff did not. I could stal
until the police arrived, but the crowds would come wit
them, and all I could think about were the innocent peopl
who might get hurt if gunfire erupted in a crowded room.

I have to talk to him, make him see that his plan won't work . .

I cleared my throat, tried to keep the nervousness out c
my voice. "Pretty clever, Javier, shaving off that big mus
tache."

"Clever?" Javier laughed. "I suppose so. But it wasn't m
idea."

"I'm sure you didn't want to. But I have to hand it to you
shaving really changed your appearance—especially sinc
your passport was so old and you had a full beard in th
photo. You got a drastically new haircut, too, I see."

"Yes, it's a whole new look."

"And you checked out of your hotel room. Very smart."

"How do you know that I—"

"But it didn't work, Javier. The police are on to you, anyway—"

"What police? What are you talking about, Ms. Cosi?"

"The authorities know about your plan. There are police all over the museum, and a personal bodyguard with Breanne. You'll never get close enough to the bride to kill her. You'll only die yourself—"

"Clare! What kind of talk is this? Have you been drinking? Is Matt's remarrying too much of a strain—"

"It was the woman, wasn't it? Matt's affair with Louisa hurt you terribly. I can imagine. But you're a handsome, successful man, Javier. Surely, there were other women since her?"

"Louisa! This is about *Louisa?*"

"She's the woman you planned to marry, right? Until she strayed with Matt—"

"Let me show you something." Javier reached into his evening jacket.

I couldn't imagine how he got a weapon past the Met's metal detectors, but he was a former commando. Maybe he knew a few tricks. It didn't matter, anyway. It was impossible to do anything now but fight or run.

Here it comes! The man's hand came out clutching—*a wallet?* He flipped the leather folder open, displayed a photograph tucked behind plastic.

"This is Louisa."

The woman had long black hair and laughing eyes. She was surrounded by children, and she appeared to weigh at least three hundred pounds.

"She's married now to the manager of a neighboring plantation. We speak often. But I am most definitely over this woman."

Javier slipped the wallet back into his tailored jacket. "And my change in appearance is easily explained. I met an American woman, Ms. Cosi." He smiled. "I have been spending my

nights with her, which is why I checked out of my hotel
Yesterday, she confessed to me that she did not like my mustache. She said it made me look like Pancho Villa." He rolled
his eyes, shrugged. "So I shaved. It was a fair exchange. She
has been even more affectionate with me since."

"You have an American girlfriend?"

"Her name is Cody. She's gone off to find the ladies' room.
We were running late and could not make the wedding ceremony. But we are happy to be here for the reception. I'll introduce you when she—"

"Javier, listen to me. A rare Colombian poison was used in
an attempt to murder Breanne. Some kind of batrachotoxin,
according to the medical examiner."

"Batrachotoxin?" Javier's face fell. "Made from the skin of
a yellow frog, yes?"

"You know about it?"

"I use it," he said.

"What?"

"Not me," he quickly amended. "Hector Pena. He is my
estate manager. He extracts frog poison then puts it on
barbed wire surrounding our buildings. It discourages bandits and FARC. Hector learned the trick from his father."

I thought about the quiet, sad-faced man. "Hector was
with you in the Colombian army, wasn't he?"

"Yes, but—"

"It *must* be him. But why would Hector want to kill
Matt's bride?!"

"Kill Breanne?" Javier shook his head. "I can't imagine
that Hector—"

"How does Hector know Matt exactly?"

"From his trips to our farm. Matteo also knew Hector's
daughter. A few years ago, she moved to Bogotá to live and
work. Matt spent time with her there, whenever he passed
through our country—"

"But Hector's daughter died, didn't she? You told us she
was murdered?"

"I did not say she was murdered. Andelina died by gun-hot." He lowered his voice. "To be honest, the young woman shot herself. But we do not speak of it. Colombia is a Catholic country. Suicide is a mortal sin, so—"

"How long ago did this happen?"

"About four weeks."

I suddenly felt sick. "Around the time Breanne raided Matt's PDA and sent wedding announcements to his old flames."

Javier registered surprise. "I never made the connection, but you are right. Matt would have had Andelina's address and phone number in his files." He lowered his voice. "Mateo was intimate with Hector's daughter, Ms. Cosi. You understand my meaning?"

Oh God. "Javier, listen to me. I think Hector's daughter killed herself over losing Matt. She must have been unbalanced already, and that stupid wedding announcement sent her over the edge."

"You believe Hector is trying to kill Breanne for this?"

"Not for sending the announcement. He couldn't have known she was behind that. No, I think Hector is trying to exact some kind of twisted justice. He wants to show Matt the pain of losing a woman he loves." I clutched Javier's arm. "Have you seen Hector today?"

"Yes." Now Javier looked sick, too. "I just saw him. He brought a gift with him, so he was delayed by security. But Hector should be inside the museum by now. I will look for him—"

"No!" I pushed Javier back against the wall. "You're my only witness to the batrachotoxin connection, and I want you to stay right here. I'll go up to the roof and talk to the police. Right now the authorities are looking for *you*, not Hector. Until I straighten that out, you could be arrested."

He frowned but nodded. "I will do as you ask."

Dozens of guests were now wandering into the Sculpture Court. Like Javier, they'd opted out of the wedding ceremony and come only for the reception. I dodged the small crowd and moved toward the exit. On my way, I scanned the

area near the table of wedding gifts, but there was no sign o
Hector there.

When I reached the elevators, I discovered they were ou
of service. Security was holding the cars on the roof until th
end of the ceremony! I cursed and searched for another wa
up. I followed a long, empty corridor before I finally foun
the steel doors to the stairwell, right beside a glass emer
gency exit that opened onto Central Park.

I entered the gloomy stairwell and nearly fell on my face
My feet had become entangled in torn wrapping paper and
length of scattered ribbon. As I freed myself, I spied a gif
box on the ground, packing tissue scattered around it. Lean
ing against the wall, I saw the metallic gleam of a silver bow
and large brass candleholders.

I heard footsteps above me and looked up.

Hector Pena stood at the top of the stairs, staring down a
me. He wore a black tuxedo and gripped a small gun.

In a flash I knew how he'd managed it: the wrapped gift
The metal bowl and candleholders might have shielded th
entire shape of the gun in the X-ray machine. Or he coul
have simply broken the gun down into pieces and reassem
bled the weapon here in the stairwell.

I gasped as our gazes met. Hector's flesh was more sallov
than I remembered, and the circles under his eyes seeme
more prominent, too. In the shadows his face seemed skele
tal, like a death's head. In a blink, he saw recognition in m
expression, understanding, too.

He knows that I know.

Hector lifted his weapon as he raced down the stairs, tw
at a time. I whirled and threw open the door. The corrido
was still deserted. If I tried running back to the Sculptur
Court, Hector could shoot me in the back. Someone *migh*
hear the shot. Or they might not. Either way, I wouldn't b
around to worry about it. I'd be *dead*.

I heard Hector opening the heavy stairwell door behinc
me. With no other way to escape, I pushed through the glas
fire exit and staggered outside the museum, onto the sof

rass of Central Park. The door closed behind me. Hector rashed into it a split second later. I thought he was going to hoot me through the clear pane, but he smiled triumphantly instead.

I heard a muffled burst of applause from inside the museum and realized the wedding party had finally come down rom the roof! Hector realized it, too. He tucked the gun inside his black evening jacket and turned around. As soon as e was out of sight, I ran back to the door. It was locked! Hector *knew* I was stuck outside, and he didn't care. Which meant he was on his way to kill Breanne—and maybe Matt, oo—right *now*! He was gambling I wouldn't have time to varn them!

No!

I stumbled across the lawn, my low heels sticking in the till-damp ground; then I reached the sidewalk and took off t a dead run. The Metropolitan Museum covered five city blocks, and I had to travel at least half of that distance to each the front entrance.

Panting, I cleared the modern art wing and blew past a bronze statue of three bears nestled among a circle of benches. Fifth Avenue and Eightieth Street were just ahead.

wended my way through a mass of exiting tourists, printed the long flight of stone steps, and burst into the museum's lobby. Breathlessly I stumbled up to a tall African American man in a guard uniform and flashed my events bass.

"Help, please . . . there's a man . . . he's armed . . . in the Sculpture Court . . ."

The guard tensed. "The wedding?"

I nodded. Clearly, he'd been briefed. He grabbed my arm and spoke into the radio headset he was wearing. As we ran toward the back of the museum, I told him everything I knew. He related the information over the radio to the NYPD.

Two minutes later, we were entering the European Sculpture and Decorative Arts wing, and the guard visibly relaxed.

"They have him in custody, ma'am," he told me, tapping h
earphones. "He tried to approach the wedding party, and the
grabbed him."

"Oh, thank goodness." I gasped, the tension flowing ou
of me.

Although the public was still milling around the museum
the European Sculpture Court was closed for our private part
I saw its atrium ahead, the waning sunlight glinting off it
marble figures. Tired as I felt, I increased my pace.

Entering the court, I spotted a flurry of motion near th
table of wedding gifts. Sully and Lori Soles had a tuxedo
clad man in handcuffs. As the detectives turned him around
I saw his face.

"You've got the wrong man!" Javier Lozado cried. "Liste
to me! Why won't you listen?"

There was no time left. I raced forward, toward the coffe
and dessert station. Matt and Breanne stood there alone
framed against Nunzio's star-crossed fountain. The guest
were at least ten feet back, clearing the area for the photogra
phers to snap away. Madame was stepping up to the couple
her sterling silver gift tray in her hands, two freshly pulle
shots ready to be served.

That's when I spotted Hector, hiding behind a camera
man. He was reaching into his evening jacket! I was too fa
away to do anything more than shout at the top of my lungs
"Matt! It's Hector! Hector's got the gun!"

Matt turned at the sound of my voice, but the phot
flashes had limited his vision. He couldn't see Hector in th
crowd! Breanne froze with stark fear, but she didn't knov
where to look, and her bodyguard had stepped far back fron
the couple so he wouldn't be in their wedding photos!

Madame was right beside them now, and she knew wha
Hector looked like. Spotting him, she lurched forward as h
raised his weapon and aimed for Breanne. The gunsho
boomed, the sound echoing inside the massive space. Bre
anne, Matt, and Madame all went down in a tangle. The sil
ver tray clanged against the floor; dark liquid seeped acros

the white marble. Screams and shouts lifted up, echoing off the pitched roof, drowning out the mannered music. The crowd shrank back, and I rushed forward.

A scuffle broke out: Rocky Friar wrestled with Hector Pena. The Colombian refused to release his small-caliber weapon, even as the muscle-bound detective squeezed his wrist.

"Give it up!" Rocky cried.

"You heard him!" Sue Ellen Bass shouted, rushing forward to Rocky's aid. Together, the two disarmed Hector and cuffed him.

I turned at a new sound: my partner's voice. Matt was sitting up now, clutching his new bride in his arms, wailing like a man who'd lost his one true love.

"No . . ." I whispered.

I saw the dark stain on Breanne's delicate white wedding gown, right over her heart. The liquid bled slowly across the handmade silk. Then Breanne's royal blue eyes fluttered, and I saw the empty espresso cup in her lap. The dark fluid wasn't blood! It was coffee!

But if the bullet missed Breanne, who did it hit?

I whirled. Madame was still on the white marble, Otto Visser bent over her, his face twisted with emotional pain.

My God, no! Not my mother! I rushed to her side, fell to my knees. "Madame? Are you . . ."

Her gently creased face turned toward mine. She pointed to the sterling silver tray on the floor. The metal was badly dented: the tray had deflected the bullet!

"You saved Breanne's life!"

"Your cry saved her, Clare. And Matteo, too . . ." Madame grabbed my arms, pulled me in. "Thank you . . ."

Relieved beyond words, I hugged her tightly. When we parted, Otto and I helped Madame to her feet. We took a moment to check her out, make sure nothing was broken.

"I'm afraid *my gift* is broken," Madame said, shaking her silver head at the dented tray.

"On the contrary." Otto laughed. "I think the couple will cherish it for years to come."

Nodding in complete agreement, I looked around, wondering where the bullet had ended up. Noticing the slight damage to a nearby stone pedestal, I pointed. "Thank heaven no one was hurt. Not even a sculpture."

Otto smiled and squeezed my shoulder. Then Madame's gaze shifted—and she gasped. "Look, Clare," she whispered, "Look at them *now*!"

I turned to see Matt still sitting on the stained marble floor, holding Breanne close, kissing her, petting her, telling her he was there for her.

"Madame? I don't understand. What is it?"

Her blue eyes had dampened. "It's love, my dear."

Otto laughed. Then he put his arm around his girl and kissed her, too.

"I'm so happy, Otto!" Madame declared as they headed for the bar. "My son *does* love his bride . . ."

Still uneasy, I remained behind, surveying the crowded room. When I saw Hector being led out in handcuffs, I finally sagged against my perfect coffee and dessert table.

Matt was still holding his new bride in his arms, kissing her with a passion I hadn't seen him display since our own Hawaiian honeymoon.

It was then I finally noticed our daughter in the crowd, watching her father, her pretty young face full of mixed emotions. I knew how Joy felt. It was surreal, given all that had happened, all that we'd been through.

Oh, sure, on the scale of human history, you could hardly deem the wedding of my ex-husband a significant event. Not like, say, Christopher Columbus discovering the New World. In my own little life, however, it was a moment that changed everything. This really was good-bye to the handsome groom of my youth; the swaggering father of my child; the globe-trotting spouse who liked to pretend that, no matter how many women he slept with, I was his only love.

For a fraction of time, I felt a sadness grip me, the quaking that comes from unforeseen loss. But the seismic shift was a small event, and when it was over, I heard another man call my name.

"Clare! Over here! I'm over here, sweetheart!"

I saw Mike then, breaking through the crowd. With a sure and steady voice, I answered him, because now I was ready—*more* than ready—to explore his new world.

EPILOGUE

~~~~~~

DESPITE starting off with a bang (literally), Matt and Breanne's wedding reception came off quite well. The champagne started flowing, and the well-heeled crowd was soon buzzing with the realization that they now had a fabulous new saga of urban survival—a wedding favor that would keep on giving with retellings at cocktail hours and dinner parties for months to come.

Nunzio's fountain turned out to be the biggest draw of the night, making our coffee and dessert bar a huge hit. Janelle received no less than thirty requests for her business card. And Matt's passion fueled Breanne's emotional recovery. Giddily soaking up her groom's repeated, ardent kisses, the usually restrained, ultra-cool sophisticate was feeling no pain, laughing and animated and uncaring that her exquisite Italian silk creation had been stained like a *macchiato*. I had to give the woman credit, she wore the espresso like a badge of honor—even insisted more photos be taken with the damaged tray and the spattered gown.

"Hector's shot missed Breanne," I told Madame as the evening wound down, "but it killed bridezilla for sure."

As for the sad-eyed Colombian murderer, I had to wait two more days to hear what the police finally got out of him . . .

* * *

Suicide by cop?" Mike told me.

"Suicide by what?"

"You've never heard of it?"

I shook my head.

Mike paused to sip the latte I'd made him. "It's when a
perp commits a crime, expecting the police will gun him
down."

"And that's what Hector told the Fish Squad? That's what
he thought was going to happen at the wedding reception after he shot Breanne?"

Mike nodded.

It was late Monday evening. I'd taken so much time off
work before the wedding that I was giving my baristas a break
and closing myself for a few nights in a row. Mike and I were
the last ones in the Blend. While I finished wiping down the
café tables, Mike watched me from the coffee bar, where he'd
been filling me in on the details of Hector's interrogation.

Distraught and unbalanced, Hector had broken down
fairly quickly, spilling everything when Lori Soles and Sue
Ellen Bass played the "sympathetic ear" gambit.

Just as I'd guessed, Hector confessed to wanting to kill
Matt's bride in order to cause him pain—as much pain as he'd
felt when his own daughter had been (in his words) "driven to
suicide by the wedding announcement she'd received."

Apparently, Andelina Pena had left a long, rambling note
professing her love for Matteo. Hector saw the note, saw
Matt's name, and focused on the idea of vengeance. To him,
the wedding announcement was salt in a wound—a cruel
trick. The fact that it was clutched in his daughter's hand
when she took her own life hadn't helped, either.

"Hector Pena believed he had nothing to lose," Mike said.
"He'd already been diagnosed with cancer. Knowing he
didn't have long to live, he became obsessed with the idea of
avenging his daughter's death."

"Then Hazel Boggs really was a case of mistaken identit just like Matt thought?"

Mike nodded. "Soles and Bass linked the crime throug ballistics on Hector's small-caliber weapon. He hadn't mean to kill the innocent young Hazel. After that, he was eve more distraught. He was also reluctant to use the gun agai The poisoning would have worked if Breanne had gone int the office that morning. Instead, Monica Purcell was the on who died."

"What about Machu Piccchu?"

"Hector attended the luncheon at Javier's urging," Mike said. "He hadn't planned on an attack there, so he didn have his weapon on him. But when he heard that Breann had been behind sending that wedding announcement to h daughter, he became enraged. After Matt ran off and he wa asked to help find him, Hector broke away from the othe men, doubled back, bought a coat and ski mask from a cloth ing store near the restaurant, and slipped inside to wait i the ladies' room—"

"Where I found him, still enraged, trying to strangle Bre anne."

"By the wedding day he was nearly crazy with rage an frustration. He felt sicker than ever, too, and just wanted t die himself."

"So that's why he was so brazen. He expected to be sho after killing the bride."

Mike nodded, took another sip of his latte. "Suicide b cop."

It was a tragic case on both sides, and I wasn't exactl cheered by the body count. "It's hard to believe one simpl act could end up causing so many deaths."

"One simple act?"

I nodded. "Breanne sending out those wedding announce ments to Matt's old flames."

Mike shook his head. "Matt had a lot of old flames Clare. Only one of them chose to make that a reason to kil herself."

"What are you saying?"

Mike shrugged. "Life's messy."

"That's it?"

He arched an eyebrow. "Can you foresee the harm of every choice you make?"

"No, but while I grant you Matt's a cad where women are concerned, he isn't a cruel man. After the reception, he told me that he'd broken up with Andelina months before he'd proposed to Breanne. He said he'd done it as gently as he could, but the young woman had been unstable for a long time, was seeing a therapist, and taking medication." I shook my head. "Still, Breanne had to know she would cause a lot of women a lot of indigestion."

Mike shrugged. "I can't argue that some people are better at making messes than others."

"So why is it people like us always have to clean them up?"

Mike caught my arm, and suggested I *stop* cleaning up for a while. "Take a break, Cosi."

I did, plopping myself next to him at the espresso bar. I noticed the *New York Journal* at the end of the bar and slid it over to him. "Speaking of dirt, guess what's in here."

"Oh, right, that big exposé of Randall Knox's. Now there's a man who not only *likes* dirt, but *feeds* off it."

"Can't argue there, but get a load of this. The coverage of the wedding in the paper is all sweetness and light. Not a word in here about Breanne's sordid past or her connection to the dead stripper Hazel Boggs. Guess why?"

"Knox turned over a new leaf? From now on, he's only going to report good news?"

"I wish. No, it seems Knox wasn't the only one with a file in his desk. Breanne finally admitted to me that she'd compiled a thick file on Knox—and not alone. Remember that suspicious-looking guy I saw outside of Fen's and later at Breanne's office, asking for her?"

"The big guy with the too-tight suit? Yeah. He factors into this?"

"He's a private investigator. Breanne hired him to dig up

unsavory history on Knox, some of which could land gossip boy in prison if she ever decided to release it to the press. It was enough to bring Knox to heel. He agreed to bury Breanne's own file as long as his remained under wraps."

"My ears are still ringing from unsavory allegations that can land him in prison. Anything you want me to look into?"

"Breanne won't say."

"Well, I think you and I might want to watch the guy anyway. Or we can sic the Fish Squad on him, or maybe even the pit bull for all those unpaid parking tickets I saw in the system."

I smiled at the mention of the Sixth's tough lady beat cop they called the pit bull, which got me to wondering. "Mike, I've been wanting to ask you—if I were a dog, what breed would I be? I've always thought of myself as a Jack Russell terrier."

He laughed. "A Jack Russell's not bad for you, but I think you're more you of a border collie."

"A border collie! Aren't border collies, you know . . ."

"What?"

"Stupid!"

"No! They're extremely smart. They just get a little neurotic if they don't have enough to do, but farmers have used them for generations to protect their dim-witted sheep. They're also pretty adorable."

"I'm a border collie?"

"You're adorable . . . and smart and gutsy and loving and . . . C'mere . . ."

Mike's mouth was still warm and slightly sweet from the latte, and his lingering kiss made the collie thing suddenly seem a whole lot easier to take. When we parted, he gazed down at me, brushed back my chestnut hair.

"I just want you to know, Cosi . . . I'm well aware you had a choice, and I'm glad that I'm the man who's here with you now."

"I am, too, Mike. Very glad."

He smiled. "So what dog am I then? Golden retriever? Irish wolfhound?"

"Rottweiler."

Mike laughed. "A police dog, huh?"

"Guard dog. A tough and hardy breed. Dependable, lovable"—I raised an eyebrow—"usually trustworthy . . ."

"Okay. I get it." He raised a hand. "And I'd rather you quit while I'm ahead. Besides, didn't you say something on the phone earlier about an empty apartment upstairs that you've finally got all to yourself?"

I nodded. The bride and groom were off on their honeymoon, Joy was spending the night at her grandmother's, and when my hand reached into my jeans pocket, it came out holding a small piece of shiny metal.

"See," I said. "Before he left for Barcelona, Matt handed over his key."

"And you've got the whole place to yourself tonight, right?"

"That's right, Lieutenant, including the bedroom."

"Come on then, sweetheart." Rising from the chair, Mike tugged my hand. "Let's see if it works."

It did.

I'm happy to report the bedroom worked like a dream—all night long.

RECIPES & TIPS FROM THE VILLAGE BLEND

Visit Cleo Coyle's virtual Village Blend at
www.CoffeehouseMystery.com
for coffee tips, coffee talk, and more recipes!

Generous trays of cookies, baked by the women of my family, were a delicious and important addition to our Italian wedding feasts. But cookies aren't just eaten at special occasions in Italian culture. Biscotti, pizzelles (sweet waffle cookies), and many other kinds are enjoyed at all hours of the day: at breakfast with cappuccinos, in the afternoon with an espresso pick-me-up, or after dinner on a dessert dish.

Anginetti

(Glazed Lemon Cookies)

The *anginetti* are a satisfying treat to have with coffee. Light and buttery with a sweet lemon glaze, they often make their appearance during the holidays, and the (optional) sprinkle of nonpareils (*confetti* in Italian) over the glaze makes them an excellent wedding cookie, too, since the colorful sugar balls call to mind the long-standing wedding tradition of giving guests almonds coated with hard-sugar shells as favors. (The bitterness of the almonds and the sweetness of the sugar represent the bittersweet truths of married life.) While recipes for *anginetti* vary—some bakers shape figure eights from a rope of dough, others simply create lemon drops—my version uses the ring shape in honor of Nunzio's wedding rings. My version is also a bit sweeter than more traditional recipes.

Makes between 3 and 4 dozen cookies
(depending on size and shape of cookie)

> 6 tablespoons butter
> ¾ cup granulated white sugar
> 1½ teaspoons pure vanilla extract
> ½ teaspoon lemon extract
> 1 teaspoon fresh lemon zest (grated from rind)
> ⅛ teaspoon salt (pinch or two)
> 3 large eggs
> ¼ cup whole milk
> 2½ cups all-purpose flour (sifted)
> 4 teaspoons baking powder

With an electric mixer, cream the butter and sugar together with vanilla and lemon extracts, lemon zest, and salt. Add eggs and milk and beat for a minute or two until light and fluffy. Add flour and baking powder, blending well with mixer until you have a dough (be careful not to overmix the dough or cookies will be tough). Dough should be soft and sticky. Chill for at least one hour; cold dough is easier to work with.

Preheat the oven to 350°F. Line baking sheet with parchment paper or silicon sheets, or spray surface with cooking spray. With well-greased hands (I rub butter over my fingers and palms), shape bits of dough into small ropes (about the thickness of a woman's wedding ring finger), make a ring with the rope of dough about 2 inches in diameter, and press the ends together on the baking sheet. Or for lemon drops simply roll pieces of dough into balls about 1 inch in size and place on baking sheets. (If you want to go really rustic, then don't even bother chilling the dough. Simply drop teaspoonfuls of the sticky dough onto the baking sheet.) Bake about 10 to 15 minutes. Don't overcook. Baking time may vary, depending on your oven! Let cookies cool before glazing and decorating.

LEMON GLAZE

2 tablespoons butter
4 tablespoons water
2 teaspoons lemon extract
2 cups confectioners' sugar (sifted)

In a nonstick saucepan, place the butter, water, and lemon extract over low heat. Stir slowly until butter melts (do not let butter brown or burn). Add confectioners' sugar, a little at a time, stirring constantly. Wait until sugar dissolves before adding more. Continue until all sugar has been added. Stir or whisk if needed until your glaze is smooth. Use a pastry brush to glaze your cooled cookies. (Optional: If you wish to add decorations to your cookies, such as nonpareils or colored sugar, be sure to sprinkle while glaze is still warm. I actually prefer the cookies without any decorations, just the lemon glaze.)

TIPS: Lemon glaze must be kept warm to stay a liquid. If i hardens up on you, simply warm up the glaze again, stirrin or whisking to regain the smooth, liquid consistency. If yo like a thicker glaze on your cookie (like I do), try "painting a second or even a third layer of glaze on the cookie after th first layer hardens. Enjoy!

Baci di Romeo

(Romeo's Kisses)

Rich chocolate ganache seals the kiss of two delicious almond-flavor cookies.

Makes about 2½ dozen sandwiches

> 1 cup (2 sticks) butter
> 1 cup confectioners' sugar
> 2 teaspoons vanilla
> 2 teaspoons almond extract
> 1 egg
> 2 tablespoons milk
> ¼ teaspoon salt
> 2 cups all-purpose flour
> ½ teaspoon baking powder
> ½ cup ground, toasted almonds*

---

*TIP: Be sure to start with blanched almonds. (To save time, look for slivere almonds in the store, which are already blanched). Toast the almonds b spreading them on a cookie sheet and baking them in the oven for about te minutes (350°F.). Then you can grind the almonds in a food processor, or jus put the nuts in a plastic bag and bang away at them with a cleaver until yo have a powder. (I use a small coffee mill to grind my nuts and spices, but I onl use it for that purpose. The mill you use to grind your whole bean coffee shoul *only* be used for coffee.)

Cream butter and sugar. Add vanilla, almond extract, egg, milk, and salt; mix until light and fluffy. Add flour, baking powder, and ground almonds. Mix just until blended (don't overmix at this stage). Chill dough for 30 minutes (makes it easier to handle). Preheat oven to 350°F. Roll out dough into 1-inch balls. Roll them in sugar, place on lined or greased baking sheet, and flatten balls with bottom of a glass. Bake 10–12 minutes (watch your oven!). If cookies overbake, they will be dry.

CHOCOLATE GANACHE "KISS"

½ cup heavy cream
5 tablespoons sugar
4 tablespoons butter
12 ounces semisweet chocolate chips
or chopped bittersweet chocolate
2 teaspoons vanilla extract

Heat the cream, sugar, and butter in saucepan. Stir until butter melts and liquid simmers, but *do not* let mixture boil! In a separate bowl, pour hot cream mixture over chocolate. Waiting two minutes, whisk well until smooth, and whisk in vanilla. Let ganache cool for a half hour in fridge, no more! Next drop (or pipe with pastry bag) about a teaspoonful on the flat side of one cookie and gently sandwich together with a second cookie's flat side. Press lightly to seal the kiss! Repeat until all cookies are kissing. (*Optional use:* while still warm, ganache can be used as a glaze for a cake.) If ganache harden too much, reheat. Makes about 2 cups.

Bellini

Like Nunzio's *Lover's Spring*, this classic cocktail was created in Italy. It was invented in 1943, at Harry's Bar in Venice during an exhibition of art by the fifteenth-century Venetian painter, Giovanni Bellini.

According to the man who created the drink, Giuseppe Cipriani, the cocktail's color matched the hue of a toga in one of Bellini's masterpieces, so he named the drink after the artist.

The Bellini is traditionally made with pureed white peaches, but in America (due to the limited availability of the white variety) yellow peaches are often substituted. Sometimes a touch of cherry or raspberry juice is added to blush the drink into an especially vibrant color.

Prosecco is the sparkling wine of choice when making this cocktail. Other sparkling wines can certainly be substituted, but the heavier flavor of French champagne doesn't pair as well with the light, fruity taste of the peach.

> 1 part well-pureed peaches (remove skins)*
> 2 parts *chilled* sparkling wine or champagne (Prosecco is best)

Peel the peach and puree it in a blender. Pour the puree into a pitcher (or a single glass), add the well-chilled Prosecco (or champagne), and stir well. Serve in chilled champagne flute.

---

*For a quick shortcut, use peach nectar.

Machu Picchu's Paella

This hearty and tasty dish is brimming with Spanish flavors. To give it the Peruvian flair, follow the example of Machu Picchu's chef and exchange the rice in this recipe for quinoa. The *paella* name, by the way, comes from the paella pan in which it is prepared and served (large, flat, and shallow like a frying pan). It's traditionally cooked with a variety of meats and shellfish, but this is a versatile enough recipe for you to experiment. You can add fresh seared chorizo instead of dry, or try substituting different types of seafoods and meats to make it your own!

Serves 8

1 large Spanish onion
1 large yellow onion
1 large green pepper
1 large red pepper
6 ounces hot, dry chorizo (Spanish sausage)
5–7 cloves fresh garlic
½ cup scallions
1 large red tomato
12–15 clams
1 pound mussels
8 ounces green peas
2 skinless, boneless chicken breasts or 1 pound chicken tenders
1 tablespoon sea salt
1 tablespoon freshly ground black pepper
12–15 large shrimp
⅓ cup extra virgin olive oil
4–5 cups (at least 32 ounces) chicken stock, more as needed

1 pound white rice*
2 teaspoons crushed Spanish saffron

Dice the Spanish and yellow onions, the green and red peppers, and the chorizo. Mince the garlic and thinly slice the scallions. Peel and slice the tomato. Clean the clams. Clean and debeard the mussels. Cook the green peas. Cut chicken breasts into strips and season with salt and pepper. Peel and devein the shrimp, but keep the shells.

In a large pot, sauté the shrimp shells in ⅓ of the olive oil, until they turn pink. Add the stock and saffron, and simmer for thirty minutes. Strain out the shells and set aside the hot liquid.

Add another third of the olive oil and heat to medium high. Sauté the chicken, browning on all sides, then remove.

Add the remaining oil, the onions, tomato, red and green peppers, and sauté for 3–5 minutes. Add the garlic and sauté for another minute or so. Add the chorizo (dry or fresh) and rice. Make sure to stir the pot to coat the rice with oil.

Add the hot stock, the chicken, and the clams to the pot. Cover and reduce heat. Cook for 5–6 minutes, until the clams open. Do not stir during the cooking process.

Add the mussels and shrimp to the pot. Cover and cook for 6–8 minutes. Add more stock during this stage if necessary. With 1 minute left, add the precooked peas to reheat them. Garnish with scallions and serve immediately.

---

*The highly nutritious grain quinoa (aka Inca rice, still popular in Peru after 5,000 years) may be substituted for regular rice in this recipe.

Lomo Saltado

This hearty dish is the Peruvian version of meat and potatoes. It's a "mom and pop" meal with versions served in virtually every restaurant and home in Peru. Like spaghetti sauce, Mulligan stew, or shepherd's pie, no two versions of *lomo saltado* are exactly alike. Make this dish your own by tossing in additional ingredients, such as a pureed tomato, or try different types of peppers. You can even marinate the meat for an hour prior to cooking. Use your favorite beef marinade recipe, or try soy sauce, or even cold coffee, which will impart an earthy note and help tenderize the meat.

Approximately 6 servings

Sirloin tips sliced thin, approximately two pounds
2–3 russet potatoes
4 tablespoons vegetable oil
4 cloves garlic
Tomato purée (optional)
1 teaspoon sea salt
1 teaspoon ground pepper
2 tablespoons of soy sauce
2 yellow onions
2 red onions
2 red peppers
2 yellow peppers
1 large (or 2 small) jalapeno pepper
1 tablespoon fresh oregano
⅓ cup chopped cilantro
1 cup white rice (optional)

Cut the meat into thin strips and marinate for one to two hours (if desired).

Julienne and fry the unpeeled potatoes in a separate pan and keep them warm.

Now place a nonstick pan over medium heat and add the oil. Sauté the minced garlic and add the meat. When cooked through (two to three minutes) reserve the juice in a separate container.

Add the tomato purée (if desired), the sea salt, and ground pepper to the meat in the pan. Cook for a few minutes, then add the soy sauce while stirring the contents of the pan. Next add chopped onions, chopped peppers, oregano, and the chopped cilantro. Return the reserved juice from the meat to the pan. Cook, uncovered, over medium heat for 3–5 minutes.

To serve, place meat and vegetables in a large serving dish and garnish with fried potatoes. In Peru, this dish is also served with cooked white rice.

Here's a preview of the next book
in the Coffeehouse Mysteries by Cleo Coyle . . .

HOLIDAY GRIND

Coming November 2009 in hardcover
from Berkley Prime Crime!

PROLOGUE

〜〜〜〜〜〜〜〜〜〜〜〜〜〜〜〜〜〜〜〜

SANTA'S been naughty . . .

He also had a pattern, and the shooter was counting on it.

*Out the door at noon, then a bus downtown. By one, the white-
bearded wanderer was checking in at the depot near Union Square,
picking up his green plastic "sleigh," starting his six-hour shift.*

*Slowly, Santa made his way down Sixth, ringing his annoying
bells, collecting his precious change. At close to three, he turned west.
On Hudson, he parked his little wheeled cart and disappeared inside
that Village Blend coffee shop. One interminable latte break later,
the wannabe saint was back on the street, ho-ho-hoing his chubby
heart out.*

*Step by agonizing step, the shooter watched while ducking into
doorways, hugging dirty buildings, keeping humanity at a chilly
distance. When twilight descended, snow began to fall, the temperature dropping with it, and the watching got harder.*

At least the bulky overcoat was thick and warm, the shoot thought. Ratty, too, because it came from a thrift store, but it wou soon be trashed, along with the hat, the scarf, the eyeglasses, ar other pieces of disguise.

Before long, the wasted hours would finally pay off. Santa wayward travels led him down a stretch of deserted cobblestones. T street was quiet, secluded, frozen over in white. Everything was s now, except for the gloves.

Thick with insulation, the gloves had provided warmth to spa on this long, cold slog, but now they posed a problem. Any paddin between trigger and guard could make life difficult—or death, this case.

So off came the right glove. A bit of anxious sweat on the finge tips slickened the surface of the pocketed weapon. The season weather swiftly solved that glitch.

Icy metal. My new best friend . . .

Impatient now, the shooter moved to finish the job. Then th ridiculous getup could be discarded, replaced with personal oute wear—garments now sitting inside the newly purchased gym ba which would also be tossed.

Next the gun would be wiped clean and carefully placed. F nally, the alibi would be established: an appearance at a publ place, one previously frequented. A register receipt would confir date and time.

And speaking of time . . .

The shooter's big boots crunched firmly through the sidewa snow. The air was cold but blood turned colder when stiff finge tightened around frosty metal.

It's time to end this problem, the shooter thought. Time silence forever the rest of Santa's nights . . .

～～～～～～～～～～～～～～～～～～～～～

"**W**HAT does Christmas *taste* like?"

That was the question I'd posed to my top baristas the night I discovered Alf Glockner's body. Until I stumbled over the man's remains, however, I hadn't been thinking about murder or corpses or crime-scene evidence. My mood hadn't plummeted; my worries hadn't started; my buoyant holiday spirits hadn't crashed through the floor.

I, Clare Cosi—single mother of a grown daughter and manager of the landmark Village Blend—still believed this was a season for celebrating. Which was why, on that particular December evening, my mind was not focused on clues or suspects or the riskier aspects of defying a cocky NYPD sergeant, but on the much simpler problem of my shop's bottom line. Hence the question to my staff—

What does Christmas taste like?

"Well, nutmeg's a must," Tucker replied.

An itinerate actor-playwright and my most reliable employee, Tucker Burton was lanky as a floor lamp, his lean form topped by a defining shock of floppy brown hair. Sitting across from me in our empty coffeehouse, he tossed back the signature hair and added—

"Cloves. And cinnamon. *Definitely* cinnamon."

"Festive spices all," I agreed. "But we've got them covered—" Turning in my chair, I tipped my pen toward the chalkboard behind the espresso bar. "Our Eggnog Latte's got the nutmeg; the Caramel Apple Pie is loaded with cinnamon; the Pumpkin Spice includes all three—"

And that was the problem.

Those drinks had been on the Village Blend's seasonal menu for years now, and they were starting to feel tired. With the sluggish economy taking its toll on everyone's wallets (mine included), I needed to accelerate the ringing of our registers before we rang in the New Year. And, *yes*, I had a strategy.

Later tonight, I was holding a private latte-tasting party; and first thing tomorrow I planned to place a new menu of tempting holiday coffee drinks on a sidewalk chalkboard in front of the coffeehouse. I even had an Excel spreadsheet ready to go. Come January, after the halls were no longer decked and Santa had sent his red velvet suit to the cleaners, I'd start analyzing our sales results to get a handle on the better-selling flavors for next year.

"What *else* tastes like Christmas?" I repeated. "Come on, people, think back to your childhoods!"

My own foodie memories were as treasured as that overused reference to Proust's madeleine—from my grandmother's anisette-flavored biscotti to the candied orange peels in her panettone. And, of course, there was her traditional *struffoli*: I could still see those cellophane-wrapped plates lined up in Nonna's little Pennsylvania grocery, the golden balls of honey-drenched dough mounded into tiny Italian Christmas trees (just waiting to help make me the chunky monkey I'd been until my midteens).

Unfortunately for me, *Fried Dough Latte* just didn't sound like a winning menu item.

"What I remember is the pralines," Tucker said.

"Pecan pralines?" I assumed, because he'd been raised in Louisiana.

"Of course. Every year, our next-door neighbor made them from scratch and gave them out as presents. Another woman on the block was German, and she made up these delicious gift tins of frosted gingerbread cookies—"

"*Pfeffernsse?*" I asked. " *Lebkuchen?*"

"*Gesundheit.*" Tucker replied. "Of course, my *own* mama, being a former Hollywood film extra, was obsessed with Bing Crosby and *White Christmas*, so we had all that traditional Yankee Yule stuff—fruitcake, candy canes, sugar cookies. And, of course, bourbon."

I smiled. "With my dad it was Sambuca shots."

He poured them like water for the army of factory guys who dropped by to place bets during the Christmas season. (Among other things, my father ran a sports book in the back room of his mother's grocery. I'm fairly sure the "other" things weren't legal, either.)

"In my house, it was rum," Gardner offered.

With a voice as smooth as his jazz playlists, Gardner Evans had the kind of mellow attitude any New York retail manager would value—and I did. No amount of customer crush could frazzle the young, African-American jazz musician, who seemed able to calm our most wired customers (especially the female variety) with little more than a wink.

"Rum?" Tucker said.

Gardner nodded. "Oh, yeah. If you're talking *taste* of Christmas, you've got to have rum."

Esther Best—zaftig grad student, local slam poetess, and latte artist extraordinaire—peered at Gardner through a pair of black rectangular frames. "What do you mean, rum? Like the stuff pirates drink?"

"Like hot buttered rum," Gardner said, stroking his trimmed goatee. "Like the rum in mulled cider and spiked eggnog. Like the Jamaican rum in my auntie's bread pudding and black cake. Ever have Caribbean black cake, Best Girl?"

"Haven't had the pleasure."

"Well, it's a lot like you."

"Like me?"

"Yeah." Gardner's smile flashed white against his mocha skin. "It's dark and dense with powerful *flav-ah.*"

Narrowing her perpetually critical gaze, Esther replied, "I am *not* dense."

"But you *are* dark," Tucker pointed out. "Besides, the man said *dense* with *flavor*. Or are you too dense to understand Gardner's derisive gangsta-rap inflection?"

"Bite me, Broadway Boy. My boyfriend's the *top* Russian rapper in Brighton Beach. I think I can recognize the mocking of urban street slang when I hear it—" Esther held a palm up to Gardner. "And *do not* give me another musicology lecture. I know you've got a major grudge against gangsta rap."

Gardner folded his arms, leaned back in his chair, and shrugged. "Whatever."

"Anyway—" Esther turned to face me. "We can't put *rum* in a latte. Right, boss? Rum is alcohol. And unless I missed the memo, you haven't gotten a liquor license for this place, have you?"

"No *duh*," said Tucker. "We can use rum *syrup*. Why do you think I used peppermint syrup for my Candy Cane Cappuccino? I would have used actual crème de menthe if it were legal!"

"Now that you've brought it up," Esther said, "I think we should eighty-six Tucker's Christmas Cap." She held up one of the many paper cups holding the evening's first round of samples. "His Candy Cane Cappuccino's *way* too sweet. If we put this on the holiday menu, I guarantee two out of three customers will complain to have it remade—or just spew it back out."

"A lovely holiday image," Dante Silva called from behind the espresso bar. With his sleeves rolled up to show off his self-designed tattoos, the shaved-headed fine arts painter had just begun frothing up a fresh pitcher of milk.

"Are you *serious*?" Esther shouted from our table. "Or is that steam wand drowning out your sarcasm?"

"I can see it now," Dante replied with a straight face, "a cobblestone street in the historic West Village; snow falling lightly on shingled rooftops; primary colors twinkling around the trunks of bared elms; and our customers spewing Tucker's Candy Cane Cap all over their Ugg boots."

Tucker smirked. "Now all Dante has to do is paint it for us. Hey, Dante! Why don't you make it into a stencil for latte toppings? Or better yet, just tattoo it to your billiard-ball head!"

Dante's reply was a hand gesture.

I sighed, wondering what the heck had happened to our holiday spirit. An hour earlier, when we'd been decorating the shop, things had gone so well I thought I'd been painted into a Currier and Ives print.

After closing early, my staff helped me pick out a New York white pine from the sidewalk vendor on Jane Street. As Tucker's basso crooned "O Tannenbaum," Dante and Gardner carried the tree back on their shoulders. Then I helped them set it up in the corner, we cut the bundling wires, and the tree's springy branches unfurled, filling the entire first floor with the fresh, sharp smell of an evergreen forest.

Esther (actually cheerful for once) began affixing bright red ribbons to the deep green boughs, and I dug out the lovingly packed boxes of antique miniature coffee cups and tin pots that Madame—the Village Blend's elderly owner—had collected over the years. Then Tucker replaced our shop dinger with jingle bells, and Dante laid out the big red and green welcome mat I'd purchased the week before—the one that said Merry Christmas in a dozen languages along with *Happy Holidays! Happy Chanukah!* and *Happy Kwanzaa!*

(Living in a city with as many cultural and religious differences as New York meant you were probably violating someone's belief system just by breathing. Lofty words like *diversity* and *understanding* were often bandied about in hopes of fostering open-mindedness, but after living in this roiling mini-UN for the past two decades, I was convinced that the way to universal harmony lay in a more practical philosophy. A diversity of cultures meant a diversity of foods. *Eat with tolerance,* I say.)

For a full hour, we continued decorating the coffeehouse, stringing white lights around the French doors, hanging fresh spruce wreaths against the casement windows. Finally, we put up quilted stockings over the hearth's stone mantel, where one of Madame's silver menorahs already stood, waiting for the Festival of Lights to begin.

Peace on earth had *actually* been in play, until we all began judging each other's coffee creations . . .

Now, checking my watch, I tensed. Our guests would be arriving soon to sample our new holiday coffee drinks, and we were nowhere near ready.

"Okay, that's it!" I announced in a tone I hadn't used since my daughter was in grade school. "No more bickering! Everyone behind the espresso bar! I want Christmas in a cup, and I want it ASAP!"

FORTY-FIVE minutes later, two dozen bottles of sweet Italian syrups were lined up on our blue marble espresso bar; stainless steel milk-frothing pitchers stood on the work counter behind it; and I was reviewing our hastily scribbled latte-tasting menu.

Tucker's offerings included Butter Pecan Praline, Candy Cane (easy on the syrup), Iced Gingersnap, and Old-Fashioned Sugar Cookie. Dante's flavors were Eggnog Cheesecake, Spiked Fruitcake White Chocolate Tiramisu, and Toasted Marshmallow Snowflake. Gardner's Christmas memories brought us Rum Raisin, Mocha-Coconut Macaroon, and Caribbean Black Cake. And from my own beloved Nonna's Christmases: Candied Orange Panettone, Maple-Kissed Gingerbread, Glazed Roasted Chestnut, and Anisette Crème.

Esther also had contributions: Apricot-Cinnamon Rugelach and Raspberry Jelly Doughnut because, as she quite rightly put it, "Chanukah has its own flavors." For Esther, this also included Key Lime Pie because, as she noted, "Every December my family fled to Florida."

The invited guests of our latte tasting were now mingling near the crackling logs of the store's hearth, waiting for us to whip up the samples.

Tucker was entertaining his current boyfriend, a Hispanic

Broadway dancer who went by the single name Punch. Gardner was playing host to Theo, Ronny, and Chick, the three other members of his jazz ensemble *Four on the Floor*. And Dante had invited his two aspiring-artist roommates: a pierced platinum-blond pixie named Kiki and a raven-haired girl of East Indian heritage named Banhi.

Checking my watch, I decided to give our missing guests another ten minutes to show. Esther's boyfriend—Boris the assistant-baker-slash-Russian rapper—was performing at a Brooklyn club tonight. Since he couldn't make it, she'd invited another taster, a friend named Vicki Glockner.

Earlier in the year, Vicki had worked as a barista for me. She'd loved experimenting with our Italian syrups, and I knew she'd make a good taster, but I had mixed feelings about seeing her again because she and I hadn't parted on the best of terms.

My friend was late, too—although he'd phoned to apologize and warn that he might not make it at all. I couldn't blame him. Since I began seeing Mike Quinn, I'd had to accept that an NYPD detective's work was never done.

My other tasting party guinea pig was now smacking his knuckles against the beveled glass of the Blend's front door. I moved to unlock it and realized the night had grown colder and the snow higher. Fat flakes had been falling steadily for the last hour. Now they layered the sidewalk and street with several inches of crystalline frosting. As I pulled the door wide, the newly installed jingle bells sounded above, and a chilly wind gust sent a flurry of ice diamonds into my dark brown hair.

"You actually made it?" I said with a shiver as Matteo Allegro stepped inside.

Two

꩜꩜꩜꩜꩜꩜꩜꩜꩜꩜꩜꩜꩜꩜꩜꩜

SKIN still lightly bronzed from the Central American sun, Matteo stamped the wet snow off his boots—and (happily) *not* onto the shop's restored wood plank floor, thanks to my brilliant managerial decision to buy the multicultural *Happy Holidays* welcome mat.

"You sound surprised to see me," said my ex-husband, unzipping his Italian leather jacket.

"True. I didn't think you'd show." I shut the door on the snowy night. "You only got back from Guatemala—*what?* Six hours ago?"

"Five."

"And I know how you feel about Fa-la-la-la Lattes." I smiled at the catchy term. I hadn't invented it. Alfred Glockner, our local charity Santa, had coined it. In truth, the whole "Taste of Christmas" idea had been Alf's.

Matt shrugged. "What can I say? When it comes to coffee, I'm a purist."

As an international coffee broker as well as our coffee buyer, Matt was also a coffee snob, but justifiably so. The lattes and cappuccinos were a big draw to the Blend and a healthy contributor to our bottom line. But they weren't his area of the business; they were mine—and my staff of baristas who mixed them to order.

While I roasted and served the beans, Matt was responsible for sourcing them. And because harvest quality could change from season to season, Matt was essentially a java-centric Magellan, regularly exploring the world's coffee belt—a band of mountainous slopes that circled the globe between the Tropics of Capricorn and Cancer, where sunny, frost-free, moderately wet conditions allowed for the cultivation of the very best arabica beans.

"Good thing your Holiday Blend's a winner this year," I said, knowing that our single-origin coffees, seasonal blends, and straight espressos were what lit Matt up. (No artificial oils, no sugar syrups, just his top-quality beans with natural, exotic spice notes, which I regularly roasted in small batches in our shop's basement.)

"So where's Breanne?" I asked, glancing through the front door's glass. Snow fluttered down through the light of the streetlamps, but the curb was empty. No limo. No hired car. No yellow cab with an open door sprouting an endless, designer-draped leg.

"She was supposed to meet me *here*." Matt scanned the tasting group gathered around the fire. "She hasn't shown yet?"

"No. Is she working late again?"

Matt's reply was a muttered, "When isn't she?"

"I'll bet the snow held her up," I said. "You know it's murder getting a cab in weather like this."

Matt didn't nod or agree, just pulled off his black knit cap, ran a hand over his short, dark Caesar, and looked away.

He and Breanne had gotten married in the spring, went on a whirlwind tour of Spain for a number of weeks, then spent much of the summer in a cottony cloud of sweetness that rivaled Tucker's Candy Cane Cappuccino. By early fall, however, the sugar had started to melt. Sharp bouts of bickering continually punctured their meringue of constant cooing.

I didn't actually see this as any great sign of marital doom. Sooner or later every honeymooning couple had to deal with the struggles and drudgery of workaday life.

Whether they touched down or crash-landed, newlyweds have been traveling the same trajectory for centuries.

"Maybe you should call her?" I suggested.

"Forget it," he said, then changed the subject. "You know, Clare, our Holiday Blend's a winner this year because of *you*. You created the blend; you perfected the roast."

"But you found the beans, Matt. *Your* beans are incredible." I didn't mind giving away the credit for this year's exotically spiced blend. Usually, Matt was so cocky it wasn't necessary. But because he'd gone humble on me, I stated the obvious: "That microlot of Sumatra you snagged on the last trip to Indonesia was superb. You made my job easy."

Matt's weary expression lightened at that, and I was glad to see him smile—until his gaze drifted over me. In anticipation of the evening's festivities, I'd fastened a prim choker of green velvet ribbon around my neck. In hopes of seeing Quinn, however, I'd squeezed into a new pair of *not*-so-prim, form-fitting low-riders. The holly berry-colored cashmere-blend sweater wasn't exactly loose, either. It also flaunted a borderline audacious neckline. (What could I say? I liked Quinn's eyes on me.) Unfortunately, at the moment, it wasn't Mike Quinn doing the looking.

"Nice sweater," Matt said with an arched eyebrow, and before I could stop him he reached out to brush the melting snow crystals from my hair. "Have I seen it before?"

"The sweater's new," I informed him while carefully stepping beyond his reach.

Married or not, Matteo Allegro liked women. And because I was one, there was no getting around his occasional flirtations. I *could* get around his touches, however, and I'd found that a subtle dodge worked a whole lot better than a snippy lecture—it proved a lot less embarrassing in public, too.

Obviously, Matt and I had a history: the kind where you live together for ten years as man and wife. For various reason—most of them having to do with his addictions to cocaine and women, not necessarily in that order—a single decade legally wedded to the man had been more than enough for me. We did, however, still share a grown daughter as well as another kind of commitment: Matt's elderly mother owned this century-old coffeehouse and she'd bequeathed its future to the both of us. So once again Matt was my partner in *business*. I tried to keep that in mind whenever Matt's penchant for crossing lines sprang up.

Matt glanced around. "So where's your guard dog?"

"If you mean *Mike*, he's got police business in the outer boroughs. He might not make it."

Matt's dark eyebrows rose. "Too bad," he said, but his tone didn't sound disappointed. "Come on, I could use some warming up. The place looks great."

His arm began snaking around my hip-hugging jeans. I slipped clear.

"Thanks," I said. "You go ahead and hang up your wet coat in the back. I have to lock up again."

"I'll save you a seat," he said with a wink, then moved toward the back of the shop. As I turned to secure the door, however, it flew open on me.

A runway model—tall woman jarred me and our store's new jingle bells without so much as a *pardon me*.

"I'm sorry," I told her. "We're closed."

Even with half of her face mummified by a scarf the color of latte froth, I could tell the redhead was a knockout. In her midthirties, she had a stunning, statuesque figure. Peeking above the costly pashmina, her nose and cheekbones appeared daintily carved; her eyes adorably big and brilliantly blue. When I spoke to her, however, the woman's wide, doll-like eyes collapsed into slits, squinting down at me as if she'd just noticed a bug under her boot.

"Like *hell* you're closed!"

Okay, the woman's tone was a tad nastier than the angelic face she showed to the world, but I forced a smile. For one thing, she was a new regular. I'd seen her in here several times over Thanksgiving weekend—wearing the same white fur-trimmed car coat and large sheepskin boots, both of which screamed designer label. Her hair was memorable, as well. From beneath her soft knit cap her sleek curls tumbled down her shoulders in a silk stream of eye-catching scarlet, a striking contrast with the ivory car coat.

"Again, I'm sorry, ma'am," I said with polite firmness, "but we *are* clo—"

"You are *not*," she said, stamping her giant Ugg boot on my internationally festive welcome mat. "You have, like, *a dozen* people here!"

Anyone who'd spent five minutes in Manhattan realized that a percentage of its well-heeled population sashayed around the island with so much attitude that branding *entitlement* on their foreheads would have been redundant. In the presence of perceived "peers," these people could be downright charming. When dealing with no one of "significance"—say, a lowly coffeehouse manager—their behavior turned less than affable. As New York retail went, however, appallingly bad customer behavior wasn't anything out of the ordinary, so I simply stiffened my spine.

"I realize the snow's really coming down. But I'm not lying to you. This is a private party, and we *are* closed as you can see from the sign on the door—"

"Excuse me? *Who*, in their right mind, would notice some stupid, little *sign* on a night like *this*?!"

By now, the buzz of discussions near the fireplace had come to a dead stop. All eyes had turned to us, which wasn't surprising. Everyone in the Big Apple loved a scene. Not that minding your own business wasn't still a primary objective in this town, but there was an important distinction: just because New Yorkers didn't want to get *involved* in an unfolding drama didn't mean they weren't interested in gawking at it.

"I'll tell you what," I offered. "If you don't mind meeting and mingling with some new people, you can join our—"

"Whatever!" she interrupted. "You're closed!" Pirouetting like a girl who'd never missed a ballet recital, Red yanked open the door and stomped her Ugg-booted feet out into the snowy night.

I locked up and turned to find everyone still watching me. "Sorry about that."

"What do *you* have to be sorry about?!" Esther cried. "That woman was a total *be-yotch*!"

Although I agreed with Esther, I wasn't happy about ejecting anyone back out into a snowstorm. "I was trying to invite her to the party."

"Maybe if she hadn't cut you off and pitched a fit," Tucker said, "she would have *heard* the invitation! Talk about rude."

"The woman's agitation level was off the charts," Gardner said. "Looked to me like she needed her meds adjusted."

"O Valium, O Valium," Tucker sang, "how lovely are your trances—"

"That little display was nothing," Dante said, waving a tattooed arm. "Three out of the last five nights I closed, I had to physically eject some total A-holes. It's like the holiday season's pissing everyone off."

"Yeah, me included," Gardner confessed.

"You?" I couldn't believe my most reliably mellow barista had lost his holiday spirit. "Why?"

"It's these nonstop loops of mediocre Christmas tunes," he said, gesturing to our shop's speaker system. "At least three radio stations have been repeating these same lousy playlists twenty-four-seven for weeks now, and practically every store I walk into has one of them on speaker—"

"It's like bad sonic wallpaper," Esther said.

"Whatever you want to call it, it's driving me sugarplum crazy." Gardner shook his head. "Three weeks to December twenty-fifth and I'm already fed up with the sounds of the season."

"Me, too," Dante said. "The CIA should abandon gangsta rap as a torture technique and try playing 'Jingle Bell Rock' a few hundred times in a row."

"Oh, man. *One* time's enough for me," said Theo, one of Gardner's musician friends.

"Wait!" Dante froze and pointed to the speaker system. "There it is again."

Jingle bell, jingle bell, jingle bell rock . . .

"Can we *please* cut the power on this stuff?" Theo begged.

Gardner nodded and moved to turn off the 24/7 Christmas carol station.

"But it's a party," I protested. "We should have *music*." (And I actually liked "Jingle Bell Rock"—and "Winter Wonderland" and "I'll Be Home for Christmas"—even if they were played twelve times in twenty-four hours.)

"Put on my ambient mix," Dante called to Gardner, then turned back to me.

"That's nice, mellow, latte-tasting music, don't you think?"

"But it's not *Christmasy*," I pointed out.

"That's okay by me," said Banhi, Dante's raven-haired roommate.

"Yeah. Me, too," added Kiki, the pierced, platinum pixie.

I couldn't believe it. "Where's your holiday spirit?"

Everyone exchanged glances.

Finally Dante said, "Face it, boss. There's no holiday cheer out there because the holidays have become a grind. Everyone's fed up with tinseled-up stores pushing commercial kitsch."

"Yeah, what's *good* about gridlock season?" Kiki said. "Out-of-town tourists and bridge-and-tunnel bargain hunters swinging shopping bags like medieval maces? A herd of them nearly ran me over today rushing across Thirty-fourth!"

"And don't forget those corporate Scrooges all over the city," Banhi added. "I temp at an office where all they do is gripe about having to use half of their bonuses to buy gifts for their families."

"Well, don't talk to *me* about 'holiday cheer'—" said Esther, putting air quotes around the offending phrase. "I'm still gagging over my perfect, older, married sister's annual year-end newsletter about her perfect suburban life."

"I *should* have the Christmas spirit," Tucker admitted. "Given my latest gig."

"What's that?" asked one of the guys in Gardner's group.

"Dickie Celebratorio absolutely *adored* that limited-run cabaret I put together last summer, so he hired me to cast, direct, and choreograph his big holiday bash at the New York Public Library. We've been in rehearsal for two weeks now."

"Celebratorio's that big party planner, isn't he?" I asked.

Tucker's boyfriend, Punch, nodded. "It's being sold to the press as a fund-raiser for New York's public libraries, but it's really a PR event for that big-selling children's book they just turned into a movie."

"*Ticket to the North Pole?*" Esther said. "Isn't that whole thing set in Santa's workshop or something?"

Tucker nodded.

"So you've basically hired a bunch of actors to play Santa's elves?" Esther pressed.

Tucker sighed. "The money's excellent, but when you get right down to it, my job's essentially—"

"Head Elf," Esther finished with a smirk.

Tucker shrugged. "Like I said, I *should* be in the holiday spirit, but the material's just so *cheesy*."

That's it, I thought. *I can't take any more.* "Santa Claus is *not* cheesy!" I cried.

Dead silence ensued.

"You're all forgetting what this season is really about!"

Everyone stared. I'd just become Linus in *A Charlie Brown Christmas*.

"Well?" Esther finally said. "What's it about, boss?"

I threw up my hands. "Giving! Selfless giving! That's what we're celebrating! The Christ child's birth is a *gift* of *love* to a weary world! All these symbols—the tree, the lights, the carols—it all comes down to *love*!"

No one moved as my words reverberated off the restored tin ceiling and echoed through the newly decorated shop. For a full minute, we actually had a *silent night*.

I shouldn't have been surprised at the flabbergasted expressions around the room. After all, this was the age of irony, when cynicism was the conventional norm, which was why a blasphemous string of curses would have gone over without a batted eyelash. The *truly* radical act these days was *sincerity*. Consequently, our silent night continued—until a single voice boomed—

". . . all right, Breanne! I *heard* you! *Don't* come, then!"

Matt had been striding into the main room from the back pantry area. Suddenly he stopped.

Yes, Matt, the entire tasting party just overheard the unhappy end to your personal call.

His cheeks, no longer ruddy from the frosty outdoors, began reddening again for an entirely different reason. Then his pleading eyes found mine—a search for rescue—and I immediately clapped my hands.

"Hey, everyone!" I shouted with forced cheer. "You know what this Taste of Christmas party needs?"

All eyes now abandoned Matt and turned to me.

"What, Clare?" Tucker asked. "What does it need?"

"Santa Claus!"

Don't Miss the Next
Coffeehouse Mystery

HOLIDAY GRIND

Clare is quite fond of Alfred Glockner, the part-time comic and gen-uinely jolly charity Santa who's been using her coffeehouse as a place to warm up between his rounds. When she finds him gunned down in a nearby alley, a few subtle clues convince her that Alfred's death was something more than the tragic result of a random mugging—the conclusion of the police.

With Clare's boyfriend, NYPD detective Mike Quinn, dis-tracted by a cold case of his own, and ex-husband, Matt, "investi-gating" this year's holiday lingerie catalogs (an annual event), Clare charges ahead solo to look into Santa's slaying. Then someone tries to ice Clare, and she really gets steamed.

Between baking delicious Christmas goodies and fending off the attentions of a persistent professional Elf, Clare remains determined to solve her friend's murder. But she better watch out, because if she fails to stop this stone cold killer, she may just get the biggest chill of her life.

**For more information about
the Coffeehouse Mysteries,
visit the author's Web site at
www.CoffeehouseMystery.com.**